T. R. Wilson was [...] Peterborough on the [...] the University of East Anglia, and his love of East Anglia — its landscape, people and history — has always been central to his life and work. He submitted his first novel, *Master of Morholm*, for publication at the age of twenty-three, at which time he was a student on the University of East Anglia MA Course in Creative Writing, under Malcolm Bradbury and Angela Carter. His MA submission was part of the novel which was later published in 1989 as *Treading on Shadows*. His previous novels, *Roses in December* and *Hester Verney*, are available from Headline. He lives with a word processor in a small flat.

Heartsease

T. R. Wilson

HEADLINE

First published in 1993
By HEADLINE BOOK PUBLISHING PLC

First published in paperback in 1994
by HEADLINE BOOK PUBLISHING PLC

10   9   8   7   6   5   4   3   2   1

ISBN 0 7472 4271 2

Typeset by Avon Dataset Ltd, Bidford-on-Avon

Printed and bound in Great Britain by
HarperCollins Manufacturing, Glasgow

HEADLINE BOOK PUBLISHING PLC
Headline House
79 Great Titchfield Street
London W1P 7FN

For Michael Scorer

But O my native land! Gods of the soil!
Welcome me with good fortune in these ways;
And thou, paternal Home! for I thy cleanser
Come here of right, the ambassador of Heaven

Sophocles, *Elektra*
trans. Sir George Young

1830

Prelude

They had taken his father away. They had taken him first to the prison-house at the little town of Swaffham, and then they had moved him to the Castle, in the city of Norwich, where the boy had never been — but which he visited in his imagination, every night of that dark winter, his thoughts seeking his father out, in who-knew-what deep cell in the midst of how many thousand strangers, as if by that means he might bring him comfort, and show nothing of his own bewilderment and fear.

They were going to try the boy's father at the Assizes, for machine-breaking and riot. His father, Jacob Wintergreen, and Abel Jex, the cobbler, and Will Strickland, whose cottage adjoined theirs, and whose little daughter the boy had played with since they were small enough to pass beneath the field-gates without ducking their heads, and several more. Ordinary men of the village, whose faces were as familiar a part of the boy's world as the lineaments of the rafters above his bed, the grooves and knots and stains in which his childish fancy had once traced maps of unknown countries and shapes of strange beasts, and little elfin people who might have frightened him but never quite did — for near at hand were his sister and his mother and father, and fears had no power then.

The boy knew all about what had happened. His sister, he thought, did not perhaps fully understand. Charlotte was just eight, and in the sight of a perfect row of icicles hanging from the cottage eaves, or fresh rabbit-prints in the snow, could even momentarily forget the pangs of an empty stomach — which, for all the neighbours' help, the

1

fatherless family knew too well that winter. Her father was not there, and she missed him, but he would come back — her mother said so. But the boy was older. He was nearly eleven. He worked in the fields, though his father believed in schooling and had sent him to the village school as long as he could. The boy did not yet belong with the men of the village, but he knew what went on: he knew about the riot.

He worked in the fields, bird-scaring, stone-picking, anything he could get. There was not much. There had not been much work in the village for some years past — only day-labour, as undependable as the weather, and for wages that would break a man's heart. The boy knew this. He knew that his father had once tried to settle for higher wages with Farmer Hemstock; and he knew now that Farmer Hemstock had never forgotten it.

He was still known as Farmer Hemstock, though he would have had it otherwise — he was *Mr* Hemstock, and demanded respect. He was known by other names too, now — and they were not respectful. The boy knew that.

And his father was going to be tried — taken before the court of assize, a prisoner — his father! — who would sit by the hearth at night, holding the boy against one upraised knee and Charlotte against the other, and would make of that meagre fire a kingly blaze by his presence alone — by the warmth in his voice, deep-chested and soft, and in his eye the merriment that never left him quite, even as the times ground harder and brought the bones sharply to his face.

He would stand before judge and jury, as other men, other fathers were standing throughout the country. The boy knew that too. For the village heard, tardily but clearly enough, the news of the wider world. All that autumn and winter the labouring men of the villages of England had stirred, and risen: in one country parish after another, they had looked on their cold grates, their empty larder-shelves, their children's rags, and had gone out together to demand higher wages, to break threshing-machines, to burn ricks, to squeeze from the farmers and the magistrates and the poor-law overseers a few sustaining drops of justice. Some said they had a leader called Captain Swing, who was secretly orchestrating the riots. In the newspapers, which Dick Freshwater the publican-undertaker read out loud, there were tales of threatening letters signed by this mysterious Captain Swing, which had set all the rich folk on their ears with talk of revolution. But it was no captain who had led the men of the boy's village out by night to threaten and burn. They needed no leader but despair.

And now from Dick Freshwater's grave conning of the newspapers came word of the punishment that was being visited on the rioters: defeated, rounded up by magistrates and soldiers, consigned to gaols up and down the country, tried in scores of courts. In the village, people spoke in lowered voices of the sentences being handed out, and fell silent when they saw the boy near. But the boy knew.

His mother had not wanted his father to go with them, the night of the riot. They explained that they meant to offer no violence, that they were simply going in a body to assert their rights and put their case. They would take a collection from the farmers, as they had heard the men in a neighbouring village had done, and distribute it fairly, they would call on Farmer Hemstock to get rid of his threshing-machine, which took away their winter work. Work, for a decent wage, was all they wanted. The word was that in some places where the men had risen up, over on the Suffolk border, the farmers and the justices had been sympathetic. After all, weren't they all Norfolk men, living on the same land? Abel Jex had said that, standing with the others in a ring outside the cottage door, their breath smoking. They shuffled, looking eager and uneasy. There was something almost of holiday spirit about their faces, lightly lying over something strained, tense, and wounded. They were doing, at last.

3

'Don't go, Jacob,' the boy's mother had said. She fastened her eyes on his father's. 'Don't go.'

His father spoke softly. 'Remember what we ate today, Mary?' he said. 'Would it ha' filled a rat's belly? Is that right? I ask you. Is that right?' He wound his muffler round his neck.

'Think how strong the rich folk are, Jacob,' his mother said. 'They got such power.' Still she had looked searchingly into his eyes, until at last he could no longer meet her gaze. He had simply gestured in a helpless way at the lamplit ring of men before the cottage door, as if to say: They're my folk, aren't they? What else can I do? And then his glance fell on the boy, standing by the empty hearth, and he patted the boy's shoulder in brief goodbye.

Couldn't he go with them? – the boy could not speak that question. He did not know whether he wanted to. He had, even then, perhaps, a foreboding. And so he had watched his father go.

The bitter year turned, the Assizes drew near, and the boy returned in the green twilight from bird-scaring in the fields, through the village that had always been his home – his home quite as much as the four walls of the cottage where his father's empty chair stood like a mourner. In thatch and shutter, in woodsmoke mounting to the crystalline sky, in the figure of the hedger trudging down the sloping street beneath a great bundle of faggots like some prodigious hedgehog, in the geese squabbling about the half-frozen yard pond, in the skeleton of a wagon in the wheelwright's yard, in the old rooks' nests hanging like weird wintry fruit in the high trees around the church – in all these things there was such an intimacy that they might have been twined in the very fibres of the boy's heart. All how familiar, how true, how loved deep in the bones of him, yet how changed since the riot! Hard times there had been before, bitterness, gaunt resentment like harsh shapes beneath the snow, but still the village had never been less dear to him than the contours of his parents' faces seen in the chimney corner when the door was fastened against the night. Blighted now, blighted since that night and day when bitterness had flared and been snuffed out.

Several of the smaller farmers had made common cause with the rioters. They had their own grievances, against high rents and tithes. They had made a collection for the men, and one had promised to get rid of his threshing-machine: he had never taken to it, and it only threw men on to the poor-rates, which he had to pay. There had even been an agreement to a meeting at the church, to settle a new wage rate. The men had gone on, cheered with free drink, torchlit, a little light-headed.

It was Farmer Hemstock next. He farmed much of the parish, and was a man of substance − gentry almost, so he thought. He had begun to be proud, and to grasp. He was disliked, the boy knew: daily through the village, like a shiver of wind through the woods, ran the little stories of Hemstock's harshness to the labouring men whom he now called Hands, as if that were all they were − so many pairs of hands to pick stones and dig ditches when they were needed, just for a day, just for an afternoon, and then be gone. The poor-rate would keep the Hands alive, just, until they were needed again. And all those little memories of their treatment by Hemstock must have rippled through the men too, as they made their way flushed and defiant to Hemstock's farm that night. They would have a turn at Hemstock. He would meet them man to man for once.

But Hemstock had met defiance with defiance; and then had come the damage. When he refused to destroy his threshing-machine, they had done it for him; when he refused to consider their wage demands, and produced his gun, someone − there were different stories as to whom − set a torch to one of the ricks in his stackyard.

After that the end was not long in coming. Up at the

Hall, Mr Ingamells, who was a magistrate, had acted. Farmer Hemstock had ridden at the head of the special constables sworn in by Mr Ingamells, and they had swooped down on the men as they gathered at the church. The men had been taken away to gaol; and now the word was that Hemstock was claiming a reward offered by the government in London to anyone who turned in Swing rioters. Quietly, that word was spoken, in the sullen peace that had followed the riot – with authority on the watch now all over the country, and companies of soldiers sent out from Norwich, jingling in scarlet down the leafless lanes. And the men waited to be tried.

The boy could not sleep. He opened the shutter at the casement, though the air was razor-cold, and stared at the night sky. Silver clouds were streaming crazily across the moon, as if the whole firmament were in a state of panicked insurrection, and all at once the boy felt terror possess him. How far off they were, those clouds and icy stars, how indifferent to the troubled people here below! In church they said heaven was up there, but now the boy saw it all vast and alien, and knew better, and his heart beat like a snared rabbit's. Only here below, here with home and family and friends, was life secure – and now it was all set at hazard.

He felt as if he were in a frail boat in the midst of a fearful sea, drifting. They were going to try his father tomorrow.

Dick Freshwater had a cart, and he was going to take the boy's mother and Mrs Strickland to the Assize at Norwich, to see their husbands tried. There was not room enough for the boy – not if they were to leave a space to bring – Oh please God – to bring his father home; and so he was to stay at home and look after his sister and Rosa, the Stricklands' little girl. They were to start very early for Norwich, and the cart was standing before the cottage door when the eastern sky was barely alight.

Charlotte was half-asleep, and leant against the boy like a warm kitten, eyes blinking and seeing nothing. Dick Freshwater's ponies tapped their shaggy hoofs, and snorted steam, and the boy's mother climbed into the cart with Mrs Strickland.

'Do you take care of your sister,' his mother said. 'You're the man of the house now.'

'Just for now, though, Mother,' the boy said. He could not see his mother's eyes, in the dimness. 'Only just for now.'

It was a strange day. Rosa Strickland was a year or so younger than he, a lively black-haired girl, with eyes that were always laughing, dark and lustrous as berries. There was something of adventure in their having the whole day to themselves, as if they were grown up. They went stick-gathering for firewood, and made a fire and roasted the handful of potatoes that was their dinner — not enough, there was never enough nowadays, but they tasted very good. They played with Charlotte, who was an easy child, always contented; and when several of the village women looked in on them, as promised to their mothers, they said they were all right. And only once did Rosa look up suddenly, solemn, and meet the doubt in the boy's eyes.

'I wonder what's happening,' he said.

Rosa was silent a moment, and her lip trembled: then she said, 'My mother say that'll all be rightled. She say not to worry. They didn't do no wrong, not bad wrong — they never hurt nobody.'

It was late. They had gone without light as long as they could, but the boy had lit a candle at last, feeling that the shadows in the cottage house-place were stealing out like bats to brush against him. One of the village women had come by again, and pressed a hunk of bread and a paring of cheese into their hands, and looked sadly at their faces before going away again. Charlotte, tired from the long strange day, had fallen asleep on the settle, and Rosa was

7

trying to coax a fire from the scraps in the hearth. The wind was wheezing in the thatch, and a shutter was rattling, and for a moment the boy thought he was mistaken in the sound he heard outside.

Rosa cocked her head, threw back her hair.

'They're back!' she cried, and ran to the door.

At first the boy could not move. He was frozen. Rosa flung open the door to a blast of February ice-wind, and ran outside. At last his legs moved, and he followed.

Mrs Strickland had got down from the cart and was hugging Rosa in her arms. She was saying something about not seeing her father just yet; dimly the boy gathered that Will Strickland had been sentenced to two years in prison. His attention was fixed on his mother, who was still sitting in the cart and looking dully before her, as if she had neither strength nor will to climb down.

'Mother?' the boy said.

Dick Freshwater threw the reins over the heads of the steaming ponies, and half-lifted the boy's mother down from the cart. Still she did not speak; but she seemed to see the boy for the first time. She took an unsteady pace forward and put her arm around his neck. He felt his mother's weight as she wept, and the world was turned upside down as his mother leant on him for support.

Dick Freshwater's granite slab of a face, square-whiskered, leapt into relief as he lifted his storm-lantern and gazed into the boy's eyes. 'Do yew be a man for your ma's sake, bor,' he said. 'Transported. Thass the sentence: thass done now. Transported. Spit on it, as I've done, and then bear up, bor, for your ma and your sister.'

Charlotte had woken, and now, alarmed at the sight of her weeping mother, was clutching at the boy with fierce, terrified hands.

The boy remembered the night his father had left the cottage with the other men, winding on his muffler and patting the boy's shoulder: the last time he had seen his father . . . The last time.

* * *

His mother could not speak of the trial. Dick Freshwater told him the story at last.

A ringleader: that was what the authorities wanted. The boy's father had once stood up to Farmer Hemstock and asked for better wages – Hemstock had testified to that. A natural troublemaker, a malcontent.

'D'you see, bor?' Dick Freshwater said. 'They don't want to hear about empty bellies, and no work from week to week, and labouring men made paupers. They want to hear about villains stirring up trouble, and putting ideas into men's heads – as if they were no more'n babes. So then they can pretend there's naught amiss in the country at all.'

The boy saw. He saw it clearly.

'Abel Jex turned King's Evidence, see. He laid it all at your father's door, and got off light with a month in gaol in return. Ah, thass easy to judge, bor,' Dick said, seeing the boy's expression. 'We're all weak creeturs here below. Many a man would have been tempted to do the same. Thass natur.'

The men of the village who had taken part in the riot had been given various long prison sentences; Abel Jex, a single month in reward for his betrayal; the boy's father, condemned to be transported in chains to the other side of the world, whence no one ever came back.

Dick Freshwater had all the figures. In Norfolk as a whole there had been one hundred and twenty-nine rioters tried: fifty-seven had been acquitted, sixty sentenced to prison, three sentenced to death, and thirteen sentenced to transportation. The Norfolk justices had been merciful; it had been much worse in many other counties, Dick said.

The village was quiet. It had been injured, lumps of living flesh torn from its body.

'Sore times for you, bor,' Dick Freshwater said to the boy. 'You must bear up.'

* * *

The spring was slow. Dry hard winds blew, and the boy's mother was racked by a cough that sounded like the monotonous bark of a dog. She walked with Charlotte each day to Pitchford — a slum village nearby, a bad word, a place with no pride — where they recruited labour-gangs of women and children to work cheaply in the fields. The boy, meanwhile, got what work he could. There was less than ever. Farmer Hemstock would not employ the families of rioters, never mind the fact that they would have died rather than take anything from him.

On the cottage mantelshelf a letter stood. The boy's father had written it with the help of another prisoner from the prison-hulks at Portsmouth, where they were waiting to be shipped off to the convict settlements of Van Diemen's Land. The boy, who could read reasonably well, had construed the clumsy print so often he knew it by heart. His father did not blame Abel Jex, he said. It was those in authority, the masters of the village world: they had grown proud and cruel. He sent his love to his wife and children, and put his trust in God.

The boy took those words into himself, and in the emptiness of the night, all silent, he raged. What had God done to deserve such trust? God was good, then, and his father bad? Never — oh, never would he accept that.

Mr Ingamells at the Hall was their landlord. His bailiff came dunning for the rent they could not pay. The bailiff was a pompous man who parroted the squire's phrases as he flourished a silver-headed riding-crop. It was all very well, he said, to say they couldn't pay the rent because the breadwinner was gone. The breadwinner should have thought of that before he started leading riotous affrays and attacks on property — that was Mr Ingamells' view. There had been altogether too much of this sort of thing. People must not begin to think they were owed a living . . .

The boy's mother was thin now. There were bluish patches under her eyes like impressions in snow. The boy gazed earnestly on her face as she stirred the pot of watery broth over the fire. He knew that that face had been round once, with a funny dimple at the corner of the mouth when she smiled; and he was straining to keep hold of that knowledge, for it too seemed to be slipping away from him, and he must not let it go. He must keep that knowledge, inside him.

'Read the letter again, Jed,' his mother said to the boy.

He began reading, but at last her coughs made him stop, and when she was recovered she laid a hand on his arm and said, 'Your father's a good man.'

'I know it, Mother!'

'Don't think ill of him,' she went on in a low voice. 'Not even – well, not even do we have to go into the House.'

'Mother!'

She hushed him, with a motion towards Charlotte, who was sitting on the floor in the corner whispering to her rag-doll.

'We got to look it in the face, Jed,' his mother said. 'I'm not strong now: you know it. We'll not be the only ones. The Stricklands'll be on the parish afore long, I reckon; and we must remember we were sore drove to it—'

'But not the House, Mother!' he cried. 'Oh, Mother – not the House!'

He had never seen the workhouse – it was in another parish – but he knew about it. Farmer Hemstock was one of the poor-law overseers.

His mother looked at him with a world of sadness in her sick eyes. 'I know, Jed,' she said, taking his hand gently. 'I know.' Then her grip upon his hand tightened, and he felt a bracelet of pain round his wrist as his mother clenched it and said with violence: 'Remember, Jed, oh remember this! God forbid I should school my own child in bitterness, and hating – and God send there'll be a day, when you're grown, when you can stand straight in the world, and be out of the power of

Hemstock, and parson, and Squire Ingamells and all their like — when you're your own man, and can tell 'em to go hang! But no matter what come, do you remember, Jed — remember how it was, here in Heartsease! And remember that wasn't always so — they made it so. We saw better times, Jed — you know that: you know this hand that nursed you was always rough, but it wasn't always starved so, to naught but bone; you know the village was a fit place to call home, once, and that when the poor men of Heartsease rose up, that was only so they might live there like men, and not cattle; remember that, Jed — even when you can't bring to mind any more the faces of the mother and father who loved you — remember!' Her eyes held his, her eyes in which all the ebbing life of her wasted frame seemed to flare at once. 'Remember!'

1843

Chapter One

The Portrait-Painter

The shadows of the October evening were closing in apace, when the shape of a cathedral spire, appearing stencilled on the cold afterglow, signalled to the young man on top of the coach that the city of Norwich was at hand.

The young man, who had been travelling since dawn, and was chilled, weary and aching, freshened at the prospect; and took the liberty of giving a shove to the heavy head of an old man who, wedged in tightly between the other outside passengers, had contrived to fall asleep, and since their last stop at Wymondham had been snoring on the young man's shoulder in an uncomfortably affectionate attitude. The guard blew the horn, and the coach descended into a maze of lighted windows, and gable-ends, and church-towers that seemed to rear up at every turning, and winding streets still clattering with foot and horse traffic; until at length the silhouette of the cathedral, having unaccountably disappeared, loomed forth again above a massy gateway, and the coach bounced and crashed under a scarcely less ancient gateway opposite it, into the yard of the Old Maid's Head.

The outside passengers, climbing down from the roof, reeled and staggered about on their legs for some moments, like so many sailors turned ashore – the young man in particular, for he had long legs, and had spent the last part of the journey with them folded up almost to his ears. Having stamped and stretched himself into his normal appearance, which was that of a tall, slender, fair man of twenty-four or -five, loose-limbed and fresh-coloured, with grey eyes of much quickness and keenness, a lean profile, and something both humorous and innocent about his mouth − and having seen to his trunk, he went into the coffee-room of the inn and ordered chops and ale, and writing materials. When the waiter had laid a cloth in a box for him, the young man drew out a letter from his pocket, and after glancing over it began at once to write.

My dear father
I am just this moment arrived at Norwich, and feel I must write directly, for I have been thinking over your letter all the way here.

You are as generous as ever in your proposals; and believe me I am very far from seeing in them any sign that you lack confidence in my ability as an artist. You offer to help me to some other career, if the painting does not answer − and I know your good nature so well as to be sure that, if I did give it up, you would make never a murmur about all the expense you have been put to in supporting this wrong-headed design of mine. But Father, I will stick at it; my mind is made up. To do so seems the least reward I can make you for all your confidence in me − and purely from a selfish point of view, I love painting too much to leave off. It's true I had but a lean time of it in Cambridge, but I have great hopes of Norwich, which is a more populous place, and abundantly supplied, so I hear, with merchants and manufacturers and professional men, of the very sort who are great buyers of small portraits and miniatures at reasonable terms − which must still be my bread and butter.

And there is another thing: I am here in East Anglia, where everything I see puts me in mind of my idol Gainsborough, and makes me itch to get out my sketchbook — and in short, I feel that I am in the right place, that I can do fine things here. Above all, Father, don't give yourself a moment's more uneasiness about my material well-being: I eat heartily, I have clothes on my back, and (at the risk of talking cant!) I want no more than that. I go to view a studio tomorrow — will write more fully soon — and remain,

Your affectionate son,
Pierce

The letter sanded and sealed, and the ample Norfolk supper disposed of, the young man asked to see his room, and was guided thither through a creaking eternity of passageways, where everything sloped, and nothing formed a right-angle. Left alone, he lit a second candle, and drew out from his trunk an unframed watercolour landscape, and a framed oil miniature of a child in a pink bonnet, which had hung as a specimen to attract custom in several temporary studio windows in the course of Pierce Coppinger's fledgling career as an itinerant portrait-painter.

'Well!' the young man said to himself. 'Gainsborough worked his way up, after all, and had to spend years painting faces.'

He went to bed, and revisited a pleasant dream-country, in which his paintings were the triumph of the Royal Academy exhibition, and were all bought by the young Queen, who paid him in five-pound notes, with her crown on.

The noise of a great coaching-inn bestirring itself for the day woke him early, and he was up and dressed well before the chambermaid brought his shaving-water to the door. After breakfasting in the coffee-room, he went forth into the city of Norwich. The light which broke from the sky, swept with torn clouds like so much autumn leaf-wrack, struck him as peculiarly East Anglian — it had excited his eye throughout the coach journey up from Cambridge yesterday; and he got himself agreeably lost in a confusion of busy streets, where old timber-clad houses nodded their bulbous brows together over the way – some spruce and neat, others exhibiting gaping holes in their plaster, and shored up with beams and joists to prevent them from tumbling down into the road. Emerging at last from a narrow inlet of a street, Pierce came upon the market-square, broad as a parade-ground, and covered from end to end with the coloured awnings of market-stalls. A few enquiries revealed that the place he sought was on the other side, and so he plunged on straight through the market. The produce of Norfolk, like a perpetual Christmas, assailed his eyes and nose on every side: prodigious beeves, veal and mutton, sucking-pigs, poultry and game, fish enough for a sea-port, butter and cheese and eggs, dressed fowls and sweetbreads and sausage – the smaller meats set out in half-moon baskets at the feet of women sitting in florid, shawled, and garrulous rows. Once on the other side he found, in another sheltered creek of gabled buildings, the address he sought, and stepped into a wainscoted office, where a clerk lurked behind a high counter, penned in with a brass rail, as if he were a specially fine Academy picture and had to have the crowds kept off him.

The office was that of a land-agent and auctioneer, with whom Pierce had been in correspondence about renting a studio in the city. His card brought forth the chief clerk, a bald perspiring man who, shaking Pierce's hand in both his own, said, 'The gentleman in the artistic line, how d'you do, sir – I had my hand upon your last letter just this moment. You're still interested in the property we suggested, sir? Capital – we'll step over directly and see it, Mr Coppinger, if you've the mind. I think you won't be disappointed.'

Weaving in and out of the traffic, and dancing in and out of the gutters, the clerk led Pierce through the streets at a trot, halting only once, when a man with a crutch in a sailor's uniform piteously held out his hat.

16

'Pooh! Don't try that with me, you vicious object!' the clerk said, shaking a fist; adding to Pierce, as they went on: 'He's no more a wounded sailor than I am, sir. It's a dodge — there's any amount of 'em. We get 'em from London, I'm afraid,' he said, as if the beggar were an inferior imported article. 'Beg your pardon, sir — would you be from London yourself?'

'Not I,' said Pierce. 'Though I have lived there for a time.'

'Nor yet a local man, I think?'

'No — I find it hard to say where I'm from. My father was a sea-captain — he's retired at Torbay now — and my late mother used to lodge at whichever was his home port. So I was born at Deal, but I had lived at half the ports of the country before I was out of petticoats.'

'A sea-captain, sir, indeed? Then *you* will have seen through that imposter immediately,' said the clerk. 'Oh! the dodges they'll try. Rubbing themselves with gunpowder to look like they've been burnt, or shamming fits, is the least of it. I make it a rule never to give a farthing for anything less than a genuine stump, and that a fresh one.'

They had arrived at Pottergate, a long street fretted with numerous courts and alleys, and the clerk stopped at the door of an old three-storeyed house with bow windows bulging out on to the path.

'Here's the property, Mr Coppinger — first floor. You couldn't hope for a quieter or more respectable trade directly beneath you,' the clerk said, indicating the sign fixed beside the door, which read N. TRUNCH, DYER, MOURNING-STATIONER. 'Now just be careful of this little turn on the stair, sir — it's nothing when you're used to it. And here we are.'

The first floor consisted of a large sitting-room, with a bow-window, a tiny bedroom, that was all bed and no room, and a sort of pantry-cum-scullery, equipped with a blackened fireplace, a Dutch-oven, a fish-kettle, and a smell of gravy dinners. Pierce, who was well used to the inconveniences of 'bachelor apartments' and was the least fussy of men, reserved his attention for the main room, where he would work, and receive his sitters. The window, forming one end of the room, furnished an excellent light; and going to it he saw a brilliant panorama of the old city, framed by the cathedral spire and the castle atop its hill.

'Yes – this will suit me admirably,' Pierce said.

'I never doubted it,' said the clerk. 'Directly we had the favour of your correspondence, I thought of this place. Now as to terms—'

'Stay – I'd forgot – there's one thing more,' said Pierce. 'Portrait-painting is my chief trade, and I rather need to display specimens on the street to catch the eye. Is there any way . . .?'

'It can be arranged, I'm sure of it,' the clerk said. 'We'll step downstairs to Mr Trunch. *He's* got two street-windows, and don't use the half – no occasion for 'em.'

The bell above the door into the ground-floor premises brought forth a man dressed in mourning, who seemed not to have come from anywhere, but simply to have materialized from the general blackness.

'Mr Trunch,' the clerk said, 'this is Mr Pierce Coppinger, who has some particular business to discuss—'

'A parent, sir?' the man in black said, looking Pierce up and down with a mild sympathizing glance.

'No indeed,' Pierce said. 'It isn't that . . .'

'Not a wife?' said Mr Trunch, leaning further sideways. 'Oh don't say a wife, sir. Don't say it. And so young . . .'

'It isn't a bereavement at all, Mr Trunch,' the clerk said. 'Mr Coppinger is going to take the first floor – a gentleman in the artistic line, you know; and he requires a little frontage, to advertise his trade.'

'Bless me, sir,' said Mr Trunch, shaking Pierce's hand, 'you may take that whole window, for all the good it is to me.'

'Just space for a few miniature portraits and a card of terms will be ample,' Pierce said, 'thank you kindly.'

'Portraits, eh? Why, that'll be an advantage to me, to get folk to pause and look in. It's not the sort of stock to beguile the eye, sir, you'll agree,' said Mr Trunch, waving a hand at the inky interior of his shop, 'and I don't attract the browser – more's the pity.'

Mr Trunch's shop was admirably if depressingly fitted out. The more conventional items of mourning – scarves, caps, weepers, hatbands, wristbands – were the lesser part. The counter was taken up with various specimens of mourning-stationery – black-bordered envelopes, notepaper, blotters, and calling-cards, black silver-sand, black pen-wipers, black sealing-wax, black seals inscribed with various deathly back-to-front messages – whilst set out in open drawers, lined with black gauze, were samples of every small object that could possibly go into mourning: jet jewellery and hairpins and combs and buttons, black reticules and pocket-books, scent-bottles, scissors-cases, thimbles, pin-cushions, lucifer-matches, dyed hat-feathers, even japanned snuffboxes so that one might grieve while taking a pinch; and about all a crapy, stuffy, muffled atmosphere, so that every word spoken there seemed to come out as a whisper. The man who dealt in these sombre goods was perhaps no more than thirty, but was rendered older by his suit of rusty black and by a habitually commiserating expression; with a fringe of dark greased hair and a round, plump, heavy-lidded face – a face designed for an agreeable cheerfulness which in the nature of the man's business had to be continually suppressed – and a soft white complexion, as if Mr Trunch, living in his black airless milieu, had begun to take on something of the composition of a mushroom.

'It's not a cheerful trade, I can see,' Pierce said.

'It isn't, sir,' Mr Trunch agreed. 'But it's steady – that's the beauty of it. Decease can always be counted on; it don't fall off. My one regret is that people only come to me when they have to, like the doctor, and so they only think of me in a Deceased light. I've had one of the custom tell me that whenever he sees my name written up, he's put in mind of boiled ham and seed-cake — which isn't a gratifying association. And then there's having to wear mourning all the time, which I do, out of respect for the custom; and it's hard, sometimes, when you wake of a morning, with the birds on the bough, and the sun shining, and your heart singing, to know you can't do justice to your feelings with a yellow weskit, or a spotted cravat — not that my heart sings so very often, sir, on account of my affections were blighted at a tender age, by a trifler — but it *does* sing, sir, I assure you.'

Pierce said he was sure of it; and hoped they would be excellent neighbours.

'I'm convinced we will be, sir,' Mr Trunch said. 'And though I can't promise to put any custom in your way just now — as regards having myself painted, I mean, Mr Coppinger, for I've no one to give a portrait to — though there was a time when the trifler to whom I alluded might have trembled to receive a miniature of my poor likeness, and even laid it under her fragrant pillow —' here Mr Trunch showed signs of agitation — 'still, in spite of my affections being blighted, I've been known to be convivial in the little parlour behind my shop, and I'll be honoured any evening to pledge a bumper with you — say to the Muse of pictorial art (I presume there is one) — may she always attend upon you, and never prove a trifler.'

Pierce thanked the mourning-stationer heartily; and returning with the clerk to the land-agent's office, concluded the business, paying a month's rent in advance, and taking possession of his new studio at once. Going thence to his inn, he was surprised to find a crowd of people blocking the passage outside his room; and a boot-boy, on Pierce's enquiring what was the matter, made a hasty scramble backward and cried: 'Thass him! Look at his eyes — like live coals!'

The crowd parted to let him into his room, where he found a hysterical chambermaid being revived with smelling-salts by another girl, whilst an ostler stood guard with a meat-jack. 'Now then!' he said to Pierce, brandishing it rather uncertainly. 'Don't come it, you know: I look thin, but I'm wiry!' At the same moment the chambermaid, catching sight of Pierce, screamed that the monster was here, and threw her apron over her head declaring that he was going to Do her next.

Pierce saw in a moment what had happened. In taking clean clothes from his trunk that morning, he had pulled to the top his lay-figure – a jointed dummy which the painter used as a model for the set of the body and folds of clothing once the face had been filled in – and the chambermaid, coming into the room in his absence, had seen a lifelike pair of legs and an arm protruding from the trunk, and must have drawn an alarming conclusion as to Pierce's profession. Pierce, anxious to relieve the chambermaid's mind at once, and thinking her unsusceptible at the moment to a reasoned explanation, chose the unfortunate expedient of dragging the lay-figure forth from the trunk, and shaking it before the girl's eyes, turning it upside-down and banging its stuffed head on the floor to demonstrate that it was not made of flesh and blood: a proceeding which sent the girl into such a state of screaming that her colleague was obliged to stick pins in her.

At length the true state of the case was made known to the chambermaid, but she persisted to the last in calling Pierce a monster, trying to frighten innocent girls with his dummies; and declared, to the agreement of the onlookers at the door, that he had a proper Murderer's nose anyway, and had the gallows written all over him. This was unfair on Pierce, who had rather a fine nose, and who, though he wore his hair a little long, had nothing disreputable about his appearance whatsoever; but it was characteristic of him that when the door was closed at last, and his brief notoriety over, he sat down to enjoy a good laugh, and to write to his father about it.

Pierce Coppinger, as he had intimated to the clerk, had lived an unsettled life. His childhood years, when his father had been at sea, had been spent in a variety of places, and he had had a little learning knocked into him in a variety of seafaring academies, with an expectation that he would follow his father's profession – the Coppingers having been naval men since Sandwich's day. His mother had died when he was thirteen, and his father retired soon afterwards to settle at Torbay with a moderate income. Captain Coppinger had soon discovered that his son had no taste for the sea, and that all his masters agreed on his uncommon aptitude for drawing; and being a man of an individual turn of mind, the captain had ignored the unanimous advice of his friends – who counselled him, in the humane spirit of the time, to flog the boy into submission and forbid him ever to touch a pencil – and had engaged drawing-masters for his son, and eventually sent him as a pupil to an Italian painter and engraver in London. The death of Mrs Coppinger had ripened what had always been a warm and unaffected relationship between father and son, and it was the captain's idiosyncrasy to believe that the boy should be encouraged to do what he wanted to do, and that he would respect his father far more as a confidential friend than as a tyrant; and the frankness and affection between them seemed to bear this out, though there were still old shipmates of the captain's, pegging at their rum-and-water in Torbay lodgings, who shook their heads over it, and said that a boy liked you the better for giving him a good thrashing – and sighed, and looked at the clock, and wondered why their children never came to see them.

Pierce had never wanted to do anything but draw and paint. As a small boy on a visit to London, he had become separated from his parents, who had found him at last in the Royal Academy exhibition-rooms, standing in front of a Turner which he had seen on a visit there the day before. He could never recall how he had found his way there again, or how long he had stood gazing at the picture. Thus it had been high delight to him to find himself studying to be an artist in London in his late teens, and to his natural relish for the occupation he had added a determination to succeed for the sake of the father who was supporting him through his apprenticeship. But hard as he worked in the Italian's studio, and hard as he studied at the Royal Academy life-classes, he could not escape a feeling of restlessness and dissatisfaction as he came to manhood. He painted foliage and pillars in the corners of Signor Gardini's huge historical canvases, where everybody had muscular calves, and pointed significantly at things with dimpled hands, and a nor'-easter seemed always (even indoors) to be blowing their complicated draperies about. He respectfully studied engravings of the Old Masters, and earned a little money from executing vignette engravings of a rather different sort, for keepsake-books and magazines — courting couples dressed in an extremity of fashion, coming out of churches about the size of sentry-boxes, or skating on a frozen pond while smirking at each other. He admired the endless Cupid-and-Psyches and Scenes-from-*The-Vicar-of-Wakefield*s at the summer Academy exhibitions, and dreamed of a day when he would exhibit there — and felt increasingly that he was not on the right track. The Dutch landscape tradition was what he loved: he venerated Gainsborough, and he was lost in admiration of the lucid East Anglian skies of the few Constables he had seen — though not many people seemed to like them, and one of his fellow-students likened a Constable to a tank full of frog-spawn. A meeting in London with Cotman, the leader of the Norwich School of landscape watercolourists, gave Pierce the sense of a kindred spirit, and reinforced his growing conviction that the fashionable studio-bound academic tradition was not for him.

Soon after that, he secured a commission to execute a

series of topographical views of an Essex estate belonging to an art-loving baronet. Those months of freedom and open air wrought a change in Pierce. He painted several miniature portraits of the baronet's family and friends while he was there; and it seemed to him that here was a way to make a living, whilst at the same time being able to do what he loved and felt he was made for — simply painting what he saw in the country, without any nymphs and shepherdesses getting in the way, or Tamburlaine and his chariots crossing the left foreground with a lot of implausibly white horses rolling their eyes and looking unmanageable. He knew one or two fellows who had struck out for themselves as itinerant portrait-painters — travelling from one town to the next, setting up a temporary studio, and turning out likenesses on easy terms for the middle classes. It was a long-established trade, and seemed to be little threatened by the laborious and expensive new invention called the daguerreotype: but Pierce was warned that it was a grinding business, endlessly painting the phizes of grocers and their wriggling children; whilst Signor Gardini protested that it wasn't art at all. But Pierce had felt at once that it was for him. He disliked London, particularly in the summer when the smell of the river was such that one could not open the windows. He loved to be on the move, and to see new landscapes open before him — perhaps this, in a modified way, was his seafaring blood coming out; and, again perhaps because of his sailor stock, he was moderate in his material wants, and had never thirsted after grandeur and riches.

His only worry concerned his father. It troubled Pierce that his father might think this a disappointing, gypsy sort of life, and wonder whether it had all been worthwhile. Captain Coppinger gave no such signal; but he had gently suggested of late that if Pierce wanted to change to some more remunerative and settled profession, he would help him without demur. It was to this suggestion that Pierce had replied in the letter written in the inn coffee-room. There was no insincerity in what he had written. He knew that if he had gone to his father, confessed that the painting was a mistake, and asked for help, it would have been given with no reproach. Yet he would have felt his own failure. And Pierce did not think the painting was a mistake. His modest view of his own talent was matched with a sturdy optimism about his potential to learn and improve – if he could just go about it in his own way. Pierce Coppinger had a good measure of stubborn determination running through a nature that was in most respects easy-going, cheerful, transparent, and not very serious: it was not merely in his lithe and rangy physical appearance that he resembled a sapling tree whose strength lay in its flexibility.

So he was entering the second year of his travelling career, which had begun not too fortuitously at Bath – only the remnants of its fashion remained in the shape of a colony of decaying Regency pensioners held together by starch and whalebone – and continued at Brighton, where he had done well, and then at Cambridge, which he had found the meanest town in the kingdom; and so he had come to Norwich, the heart of that East Anglia of vast pearly skies and meadows and mills that had always attracted him, where he hoped to meet members of the Norwich School, and continue his landscape studies in the interim of commissions. He endeavoured, in the second letter he wrote to his father, to further reassure the captain as to his prospects; and expressed his hope that the old gentleman was in good health and spirits. He had feared at first that his father might suffer from want of company and occupation down at Torbay; but Captain Coppinger had resources against boredom in his own character, which was markedly independent, hot-tempered, and somewhat eccentric – though the latter suggestion infuriated him.

'I have *always* slept with my feet pointing to magnetic north,' Captain Coppinger had once said. 'It is the merest common sense, as I informed the doctor, that ass, that block, that painted stick without a trace of mind, who had the temerity to laugh at an eminently sensible measure which any uncertificated sawbones would have the wit to acknowledge.' The captain consulted his physician often, and never agreed with anything he said or did anything he told him. His stated creed was that a man should always think for himself, and he had carried this to the extent of suspecting that the world as a whole was attempting an imposture on him. Though rather devout, he frequently attacked the local clergyman on his own ground when he thought he saw an attempt to pull the wool over his eyes.

'Now look here,' he had said once to Pierce, thrusting an open Bible before his son, 'here is another imposture – see: "Cast thy bread upon the waters: for thou shalt find it after many days." Now what is this?' the captain cried, swelling and reddening. ' "Cast thy bread", and so forth – what nonsense is this? A brute with the merest vestige of soul or sense will tell you it is *not* so – the gulls will be gobbling the bread in an instant . . . I protest – really I protest at such an insult to my understanding – I shall tell the vicar so – I shall inform that scoundrel that I did not dodge cannonballs in the Indies to be fed such fairy-tales – bread, and waters, and many days – really I protest!' In this way he maintained a running feud with the medical profession, the church, and the law as well; and he had even fired off 'a pretty stinging letter' to the publishers of Sir Walter Scott's novels, in protest at an imposture in *Waverley*. ' "My heart's in the Highlands, my heart is not here – My heart's in the Highlands a-chasing the deer!" ' he had read out, with volcanic disgust. 'My dear boy, consider – consider for a single moment the flagrant impossibility of a disembodied heart pursuing a deer across country – mountainous, too – no, really, it will not do!' But there was evidently something sustaining in this permanent state of warfare with a world out to hoodwink him: indignation was the captain's tonic, and he came out of each quarrel like a man refreshed.

Pierce had inherited none of this; but he had inherited the tolerant belief that every man should think just what he liked, which was partly why he had not settled to a conventional artistic career; inherited too a way of looking at life with a certain youthful freshness of expectation. Accordingly he settled into his new studio with a ready optimism, covering the uglinesses of the main room with various draperies that he carried with him as backgrounds for his sitters, and with choice specimens of his own work; unpacking his paints, brushes, knives, palettes, maulstick, and canvas, with their pungent linseedy smell that never failed to give him a tingle of happiness; and hanging in Mr Trunch's window a selection of miniatures. In the evening he accepted Mr Trunch's invitation, and joined the dyer and mourning-stationer for a glass of something in his little parlour behind the shop: a comfortable nook, with a rather hectic pattern of flowers and birds breaking out like measles all over the walls and curtains, as if to keep the funereal firmly at bay. Mr Trunch dispensed hot punch with a liberal hand, until Pierce felt himself fairly steeped in lemon, cloves and sugar; and presently his host took down a clay-pipe from the mantelshelf and asked Pierce if he partook.

'Thank you, no,' Pierce said, 'but please, don't let me stop you.'

'I won't, Mr Coppinger, as you're good enough to insist,' said Mr Trunch, lighting the pipe with a black spill. 'It's my weakness. There was a time when I was proof against it — the punch likewise; bless you, there was a time when one glance from the killing eyes of a certain fair trifler to whom I have alluded was meat and drink to me for days and nights together — when if you'd put a bottle of the finest brandy in my hands, and said, Nahum Trunch, drink! — why, I would have laughed (not uncivilly I hope) and emptied the stuff to the drains. I was a young palmer in love's eye, as the poet has it — I was clean-limbed, upright, water-drinking, up with the sun and to bed with the − ' Mr Trunch cast about him − 'with the ploughman. I couldn't see a gate without leaping over it. As for tobacco, I scorned such stimulants. I was a different man from the one you see now, Mr Coppinger; the light of a vision was before my eyes, and I trod upon flowers − until I was disabused by a trifler, and fell a prey to dismal weaknesses.' Mr Trunch filled his cup again as he said this, and looked more cheerful by the moment. 'I suppose I oughtn't to indulge; I suppose I ought to resist − but bless you, where's the point in having weaknesses, if you don't give in to 'em ? Blighted as I am, I haven't got the will − and so you see the miserable creature before you,' concluded Mr Trunch, pulling on his pipe, and settling into his armchair and, judging by his appearance, not greatly regretting his fall at all.

Pierce was put in mind of a bruise made on his own heart by an elegant young lady at Brighton, whose parents had seen him off (too poor), and whom he had last seen on the arm of a Guardsman with a humiliating quantity of whisker. It was not a deep bruise − Pierce had never yet felt such, taking life lightly as he did − but the punch touched a sentimental nerve, and he sympathetically asked Mr Trunch whether there had been an objection to the trade he carried on.

'Not that as such,' Mr Trunch said, 'though there was an occasion when the lady in question (whom it is too painful for me to name) had rather a turn on coming to my shop, and seeing a mourning-christening-robe hanging up; but the real mischief was done by a villain of a law-clerk − pardon me, sir − ' Mr Trunch worked his greased hair into agitated shapes − 'I can't moderate my feelings when I speak of him − a villain of a law-clerk, who poisoned her mind against me by warning her that the fumes from the dye-vats, over the yard, fly up to the head and turn the brain; and slandering the profession by insinuating that all dyers die insane − yes, he even

28

stooped to a pun on it — which indicates his character, Mr Coppinger, more damningly than can any words of mine. Another cup, sir?'

Mr Trunch rose, a little heated, to fetch Pierce more punch; and returning, pressed a sheet of paper into Pierce's hand.

'That is she,' Mr Trunch said.

It was a watercolour sketch, of a long-nosed lady with all her teeth showing, apparently floating in mid-air next to a leaning piano.

'Not a good likeness — her sister's drawing, you see, sir — she dabbled in the polite arts — contemptible to your professional eye, I know. She was for throwing it away — but I seized it secretly, and slipped it under my coat-tails, and bore it off exulting. It's the only likeness I possess, you see, so I keep it — it's my weakness.'

Pierce, not knowing quite how to respond, said: 'You mentioned a law-clerk—?'

Mr Trunch nodded. 'It was to His embraces,' he said, 'that she fled from me.'

'Dear me,' Pierce said, 'I'm very sorry, indeed — but I'm honoured that you should show her picture to me, Mr Trunch.'

'Why, I felt you were a man to understand, sir, as soon as we met,' said Mr Trunch, 'and I've been fondly imagining today (it's my weakness), how nice it would have been to have proudly introduced to you, as my promised bride, she whose name I cannot write in fancy's copy-book without dropping a tear upon the blighted page. I would only advise you, sir — since that can never be — to beware of law-clerks, if you enter the lists of love, for they will break your lance, lame your steed, and reduce you to — ' Mr Trunch raised his cup, and beamed comfortably through the steam of it — 'to just such a miserable being as I.'

Pierce woke the next morning with a thick head and a guilty suspicion that it was late, and that a succession of people might have been knocking at his door and clamouring for portraits and going away again disgusted and spreading the word that he was unreliable, and so his career was finished. Coffee and a hot roll from a pastry-cook's over the way restored him; and he stood for some time at his bow-window, observing the street with its milling people — all of them unfortunately oblivious of the presence of a needy artist in their midst, and of the tremendous difference a quarter-length portrait or a landscape with woodcutters and a cow would make to their lives. At last he went out to find the local newspaper offices and place an advertisement; and when he came back, wet from a sudden shower, he found a man knocking at his door.

'The portrait-painter, is it?' the man said, turning to Pierce with a stiff swivel of his whole body.

'Yes, yes, do come in,' said Pierce eagerly, opening the door. 'I almost missed you — how d'you do—'

But the man did not take Pierce's proffered hand — he shook his head in the same wooden way and said, 'Oh! no — it edn't me — I was just sent. I'm just the servant.' He was a stout, tight, rigid old fellow in a surtout and boots, with a fiery face and puffs of white hair escaping from beneath a hard glazed hat, which he levered off with a gingerly motion as if he were uncorking himself and feared he might go off bang. 'I come to ask will you paint Master and Mistress and are you dear?'

'Oh, I don't think anyone's ever found my terms unreasonable — they can certainly be negotiated,' said Pierce, who was not a very astute businessman. 'Master and mistress: that would be a double portrait—?'

'Thass it,' said the man, who with great care had chosen a spot on the faded rug, and was standing there with no more give in him than a chess-piece.

'A wedding-portrait, perhaps?'

'Oh! no.'

'Well,' said Pierce, 'if the lady and gentleman would like to suggest a time when they could come for a first sitting—'

'No,' said the manservant, 'he don't go out, not nowadays: he want you to come to him, see. Thass noo goo, otherwise.'

'So the sittings would be in the gentleman's own home?'

'Noo goo, otherwise.'

'Well, certainly, I've done that before, if that's what suits the lady and gentleman,' Pierce said. 'When would it be convenient for me to call?'

'I'm to take you there now, to discuss it, if you'll come,' said the man, corking himself up again. 'Thass not far.'

It was all rather curious, Pierce thought, but encouraging – one could command a higher price for a double portrait; and pausing only to pack up a few specimens of his work, he pronounced himself ready.

The manservant turned himself about with an awkward shuffle, like a figure on a Swiss clock, and then was pulled up short in moving to the door by his right leg refusing to move.

'Oh! you would, would you?' the man said fiercely, addressing his leg and giving it some quite brutal blows with his fist. 'You beggar – you villain, you – don't start, thass all!' The leg gave in at last, and moved, and they went out to the landing, Pierce expressing some anxiety about the manservant's being able to manage the stairs.

'Oh! there's nothing amiss with me,' the man said, clumping down the stairs without apparently bending his knees at all, and bouncing off each wall as he went. 'It's this beggar as goes gammy on me – you villain!' he added, aiming another punch at his leg. '*I'm* as spry as they come. But that leg won't be told, and then there's this rascal – ' holding up his gnarled left hand – '*he's* started, lately – you rogue!' giving it a cuff with his other hand. 'They'll take liberties, do you give in to 'em – and then there's no end to it.'

This man's employer, he answered in response to

Pierce's enquiry, was Mr Childs of Cardinal's Cap Yard; and he then fell silent, giving his attention to his stumping progress through a warren of courts and alleys off St Benedict's, where the light of the sun, dim and bleary enough on this dun autumn day, got itself lost altogether in a forest of chimneys, and gables, and slouching eaves, and noisome passageways between tenements. There were little frowsy houses here built on ancient gardens, and yet littler houses squeezed, somehow, into the spaces between them, and into the corners of yards, and even right across the path. Occasionally they came across a dwarfish shop, with a window like a porthole, and a set of sunken steps to tumble down, and a low lintel to crack your head on; and often the manservant gave a grunt as they passed through some particularly sombre alley, where what seemed at first to be stables turned out to be human dwellings, and what seemed at first to be a half-starved dog turned out to be a ragged infant crawling in the muck. Pierce had begun to wonder how he would ever find his way out again, when they emerged into a broader yard, hard by a ruined church, and a signboard – JOS. CHILDS, TANNER – announced that they had reached their destination.

The house was large, and old, and made a dead-end of the yard; and one wing of it – where the signboard was fixed on a double gate, and from which came thick smoke and the reek of belly-leather – was clearly the tannery. The other half of the building seemed to be residential, though there were no signs of life at its barred and shuttered windows, and a long silent wait ensued when the manservant knocked at the door. Looking up, Pierce thought the house might have been constructed so as never to catch the sun at any angle; and when at length they were admitted by a maid after much drawing back of bolts, he was led in through so many locked and double-locked doors, and through little halls and corridors and vestibules – like infant rooms that had been confined there and been stunted and never grown up – and then through more doors, and up steps and down steps, that he had a curious feeling that he was going to come out at the other side of the house, never having been properly in it at all.

Finally, however, he found he was in a large, low-ceilinged room, without any clear idea of how he had got there; and the manservant was saying to a bundle of old clothes by a cold fireplace, 'Here's the portrait-painter — I brought him.'

The room was shuttered, and it took Pierce a moment to identify the bundle as an old man, who was beckoning him to come forward. The manservant, meanwhile, had uncorked himself again, and was very briskly rearranging the various shawls and rugs with which his master was swathed, as if he were making a bed.

'What are you about there, Ben Catbush?' the old man said irritably.

'Why, you've all come undone, you have,' said the servant, with a respectful firmness. 'And look here — you've let that fire go out. Now why didn't you ring?'

'I'd like to know how I'd pay your wage if I kept fires in October,' the old man grumbled.

'You'll go down with an ague, you will,' the servant said. '*I* know you.'

'That'll do — get gone,' his master said, flapping him away; and when they were left alone, peering up at Pierce in the gloom. 'Mr Coppinger, is it?'

'Yes, Mr Childs. How d'you do,' said Pierce, offering his hand. Mr Childs shook it doubtfully enough, as if he feared that might commit him to something, and motioned Pierce to a chair on the other side of the hearth.

'I don't get about much, see,' Mr Childs said. 'Ben Catbush tole me there was a portrait-chap come to town. I been looking out for one, see.'

Pierce said he was glad of the opportunity, growing a little uncomfortable under the piercing scrutiny of Mr Childs, who rasped a thin hand back and forth across his chin and studied him from head to foot. As his eyes adjusted to the semi-darkness of the room, Pierce saw that it was a sort of unfriendly parlour, with a closed bureau, a locked bookcase, a looking-glass chained like a felon to the wall, some stuffed birds imprisoned under a glass dome, some live birds (no more lively) in an ornate gaol of a cage, and a dismal lop-sided chandelier, like something that had climbed up there and hanged itself. Everything was so shut and sealed and confined, that the very carpet, curling at the edges, seemed to be trying to roll itself up and be put away. He saw too that Mr Childs was not as old as he had first thought — perhaps not fifty-five; but was plainly without health, so that he had the hunch, the grey complexion, and the tremulous grasp of old age. Beneath his skull-cap long yellowy strands of hair hung over his collar and over the snuff-stained shawl about his shoulders: there was a snuff-box in his lap, and snuff too seemed a dominant element in the expression of his long face which, in its raised brows and tight lips and alertly hooked nose, was that of a man about to take a pinch. The eyes that examined Pierce — so completely, so warily — were bright blue, a younger man's eyes, full of shrewdness — and, it seemed to Pierce, full of troubles.

'Now, are you dear? Because I'm not a wealthy man, you know — don't think it,' Mr Childs said in a defensive tone.

Pierce said he was sure they could agree on terms, and produced his sample portraits, which Mr Childs studied with great attention.

'These are real folks, are they?' Mr Childs said, pausing to glance keenly up at Pierce.

'Yes — various friends, who kindly agreed to sit for me,' said Pierce, not caring to admit that some were unsold commissions.

'Ah! Now here's the one!' Mr Childs said suddenly. It was a double portrait of a brother and sister (who had hated each other); the woman looking at a music-book, while the man rather idiotically showed her a flute. 'Two together – thass what I'm after. Not with a flute, though – I don't want a flute. I suppose you could do it without a flute – could you?'

Pierce assured him that a flute was not compulsory. 'The pose is up to you, Mr Childs. Perhaps there's a special occasion that you and Mrs Childs wish to commemorate – an anniversary . . .?'

'Anniversary?' said Mr Childs sharply. 'Who said anything about an anniversary? Ben Catbush? What've he been saying?'

'No, really, Mr Childs – it was just a speculation on my part,' Pierce said. 'I do a lot of anniversary portraits, that's all.'

'Well – mebbe it is an occasion, after all,' said Mr Childs more softly, 'or it will be, mebbe . . . Now look here! You know your business, I hope. I don't know the words for it. I want me and Mrs Childs together, see – faces, so as you can tell who it is, plain – I don't care about bodies – that don't signify.'

'Quarter-length then,' Pierce said. 'Certainly,'

'And I don't want one of these here little ones,' Mr Childs said, pointing to one of Pierce's miniatures, and then at a half-size sketch. 'This big, at least. I suppose that comes dearer ? Oh! well, I suppose it would. Paint don't cost nothing, I dare say. And I want us a-looking at each other – see?'

'Surely,' Pierce said. 'Perhaps with linked hands?'

'Ah! Thass it!' Mr Childs said, wheezing with animation. 'A-looking at each other, wi' linked hands – just like life – thass how I want it!'

Pierce felt there might have been something touching in this, had not the light in Mr Childs' darting eyes appeared more obsessive than tender, and had there been any sign of feminine influence, any hint of the affectionate home in that barren parlour; but had not Pierce known Mr Childs was a married man, he would have classified the room, and the house altogether, as the den of a solitary and rather miserly bachelor. He was already wondering whether Mrs Childs was quite so unprepossessing in looks as her husband, and how he was going to make the old man look anything less than grotesque, but he smiled and asked, 'When would it be convenient for the sittings to begin?'

'Why, as soon as may be,' said Mr Childs. 'I got no time to waste. You can come every day, I suppose?'

Pierce said he certainly could, if Mr and Mrs Childs would not find it too tiring.

'Oh! I can do any amount of biding still,' said Mr Childs grimly. 'Thass all I'm good for, now, with this—' He struck his chest, and produced a terrible hurdy-gurdy note. 'As for Mrs Childs, that don't signify. *She* won't be sitting.'

Pierce was taken aback a little. 'Er − the lady's shy of sitting for her portrait, perhaps? Just a short time would be enough, if—'

'Now look here!' Mr Childs said. 'You know your business, don't you? I mean, you painter fellows do all that studying − don't you? − standing afore those Old Masterpieces for days on end, and copying 'em? And there's another thing: did you ever see an elephant?'

Pierce, deliriously wondering whether this startling question was meant to prepare him for Mrs Childs' appearance, said he had not.

'Ah!' cried Mr Childs, with a cunning look, and an agitation of his fleshless jaws. 'But if I was to put paper before you − now, you know your business! − and say to you, draw me a likeness of an elephant − you could, couldn't you?'

Pierce, caught between bewilderment and professional pride, answered that he could.

'Thass all right then,' said Mr Childs, suddenly levering himself upright with the help of a stick by his chair. 'Come you here.'

Pierce gave the old man his arm to support him, and was led to a corner of the room, where a small portrait hung on the panelled wall.

'Thass Mrs Childs,' said Mr Childs.

It was an amateur drawing in ink and wash, but not badly executed, of a plump fair woman in early middle age. Pierce was just thinking that Mr Childs had done rather well for himself, when the old man gripped his arm and said: 'Dead! — dead this twelvemonth, and I wish I was with her!' Adding, his voice sunk to a hoarse whisper: 'And sometimes that more than half seem as if I am!'

Pierce looked from the picture of the dead woman to the haggard, troubled, champing face beside him — a face made yet more narrow by the shadows of the dim room, so that it seemed half eaten away — with a feeling of having stepped into someone's uneasy dream. But Mr Childs, suddenly becoming businesslike, threw him the keen look again and said, 'So now you see: I want you to paint me from the life — call it life, anyhow! — and Mrs Childs from that there picture; both together, holding hands, like we were both alive, or both dead — it's all one. Come — you know your business: will you do it?'

Pierce hesitated. 'Is it a good likeness?' he said.

'Why, I know it's her — thass what matters,' Mr Childs said. 'And suppose, when you was a-drawen of her, I was to look over your shoulder now and then, and say how she was: mebbe the nose a little more so, or the chin a little more so — that would help, woulden it? Come: you know your business!'

It was certainly the oddest commission Pierce had ever taken, but he saw no reason why he could not produce a satisfactory copy of the picture of Mrs Childs, and make a composition of it with the old man's face — and the curiosity of the whole affair appealed to him.

'I'll be glad to begin whenever you wish, Mr Childs,' he said. 'And I think it will turn out very well. There's just one thing—'

'Ah?' — sharply.

'Will we be having the sittings in this room? It's just

37

that I really will need more light. If we might have the shutters open . . .'

Mr Childs rasped away at his jaw, as if he would file down his finger-ends. 'I don't like 'em open, thass a fact,' he mused, 'but then, you know your business. What say we begin tomorrow, then, hey? It can't be too soon for me. Pull that bell, Mester Coppinger — pull hard, do Ben Catbush'll never hear. His ears are going — going like his leg, and his hand, and I don't know what-all. And yet there's more life in him, what's left of him, than in all of me — I reckon there is!'

A sound of slow stumping down long passages, and of a stout body bouncing off various walls, preceded the eventual appearance of the rigid Ben, who began stolidly to fuss around his master. 'Now then, you been gambolling about, you have — *I* know you — and getting weared out. You're too lively, thass what you are . . .'

'Leave me be,' Mr Childs said testily. 'You're an old woman, Ben Catbush. Show Mester Coppinger out. He'll be coming the morrer morning — mind you let him in.'

Pierce was conducted, by the same incomprehensible route, to the front door, and presently found himself in the sunless courtyard, the door being fastened shut behind him, with a dull rattling and clanking of locks and bolts. Again he looked up at the shuttered old house, finding it hard to believe that he had ever been in there, and received his strange commission; and it seemed to him, as he walked quickly away with an urge to seek out the busy streets, and light, and people, that Mr Childs could hardly have been more securely shut away from the world if he had lain fettered in a prison-cell.

Chapter Two

Jed's Dreams

There! There he was again!

The young weaver, having glanced over his shoulder, proceeded on his way a few paces, then ducked into the doorway of an ale-house. He counted to twenty, then inched forward and peered down the street with an effort at casualness. There were many people about — working men like himself, hurrying home in the smoky evening — and for a moment he thought he was mistaken. But no, there was the man — a stocky buttoned-up old fellow in stout boots. He was looking into a shop-window, with an appearance of never having had it in his mind to do anything but look into shop-windows from his very cradle.

The young weaver stared at him in perplexity. Surely it was the same man . . . Yet the old fellow turned never a hair, and presently waddled across the road to look in another window. The weaver shivered — it was a cold dank evening, and he wore only an old velveteen jacket over his shirt and neckerchief; home beckoned, and supper, and he wondered if hunger was perhaps making him light-headed and imagine things.

He set out again, clasping his jacket together at his throat, down the old and dilapidated thoroughfare of Magdalen Street, where there was a trampling of pattens in the mist-born mud, and where one or two hawkers still circulated with their trays round their necks, as dejectedly as if they had been millstones, and the first link-boys were lighting their pitchy torches with a sputter in the damp air. He resolved not to look behind him any more, and to have done with this fancy that he was being followed which had disturbed his rest the last few nights. His resolution held until he was on the point of turning into the dingy court where his home was, when all at once he gave in, and turned quickly about to see the self-same old fellow in the boots duck jerkily into an alleyway.

It *was* true! – he *was* being spied upon! In a flurry of indignation, fear, and he did not know what other feeling, the young weaver ran back down the street, and into the alleyway where his pursuer had disappeared.

'Hoy !' he cried. 'Now what's the game? I see you – come on!'

The alley was empty but for some stacked barrels. The young man ran down it, and peered into the stinking darkness of several cobbled passageways leading this way and that, but the old fellow was gone.

He gave it up and retraced his steps, lost in thought. His home was in a narrow court called, in all seriousness, Paradise Yard, one of several hundred such that lurked behind the streets of the city of Norwich. It was a promiscuous huddle of old merchants' houses that had been left to fall down, and then rebuilt, and left to fall down again, and now existed somewhere between those two states, carved up into crowded lodgings and forever hung with drooping banners of washing, on which the sooty air had such an immediate impact that it could be said never to be clean at all, but only to revolve through a varying cycle of dirt. The young weaver, Jed Wintergreen, inhabited a top-floor room in this healthful spot, reached by three flights of worm-eaten stairs; a room with an iron bed, a table and two bentwood chairs, a chest, a fireplace with a few pans, a couple of paper prints pasted to the wall, and a largish window giving a view of a chimney, a square yard of leads, and (usually) a dead starling. Here the young man came, panting from his recent run and from the climb, and flung himself down upon the bed in the utter exhaustion to which every day at the mill reduced him. At length the thumping and clattering of the looms – which always lingered like a ghost-sound in his head for some time after he had quitted the mill — cleared from his ringing ears, and he sat up and lit a candle, feeling the cold and wondering if he could afford a fire.

'I'll think no more of him,' he told himself. 'It's my imagination — or else he's some harmless old chap a bit soft in the head — thass all.' There was half a loaf on his larder-shelf, and cheese and some cold bacon, and he scraped together a fire to boil a kettle for tea. He had set out his meal on the rickety deal table when there was a tap at the door.

'Thass only me, Mester Wintergreen.' Mrs Carter from downstairs put her head round the door. 'There — I've stopped your supper. Yew goo on with it, dair — don't mind me.'

Mrs Carter sidled in and regarded him amiably with her arms folded on her comfortable shelf of bosom. She was a friendly old body who took in washing and sometimes cooked Jed a hot meal on her stove. She nodded encouragingly at him several times and then said: 'Just wondered if everything was all right. With yew, I mean.'

'All right enough, thank you, Mrs Carter,' Jed said. 'Dirty sort of day, edn't it?'

Mrs Carter said that it was enough to make you, without being more specific; and with more nods, added, 'I just wondered — yew know — whether everything was all right. In general. Only . . .'

'What's the matter?' Jed said.

'Well, I was asked not to say anything,' said Mrs Carter, 'only I don't hold wi' that sort of dealing. Mester Wintergreen's always been the best of neighbours to me, says I to meself, and I aren't about to start keeping secrets behind his back, not if any number of red-faced men was to ask me.'

'What red-faced men?' said Jed, pausing in his meal.

'Well, I didn't want no truck with him — I had enough to do wi' Mr Tabb's washing, and what he do with his

41

shirts I don't know but thass nothing no Christian ought to do whatever it is — and this here red-faced object in his gret boots come a-knocking and bothering me, so I nearly told him to go and boil his head, only then he say did Mester Jedediah Wintergreen live here, so I say yes — thinking it's mebbe important, you see. Only then he start asking questions — where did you work, and was you married, and that manner of thing . . .'

Jed's blood froze. 'A stout ole fellow, was he, Mrs Carter? All buttoned up close?'

'Ah, thass him. You know him, then? If I'd thought he was a friend of yourn I'd not have been so sharp with him — only as it was I didn't like the way he was asking these questions, and wanting to know all about you, specially when he said I weren't to tell you about it. Red-faced men in boots may like that sort of sneaking dealing, but I don't, and I said so. 'Course, if you know him . . .'

Jed was staring at his plate. Suddenly he could not eat. 'Know him . . . Yes, Mrs Carter, I — in a manner of speaking . . .'

'I hope I didn't do wrong, only *I* wasn't brought up that way—'

'No, no — you didn't do wrong — thank you, Mrs Carter,' Jed said. He managed at last to usher her out, and when she was gone he dropped into the chair before the smoking fire, his mind in a ferment.

It must be the same man! Not only following him, but seeking information on him . . . What could it mean? Who could be interested in a poor young weaver, the limits of whose life were this drab room and the gaunt mill by the river that claimed him for twelve hours a day? A wild and angry alarm seized him: from the unhappiness of his past, there had grown in Jed a strong revulsion from the power of authority, and now, all mysteriously, it seemed to be reaching out for him.

All at once his eye fell on the book by his bed. It had been lent to him by Jack Hall, a self-educated tailor. Norwich had a proud radical tradition, still alive in men such as Hall, who was involved with Chartism, and held meetings of like-minded working men at his house on Saturday nights. Books were like gold to Jed, and it was chiefly because Jack Hall was helping him to a little education that he attended the meetings; but he was in full agreement with all the Chartist aims, and he had joined the strikes when the worsted manufacturers, trying to compete with the machine-made textiles of the North, cut down the weavers' wages to starvation level. He remembered Jack Hall telling him of his brushes with authority, the way they kept their eye on him . . . Could that be what was happening? Was Jed too a marked man now, under surveillance?

At that thought his alarm cooled somewhat and hardened into defiance. It fitted in, after all, with what he knew of the world, which made him see it as inimical, untrustworthy, fraught with dark purposes which too often included the breaking of hearts. He had another vision of the world too — as it might be, if it were more true and just, and no doubt that was why the authorities were investigating him; and something of this twin vision was to be seen in Jed Wintergreen's appearance. At twenty-four he was tall and well-knit, robuster than many of his fellow-weavers, though pale-skinned as they all were from the long hours in the mill, and with a wiry sort of tension about his arms and shoulders, as if his overworked body could never entirely relax. His hair grew thick and dark about a high-cheekboned, intelligent face — a face that, placed above a genteel collar, against a background of ease, affection, comfort, might have formed a portrait of an attractive young man of spirit and promise. It was a face made to be generous and open, on which something urban and complex had cast a doubtful shadow. His blue Saxon eyes, with a faintly bruised and smoky touch about their orbits, looked at you with an unspoken question. There was an intentness that was warm but not restful, a capacity for passionate affection ever contending with the wariness of a young animal that has been ill-used.

He resolved at once that he would not be intimidated. Whoever this man might be who was haunting him, he would face him somehow, speak to him somehow, demand of him what it meant. Having decided this, Jed Wintergreen made himself brisk and, throwing off brooding, cleared his table, fetched water from the pump in the yard below, and washed off the grime of his long day. Then he trimmed the candle and sat down to write his regular letter to his sister Charlotte, in service at Shipden on the coast. He was an indifferent penman, but he had forced himself never to get out of practice, and the letter to his sister was important − all the love he bore her had to be concentrated in it, for they could scarcely ever get to see each other; and often he felt that those invisible, unbreakable threads linking him to Charlotte twenty miles away were all that kept his life steady, and gave it meaning.

But tonight he could not get on with the letter. He was disturbed. This business of the man investigating him had stirred his mind like a muddy pond. His was not a phlegmatic temperament: new trouble reawakened old, like the recurring of malaria, and Jed fell prey to dark thoughts as he paced back and forth about the dingy room. At some point he laid himself down on the bed; at some point he slept and groped helplessly into dreams of the past that he had hoped had left him for ever.

He was a child again, back in the workhouse, separated from his mother. He longed to comfort her, shattered as she was by the news of his poor father's death in the convict settlement; and in the dream the knowledge that she would soon die too sharpened his impotent agony. He yearned to console her, but he was always being marched away with the other pauper boys to another ward, and he could not reach her . . . Jed awoke with a lurch, sweating. The candle had burnt down to a grotesque winding-sheet, and the room was chill. He drank some cold tea and cursed. It was a long time since he had had that dream, and he hated it above all the others. That period had only been a short part of his life, yet it assumed a monstrous precedence: indeed, it determined everything about him.

They had struggled on — he, his mother and Charlotte — for a while after his father had been sentenced to transportation for his part in the 1830 riots: helped by other folk in the village, sustained by Jed's going far afield in search of more work, but hindered by his mother's failing health, and doomed at last by the news that his father had died almost as soon as he had been landed with the other convicts in Van Diemen's Land. Debility and fever, pronounced the official message: broken, amended Jed silently, broken and deprived of life as surely as if he had been hanged. It was that news that finished his mother. She had not the heart to struggle for independence any more. They had been taken into the workhouse; and his mother had, quite simply, relinquished her hold on life. Within a few months she was dead: a convict's grave on the other side of the world, and the brusque dispatch of a parish funeral, untimely closed the annals of a family, with all its mutual experience and hopes and habits and web-like ties of feeling, and left Jed and Charlotte workhouse orphans and paupers.

It left Jed, too, a bewildered, embattled young soul, trying to come to terms with a feeling that he had lived two lives — that his very self had been rent in twain. There was the life that existed before the night of the riot: poor, hard, but buttressed by massive solidities of affection and custom and loyalty, not only within his frugal cottage home but within his larger home, the village itself — Heartsease, the place where he belonged. And suddenly there was this other life, where no one cared who he was or what had been the myriad thoughts and impressions and memories that made him up, where his very identity was nothing more substantial than a name; where he was shunted about, and administered a meagre dose of food, and made to feel that he was granted existence only on the same terms as a weed in a garden. And it was of a piece with this life that he should be torn from Heartsease itself, as he had been separated from everything that nourished his being. There was little work in the village, and the parish overseers needed to be rid of him, and at last he had been sent to Norwich, where a weaver had agreed to take him as a pauper apprentice.

So he had gone, quite alone, quite ignorant of the place he was going to or the trade to which the overseers had farmed him out, leaving behind him the village of Heartsease, with all that had made his life bright entombed there, it seemed, everlastingly, and taking with him nothing but a small bundle of patched clothes, and a mental bundle of memories of which the keenest was his mother's fervent injunction to remember! Remember! He found himself in the heart of the old city: handsome enough, in the houses of its wealthy merchants and manufacturers, in the gracious closes about the cathedral, in shops and churches and assembly-rooms, but drab enough in the crowded quarter where his master lived, which to the country-bred boy appeared a frowning otherworld of brick and cobblestone with a strange climate of perpetual smoke and no sky. Conditions had often been cramped in Heartsease, but here total strangers lived on top of one another, coolly and abrasively; here the water was foul, and huge night-soil heaps festered right beneath the windows of houses, and no wind blew the noxious vapours away. The first shock soon wore off, but his mind always retained the sense of vivid contrast between the city and Heartsease, the village from which he had been effectively banished, and to the glowing memory of which his soul resorted, as a last and eternal defence against the hurts of the world.

His time as a weaver's apprentice had taken him to the edge of manhood. Jed still had dreams too about this time — the early part at least — but they were occasional fragments, painful glimpses, in which he was thirteen again, and waiting in fear and loathing for his master to come in from the ale-house, waiting to cast the single glance at the old weaver's face which would tell him whether his mood was blissful or − more usually − brutal . . . The man to whom Jed had been bound apprentice was a worsted weaver of an old-fashioned sort, running his own small premises − not very profitably − with living quarters behind containing a jumble of wormy furniture, a wall-eyed dog, and a punching-bag in slippers and curling-papers whom the weaver acknowledged in his lighter moments as his wife. Under the indentures which bound Jed to this place, the weaver, Pegg, was supposed to teach the boy all the art and mysteries of his trade, and so forth; but as far as Pegg was concerned, Jed was nothing but a parish boy − lowest of the low − who was there to have as much work beaten out of him as possible. He got to know, moreover, that Jed's father had been transported; and in his cups would sometimes regale the smarting boy with pleasantries about Botany Bay and gallows-birds and hulks, more terrible by far than the cuffings and thrashings that were the more straightforward expressions of Pegg's unlovely temper. Jed had borne it, somehow; the catastrophe that had come upon him and his family had made him temporarily apathetic, and left him feeling that justice and fairness were never to be expected any more, and it was no good resisting. But his personality, with the elasticity of youth, presently began to reassert itself; it was his nature to respond impetuously and generously to any friendliness, and Mrs Pegg, when she dared to be and when she was not pickled in gin, had been kind to him; and so there came a day when Pegg, in a mood to lay about him, and having already given his wife a black eye, found the stick snatched from his hand by his sixteen-year-old apprentice − not a burly lad by any means on the meagre victuals Pegg allowed him, but at that moment fiery and determined enough for

47

anything. Pegg blustered and threatened; met the defiant eye of the youth before him, calling on him to strike another blow if he dared; and, shamblingly, backed down.

From that time onward things were a little better. Pegg nagged and browbeat and raged at his apprentice as before, but he never went too far. All the same, it was a harsh enough life, and Jed was glad to escape it when his indentures were up. Factory discipline he found preferable to the niggling tyrannies of a small master, and he took the skills grudgingly taught him by Pegg to the mill of the Norwich Yarn Company, a brand-new building of gaunt brick, six storeys high, whose ranks of cell-like windows shed their light on to the river long into the evening. Various firms rented space in the mill, where overseers patrolled the long aisles between the looms and their toiling human servants, and where the yearned-for bell that signalled the end of work seemed like a shriek of protest that the monotonous din could go on no longer. Under this grim regimen − where for half the year he rose in darkness and trudged home in darkness, seeing no more of the sun than a mole − Jed Wintergreen felt his transformation of self to be complete. The boy who had lived in the lost community of Heartsease, amidst field and hedgerow and heath, seemed dead − dead as his poor wronged father and mother.

Yet Jed remembered − remembered as his mother had exhorted him to − remembered with a piercing clarity. Remembered not only the oppression and injustice of the time of the riot, remembered not only the names of those proud cold men who had wielded the power − Farmer Hemstock, Squire Ingamells, and his father's betrayer, Abel Jex: never, oh! never would he forget those names! He remembered too the world before the fall. His eyes watched the shuttling loom, while his mind's eye saw ploughed earth touched with frost, and copses like smoke on the horizon, and old Dick Freshwater's cart trundling and jingling down the village street. On Sundays he tramped out into the country — he had long rejected the church, and while Jack Hall and most of his friends were Dissenters, Jed wanted none of that either. He wore himself out trying to leave the city behind, and to get out of sight of the cathedral spire and the many church towers that beaconed over the sheep-meadows, and called him back at last. And such was the stuff of Jed's other dreams — healing dreams of a better place, open, green, and generous, dreams from which he woke with a sense of loss and longing . . .

Now Jed scattered the ashes on the fire and took a turn about his narrow room, troubled in his mind. His eye lit again on his letter to Charlotte. He must finish it tomorrow. Should he perhaps say something about the man who was following him? But no — it would surely worry her. Little as he was able to do for his sister, separated by twenty miles as they were, he felt a great protectiveness towards her, the stronger perhaps because his power to help her had been so limited. Not the least part of his agony in being sent away from Heartsease to work at Norwich had been the thought of leaving Charlotte behind in the untender care of the poor-law authorities; and when she had finally been sent out to service, as an underfed skivvy at a farm in the middle of nowhere, she had been as lost and miserable as he feared. Fate had ultimately relented towards her: her mistress had relatives who kept an inn in the fishing-town of Shipden, and they had offered to take the unhappy girl as a general servant. It had been a change greatly for the better. Her new master and mistress were kind, and now that she was grown she occasionally made the journey to Norwich for a day to see Jed, travelling there and back on the carrier's cart. There was joy in those days for Jed: he seemed to feel the touch upon his heart of the better old times, a kindly caress across the years, and he wished he could believe that the injured shades of their parents could see them together — survivors whom the harsh laws had failed to separate, and whose natural affections they had failed to poison. No, he would not disturb Charlotte's peace of mind.

He threw open the shutter for a look at the sky – a ration of sky, like a narrow town garden – before turning in. The mist had thinned, and there were stars above the chimney-stacks and jagged rooftops. A wish moved in him for someone in whom to confide his disquiet. Oh, there were friends, amongst his workfellows and at Jack Hall's, but in Jed's dreams of a better place and a better time, he sensed too the elusive presence of a friend he had never yet made, and of a heart that opened to his alone. But not here, not now: only the night received his thoughts, and the old cold stars so far away.

Chapter Three

At The Crab Pot

Charlotte Wintergreen had not been quite herself all day. A little nervous and excited, it seemed: she had even upset a whole basin of dried peas all over the kitchen floor, and usually she was the quietest, calmest and deftest of girls. So thought Mrs Skeels, the landlady of the Crab Pot Inn.

'I hope you're not starting a fever,' Mrs Skeels said. 'You look a mite hectic to me. I don't want you going into a swoon tonight — with a house-full, I shouldn't wonder, what wi' Toby Dane's coming of age an' all.'

'I'm all right, Mrs Skeels, truly,' said Charlotte. 'And you know I've never swooned.'

'That don't signify. I'd never been married afore I married Skeels — and look at me now!'

'Why, you do sound as if you regret it, mawther,' said Mr Skeels, with a wink at Charlotte.

'Now it's not fair if I'm to be took up wrong,' said Mrs Skeels, drawing herself up in her most severely reproving fashion. 'Never, Skeels, have I given you any hint o' that. No one could lay *that* at my door — they might accuse me of anythink else. I say anythink — forgery, murder, I shouldn't mind.'

'Not murder, mawther,' said Mr Skeels, 'surely!'

'I say murder. Now I won't be took up wrong, Skeels. It's all very well, but you wouldn't put up with it — you know you wouldn't.'

Mrs Skeels was a lean, perpendicular woman of fifty, rather sunken about her cheeks and bosom, and very starched about her cap and apron, with measured indignation expressed in every angle and knob of her body. She had an airily strict manner, which she

51

presented to everyone from her husband to the fishermen who came to the bar of the Crab Pot for their mugs of ale; and none of them minded it, knowing that her heart was as tender as her exterior was flinty. It was her whim to be perpetually on a moral high horse, and always fancying herself being knocked off it.

'And you'll wear *that* away, afore you're done,' Mrs Skeels said, as Charlotte for the fifth or sixth time smoothed and refolded an embroidered neckerchief that lay in waiting state on the kitchen table. 'And when you do, I hope you won't say I didn't warn you − I hope you'll not accuse me of *that*.'

'That do look all right, though − don't it?' Charlotte said. 'I never made anything to give to somebody before. Don't it, Mr Skeels?'

'Why, I should be glad of one like it,' said Mr Skeels.

'Well! I hope, Skeels, you don't mean to suggest you've never been anythink but well turned out since you married *me*,' huffed Mrs Skeels. 'No one could lay that at my door, I hope. Anyone might look in my closets. I'd go and drop myself in the sea directly, if I thought otherwise.'

'Never mind, mawther,' said Mr Skeels, with another wink at Charlotte. 'It's all according.' This was an habitual soothing formula with him. 'Well, well, young Toby twenty-one and all! That don't seem a candle's-length since he used to take this gal of ourn a-looking for shells on the beach, when she first come here, a little shrinken mouse who'd jump at a shadow!'

'Ah! Bringen shells home, indeed, when she ought to have been a-scrubben, and earning her keep!' snorted Mrs Skeels, omitting to mention that she had kept the shells, and had them still. 'They said to me, you'll spoil that gal − surely!'

'She's not spoilt, though, mawther, I reckon?' suggested Mr Skeels mildly.

'Well, I hope I know my business better than that, Skeels,' his wife said, more than ever indignant. 'I hope no one could ever accuse *me* of paying heed to other folk's clicketen, and not knowing how to train up a gal so as to be a credit to me. I'd step off a cliff afore that.'

Dinner being ready, Charlotte laid places for Mrs Skeels and herself at the table which filled one end of the long brick-floored kitchen; and set before Mr Skeels a sort of high stool with a broad top, off which he ate his meals. For Silas Skeels had lost the use of his legs some years ago in an accident, and now he spent his days sitting in a strong fishing-net, suspended in a loop from the ceiling beams, his feet dangling just above the floor — the most comfortable position for his crippled body. He was a burly man, with curly hair and a big, smooth, pink face, that seemed not to have aged at all during the years of his immobility. Before the accident he had owned fishing-boats as well as being proprietor of the Crab Pot, and had been known in Shipden as a middling-comfortable man; and it was whilst he was out in one of those fishing-boats that the capricious sea had turned against him, and had smashed both man and boat like toys. Seldom had he murmured against this stroke of fortune: only when he saw his wife and Charlotte overworked — for money was tighter nowadays — did he mourn his uselessness, for there was little he could do in a practical way, beyond a little net- and sail-mending. There might have been a greater pathos in the sight of this big man, with the marks of a hale and active life upon him, forever suspended like a great doll, were it not for his sweetness of temper, and his insistence, as he drank his rum and smoked his pipe and stared out to sea, that he was only doing a few years early what most Shipden men greatly looked forward to.

The little fishing-town of Shipden clustered at the mouth of a bay on the north coast of Norfolk; a coast of austere and uncompromising beauties, which the Newcastle coal-brigs, beating their way round from the Wash, were glad to keep at a distance, so many were the sailors' graves planted at the feet of the grey-towered churches there. Shipden itself was dominated by its church, which was so huge and lofty that it seemed every house in the place could comfortably have been fitted into it; for it was a modest town, of fishermen's cottages, squat and pebbled, and a few inns and genteel houses tucked into muffled streets. A little circulating-library and a few bathing-machines were all that was offered by way of amusement to the visitors who used it as a sea-bathing place; for these were few, wealthy, and exclusive, and would have recoiled if Shipden had broken out like Weymouth in card-rooms and assemblies. On either side of this little enclave, with its bright-painted crab-boats drawn up on the beach, rose high and grand cliffs, clad inland with heather and fern, and then giving way to a rolling wooded country where nobody seemed to live, where you might tramp the lanes all day and never see a dwelling, except for a glimpse through the trees of some improving landlord's mansion, surrounded by all the frigid imbecilities of landscaping, and guarded by gatehouses like monstrous salt-cellars in case anyone should be dull enough to want to go there. With this secretive country at its back, Shipden looked entirely to the sea – a quiet enough sea when it chose to be, washing mildly on the beach of a summer day, as if it were far too unassuming to come any nearer; but capable of much, as the massy sea-wall testified – capable of much, as witnessed the many sheds, outhouses and fences made of ships' timbers.

Tarry timber was much in evidence in the fittings of the Crab Pot Inn – which directly overlooked the sea-wall – and contributed to the darkness within. It was as dark as a house could plausibly be without actually being underground. The walls were so thick, and the bull's-eye windows so small, that opening them from the inside was like climbing into a short tunnel. The smoke-stained beams of the bar-parlour were so low, and its narrow dimensions were so crowded with furniture of seasoned oak, that the fishermen who formed the main clientele were forced to move about with a perpetual bowing and stooping and shufflings and walking backwards, like so many sou'westered courtiers. Not that they minded the dimness and chokiness: 'snug' was how they liked things, and the visitors who thought there was something special about fresh air were a mystery to them.

The Crab Pot had been home to Charlotte Wintergreen for so long that it seemed to her that she had never had any other. In casting her eyes back over her past life, she could see, beyond the contented years at Shipden, a terrible wilderness that marked the death of her parents, and the workhouse, and anguish — and on the other side of that was her infancy with her family in Heartsease: a sweet prospect, certainly, but so distant now, so blurred in its features with the passage of time, that it seemed rather something she had been told about than lived through. It seemed strange, too, to recall how alarming her first coming here had been: Mr Skeels so huge and bluff, Mrs Skeels so severe; the fishermen in the bar-parlour staring fixedly at her over their pipes (she knew now there was nothing rude in this — it just meant they found you as pleasant and interesting an object to look upon as anything else); her little bedroom directly above the inn-sign which swung in the wind with a long human whine, as if it cried 'Ple-ease!' at each new buffeting; and all night long the unaccustomed sound of the sea surging up the beach, and every now and then seeming to make a rush, so that more than once that first night she started up in bed trembling, convinced that the inn must be marooned. And now she was turned twenty, and Shipden was dear to her: she knew by heart the music of the sea and wind with all its modulations; beloved, too, was the little bedroom with its bright ragwork counterpane and bowl of coloured pebbles and ship's chest — and she wondered how she could ever sleep without the companionable sound of the swinging inn-sign. And Mr and Mrs Skeels seemed to her more like an uncle and aunt than her employers.

The ripening of their relationship had been slow — everything was, in Shipden — but steady. The Skeels, who were childless, had progressed from treating their servant girl considerately and fairly, to treating her with an easy familiarity, and thence to treating her as one of the family. Charlotte loved them for their kindness. It would never have occurred to her that the kindness shown her might have something to do with her own qualities, that the Skeels could not help but warm to her for her willingness and good humour, for something gentle and uncomplicated at the core of her nature. She had lost her early timidity, but there was still a quality of modest self-effacement about Charlotte. Like her brother Jed, she had dark, fine looks, candid-eyed — but they lacked his disquiet. Only today — as, having finished dinner, they got the inn ready for the busy evening — was there something flushed about her face, something high-strung about her neat movements.

'I say, gal,' Silas Skeels said to Charlotte whilst his wife was in the parlour. 'Broach the cask of Old Parvo, will you? — Toby shall have a pint or two of that, in honour of his birthday. He's old enough to meet it now, I reckon — though that ale is a Blinder. Not that I don't reckon he'll like his other present best, I shouldn't wonder!' Mr Skeels said, smoking his pipe tremendously, in a sort of humorous cloud. 'How long, now, was you a-broidering of that? Come: tell me in my bad ear, that won't signify.'

Mr Skeels was a little deaf in his left ear, and seemed to suppose that what was heard indistinctly was not really said — and indeed perhaps did not exist, for if there was bad news of any kind, he always demanded to be told it in his left ear. Charlotte, a little confusedly, told him, at which he was all the more amused and smoky.

'Seven weeks, eh? Well, if a gal had spent so long a-broidering me a neckercher when I was young, I should ha' thought myself an uncommonly lucky chap — I would, though!'

Charlotte laughed, and said it whiled away the evenings; and was glad to escape to the cellar.

The lamps had already long been lit in the Crab Pot when the autumn twilight gave way to night, bringing the fishermen for their ale. They were taciturn, phlegmatic people, who could sit for hours on end, winking their eyes in the smoke and saying not a word – so massively relaxed, it seemed barely credible that their daily occupation was a dangerous joust with a temperamental sea. In their thick-set blue-eyed fairness you could see their ancestry – raiders who had crossed that sea from northern shores in ships little different in design from their descendants' crab-boats; but Toby Dane, in spite of his name, was something of an exception to the general physiognomy. He was dark and slight and quick. There was something livelier and more full-blooded about him: there was fun in his eyes, which were almost black beneath wry arched brows, and sometimes a hint of impatience with the stolid ways of his fellows. But he was well-liked, and there were many shouted congratulations on his coming of age when he walked into the inn with his father.

'Thank ye – thank ye,' Toby murmured, shaking hands all around, while his father, Skipper Dane, announced: 'Partners now – thass what. We been down to Yarmouth the smorning to see the notary, and had it all signed proper. Equal shares – equal partners in the boats now, father and son.'

'Equal, eh, Skipper?' said a voice.

'Thass it – except he do do everything I tell him or else,' said Skipper, to a general laugh. Skipper Dane's real feeling for his son, however, was plain to see. Cholera had carried off his wife and two other children at an early age, and there was a sort of fond apprehension in the way this stout leathery man looked at his son, as if he were never free from a fear of losing him too.

'No, no – put that money away, bor,' said Mr Skeels, who every evening was carried by his wife and the potman to the bar-parlour, where there was a second hook for his hanging seat. 'The Crab Pot's in the chair tonight, and you shall make the acquaintance of Old Parvo. Watch him – he's smooth, but he kick!'

Mrs Skeels had taken up her usual evening position at the bar, where she stood, straight as a fire-iron, in a sort of starched daydream, occasionally throwing a distrustful glare over the whole company, as if those staid fishermen, scarcely stirring a whisker, were liable to all manner of high jinks. Charlotte brought a jug of the celebrated Old Parvo up from the cellar, and Mrs Skeels poured for Toby, wishing him happy returns with austere suavity, and presenting the compliments of the house.

Toby tackled the ale with appropriate respect; and meeting Charlotte's eyes over the rim of his mug, gave a broad smile and said, 'Well, Charlotte! What do you reckon to me being a partner? I can't get used to it!'

'I'm glad for you, Toby,' Charlotte said. 'Congratulations!'

'And what do you reckon to us having another boat built? Aye, expanding – there'll be a fleet before you know it. And I'll tell you what: we shall want a name, and you shall name her. What's it to be?'

'Oh! I shall have to have a good think about that,' she said, pleased. 'It wants a good name – a lucky name.'

'Why, what's that you've got there?' said Toby.

She had been hesitating over the neckerchief, half-deciding not to give it to him – it wasn't much of a thing . . . 'Well – I embroidered it,' she said confusedly. 'As a present for your birthday.'

Toby took it gently from her hands. 'Charlotte,' he said quietly. 'Why, it's the handsomest thing – and all the work that's gone into it!'

'Charlotte's handy with her needle,' Mrs Skeels said. 'I believe I can take a little credit for that, having taught her myself. You may call me anything you like except a bad needlewoman.'

'Now I'm a Swell as well as a partner,' said Toby, tying

the neckerchief on above his striped guernsey. 'Thank you, Charlotte . . . Fancy you thinking of my birthday so far ahead! What d'you reckon to it, Dad?'

The other fishermen soon called him away with talk of the new boat; and Charlotte was busy fetching and carrying. Presently an old man played the fiddle, and Toby was called on to sing.

'As we were a-fishing off Haisboro' Light,
Shooting and hauling and trawling all night,
It was windy old weather, stormy old weather;
When the wind blows, we all pull together.'

It was an old favourite. Toby had a slightly husky tenor voice that carried a tune well: Charlotte loved to hear it. Even Mrs Skeels unbent so far as to tap a single finger in time.

'I think what these fishes are saying is right;
We'll haul up our gear and we'll steer for the light.'

She could have listened all night, her eyes fixed on Toby's dark head in the midst of the lamplit ring of faces. But at last the company broke up, with an early tide to catch; and she had pots to wash in the scullery.

She was humming the tune to herself as she worked the pump-handle, when Toby put his head round the scullery door.

'I say – Charlotte! That boat you're to name – will you come and see her a-building? Say tomorrow afternoon. You'll be going over to Granfer's usual time, won't you? I'll meet you then.' He smiled and patted the neckerchief.

Granfer's was a shop kept by an old sailor in a hamlet along the cliffs, Upper Shipden, whither Charlotte walked to buy Mr Skeels' special sulphurously strong brand of tobacco. The next day Toby was waiting for her at the top of the cliff path. There was a powerful wind blowing off the sea, which made them stagger about and laugh at each other. Gulls were careering crazily about the grey sky as if they were enjoying it too.

'I put it on special,' Toby said, indicating the neckerchief. 'Not when we went out this morning though — ' meaning when he and his father had gone out in the crab-boat — 'too smart for that.'

'Oh! but Toby — I wanted you to,' Charlotte said.

'Did you? Why so?'

'Well—' She brushed her hair from her face, and with a half-laugh said, 'I sewed some magic into it. So it would always protect you from harm when you went to sea. Like the magic cloak in the tale — did you never hear that? I always remember it. I reckon my brother Jed must have told it to me, in the country when we were small. He was a rare teller of stories — he could make you see things, just as if they were right there before your eyes.'

'Have you heard from him lately? Here, take my arm — you'll be blown away.'

'I had a letter last week. Jed never misses.' It had been a slightly odd letter: Charlotte had sensed some underlying trouble in Jed's insistence that everything was all right. 'You will wear it, though, Toby — won't you?' she said, half-laughing still, but serious.

'I will,' Toby said. 'Not that I'll come to any harm, you know — not with a seaman like Dad.'

'No,' she said, and she could not speak of the times when she woke in the night and listened to the long-drawn breath of the sea, and wondered whether there was treachery in that soothing sound; whether, at that very moment, it had turned spiteful out beyond the bay, and was playing cat-and-mouse with some valiant little boat on the night tide.

'But then,' Toby said, 'I never had no one to tell me stories like that. Unless Mother did: I'd be too young to remember. I know I used to play make-believe with Meggy . . . but after that it was all Dad, and getting a living from the sea, and being practical.'

Meggy had been Toby's twin, who had died as a child. He seldom spoke of the loss of his sister; but he had once said to Charlotte, of the time when she had come to Shipden as a girl and he had taken her hunting for shells and starfish along the beach, that that had been like gaining a new sister in her place. Charlotte remembered this now, with a rough-edged sort of pleasure.

'Thass a pity you can't get to see Jed more often,' said Toby. 'Is there no chance of him coming to Shipden for a day or two?'

'I don't think so — they work him so hard at the mill. I know he'd like to — he don't like the city, though he've been there so long. He always talk in his letters about when we were small in the country — and somehow he make me see that too; the village, and the way it was. Thass so important to him, and I don't like to admit I can't really remember it — not the way he do.'

They came to the boat-builder's yard at Upper Shipden, where the skeleton of the new boat, a double-ended clinker design, lay on the stocks in a wind-whipped nest of wood-shavings. Charlotte's mind had been running on Jed and her childhood; and as they walked round her she suddenly said: 'What about calling her *Heartsease*?'

Toby cocked his head on one side. '*Heartsease* . . . D'you know, I like that. Thass a lucky sound . . . *Heartsease* it is.'

'She'll be the smartest boat on the coast.'

'Aye — a tidy craft . . . But Dane and Son will have a grander one than this some day, you'll see. And I've already got a name for her.'

'What?'

'Why, the *Charlotte,* of course,' said Toby with a gleam of mischief. 'Come on — I'll race you to Granfer's.'

They were some time at Granfer's shop, where the old man told them in great detail about his rheumatics. When they set out for home again the wind had shifted and the sky was dark with converging masses of cloud: there was a heavy swell on the sea.

'Stormy tonight, I'll bet,' said Toby. 'Hullo, what's that?'

Something delicate and filmy was blown by the wind across their path. Toby chased it and caught it as it snagged on the heather; it was a black net mantle, very fine. At a distance Charlotte could see the figures of two ladies, quite close to the cliff edge: one was waving.

They went to them. To the elder − a tall muscular dame in steel spectacles who advanced to meet him − Toby said, 'Did you lose this, ma'am? It's all right − it's not torn, I think.'

'It's mine,' said the younger of the two women, who was seated in a wheeled invalid-chair, and who extended a small gloved hand to take the mantle from Toby's very brown one. 'It is torn, I'm afraid − because I tore it. I threw it off in a temper.'

'We're much obliged to you, I'm sure,' said the older woman dismissingly, with a Shoo! motion as if Toby and Charlotte were farmyard animals. But the young woman in the invalid-chair, fixing her eyes on Charlotte, said, 'Do you live in this place?'

'Surely, miss,' Charlotte said. The young woman − no more than her own age − was dressed in a fur-trimmed pelisse and veiled bonnet, with coppery ringlets framing a pale, beautiful, displeased face, on which the skin was as translucent as paper on a fan. The eyes that held Charlotte's were so large, so glowingly assertive, that they seemed to have drawn into themselves all the vitality of her delicate frame.

'Then perhaps you can tell me,' the young woman said, with a sort of scornful twist of her body in the chair, 'why I mayn't go up *there*?'

She pointed to where a rough path wound steeply up between ferns to a high promontory − the highest point of these cliffs, crowned with broken turf.

'I think we had better be going, my dear,' the older

woman said, simpering and shooing at the same time. 'There'll be rain soon.'

Ignoring her, and addressing herself still to Charlotte, the young woman went on: 'I want to go up there, but Mrs Vickers — she's only my nurse, so don't take any notice of her airs — refuses to take me for some reason. Do you know the spot? Am I wrong in wanting to go there?'

'Well, thass the finest view 'twixt here and the Point, miss,' said Toby.

'My dear Miss Ward,' the older woman said, ignoring Charlotte and Toby as resolutely as her charge was ignoring her, 'I really don't think it possible to get the chair up there — your grandparents would never forgive me if—'

'Do you think it possible?' said the young woman, looking from Charlotte to Toby, with the first suggestion of a smile — uneasy but startlingly beautiful — beginning to light her wintry face.

'I'll push the chair, miss, if you like,' said Toby readily. 'There's a fair path, and it's worth seeing.'

'There!' the young woman said, her face sensationally transformed by the smile in its completeness. 'Let's do it.'

'Miss Ward, Miss Ward,' clucked Mrs Vickers, 'this won't do . . . Much obliged I'm sure — ' with a reluctant nod to Toby and Charlotte — 'but my dear, do consider, we do not *know* these people.'

'Very true,' the young woman said, briskly extending a hand to Charlotte and Toby. 'My name is Loveday Ward. What are your names? . . . Charlotte Wintergreen, how d'you do. Toby Dane, how d'you do. Now that's over, so let us go!'

Toby, with a glance of wry surprise at Charlotte, turned the chair about — plainly the young woman was as light as a bird — and they set off up the steep path. 'Take my hand as we go, will you, Charlotte?' Loveday Ward said as Charlotte walked beside the chair. 'That's it . . . How warm your hand is, and no glove! Now I am fully supported and protected, I think, and Mrs Vickers may fly away on her broomstick.'

Mrs Vickers, toiling along behind them, exerted herself greatly in pretending not to have heard this.

The wind up here was more boisterous than ever, but glints of sun shone out from beneath the low eaves of cloud, and traced the heaving ribs of the sea. The view never failed to thrill Charlotte, and now she seemed to see it afresh, as if through the eager eyes of the strange girl in the wheeled chair — so frail a piece of humanity, confronted with so much that was huge, bracing, and everlasting.

'Oh! it's fine up here,' Loveday Ward said. 'We must be so high — higher than—How high do you suppose?' she asked Charlotte, with the brilliant smile again. 'Never mind. I shall walk. Toby, will you give me your arm? Oh! yes, I can walk. It isn't my legs.'

'My dear Miss Ward, really . . .' spluttered her nurse.

'Well, what's the matter? I'm supposed to be here for my health, am I not? How am I to get strong forever lying in that chair?' Loveday got to her feet with a swift impatient motion: she seemed to Charlotte to faintly quiver like a taut string as she stood there erect, her skirts billowing about her, gazing out to sea. Toby, after a moment's hesitation, gave her his arm with a wondering look.

'That's it,' Loveday said. 'Now Charlotte, let me put my arm through yours. So.' They began to walk along the grassy cliff-edge, with Mrs Vickers fussing in the rear. 'How warm you both are! Don't you feel the cold?'

'It's because we're used to it, I reckon,' Toby said. 'Shipden's not a warm spot, generally.'

'I've tried warm spots,' Loveday said. 'For my lungs. France. Italy. They're no good. So the doctors said sea air: Brighton — Lyme — Broadstairs — Ramsgate — Shipden. I keep going to different places, trying to find my health. Just as if my health ran away from me, and hid somewhere, and I must hope to come across it! Well, it *ought* to be pining for me — it's been away from me for long enough,' she said, in a tone that was at once bitter and humorous. 'Do you suppose it might be here — lurking? Oh! I shall have sharp words with it, if it is.'

Charlotte, who had never had a day's illness, regarded her with quiet pity. 'Are you all alone?' she said. 'I mean—'

'You mean apart from Mrs Vickers, who doesn't count. No, I have grandparents. We've taken lodgings in the town. They do what they can for me, but they're old and not strong. And my late parents weren't strong either. Quite a set, aren't we? We've any amount of money — but no good, no good!' The wind had brought a flush to her white face, an access of colour so sharp that it looked as if it must actually pain that transparent skin. 'If only I had a little of your strength, Toby! I'm sure you have some to spare.'

Toby said, colouring: 'I wish I might give it to you, miss, if there was a way.'

'Lots of people come here for their health,' said Charlotte, 'and lots of them do well, and go away recovered.'

'And some of them don't, eh?' Loveday said; and then, squeezing Charlotte's hand, 'Don't mind me — I get in bad humours tied to that wretched chair, and this bad humour is lifting moment by moment. It's wonderful to see young faces about me. Tell me where you live, and what you do.'

Toby and Charlotte told her in turn, the girl staring motionless out to sea with the hectic colour in her face as she listened, and seeming to drink in their accounts of their young lives, as if they too might nourish and revive her. Then she stirred and said, 'What am I thinking of — I must be keeping you from your work. I tend to think everyone is like me — with great empty days waiting to be filled. And perhaps I am a little tired now, though I shan't admit as much to Mrs Vickers.' Drawing Charlotte and Toby close to her, she whispered, 'Her husband bolted, you know. All the way to India. What *can* she have done to him?'

They made their way back down to the lower cliff path, Toby pushing the chair; and Loveday, seeming to sink listlessly into herself again, allowed Mrs Vickers to fuss about her with shawls, and reassert her authority. But at parting the sick girl put out her hand again to Charlotte and Toby and said, 'Let me see you again − will you? I like to see your young faces. I like to hear you talk. You do me good. I am an invalid, you know − ' this with that twist of cool self-mockery − 'and so I must be humoured. It's traditional. I shall be here − or on the beach − looking.'

Toby and Charlotte were quiet for some time as they descended towards Shipden − the church tower with its nursling brood of cottages gathered round it, the wooded land beyond, the low cloud beginning to spit rain.

'Young faces,' Charlotte said. 'And yet she must be no older than me . . . How sad!'

For some moments Toby was silent. Looking sidelong at his face, Charlotte saw his humorous brows were drawn together in the inward, rapt expression he sometimes wore.

'I tell you what,' he said with decision. 'I think we *can* help her. It can't be no help to her, forever surrounded by old folk: thass no wonder she don't get on. She don't look so very ill, just weak. I reckon I could give her a bit of my strength somehow, like she said − I reckon she could get better, with our help. Don't you think?'

Toby was, perhaps, rather too good at finding reasons for what he wanted to believe − so a dispassionate observer might have felt about his character, anyhow; but Charlotte was not dispassionate about Toby. She said yes, in her quiet way; and in the same quiet way, when they parted cheerfully at the Crab Pot, she noted that he seemed to have quite forgotten about the *Heartsease,* and the neckerchief, and the magic sewn into it.

There was a minor disaster in the cellar of the Crab Pot that evening, when a bad cask of ale could keep its secret no longer, and expired with a frothy bang. Mrs Skeels did not take the news well.

'It's all very well you saying never mind, Skeels! It ain't right I should have to put up with it! There's her up at the King's Head — no decent woman could look in *her* closets without swooning in shame, and I state that as a fact and not a rumour — and here's me who'd rather die than see a cobweb on my shelves — I'd cut my throat with your razor afore that, and cut deep — and yet this happen to me and not her!'

In the meantime Charlotte, with buckets and mops and a minimum of fuss, cleaned the cellar up so thoroughly that even Mrs Skeels was mollified, and declared that if her at the King's Head had trained her servants half as well, her customers wouldn't find so many little teethmarks in their cheese.

'I begin to wonder,' Silas Skeels said, as Charlotte cleared the bar tables at the end of the night, 'what we should do without you, gal.'

Charlotte smiled at him. 'Well, I ain't going nowhere, Mr Skeels.'

'We-ell, no . . .' Mr Skeels whistled a few bars of the song Toby had sung last night. 'Only . . . do a gal get to your age, it often happen she get another prospect before her. And do a gal get that prospect, she ain't to think twice about it, you know, and wonder how other folk are going to manage — specially when them other folk have got to thinking of her like one of their own, as often happen, and what'd make them happiest is for the gal to be happy, whatever it be — thass all.'

Having delivered this rather cloudy speech, Mr Skeels sent up such a cloud of pipe-smoke as a complement that he practically disappeared behind it. Charlotte found him, however, and kissed his cheek, saying again very calmly, that she wasn't going anywhere.

But when she went at last to her own bedroom, and the

inn-sign creaked its greeting to her, and she was able to fasten behind her the warped old door of ship's-planking, and be alone — then she was not quite calm; and for some time she knelt on the trunk below the window, looking out at the great murmuring darkness that was the sea, and the vaster darkness above. The last torn rags of storm-cloud were gone, and the stars shone — so mildly, it seemed to Charlotte — as if they looked with a little pity at the many unspoken longings that were lifted up to them, and at the many overburdened hearts on which their light shed a little healing.

Chapter Four

Letting Go

While the infirm year tottered into winter, Pierce Coppinger worked at his unusual commission for Mr Childs, the tanner of Cardinal's Cap Yard. He went there every morning, and though he secured one or two other commissions for miniatures, and gained introductions to members of the Norwich School, the work he was doing in that dungeon of a parlour, with his live sitter and his dead sitter taking shape together on his canvas, occupied the forefront of his mind, and cast on him a weird fascination.

For the sittings Mr Childs wore – about as comfortably as a noose – a clean collar, and a shiny old coat smelling of mothballs. It was plain that the old man was close with his money, and that there was a tidy bit to be close about. Occasionally his manservant, Ben Catbush, would come bearing tradesmen's bills; and Mr Childs would grumblingly extract from the bureau a strong-box, the weight of which nearly pulled him over, and enact complicated rites with a mass of keys, jealously glancing at Pierce while Pierce tried not to look.

'Coals? They ought to be diamonds, for what he charge,' Mr Childs complained, wincing as he counted coins into Ben's palm. 'They'll see me in the workhouse yet – or the debtor's prison,' he added with a glance at Pierce.

Pierce, thinking that Mr Childs' material position would hardly be different in such a situation, coughed and wiped his brushes.

'Tell them in the kitchen no cooking of a Saturday any

more,' Mr Childs said. 'Cold meats won't hurt us once in a way.'

'Why, thass a poor do,' Ben Catbush said. 'You know what the doctor said — you're to have feeding food. Stews and hot broths is what you want, you know.'

'Ben Catbush, you old woman — I shall eat what I like. Why, I knew a time when any meat was a feast to me, and roast beef would have made me weep. What d'you think of that?'

'I don't think anythink of it,' Ben Catbush said, rearranging his master's shrunken legs. 'But I'm just an old woman.'

When he had gone they resumed the sitting: Mr Childs muttering under his breath about coals, roast beef, and the debtor's prison, until at length he was convulsed by a sneeze.

'Here,' he said to Pierce, 'you didn't paint that, I hope?'

Pierce assured him not.

'Only I want to look normal, along of my old gal. Normal as may be, anyhow. I know I'm sickly — you know it, Mester Coppinger. I shan't last, and it's lucky you ain't a slow draw-er, else I reckon the picture would never be done — not from the life, anyhow. Though if it was from the Death, I don't reckon it would be any different!'

Pierce had grown used to these morbid plunges of Mr Childs', and knew now they required no response beyond a sympathetic look.

'My old gal'll be waiting for me, anyhow,' Mr Childs mused. 'Leastways, I hope she will — I hope she'll have put in a good word for me . . . She was my mascot, Mester Coppinger. Things were all right with me when she was here below. Mrs Childs was a good woman — anybody'll tell you so; and she liked me, you know — liked me a lot — anybody'll tell you that, too; so I can't have been such a bad sort, after all — can I?' His foxy eyes glittered at Pierce. 'Can I, Mester Coppinger?'

Pierce, vainly struggling to picture Mr Childs as a Charmer, contented himself with saying that the late Mrs Childs — whose portrait was propped on a second easel beside him — had a lovely face, and he hoped he would do her justice.

'Justice!' Mr Childs seized on the word. 'D'you believe in that, Mester Coppinger? D'you believe the world trundles along on tracks of justice — like these here railways they're a-building to Norwich, so I hear — always going straight to the ends we deserve, and no getting off? Or does the world work different — all over the shop, hitty-missy like the blind man shot the crow — the good luck coming to some as deserves it, and some as don't?'

Pierce, who was something of a freethinker, said: 'I'm afraid there is a lot of injustice in the world, Mr Childs. I dare say it will all be set right in the next world, but I confess I would rather see it set right here and now.'

'*Would* you?' cried Mr Childs, with such energy that Pierce jumped. 'Here and now, eh . . .?' He fell to stroking his stubbled jowls, startling Pierce however by suddenly crying again, '*Would* you?' and then, after another long brooding silence, '*Would* you though?' until Pierce wished he had never said anything.

'I suppose,' Mr Childs said at length, 'you think there's mebbe a touch of the miser about me?'

Rather staggered by this understatement, Pierce said there was nothing wrong with a man being careful.

'Careful! Ah, thass it — I have to be careful, always I've had to be careful,' said Mr Childs, with a glance at the barred window, which he reluctantly permitted to be unshuttered for the sittings. 'Wouldn't you say, now, that a man may do what he likes with his own money?'

'I would, indeed,' said Pierce.

'*Would* you?' Mr Childs cried again (Pierce was ready for it this time). 'And if a man may do what he likes with his money when he's alive, he may surely do what he likes with it when he's dead, hey?' Mr Childs gave the shrill

71

wheeze that in him passed for a laugh, and abruptly fell to brooding again.

He sat on quite still, hunched over in his chair, lined and sallow in the winter sunlight that burgled its way through the barred window; and Pierce tried to make the flesh on his portrait look a little more wholesome, and hold back on the gamboge; and as chill grey day succeeded day, and the picture progressed, and Mr Childs brooded and spoke cryptically of death and justice, the young artist was increasingly gripped by an odd fancy that it was not only a deceased woman he was painting — that he was painting a dead man, or a man more dead than alive, and that there was something posthumous about the whole enterprise; and each day when he left Cardinal's Cap Yard he had the sensation of surfacing, Orpheus-like, from the underworld, and felt that if he glanced back there would be a great slamming of gates and portals.

These feelings were reinforced one day by Mr Childs' telling him that he was expecting a visit from a Nonconformist minister, with whom he wanted to talk about things: 'Serious things,' he said, 'what I got to think of afore it's too late.' The minister was a thin dusty stork of a man who crossed his long shanks in front of the fire and ate toasted muffins with all the relish of a man who preaches self-denial.

'It's thinking over my life, you see,' Mr Childs said. 'Thinking of things I done, and didn't do — that give me no rest.'

'Think of Eternity, my dear sir,' said the minister.

'No — I shan't — I done that, and it don't answer,' said Mr Childs. 'It's the here-below I'm thinking about.'

'All flesh is grass,' said the minister, licking butter off his fingers. 'My dear sir, what the Lord asks of you—'

'Aye?' Mr Childs said eagerly. 'Now, you know your business. What do He ask?'

'Repentance for your sins,' said the minister

impressively. 'It is not I that can save you, Mr Childs: your salvation lies in your own hands. Repent your sins, sir. Be washed in the blood of the Lamb. It cleanses and purifies,' he added, as if of a superior brand of soap.

'Why, I believe I do repent of 'em,' said Mr Childs thoughtfully, 'at least, I — I'm sorry . . . But look here! you know your business: what if a man's profited by his sins, as you call 'em? What then?'

'"Be sure your sin will find you out",' said the minister, dabbing crumbs off his plate, and seeming to refrain with difficulty from picking it up and cleaning it like Jack Spratt.

'No answers!' Mr Childs said to Pierce, when the minister had eaten everything and gone. 'I reckon I were looking in the wrong quarter there, altogether.' And so next day Pierce met with further evidence of Mr Childs putting his affairs in order. When he arrived for the sitting he found another man just leaving, whom Mr Childs introduced as Mr Veazey, his lawyer.

This Mr Veazey was a short, spruce, bracing, fresh-coloured man of forty, broad across the chest, with a great deal of watch-chain on view, a great deal of bustle in his system, and light hair very stiff and upright, as if there were no question of its lying flat on top of such a brisk man. 'Mr Coppinger, how do you do? Our friend has told me about you,' the lawyer said, coming at Pierce somewhat like a wrestler, and seizing his hand as if they were going to try a few throws. 'Quite a surprise to find our friend a patron of the arts, but then why not? There's no end to him — I've often told him so. And how does the portrait go on? Will you allow me to see it?'

Pierce uncovered his easel.

'It's our friend to the life!' Mr Veazey said, squaring up to the canvas. 'Now I call that uncanny!'

'To the life, you say?' grunted Mr Childs. 'Then it can't be much like — there's little enough life in me!'

'Ha ha ha! My friend, you're a pessimist — that's what you are,' said Mr Veazey. 'But I know you don't mean it

for a moment. Why, when you and I, Mr Coppinger – '
the lawyer took Pierce confidentially by the buttonhole
– 'when you and I are silver-haired, and past everything
but sitting in the sun – say in a rose-garden – and
feeling the rays pleasantly on our faces, and talking over
old times together – what a charming picture that
makes! – why, even then our friend will still be going
strong. There's no end to him!'

'Thass not what the doctor say,' said Mr Childs, with a
sort of grim satisfaction.

'Now I'll tell you what it is about our friend,' said Mr
Veazey to Pierce. 'He's got too much imagination. He
fancies things. But there – didn't I say there's no end to
him? But I must let you get on with your sitting. Our
friend, sir – is he a good sitter?'

'A very obliging sitter indeed,' Pierce said.

'Obliging! You don't surprise me in the least! That's
our friend all over!' cried the lawyer. 'Well, my good
friend – ' darting over to shake Mr Childs' hand – 'I
shall be back tomorrow, and in the meantime you may
rest assured that I shall put the business in train with the
greatest dispatch – I shall give it my personal attention.'

'I should think so,' Mr Childs growled, 'for you charge
enough.'

'Charge enough! Ha ha ha!' Mr Veazey laughed with
the greatest enjoyment. 'You're a tonic, my good friend
– that's what you are! I call that diverting! No, you
needn't ring – *I* know my way,' and seizing his hat and
cane as if he were taking a turn at the dumb-bells, the
lawyer left them.

'I suppose you'd like to know what that business is,'
said Mr Childs when he had gone.

Pierce and Mr Childs had by now reached a sort of
accord: Pierce growing so used to the old man's habitual
wariness and suspicion as not to mind it, Mr Childs
seeming to like firing off his veiled confidences during the
sittings; so Pierce simply said: 'If you choose to tell me,
Mr Childs – I don't mind.'

'Why, I may as well at that, for you're not someone who'll gain or lose by it . . . I'm making my will, Mester Coppinger, thass what. A big step for a man, that — ain't it? You know, I *have* got a little money, a little property — not *so* much, mind, but such as a man's children would be glad of when he was gone — if he had any, which I ain't . . .' Mr Childs paused, with his pinch of snuff half-way to his nose, and burst out in an agitated voice: 'I wisht my ole gal was here! It was different then: when she were alive, I never thought of it overmuch — but now I keep thinking of this money I got, and how there's places it ought mebbe to go, and things it ought mebbe to do . . . But thass so hard to let it go! I didn't always have money, see; and so once I got it into my hands, I — I couldn't a-bear to let it go!'

The old man fell silent, but his gnarled hands made convulsive clawings at his shawls, as if his burdened mind would not even allow him the liberty of being still.

Mr Veazey was often at the house over the next few days, consulting with his client; always as fresh and pink and buoyant as if he had just come from a Turkish bath. One morning as Pierce was leaving he met the lawyer in one of the gloomy panelled passages, and was promptly buttonholed.

'And how is our friend this morning, Mr Coppinger? In spirits, would you say?'

'About as low as ever, I'm afraid,' said Pierce.

'As low as ever! That's it! You're an artist in words as well as paint, Mr Coppinger — that's what you are.' Lowering his voice Mr Veazey said, 'Between you and me and the doctor, who favoured me with a word, there's not much that's hopeful about our friend's condition. But he's full of surprises, sir — he might surprise us yet, you know!'

'I wonder if a change of air might benefit him,' Pierce said. 'He's so very close-confined.'

'Close-confined! You've hit it! But that's always been his way, Mr Coppinger. All through our association. One

75

might almost suppose he has a secret − eh?'

'It had crossed my mind.'

'Crossed your mind! Ha ha ha! You're a diplomat, Mr Coppinger − that's what you are. And you'd suppose a man's lawyer, who's drawing up his will, would be let into his secrets, wouldn't you? But that's shop-talk: you don't want to hear that. What you want to hear is this: that I've half a mind, having seen your portrait of our friend and his late wife— And isn't that a quaint notion of his? Really there's no end to him! − I've half a mind, I say, to ask you to immortalize Mrs Veazey in like fashion. Oh! don't worry − Mrs Veazey's a live subject, sir. Nothing uncommon in this commission. Though I should add, sir, that Mrs Veazey − if you can believe it − was once a Miss Brocklehurst.'

'Was she indeed!' said Pierce, opening his eyes wide; the name meant nothing to him, but Mr Veazey seemed to expect such a reaction.

'You wouldn't suppose a humble provincial solicitor could aspire to the hand of a Miss Brocklehurst, would you? A dramatic history, sir. Opposition to the match from distinguished parent. Love-notes smuggled in by parlourmaid under a dishcover. Distinguished parent cuts off all communication. Humble provincial solicitor strives to get on in his profession, and make a name for himself, so as to support his heart's delight in the style to which she has been accustomed, in order to mollify distinguished parent.'

'Who must surely have been reconciled, at last,' said Pierce.

'Ha ha ha! You're the soul of civility, sir! I call that polite! And he was reconciled: which has never, however, lessened my sense of wonder, that a former Miss Brocklehurst should do the honours of my breakfast-table. It may seem surprising to you that a former Miss Brocklehurst should never have been painted − but she ain't: and you're the man to do it.'

Pierce said he was very sensible of the honour.

'Honour! That's like you! Dear me, how very pleasant this is! Now suppose Mrs Veazey was to call on you in the afternoons, after she's finished her shopping (silk and lace, sir — how can I stint a former Miss Brocklehurst?) — when you're free of our friend? Of course, I don't know how long your engagement here has to run — but I don't think, you know, it will be long — I really don't!'

Mrs Veazey turned out to be a very elaborately dressed lady, not young, who gave the impression of having been told in her youth by an admirer that she resembled a startled fawn, and of never having forgotten it. She was as garrulous as her husband; and so Pierce found his days well filled. He was gratified to be getting on so well, but a little frustrated, too, that he had been unable to go sketching in the country before the winter took hold; and he was tantalized by the mystery of Mr Childs, who, as his body grew daily weaker, seemed increasingly to chafe and agonize over some unspoken trouble. The old man might be unlovable, but Pierce could not help but be wrung with pity for him — which, combined with his curiosity, led him to hope Mr Childs might unburden himself to him; but Mr Childs kept his counsel. Sometimes he was closeted with Mr Veazey in a little lightless office that led off the parlour while Pierce waited to begin the sitting — and he had to forcibly turn his attention to his nearly-completed picture and restrain himself from listening at the door.

The picture had turned out well enough: Mr Childs was delighted with it and, so Ben Catbush told Pierce, spent the whole evening gazing at it; but Pierce was not satisfied. It had been difficult to handle the shadow, in combining a sitter from the life and a copy of a portrait — no matter what he did, the two figures seemed to be dwelling in different worlds. And the linked-hands pose, with Mr Childs' cadaverous face glowering out, made but a grim sort of composition. It reminded Pierce of those portraits of the early seventeenth century, when people apparently liked nothing better than to dress up in their stiffest ruffs, and sit looking over their shoulders with skulls in their laps.

A bitter dry Christmas was at hand, and huge waggons of geese and turkeys, live and dead, were perpetually trundling out of Norwich bound for the London market. In his lodgings Pierce was obliged to heap his clothes on the bed to keep warm at night, and downstairs the very dye in Mr Trunch's vats froze, and looked like funereal sorbet. At Mr Childs' house old Ben Catbush seized up, as he put it, in the cold, and it took him longer than ever to creak his way down the long corridors, colliding with doors, and rebounding off walls in quite an alarming manner. A large fire burnt constantly in the parlour grate, but the cheerless room was never warm: draughts always pervaded it, as if the wind, having penetrated that complicated old fortress of a house, could not get out again, and was doomed to bluster about in there, slamming doors in its frustration, and worrying at the musty drapes like a pent-up hound.

It was on such a dark howling morning that Pierce put the finishing touches to his portrait of Mr and Mrs Childs. The old man was huddled as close to the fire as he could be without falling into it − winking at the blaze, exploring his jowls with his fingers, and occasionally giving a little grunt to himself.

Pierce had found a way of modifying the shadow moulding Mrs Childs' face, and was absorbed: he paid little attention when Mr Childs stirred and said, 'Are you superstitious, Mester Coppinger?'

'No, not I.'

Mr Childs subsided: then got up with surprising sprightliness. 'I shan't be a moment − no, I can manage, thank ye − you bide where you are.' Pierce saw that he was going over to his bureau, which no one was suffered to come near; and returned his attention to his painting.

He heard Mr Childs rattling at locks and clasps − muttering, in the intervals of his terrible long-drawn gasps at breath, 'Thirteen − thirteen − yes, thirteen

years. Oh, yes!' And then, after a pause: 'Not too late —
no, not too late!'

Pierce stepped back from his picture. Now *that* was
better: he had unified the composition, and now Mr and
Mrs Childs at last looked as if they were inhabiting the
same world. He was about to ask Mr Childs if he would
like to look, when the old man gave a deep groan,
wavered where he stood, and then before Pierce could
rush to catch him, fell heavily against the bureau and
slumped to the floor.

With his heart in his mouth Pierce bent over the prone
figure; but the last embers of life in Mr Childs had
winked out, and one hand lay limply open, the bunch of
keys fallen from it. The old man had let go at last.

Ben Catbush had come, and with tears streaming down
his expressionless face had moved his master to the
couch. Pierce had asked him whether Mr Childs had any
family. 'None — not a soul!' was the reply; and so Pierce
thought it best to send not only for the doctor but for Mr
Veazey, who very soon arrived, bright as a bee.

'Lucky I was at home — very lucky! Ah, dear me, dear
me, this is a very sad business. Little did I think, my old
friend, that our next meeting would be under these
circumstances!' he said, addressing the lifeless form of
Mr Childs. 'You've sent for the doctor, Mr Coppinger?
Of course: though I'm afraid it's all over. Not that it's
such a surprise, alas.'

'My ole master's gone!' moaned Ben Catbush. 'I been
with him a dozen year! What's to become of me?'

'Don't you fret, Ben Catbush,' said Mr Veazey.
'You're the soul of loyalty — that's what you are. You
mind your duties, just as if our friend was still with us,
and you won't go far wrong. Go on down and wait for
the doctor, like a good fellow.'

Poor Ben, his navigation made worse than ever by
tearful eyes, ricocheted about the room for a while before
getting to the door and departing.

'I call that affecting,' Mr Veazey said. 'Faithful retainer — humble fidelity. Dear me! And what *is* to become of him, I wonder?'

'Ben tells me there is no family,' said Pierce.

'No one in the world. My dear sir, this is unfortunate, you being involved in this way — you look quite knocked up. Take a seat, sir.' Pierce did as he was bid. He had no experience of death, for that of his mother had taken place when he was away at school, and he felt a little shaky. 'I did not know Mr Childs well, but all the same . . .'

'Most unfortunate! And your picture, I believe, just finished. You had yet, I think, to be remunerated? Well, all that will be settled — as our late friend's solicitor, I can assure you of that. Our late friend — dear me, how sad those words are! — was very diligent in setting his affairs in order. Ah, is that the doctor I hear? I think the best thing for you, Mr Coppinger, would be to go home and take a little rest. I can do the necessary here. I've friends in, dear me, the undertaking profession. And now here's an idea — what would you say, my dear sir, to dining with Mrs Veazey and myself tonight?'

'Why — thank you — I would be glad to,' Pierce said. The prospect of the evening in his lodgings, haunted no doubt by the thought of the old man lying in the dismal house with no family to mourn him, certainly did not appeal.

'Capital! Mrs Veazey has given you our card, I believe — speaks very well of you, by the way. A fine subject for your brush, is she not? An unmistakable Brocklehurst face . . .'

So that evening Pierce, washed and shaved and dressed in his one evening tail-coat, and having shaken off a little of the horrors caused by the events of that morning, repaired to Mr Veazey's house in Tombland near the cathedral. It had long been said that Norfolk people were the most litigious in the land, and that they would go to law for their neighbour's horse looking over the fence:

certainly Mr Veazey had done well for himself, judging by the interior of the house, which was all prosperous glass and silver and rosewood, and in which the host and hostess were not the least shiny and polished items. There were three little girl-Veazeys, still in long frilled drawers, who were brought down to curtsey and exhibit the Brocklehurst features, and then sent up again to dine — as if they were more owl than infant, and would only feed on a high perch. Mrs Veazey was dressed very finely, and was hung about with such a quantity of glittering jewellery that she might conceivably have changed places with the great chandelier above the dining-table; but she was very civil to Pierce at dinner, smiling on him with the strong teeth and aquiline nose that were giving him such trouble in the miniature he was painting of her, and asking him if he was quite recovered from the shock of that morning.

'Thank you, Mrs Veazey,' Pierce said. 'It did give me rather a jolt. I'm afraid I'm not much use in such a situation — I keep wishing there was something I could have done for him.'

'Ah, don't think it!' said Mr Veazey. 'Our friend's time was up, you know, Mr Coppinger — you must have observed it yourself. I believe he knew it himself. Very careful and extensive preparations, settling his affairs. In that connection, my dear sir, I would suggest you come to Mr Childs' house tomorrow evening, when I read the will — as you are a creditor with a claim on the testator, as well as an associate of his last weeks.'

'Certainly, if you think it best. It seems a little — well, odd, and sad, to claim a fee from a man who's no more, and will never have the enjoyment of the picture.'

'Oh! but he did, you know, even in its uncompleted state — he told me so. Remarkable devotion to the memory of Mrs Childs, wasn't it? Our late friend was — shall we say — a little rough-edged, but where Mrs Childs was concerned, the soul of fidelity! You may not know, Mr Coppinger, that he even took her name.'

81

'Then his name was not Childs?' said Pierce in surprise.

'Not a bit of it! In law, that is — though a man may choose to go by what name he likes. Mrs Childs, you see, was the young widow of Joshua Childs, the man who founded that tannery, and left it to her; our friend married the widow, and thus the business became his. He never changed the name of it, never took down the sign, and in due time began to use the name Childs himself. I break no professional confidence here — there was no secret in this.'

'I had no idea,' Pierce said. 'I had thought — well, that he was a self-made man.'

'A self-made man! I call that apt! Because in a way he was, Mr Coppinger — marrying Mrs Childs was the making of him. I don't say it wasn't a love-match; but it gave him possession of a comfortable little property, you see, which he proceeded to make the best of, and prospered. Certainly his previous sphere of life had been different, quite different. I may say it cost him the greatest pain to allude to it. One might almost suppose, fancifully, that our friend wished to change his identity altogether, stop being the person he had once been, and submerge himself, as it were, in his wife's name. But you'll hear more about that, I think, tomorrow.'

This was highly tantalizing to Pierce's curiosity; but the lawyer turned the conversation to painting, and there was nothing for it but to wait till tomorrow. The dinner passed pleasantly, with Pierce being treated to many encomiums on the illustrious family of Brocklehurst, without ever finding out what they were illustrious for, and afterwards in the drawing-room, where there was a piano, Mr Veazey called for music; and Pierce politely seconding this, coaxed an admission from the former Miss Brocklehurst that she sang a little. It would have been more exact to say that she sang a lot. But Pierce was grateful for the friendly welcome they had given him, and was considerably more tolerant than most men of twenty-five; and he presented what he hoped was an attentive face through a succession of songs and a *canzonetta* with a dismaying number of verses, all of them in Italian.

It was as Pierce was leaving, with many thanks for a pleasant evening, that his mind reverted to what the lawyer had said earlier and, turning to Mr Veazey on the threshold, he said, 'I've just thought – what *was* Mr Childs' real name?'

'His name? His name was Abel Jex. Good night, Mr Coppinger!'

Jed Wintergreen came home from work in a hurry. There was a lecture at the Mechanics' Institute that he wished to attend, and he would only just have time for a wash and a bolt of bread and cheese. He came into Paradise Yard at a trot. It was dark and foggy, and just in front of the entrance to the tenement he ran into a hard obstruction that turned out to be a man.

'Beg pardon,' he said. 'Can't see a hand afore your face tonight—' He stopped. 'You!'

It was the buttoned-up old fellow in boots – the one who had been keeping watch on him. Just lately he had not seen him – but had suspected that his pursuer was simply covering his tracks more carefully. Now he stared into the red knotty face, and was filled with anger.

'Now – I caught you at last!' Jed said. 'I know you been spying on me: you needn't pretend. What's it all about, eh? What d'you mean by badgering a man like this?'

'Mr Jed Wintergreen?' said the old man, unmoved.

'You know who I am all right – you been asking about me. Don't deny it.'

The old man levered off his hard hat – Jed noticing for the first time that there was a mourning-band around it – and took a letter from his pocket. 'I'm to give you a message, sir,' he said. 'From Mr Veazey, solicitor, of Tombland. What begs you to do him the favour of waiting on him at the house of Mr Childs, Cardinal's Cap Yard.'

'A lawyer?' said Jed, alarmed. 'What can he want with me? I ain't broke no law.' At the same time he realized that the old man had called him sir. What the devil did that mean?

'Perhaps you'd like to read that there letter, sir,' the old fellow said.

Jed glanced at the seal. It looked highly official. 'I suppose you'd best come in,' he murmured.

He led the way up to his room, where he lit a candle and opened the letter while the old man waited.

Dear Mr Wintergreen,
Pray forgive the liberty of my thus addressing you, whom I have yet to have the pleasure of meeting. The bearer of this note will have communicated to you what may seem a rather strange invitation — which I hasten to assure you is extended with a view to your own best interests. I have some business on hand which nearly concerns you, and if you will do me the favour of attending at the execution of it, you will I believe learn of something to your advantage.

I am, sir, your obedient servant,
GILBERT VEAZEY

P.S. I believe the name of ABEL JEX may be familiar to you, and may serve to reassure you that this matter does indeed concern you most particularly.

Jed put down the letter with an unsteady hand. Abel Jex! — the cobbler of Heartsease, who had turned King's Evidence and helped send his poor father to his undeserved fate. As with everything connected with the time of the Heartsease riot thirteen years ago, the name spoke across the years with the clarity of a trumpet-note: for Jed it might all have been just yesterday. He glanced up at the message-bearer with a new keenness. Abel Jex . . . He had never heard anything of Jex since that time: now it occurred to him, confusedly, that his father's betrayer might have come to some trouble at last . . . and a lawyer wanted to speak to him . . .

He would go. If it was Abel Jex in trouble with the law, Jed would not weep. Oh, he would far from weep.

'All right – I'll come,' he said, pocketing the letter. 'But here, what have *you* got to do with all this? I suspected you was—'

'I don't know nothink,' said the old fellow. 'I'm just to bring you. I don't know nothink – except my ole master's gone – and I don't know what's to become of me.' And, to Jed's surprise, tears glistened in his eyes.

They set out. Here and there gaslight smeared the freezing fog to dimly show their way; and as they went Jed looked up at the secretively glowing windows of houses, with his usual feeling – but stronger than ever now – of wonder and bafflement at what the people within were doing, and a sense of terrible distance, as if they were as mysterious and alien to him as Red Indians.

Was Abel Jex, then, in Norwich? He had never seen him in all his years here – and he would have known him immediately. Oh, yes, he would have known him. But then it was a city of some fifty thousand souls . . .

He did not know the dark court into which he was conducted: you might live all your life in Norwich and never be familiar with all these warrens. A misgiving touched him as he followed the old man into a big darkened house: was this all some bizarre trap? The persecuting authorities drawing him into their web . . .?

He was ushered into a dusty parlour, well-lit with candles, and a short crisp bustling gentleman was advancing to shake his hand.

'Mr Wintergreen? Mr Jedediah Wintergreen? Heartily glad you could come, sir. I hope I haven't inconvenienced you, but it is a matter of some importance. Some considerable importance. My name is Veazey.'

Jed was so unused to being addressed in this manner that it had the effect of deepening his suspicions. 'You're the gentleman who writ me this?' he said, producing the letter.

'Quite so! And very surprising it must be to you, I'm sure. I wish I could have been more explicit, but it's a ticklish business, sir. I am the solicitor administering the estate of the late gentleman who owned this house – generally known as Mr Childs, christened Abel Jex. I think you know the name, sir?'

Jed stared at him. '*Late*, did you say?'

'I'm afraid so. Mr Childs – Mr Jex, I should say – was gathered to his final rest yesterday. And I was directed on his instructions to summon Mr Jedediah Wintergreen. To be brief, my dear sir, it's a matter of the late Mr Jex's will. In which you are mentioned.'

For the moment Jed's mind refused to take in the implications of this. He gazed round the room. The old servant was standing by the door; and there was another man here – a long-legged fair young man with a frank open face.

'This is Mr Coppinger, who happened to be with Mr Jex in his last moments,' the lawyer said. 'And now I think we may begin. My dear sir, do take a seat – don't be perturbed, I beg.'

Hardly knowing what he was doing, and too much in a state of wonderment to be conscious of his rough clothes, Jed sat. 'Abel Jex,' he said. '*This* is Abel Jex's house? Why, I never knew – I can't believe—'

'Mr Jex was known to you many years ago – in your childhood in the country, I think?' said Mr Veazey. 'Quite so. Don't be perturbed, my dear sir. In his last weeks, sensible of his approaching end, Mr Childs – Jex rather – began at last to confide to me the circumstances of his past, with which I believe you are familiar, Mr Wintergreen. Mr Jex served a short time in gaol in the year 1831, for his part in the agricultural disturbances of the previous year, picturesquely known as the Swing Riots. Mr Jex was at that time a cobbler, of the village of Heartsease, about eighteen miles from this city. A number of other men from his village were also convicted at that unhappy time − one of them sentenced to − dear me! − transportation: name of Jacob Wintergreen.'

'My father,' said Jed, with a proud glare at the lawyer, and at the fair young man.

'Your father, sir − don't be perturbed, I beg you! − who, I believe, did not long survive his arrival in the Antipodes. It appears, from the somewhat emotional account given me by Mr Childs, Jex I should say, before his death, that he felt responsible for this. It appears he turned King's Evidence at the trial and, to use his own phrase, fingered Jacob Wintergreen − your father, sir. You of course were a child at the time − but this was known to you?'

'It was known to me,' said Jed sombrely.

'Well! Mr Jex, on his release from gaol, did not return to his native village but settled here in Norwich, where he soon married a widow, Mrs Childs, who possessed a tidy little property in the shape of a modest tanning business, took her name, and thus as time went on he prospered.'

'So I can see,' Jed said with rising bitterness.

'Now it appears,' said Mr Veazey, 'that in his last illness Mr Jex was troubled by thoughts of the unhappy events of thirteen years since. He confessed that they preyed on his mind, and his habits, always close, became eccentrically so. He began to feel a certain guilt at his good fortune − unmerited good fortune, it now seemed to him; and it occurred to him to wonder what had become of the family of that Jacob Wintergreen whom he had, ahem, fingered.'

'Did it indeed!' breathed Jed. 'Rather late, I reckon!'

'Rather late − quite so. Mr Jex felt at last that it was a case of better late than never, as it were; and secretly made enquiries as to the whereabouts of Jacob

Wintergreen's children. He had heard that Mrs Wintergreen had not long survived her unfortunate husband — don't be perturbed, sir! — and had reason to believe, alas, that their orphaned children, two in number, had been left to the mercies of the parish, and consigned to the obscurity of poverty.'

Jed was silent, his jaws working. It was still like touching a raw nerve to hear this spoken; but he was able to be grateful, at least, that the fair young man had considerately averted his eyes.

'His enquiries at last discovered the whereabouts of the two children, now grown of course — by name Jedediah or Jed, and Charlotte,' Mr Veazey went on. 'Finding that Mr Jed Wintergreen — yourself, sir — was living at no great distance from him, he set his servant Ben Catbush to discreetly look you out, and observe your condition of life.'

Jed glanced at Ben Catbush, and managed a smile. 'Tweren't *very* discreet,' he said.

'Not very discreet! Ha ha ha! I call that dry!' said the lawyer. 'You're a philosopher, sir — that's what you are. Mr Jex looked you out, Mr Wintergreen, with a view to — in short, to providing for you after his death, as a recompense for the injury which he felt he had done to you in life.' Mr Veazey went to the table, and picked up a parchment. 'Mr Abel Jex's will, sir, makes you sole executor of his estate: inheritor, with your sister Charlotte, of his property; in short, Mr Wintergreen, it makes your fortune, and before I read it formally, allow me to congratulate you.'

Jed's head was swimming. Mr Veazey had finished reading the will, with its tangled legalistic phrases, but Jed had taken in more of it than the lawyer thought. What was making him stare so blankly into the fire was the rush of memory that was assailing him: the events of thirteen years since, always fresh, were before him again with painfully new vividness. And over and over he kept thinking of his mother's cry, shortly before she went into the workhouse to her death: 'Remember!'

'My dear sir, this is, I appreciate, vastly unexpected,' said Mr Veazey, brightly regarding Jed. 'Take a little time to collect yourself. Ben, did Mr Childs, Jex rather, keep spirits, I wonder? Of course, Mr Wintergreen, it is not for me to dictate in your own house.' He nodded, smiling. 'Your own house, Mr Wintergreen. If there are spirits, they are yours to dispose of.'

Jed seldom drank, but he needed one now. He looked at Ben Catbush.

'There's rum,' said Ben. 'And brandy. And canary and mountain in the cellar—'

'Oh! I'll take a drop of rum, if it's all the same to you,' said Jed with difficulty. This was like no dream that even he had had. He looked helplessly at the other two. 'I don't know what – Name what you like . . .'

'Well, now, I call that hospitable,' said Mr Veazey. 'Mr Coppinger, what do you say to a glass of canary?'

'Why, yes – thank you,' the young man said, to Jed rather than the lawyer.

Ben stumped off to fetch the drink. Jed stood up and rubbed his hands over his face. It was true. Just a couple of hours ago he had been working in the mill as usual, in that inhuman noise and stuffiness and gas-glare . . . and now this . . . Abel Jex, who had betrayed his poor father; Abel Jex, whose name had been one of those he had carried in his head like a curse all these years, obeying his mother's injunction to remember; Abel Jex had prospered, and grown guilty in his prosperity, and now he had left everything to the children of the man he had wronged . . . The will directed that all his property be shared between Jed and Charlotte: she not being of age, he was to be sole trustee in the meantime, but there was to be a guaranteed income for her whatever he decided to do with the property – which amounted to this house, the tannery, which Mr Veazey had said was a going concern under a trustworthy manager, and an undisclosed sum partly in Gurney's Bank and partly in 'Mr Childs'' own strongboxes. The only other legacy was a small sum to his faithful servant Ben Catbush, and the return to Mr Pierce Coppinger of his own painting, and any other pictures in the house he might fancy.

Like a man who finds he is still holding his face after his toothache is gone, Jed was even now thinking that he would surely be late home, and would not be up in time for work in the morning . . . He had to force himself to confront the idea that he – and Charlotte – did not have to worry about such things any more. Charlotte . . .

Ben Catbush came in with a tray. Jed took a stiff peg of rum; and when Ben had served the canary said to the old man: 'Well, Ben – if I might call you that – won't you have a tot of rum, too?' As Ben looked startled Jed said, 'Oh! I don't know the ways and manners of these here things – take a tot with me, anyhow: I was hard on you, I'm afraid, but I didn't know what it was all about then. I thought all sorts of wild things, when I saw you a-spying on me.'

'A ticklish proceeding,' said Mr Veazey, 'but I believe Mr Jex was anxious to do good by stealth, as it were, Mr Wintergreen – and to, ahem, avoid seeing you himself.'

'I can understand that. I can't deny I've had bitter thoughts about Abel Jex over these years,' said Jed grimly. 'Not that our misfortunes was all down to him . . . Just yesterday, you say?'

Mr Veazey nodded. 'He, ahem, lies upstairs. A professional woman has been engaged. Mr Jex gave me all the directions for his funeral. He is to be laid beside his late wife.'

'Well . . . thass hard to feel hateful about a man who's just left this life,' said Jed softly, 'leave alone when he's – when he's done this thing . . .' His eye fell on the easel, with the portrait still on it, covered. 'You was painting his picture, you say, Mr – Mr Coppinger?'

'Yes, I'd been coming to the house for some weeks,' said the fair young man, 'which was how I got to know him. He was, I'm afraid, a very sick man, but he insisted on the sittings.'

'Sick, was he? I suppose he must have changed a lot since I was a boy. D'you mind if I look at the picture?'

'Not at all,' Pierce said, uncovering the canvas.

Jed stood pensively gazing at it for some time. Yes, he recognized it as Abel Jex, all right, yet if it was a good likeness — and as far as he could tell it was a wonderful skilful picture — then how aged the man had become, how haggard and ground down . . . It dawned on Jed that for all Abel Jex's unmerited good luck, his own family had perhaps not been the only ones to suffer.

'Did you get along well with him, Mr Coppinger? What sort of man did he seem?'

Pierce considered. 'We got on quite well in the end. It was curious . . . I don't think, somehow, he was a very happy man.'

Jed nodded, looking again at the portrait. Then he turned to Mr Veazey and pointed to the will. 'I suppose there's no chance of a mistake about this, sir?'

'None whatsoever, Mr Wintergreen. I drew it up myself: Mr Jex was quite clear in his wishes; it is as tight as a drum.'

'Only, you know,' Jed said, restlessly pacing, 'you must know what my first thought was — is . . . This money — this fortune — would you say fortune?'

'It is sufficient to set a man up comfortably, with the right advice,' said Mr Veazey.

'This fortune, then, comes from Abel Jex. You've already told what Abel Jex did that he felt so guilty about. I were a child when those things happened — but not an infant. I knew. And the feelings — they've stayed with me to this day. Hurt, and anger, and — so forth.'

'Very natural,' said Mr Veazey urbanely.

'I'm a weaver,' Jed said, 'and I'm — I'm poor, and I'd be a liar, and ten sorts of fool, if I said I wanted to stay poor, and didn't care to have money. And yet there's my father buried in a convict's plot over tother side of the world, and here's Abel Jex done so well for himself, and so — so something in me say, Be damned to his house and his money! It's tainted — let it rot . . . D'you see?'

He had spoken passionately, and Pierce was moved; but Mr Veazey rubbed his pink hands in his briskest way and said, 'My dear sir, knowing the outlines of your history as I do, I fully comprehend these sentiments. You're a feeling man — that's what you are. But allow me, speaking as a professional man who has much to do with inheritance, to assure you that money and property in themselves are neutral. They can carry no taint or stain. From the moment the testament is proved, the property is yours and not Mr Jex's: one might almost say it has never been Mr Jex's at all. Yours to use for good or ill.'

Jed nodded. 'And then there's Charlotte, of course,' he said.

'Your sister — indeed. We have yet to convey the news to her. She is in service, I believe, at a place on the coast? So Mr Jex's enquiries revealed. I shall notify her formally, but you may feel, sir, that you would like to send a covering letter — to gently prepare her for this wonderful news. And it *is* wonderful news, Mr Wintergreen, is it not? Without doing violence to your . . . understandably poignant feelings, still I believe you will wake on the morrow with — in short — with a heart like a balloon, soaring!' Mr Veazey consulted his watch. 'Well, I must be on my way. Here is my card, sir. If you will call on me tomorrow, we may settle the business. Our late friend's funeral is set for noon: perhaps if you will come in the morning, we may go together thence to see Mr Jex to his rest — if, ahem, you would care to?'

'Yes,' said Jed. 'I'll come.'

'Capital. Our friend Ben Catbush is at present entrusted with the keys — none better, believe me, sir: perhaps you would care to see over your property?'

'Oh, I—' Jed glanced round at the drab parlour, which

the many candles still could not brighten. 'Nay — I reckon I'd prefer to leave that while daylight, if it's all the same to you.'

He felt a vague unease at the thought of staying in the house with its late master dead upstairs; and elected to go back to his lodging. Ben Catbush lit the three of them down to the front door, where Mr Veazey shook hands with him again, and bustled off into the fog. Jed looked up at the dark house.

'I used to tell my sister stories, when we was little, about goblins and ogres who lived all shut up with their treasure,' he said. 'Now I feel like I've stepped into one.'

'It will have a happy ending, I'm sure,' said Pierce, smiling.

'D'you think so? Perhaps it will.' Jed looked at the fair young man, who was genteelly dressed though not wealthy-looking, and said diffidently: 'Will you walk a way with me, Mr Coppinger? My head's still spinning a bit, and I'm sure I shan't rest . . .'

'Certainly,' Pierce said. 'In fact — my lodgings aren't far — will you come in and drink a glass with me? I'm sure you could take another drop of something — I know I would, if I was in your position.'

Jed Wintergreen, who had found the world so generally disposed to treat him as an enemy, always responded warmly to any friendliness; and he felt greatly in need of company. The young painter had a genial manner, and in his studio he soon put Jed at his ease, pressing him to a chair, stirring up the fire and mixing him a hot toddy.

'These pictures are all your work?' Jed said, looking with admiration at the specimens on the walls.

'Unsold ones, I'm afraid,' Pierce said. 'Sometimes people don't like the way their portrait turns out, and won't pay a farthing for it: and the landscapes I paint for pleasure. I'm longing for the spring so I can get out in the country again.'

'You love the country too?' said Jed. 'I'm glad of that.

I were brought up in the country, as you've heard, and I don't reckon a day's gone by, since I've been penned in this here city, that I ain't thought on it. Heartsease — that's my village. Nothing out of the common, mebbe, to anyone who didn't know it; but to me, even though I ain't been there for thirteen year, it's all lit up with special feelings, every leaf and stone of it . . . Is there no place like that for you, Mr Coppinger?'

'I've never lived in one place long enough to call it home. Perhaps I'm still looking for a place like that. You certainly make me want to see it, anyhow. Please, call me Pierce.'

'Jed, then. Oh! I'd dearly love for you to see Heartsease. I'd love to see it again myself, but I been so long here tied to the loom—'

'Well, now you can,' said Pierce.

Jed looked up, transfixed at the thought. 'So I can . . . Even now, a few minutes go by and I sort of forget again, forget how everything's changed. I suppose now I — I can come and go as I like.'

'Well, according to Mr Veazey the inheritance should set you up comfortable. I doubt whether you need worry about being on time at the mill tomorrow.'

Jed smiled. 'That's a good feeling — a rare good feeling. Pity the poor chaps who'll still have to go on there working their lives away . . .' He sighed and ran his hand through his thick crop of hair. 'I don't know as I shall ever get used to it. Everything'll be so different, and I reckon I'll be a regular fish out of water at first. But I *am* glad of it: mebbe I seemed sort of awkward and ungrateful before; only it was the thought of Abel Jex, you see, and what he done . . .'

'It's a sad history. I'm only sorry you had to sit there and hear it told again in the presence of a stranger.'

'Nay, I don't mind that: it's no secret. Though I suppose it was for Abel Jex.'

'Well, I didn't know him for long, but looking back I can see now how his mind was dwelling on it; and I do believe, Jed, that he really felt a genuine remorse — late as it was.'

Jed nodded. 'I remember as a boy being told not to be too hard on him — that other men might have done the same. Cast into gaol, no knowing what was to come — and then being given a chance to save your own skin. Even do it mean ratting on your friend and neighbour . . . It was a bad time altogether. And there was some who played a worse part in it than Abel Jex.'

'Perhaps, after all, there is a sort of justice in you and your sister getting this inheritance,' said Pierce. 'Too late to help your father and mother, I know — but it is a sort of setting to rights.'

'Mebbe it is at that,' said Jed thoughtfully. 'I've gone so long believing that there ain't no justice in the world at all, but mebbe this show . . . mebbe other things can be set to rights.'

'Shall you live in the house, do you suppose? You and your sister?'

'I hadn't thought. I can't say that place exactly appeal, from what I saw of it.'

Pierce laughed. 'It gave me the shivers too.'

'But just to set up home with Charlotte — not to be always apart, and waiting for a letter — by, I've dreamed of that. New clothes for Charlotte — that shall be the first thing I do with the money. Anything she want, anything in the world that money can buy. And she can leave service now — there's another fine thing! It's been a good place, but still, she's at their beck and call, and thass not the same as being free.' He looked at Pierce with eyes from which the smoky perplexity had for the moment gone, and grinned. 'Free!'

'A good word,' said Pierce, 'and worth toasting in another glass.'

He mixed more toddy, and they drank and talked a while longer; and at last when Jed prepared to go he put out his hand and said: 'It's been right friendly of you, Mr — I mean Pierce. I don't know how I should have gone on if I'd had to go straight home, and sat there with this here business burning and burning through my mind.'

'I'm very glad to be of help,' said Pierce. 'You'll be very busy soon, I don't doubt: if there's anything I can do . . .'

'Well — I don't know quite how to say it — but I will ask something of you. I suppose I shall be living — dear God, how strange! — in that there gaol of a house soon; rattling about like a pea in a hogshead, I shouldn't wonder; and if you wanted to come, any time, and see me — for a glass, and a chew of the fat, or whatever — why, I'd be grateful. Mind, I know you got your work—'

'I shall certainly come,' said Pierce. 'My work isn't such a tyrant as to keep me from my friends. And after all, we were so strangely thrown together it almost seems like fate or something — and we can't go against fate, can we?'

'That we can't,' said Jed with half a smile. He left Pierce's lodging with a wave of his hat; walked away down Pottergate with a light step, and was swallowed up by the fog, which would spit him out again as a new man, in a new life.

Chapter Five

Lost And Found

Two young men entered the office of Mr Veazey the solicitor in Norwich's Tombland one spring morning. One was a tall limber fellow, his fair hair worn, artistically, a little long; the other slightly less tall, dark-haired and pale-complexioned, on whose well-knit frame a good frock-coat and black silk cravat sat with just a fraction less than perfect ease, but whose face wore an attractive expression of alert expectancy that lit the deep shadowed eyes.

They were greeted by Mr Veazey and received into his highly polished office, a perfect temple of beeswax.

'So, gentlemen, all ready for the fray, eh? How do you go? Do you ride?'

'I've hired a gig from Harrison's livery-stables just across the way,' said Jed Wintergreen.

'Hired a gig! I call that dashing! Well, sir, I've written Mr Ringrose, and he knows when to expect you. He's not often from home, it seems: chooses to live in a retired way, something of a scholar, dabbles in sundry amateur pursuits. My colleague has handled his affairs since he came to Norfolk ten years ago – very agreeable gentleman, he tells me – you couldn't hope to do business with a more liberal-minded man. If you do business, that is. It is merely an appointment to look over the property, sir – nothing more: don't feel you must commit yourself. It's not often, certainly, that such a property will come up in such a small country community – but even so. Take time to look about you.'

'I mean to do just that,' Jed said with a smile.

'Quite so. Aha, Mr Coppinger, I think I spy a sketchbook in your pocket.'

'I hope to make some landscape studies at last, now that the everlasting winter has left us,' said Pierce.

'Everlasting winter! You've hit it! It hasn't suited Mrs Veazey — the Brocklehursts have never stood up well to the cold. It's the blood. By the by, Mr Wintergreen, I've heard again from the leather gentleman — quite committed now to putting in an offer for the tannery *and* the house. It's a reasonable price he names, though I believe I can push him up further.'

'Well, if it's a fair price for the property, I don't see as we need press,' Jed said meditatively.

'Oh, but my dear sir, you must *always* press,' said Mr Veazey with a gurgle of amusement. 'This gentleman has, say, x amount of money in his possession, with which he seeks to buy y of you: what you must do is try to get as much of x into *your* pockets as possible, and give him as little of y as possible in return. That's business, my dear sir!'

'Is it fair dealing, though, I wonder?' said Jed to Pierce, when they left the lawyer's office and walked over to the livery stables.

'I think Mr Veazey would say that fair dealing is anything you can get away with,' said Pierce.

Jed laughed, shaking his head at the same time. 'I reckon he think I shall end up thinking that way myself. God forbid!'

Jed drove the gig. It felt good to him to be bowling out of the city, leaving behind the smoky artisan suburbs that had grown up outside the old walls, and seeing about him the greening sheep-meadows, and the wooden sails of windmills turning on the horizon: it felt fine. As Pierce remarked, it was a base slander to say Norfolk was flat. Away on the western edge, where the Ouse entered from the Wash — *that* was flatness if you liked; but to travel on these quiet roads was to be tucked into gentle folds of patchwork country, woods and water, field and lane, at once broad and intimate.

Jed felt fine, and it was already an effort to remember the profound sense of dislocation with which he had moved into Abel Jex's old house five months since. He had not actively regretted his turn of good fortune, but in the first strangeness it had seemed to wear a decidedly speckled aspect. Never had he thought he would be wistful for the regimented certainties of the mill, but just for those vulnerable first days, stranded in that echoing house where everything met his gaze with a blank indifference as if it knew him to be a stranger, and the days had no shape . . . It had soon passed. For one thing there was the taut mainspring of Jed's nature, which just as it had in the terrible passage of his childhood when his family had been destroyed, and just as it had when the drunken weaver to whom he had been apprenticed had finally gone too far, had caused him to meet his new circumstances head-on, to turn his face nakedly to all that they entailed. For another, there was the friendship of Pierce Coppinger, which had been generously given and deeply appreciated – how deeply it was beyond Jed to articulate, for in affection and loyalty he was as fierce and steadfast as he was in remembering an injury. He thought and felt in absolutes: the biblical phrase about no man having greater love than he who lays down his life for his friends would have struck Jed as no more than a simple definition of friendship – nothing less was worthwhile.

There was much to separate the two men – education, upbringing, experience – but in practice these had a way of evening themselves out. Pierce was at home in the world in a way that Jed was not; yet in suffering known and adversity undergone, Jed had the advantage, if such it could be called: in those terms Pierce was an innocent boy beside him. Both, moreover, were somewhat solitary by temperament; and if Pierce could be judged to be separated from his friend by simple application of the word 'gentleman', it was in a rather marginalized sense.

His profession was neither fish nor fowl, and still obscured by a faint haze of the not-quite-respectable; and his youth had been spent with a father who could not see a convention without firing a broadside at it. Thus they were both men who took as they found – and besides that, they liked each other.

Mr Veazey it was who acted as agent between Jed and a complex new world that came with suddenly owning more than the clothes he stood up in: Pierce helped him with less tangible things. At first Pierce tended to be casually cheerful in his advice – 'Oh, just wear what you like, my dear fellow' – until Jed signalled to him that that was not what he wanted: it was precisely because he lacked that inbuilt assurance that he asked for guidance. With Pierce to help him the growth of Jed's confidence was swift. He soon met the manager of the tannery, and the various tradesmen, without constraint on either side. He kept Ben Catbush on, and established a rapport with the old man who had once seemed a sinister figure in his life; and the maid-of-all-work never failed to look surprised when Jed wandered into the subterranean kitchen to chat with her, and help her take the bread out of the oven.

For he was not changed: he was still Jed Wintergreen, whose shaping influences had been earth and labour and kin; he had no wish to put off his old identity and don a new, to use his money as a philosopher's stone to transmute his nature. It was wonderful no longer to be poor – daily, hourly wonderful – the shine never came off it; only those who had been poor, as Jed had all his life, knew the way that that one fact dominated your whole existence. It was as if he had been carrying a heavy pack on his back all his life and only now did he know what it was like to stand straight. But Jed did not seek to fly from his past, far from it, and therein lay the third and most important factor in his adjustment. There was the element that made him wake each morning with a brilliantly glad consciousness of his new life – the idea that his money could take him back to Heartsease, and restore his lost world.

He could not say when this idea had first suggested itself to him as a potential reality. Oh, the return to Heartsease had always been the sweetest of his dreams, but it had also seemed the wildest and remotest, so complete had been the wreck of his youth there, so brutally severed and torn had been his every tie to that place and time. It was perhaps when he was discussing his inheritance with Mr Veazey, early on, and the lawyer had mentioned his freedom to sell up, 'in favour of some new property, in Norwich or elsewhere'. For until then it had not fully occurred to him that he was not tied to that house in Cardinal's Cap Yard as he had been to his loom, that he might go to some other place. And almost before he had framed the question *What other place?* had come the answer: *Heartsease*.

From then on all the desires of his heart were contained in that one idea. It had a perfection of inevitability about it — it simply must be. He employed Mr Veazey in making enquiries about property in the village of Heartsease — an obscure enough place, in the heart of Norfolk, and the solicitor had suggested that he might spread his net a little wider, if it was a country property he sought . . . Jed had been firm. That place: no other. At last Mr Veazey had heard from a fellow-lawyer of one of his clients, a Mr Ringrose, who was seeking a tenant for a modest holding in the village of Heartsease, house rather out of repair, but good land attached, a long lease . . .

This Mr Ringrose lived at the Grange — a small manor just outside Heartsease, which in Jed's day had been a run-down place inhabited by two decaying spinsters. Some small tenancies belonged to it: the bulk of the village was of course owned by the Hall where, it seemed, still lived that same Squire Ingamells whose ill name was branded on Jed's memory. The thought of gaining a foothold in the village outside the baleful influence of the

Hall added an edge of exultation to Jed's excitement. He had listened respectfully to Mr Veazey's advice not to rush into anything, but privately he was determined that unless this property was a sheer hole in the ground he would take it.

There was only one slight disappointment to lay a bar of shade over the brightness of Jed's mood as he drove westward on the Colney road to reclaim his murdered youth. It concerned his sister Charlotte. Charlotte had, of course, been overwhelmed and delighted at the news of their being provided for − delighted, he noticed, chiefly for his sake rather than her own, which was typical of her. 'Now you can leave the mill, and not be forever tired and worn,' she had said, 'and you can have books of your own, and eat well, and − oh, Jed, it's wonderful, ain't it?' He had visited her in Shipden, and she had stayed with him in Norwich, and he had taken her round the shops and made her choose whatever she wanted, and they had had supper together in Abel Jex's gloomy dining room, both dressed in their new clothes, and had laughed to see each other so fine across the table. He had arranged to have her share of money paid monthly, and had laughed again to see her eyes widen when she saw the figures on the banker's draft.

'But this mean we're rich!'

'No,' he said. 'Rich is something different, my dear. But it mean we're finished wi' being poor. It mean the cruel times are gone for you and me, Charlotte.' And she had hugged him − both thinking of their mother and father in their dishonoured graves, and neither needing to speak of it.

And yet Charlotte let him know, in her own gentle way, that she was not ready to leave the Crab Pot permanently just yet. He saw clearly enough, when he went there, how fond Mr and Mrs Skeels were of her, and how her servile status had melted into that of one of the family. Jed well understood the quiet loyalty that bound his sister to them − it was a quality he was fitted to appreciate, and no one possessed it more surely than Charlotte. She would not have been the Charlotte he dearly loved if she had turned on her heel and left them at once.

And yet, and yet . . . She said she wanted to see the Skeels and the Crab Pot comfortably settled before she left them, but it seemed to Jed that money could do that. Now she could continue to help them in all sorts of ways, without actually having to go on living there. He did not think that the Skeels were mulishly clinging on to her either. He had told her of his plan to go back to Heartsease, and she had thoroughly approved it – and yet, in spite of all this, she was reluctant to leave Shipden. He did not understand; and when he had pressed her, Charlotte, whose nature was normally as raindrop-clear and uncomplicated as her eyes and her generous smile, had coloured in confusion.

Perhaps, he thought, her reaction to their unexpected inheritance had contained more of bewilderment and shock than he had supposed, and she was holding on to the familiar. It was perplexing, but he hoped in time she would come round. And, he thought, it would give him the chance to make the house in Heartsease ready, so that it would be a true home when she came to join him there – a home such as they had once had. There was warm pleasure in the thought of that – and also triumphant vindication, in the face of those masters of their fates who had exiled them from Heartsease thirteen years ago.

He thought of them as the gig crossed a bridge over the infant River Yare between trees lacy with spring bud. Mr Ingamells, at the Hall: so he was still there, the squire and magistrate who had ridden through the village in a closed carriage and was as severe on men driven to crime by hunger as only the descendant of a Norman bandit could be. And Farmer Hemstock – was he still there? The big farmer who had grown so stiff-necked with wealth that he could not bear to speak with the men who dug his ditches except from behind a gun; who had reaped a fat reward for turning over to the merciless authorities the desperate men he had pauperized . . . Jed remembered Ingamells and Hemstock and their deeds all right − his poor broken mother, wherever she might be, need not fear he had forgot . . .

Jed's hands had grown damp on the reins in thinking of these things; and with an effort he turned his mind to the happier associations of his project − seeing the village in his mind, the Spanish chestnuts near the church, the spinney by the stream where the butterfly-orchis grew, the forge with the thick outer wall that was always warm to the touch − how well he remembered stopping to press his cold hands against it on a winter's day! And he might meet old friends too: Dick Freshwater, the publican who also did undertaking, had been good to him − was he still about? He had seemed old then, to the boy, but had probably been less than fifty.

They were in a quiet country now, the roads empty but for the odd farm-cart; but here and there in the distance, briefly appearing between hedgerows prinked with infant blossom, a commotion was visible as if an army were on manoeuvres in mid-Norfolk. After splashing through a ford they came to a piece of rising ground with an open view across the fields, and Jed pulled up beside the road to have a look. Away to the south there was a great scar on the land, cutting brashly across the pattern of field and hedge and path. Massive banks of raw earth had been thrown up on either side of it, all shored about with bare timbers, and criss-crossed by crazy promenades of planking, among which could be seen the hangman silhouettes of derricks and tripods, and lines of rickety sheds that climbed in and out between heaps of rubble and ashes. Over all the scene moved a human swarm, distinguishable even at a distance as dressed very differently from the usual smocked country workers, and seeming too to betray something different even in their motions with pick and barrow and shovel − something both single-minded and reckless.

'Building the railway from Norwich,' said Pierce. 'East Anglia must have them like everywhere else, I suppose.'

'I hope it won't pass near Heartsease,' said Jed. Though a scene of devastation, it was also an exciting sight: there was a thrill in seeing that giant thrust of power and confidence flung across the land. But even as he felt the thrill, Jed's heart misgave him. He was a child of the new age: steam power, iron, gaslight, these were a part of his world as they had never really been for his parents, yet for Jed the transition to this new world, if such it was, was all tied up in his mind with the central transition of his own life, the destruction of his family, the great trauma of thirteen years ago. He could not forget that his father and the others had rioted against a machine, the threshing-machine that impoverished them. Machines had pauperized the Norwich weavers, too, and in the Yarn Company Mill he had been their exhausted, numbed servant. Jed could never take the impersonal view of experience; and the interruption of this journey back to a better past by the sight of the devouring railway seemed to him almost like a personal menace.

'My father thinks the railway boom will end in disaster,' said Pierce. 'He insists that travelling at such speeds will cause displacement of the bones, and the next generation will be born with their heads facing the wrong way.'

Jed laughed. 'I'm not sure that *this* generation's got their heads facing quite the right way.' He flicked the reins.

They had been travelling some time in companionable silence when all at once Jed knew he was home. It was no dawning recognition of a landmark here and there: quite suddenly, every tree and field — every leaf he would have said — was unutterably familiar to him. It was as if the thinnest of transparent skins separated him from his past, and he had simply stepped through it.

'We're here,' he said to Pierce.

It was unchanged — more purely unchanged than he had dared to hope. The curious dog's-leg row of cottages as one entered from the east, which did not seem to face anywhere, and trailed their short gardens in the stream; the main street, comfortably broad, with Dick Freshwater's Wheatsheaf public-house self-importantly protruding like a pot belly at the first turn, with the stone hitching-post and trough before it; the high grey church big and massy enough for a town; the turning to Splash Lane that was always flooded, with the track to Madhouse Heath beyond; the wheelwright's yard, all a fascination of tortured timber and iron; the cottage dormer windows looking blearily through the ragged thatch; even the boy in the peaked cap leading a pair of horses who stopped to stare at the gig might have been a facsimile of his young self. Heartsease. Here it was: it had been waiting for him.

Wait. It was not quite the same.

He had slowed the horse to a walk as they came to the western end of the twisting street, and now Jed pulled on the reins and took off his hat and wiped his brow and stared.

The house where he had lived as a boy was gone. The whole row of three cottages, with their lean-tos and gardens, had vanished. The ground where they had stood had been fenced into a close and set to grass which still had a faintly callow look against the older pasture.

'What's wrong?' said Pierce.

Jed came to himself, and gave a faint smile. ''Fraid I can't show you the house where I was born, Pierce.' He gestured towards the fence. 'It was thereabouts, anyhow.'

'There? Are you sure you're not mistaken, and—' He glanced at Jed's face. 'Of course you're not — silly thing to say.'

Jed was silent for some moments, turning the reins over and over in his hands. It was on his lips to say that it was really no surprise that they had pulled down his parents' cottage, as they had destroyed everything else; but though the feeling was real, it would come out maudlin, and he checked himself. It was only a house, after all, only so much heaped rubble and straw: it was lives that mattered; and already the flood of intolerably poignant memory that had swamped him as he came into the village had been channelled into something more concentrated and purposeful: a determination that he would make *his* life here, on his own terms – and just let them try and stop him.

'Do you want to look around for a while?' said Pierce.

'We'll do that later,' Jed said. 'Let's meet this here Mr Ringrose.'

The Grange was a modest ivied house of Dutch gables and leaded windows which lay at the end of its own carriage-drive, half a mile out of the village. Its owner, Mr Ringrose, turned out to be a stoutish man in early middle age, with a tonsure of reddish hair, an expanse of white waistcoat, a mouth that was generally either smiling or pursed in a soundless whistle, and hands that seemed always to be itching to go into his trouser pockets. Altogether there was something ambling, abstracted, and good-naturedly round-shouldered about the man. 'Bachelor Hall here, I'm afraid, gentlemen,' he said, inviting them in. 'I don't often receive visitors – pity – but comfortable, I think, comfortable.'

The house might have fairly have been expected, from the exterior, to have contained all the hideous authenticity of carved panels and pendants like wooden droppings and fly-blown stags' heads: instead it reminded Pierce of rooms he had seen at Bath – cool and uncluttered, arched recesses containing numerous books and separated by chaste plaster medallions, and several white busts.

'Fox, of course,' said Mr Ringrose, as he saw Pierce looking at one of these. 'Rather before your time. Saw him several times from the gallery of the Commons when I was a lad. Eh? Very fair likeness. I would like to have met Fox. You're a connoisseur of sculpture, sir?'

'I admire it greatly,' Pierce said, 'without quite understanding. I am a painter by profession.'

'Painter, eh? Splendid — you know, I've always been interested in painting myself. I've one or two drawings by Rowlandson you must see — rather warm for this age, apparently; déshabillé, and nightshirts, and so forth — we seem to have rather buttoned up since those days.' Mr Ringrose trundled over to the window, where the sight of his garden caused him to disappear into soundlessly whistling abstraction.

'Er — I think Mr Veazey wrote you, sir, about the vacant property,' said Jed.

'Splendid — so he did, so he did. Yes, the house has been vacant some little time, I regret to say. Not as spruce as you might wish. First there was the old tenant letting it go rather. Drink, I'm afraid. Not that I don't reckon there are worse things. Eh? Fox, now — he used to tipple rather. Gambling too. Thousand guineas on the turn of a card and so forth.' Mr Ringrose's round blue eyes looked wistful. 'We don't seem to go it like that, these days. Band of Hope and so forth . . . And then I had another prospective tenant who changed his mind. So I don't mind telling you the place needs work, rather.'

'Oh, I don't mind that,' Jed said. 'I'm prepared for that. Mr Veazey said there was a good holding of land . . .?'

'Been let go rather, too,' said Mr Ringrose. 'Choked — wants clearing. But it can make a tidy little farmstead, in good hands.'

'Thass what I want,' Jed said. 'A little place to farm on my own account, proper.'

'Ah, you're interested in farming, sir? I've always been rather interested in farming myself. Turnip Townsend — I would have liked to have met him. I've set up a little experimental enterprise here at the Grange — a poultry-farm. Eh? Turkeys, fowls, ducks. I must show you my poultry-farm. All on modern lines—'

'Thass good of you,' Jed said. 'But I'd dearly like to see over the property, if I might.'

'Certainly you shall,' said Mr Ringrose. 'We'll stroll over there now.'

Jed was so impatient to see the house that he would much rather have run than strolled, but Mr Ringrose moved at his own pace, stopping several times on the way out to point out to Pierce various pictures that hung in the hall.

'Byron, you know,' he said, indicating an engraving. 'I wish I could have met Byron. Rather a scandalous fellow, but still. We don't seem to breed 'em like that any more.' He sighed, and Pierce seemed to detect in Mr Ringrose a smothered longing to have been a Regency buck, toasting Bonaparte and being dissipated in a starched cravat, together with a wistful consciousness that he had been born just a little too late.

'Shelley – there was another,' pursued Mr Ringrose, having taken up his hat and cane in the same clubmanlike manner, and led them out by the front door. 'Sent down from Oxford – atheism, you know. A little strong, I feel. Eh? I tend to take the liberal view of things myself . . .'

Musing thus on a lost time, Mr Ringrose conducted them through the village, Jed dwelling the while on his own lost time, and feeling it steal closer to him with every thatch-eave and door-post that met his eye. The narrow turning down which Mr Ringrose led them was Splash Lane, and was made shady by hedges of hawthorn and bramble. Jed remembered gathering blackberries here.

' . . . Rather a curious name the property has,' Mr Ringrose was saying. 'I've always been rather interested in the origin of names. Plague House – not an appealing name, I confess—'

'Plague House?' said Jed. 'I remember it.'

'Ah? Splendid. Nothing unhealthy about it, of course – eligible situation – the name dates, I'm told, from the time of the Great Plague, when the then inhabitants of the house had the misfortune to bring the plague to the village, on returning from a visit to London where it was raging. Quaint story.'

Jed remembered Plague House — a neat and well-kept little farmstead with its timbered gable-end looking directly on to the lane; but if he needed any further evidence that thirteen years had not gone by without change, Plague House as it now was supplied it. The thick walls looked as if they were suffering from some terminal disease — a plague indeed — of which ghastly eruptions of decaying lath and plaster were the chief symptom. Most of the window-panes were gone, leaving the window-frames nothing to do but follow, while the thatch of the roof had become merely a sort of ineffectual obstacle to the free passage of bats and owls. The main door, at the back, was reached via a tangled tunnel of honeysuckle and hollyhock, and opened very reluctantly, to the sound of a dainty stampede and a whisking of long tails.

There was a large kitchen and scullery, a parlour of snug dimensions and, plainly the oldest part of the house, a hall with a staircase held aloft on massive wood struts. To Pierce the antique darkness and decrepitude, the musty, mouldy, mildewy smell, the cobwebs depending like great hammocks from the beams, presented a dismal and discouraging aspect, and he was strongly inclined to get outside into the fresh air. But a glance at Jed was enough to tell him that his friend saw it all with very different eyes — that, indeed, he was not seeing it in its present state at all, but as it would be.

The upper storey was in slightly better condition; and Jed threw open shutters and delved into closets with such enthusiasm that he seemed ready to begin renovating the place there and then.

'It wants airing, of course,' Mr Ringrose said mildly, with his hands in his pockets. 'The structure's very sound; and then of course there's the stable and barn —

they're more recent. I'm a liberal man, as I say: I don't
hold with these profit, profit ways of dealing. Eh? If you
were to put the property in a good state of repair, Mr
Wintergreen, we might well consider that in the rent. And
the farming, now – you can see from this window, the
land extends over beyond the stream there, a nice
compact enclosure, you know – I can help you there, I
want to see it cultivated again. Let me see, is there a
family, sir?'

'I'm not married,' said Jed. 'But my sister would be
coming to keep house with me.'

'Splendid – splendid – a woman's touch, and so
forth,' said Mr Ringrose, gesturing at the gaping plaster,
as if it were no more than a curtain that needed tying
back.

Jed gazed out at the fallow fields. Pierce's conjecture
had not been wrong: Jed was in a state that could fairly
be called visionary. Paths of destiny as straight and true
as the new railway seemed to have brought him here. He
turned to Pierce. 'What do you think?' he said.

'I think,' Pierce said with a smile, 'that your mind's
made up.'

Jed returned to the Grange with Mr Ringrose to talk over
the business: Pierce wandered off to go sketching. An
agreement was soon concluded, that Jed Wintergreen
would be the new tenant of Plague House, and Mr
Ringrose would instruct his solicitor at once to prepare
the lease. He invited Jed and Pierce to join him for an
early dinner, and Jed, gladly accepting, went out to look
round the village and to find his friend.

Passing along the dirt road, he felt he wanted to shout
aloud: swung himself about instead, to feel the air of
Heartsease blowing on his face and through his hair, and
saw that someone else had just left the Grange and was
walking in the same direction as himself. He wondered if
it was someone he knew, and resolved to greet her
anyhow, for he felt the need to speak to someone here,

to reclaim his origins, to proclaim somehow that he was Jed Wintergreen who had been banished and was returned . . . He took off his hat as the young woman came towards him — started to speak, stopped, and gazed.

'Rosa!' he said.

His first reaction was astonishment: not at the fact that she was grown and changed, but at the fact that he recognized her so immediately, after thirteen years. Rosa Strickland: the little girl from the next-door cottage, with whom he had waited that unforgettable night for news from the Assize about the trial of their fathers, and who had been his playfellow in the lost days before the catastrophe.

'Sir?' she said. She was clad in a coarse short-sleeved woollen frock and linen apron, and was bare-headed; but at that moment Jed was quite unconscious of his new clothes, and he said, spreading his arms wide and smiling, 'Don't you remember me, Rosa?'

She looked at him suspiciously, and almost seemed about to hurry past him. His smile faded at that — and something about that change in his face made her pause, and look again, and slowly breathe: 'You — *can't* be Jed Wintergreen.'

'Why, I thought for a moment you were going to pass me by,' Jed said, laughing and taking her hand. 'Have I really changed so much?'

'You *can't* be,' she said again, giving him her hand absently, and studying his face.

'I dare say it do seem that way,' Jed said. 'I never thought to be back at Heartsease myself, let alone all — well — all fligged up so,' he added with a wry gesture at his clothes.

'You just come from the Grange?'

'Thass it. Seeing Mr Ringrose, about renting a place here. I've wanted, always I've wanted to come back to Heartsease . . . D'you work at the Grange?'

'Some of the time,' said Rosa. 'I help at Mr Ringrose's

112

poultry-farm . . . Jed Wintergreen. I wouldn't have known you.'

'Well, I knew you straight off,' said Jed, colouring a little as she scrutinized his clothes.

'Ah, but I been here all the time. I've known a lot of folk leave Heartsease, but you're the first to come back. And when you've made your fortune, and all, by the showings of you.'

'It was made for me. By someone you knew . . . Where are you going, Rosa? Can I walk a ways with you?'

'I'm for Farmer Gage's, over Pitchford way – see if there's any weeding agoing. You can walk along o' me, do you like.'

They went on together, each occasionally stealing a glance at the other. Rosa Strickland, who had been dark as a child, was yet darker. Her hair, parted and tied back but still falling abundantly about her shoulders, was blue-black like coal. Her skin was very fine and clear – one might almost fancy one saw the blood pulsing through it – but lightly tinted by sun too, so that altogether it gave off a rich glow. Jed remembered her eyes as wonderfully brown and soft and laughing when she was a girl; but though those eyes were as beautiful as they had promised to be, beneath a smooth forehead and dark brows they no longer seemed to laugh. They were steady and luminous, they were intelligent, but they were not easy. Neither were her lips, which seemed very slightly to draw into themselves, as if to deny their red fullness. Her figure was tall and well-rounded, and, with a certain taut upright pride in her way of holding herself, merited the word statuesque, her hands quite slight, and marked with labour. The old brightness, in maturing into beauty, seemed to have become shadowed by a watchful constraint. In fact if Jed had sought a comparison for the oddly challenging way in which she tilted up her oval face, he need have looked no further than his mirror: as it was, it struck him that insofar as Rosa resembled the flower of her name, she suggested one that, touched by some chill or canker, had not quite opened fully.

He told her as they walked of his life in Norwich since he had left the village, and the unexpected stroke of fortune that had suddenly ended his impoverishment, and the man who had been responsible.

'Abel Jex . . . just fancy . . . We never heard nothing of him in Heartsease — he never come back after that time,' said Rosa. 'Knew he wouldn't be welcome, I dare say.'

'Aye. You can imagine what went through my mind at first when I found twas him as had died, and wanted to provide for me. The way I — well, the way I wished I might throw it back in his face.'

Rosa stopped. 'Why, you fool!' she said vehemently.

'Why so? You know the story, Rosa — none better. You couldn't expect me to feel no love for Abel Jex.'

'No reason to turn down his money,' Rosa said dryly. '*I* wouldn't. No matter where it came from. There's nothing noble about being poor, Jed — don't think it.'

'No,' he said, 'and so I came to see. Oh, I'm glad of the money, mortal glad of it — only it brought back those memories of my father and all . . . not that they'd ever been far away, since that time . . . What of your father, Rosa? I was sent away to Norwich while he were still in gaol, I think.'

Rosa seemed to draw herself up a little straighter, and narrowed her eyes as she looked forth at the sown fields opening ahead of them. 'He come out of gaol at last — not well: not the man he had been. He couldn't get much work around here — not after taking part in the riot, and being a gaolbird. He didn't live long after that.'

'I'm sorry,' said Jed. 'Your mother . . .?'

'She washed, and scrubbed, and skivvied — until she couldn't do it no more.'

Jed said, 'I'm sorry,' again, helplessly.

Rosa turned her dark eyes full on him. 'They were well out of it, I reckon. I was earning by then, and could manage. What was there in life for 'em by then that was so worth clinging on to?'

She spoke harshly. Jed thought he saw a wetness shine in her eyes, but she turned her face from him.

'What about the others who was put in gaol? How did they fare?'

'Oh! that weren't so bad for them — they was single chaps, got work elsewheres. There's not much to remind folk of that time now. Except your coming back, mebbe. A Wintergreen back in Heartsease . . .'

'I wouldn't have thought folk could have forgot so soon,' said Jed.

'Oh, I never said they'd forgot. Only when there's no use in remembering, nothing to be done—' She seemed about to say more, but stopped abruptly.

'Well, one way of making sure folk are forgotten is to knock down their houses,' said Jed, his bitterness surfacing a moment. 'Did we have a pest or summat, that they had to do that? Summat catching?'

'That were Mr Ingamells. He thought it weren't worth the risk of bringing in more families on the poor-rate. His bailiff say there's too many folk in Heartsease already.'

'Do he! Them who pay rents, and work the fields, and keep Ingamells nice and comfy in the Hall, for instance!' said Jed hotly.

Rosa regarded him sceptically, then touched his arm and smiled. He was glad to see the smile: there was in that smile a breaking of tension which you found you had been waiting for without being aware of it. 'Poor Jed,' she said. 'You've been away a long time . . . But *you* won't be on the poor-rate. Is this money enough to set you up proper? What are you going to do?'

'I'm taking Plague House — it still seem strange to me, to just say something like that! — and I shall settle there, and farm, and — and live the life I've always wanted to, working the land, fair and honest, the way my poor father — and yours, Rosa — would have wanted. Mr Ringrose have took the state of the place into account in the rent: he seem a decent chap. Is he?'

Rosa nodded. 'He treat me well enough. He got no enemies here, I reckon — but then, he ain't got so much power. Thass still Mr Ingamells who rule here — that don't change.'

'What about — ' he felt a sick shudder as he spoke the name, as if momentarily plunged into one of his black dreams of the past — 'what about Farmer Hemstock?'

'Oh! he thrive.' Rosa's mouth was tight. 'He thrive, Farmer Hemstock. You can see his house — thataway — see beyond the trees there.'

Jed frowned into the sun. A large and handsome house, quite new, buttressed and pilastered. It looked more like a villa than a farmhouse. 'There? Do he still farm? I thought—'

'Oh, he farm most of the land here,' Rosa said. 'He moved out of the village proper, and built that place, away from us. Don't let him hear you say *Farmer* Hemstock. *Mister* Hemstock, if you please.'

'I remember he were proud, back then. Why, that look as though he's half-way to a squire himself.'

'So he'd like to think. He keep himself well aloft whenever I've worked for him — no heavy boots near *his* door, but that suit me.'

'Rosa! You don't mean to say you work for him — after what he did, my father, yours—'

'When I have to,' Rosa said. She shook her head at him, and said again: 'You've been away a long time, Jed. I wonder if . . .'

'What?'

She did not answer, instead she said, 'You could have done anything you liked with this here legacy, I suppose?'

'I could. And I'm doing what I like. Coming back to Heartsease. Is that so very strange?'

'Mebbe not. Mebbe I'd feel the same . . . Only I can't help but smile, Jed, at you wanting to come back — when all the time I've wanted to get away.'

'Only because of what they made of Heartsease,' Jed said, gesturing towards the Hemstock place. 'It don't have to be like that. It wasn't like that, once. Mebbe if folk can begin to stand up for theirselves . . .'

'Like they did before?'

'Not — not necessarily. There'll be one place in Heartsease, anyhow, where there's fair dealing, and where the Wintergreens'll hold their heads up again — thass for sure.'

'More'n one?' said Rosa. 'Are you wed now?'

'Nay. I mean Charlotte — she'll be coming to keep house for me.'

'Charlotte!' said Rosa, softening. 'She were a sweet girl — so quiet and gentle-like — I've often thought about Charlotte.'

'The best — the best girl there ever was. If I had any doubts about this money of Abel Jex's — about what it could do for good or ill — it was the thought of making Charlotte happy that stopped 'em. If anyone deserve to be happy, it's Charlotte.'

Rosa nodded. 'Some people are meant to be happy, I reckon. It's in their faces. And some people—'

'Why, *everybody*'s meant to be happy, Rosa,' said Jed fervently. 'And here on this earth — not in some never-never in the sky like the parson say. Thass what I— ' He broke off, seeing a figure in the lane ahead. 'Rosa — thass my friend Pierce Coppinger. I don't know what I'd have done without him, these past months when it were all new to me, and I felt so strange and awkward. Pierce! I want you to meet him . . .'

Rosa began to protest, but Jed was already hailing the young man, who came to them with an open sketchbook under his arm.

'Pierce — look here — I met up with Rosa Strickland, you remember, I told you the Stricklands were our neighbours all them years ago . . .'

'Of course, how d'you do,' said Pierce, snatching off his hat, in his honest courteous manner; which Rosa

117

acknowledged in a confused way, from behind a sort of veil of constraint.

'Pierce is an artist,' Jed said. 'I been telling him how handsome the country is round Heartsease, and he come to see for himself.'

'I could stay all day — I found a most perfect view — it's just the way I imagined it,' said Pierce eagerly. 'The light — I can't get over the light.'

'Well — let's see, then,' said Jed, pointing to the sketchbook.

'Oh, well, it's a very unformed sketch, you know — just the outlines . . .'

Jed held the sketchbook at arm's length. 'See, Rosa — and you ought to see 'em when he works 'em up into proper paintings. I don't know why he ain't famous, but he reckon he's only a beginner.'

Rosa regarded the sketch soberly. ''Tis handsome drawn,' she said at length. 'Only you left out Art Martin's old timber-pond.'

She spoke, it seemed to Pierce, with a curious sort of challenge, though she did not look at him. He was a little nonplussed. 'Yes, I — it rather spoilt the composition.'

'It's there, though,' said Rosa, with a slight smile, meeting his eyes for the first time.

'Oh, these artists see things different, you know,' said Jed. 'I tell you what, I shall have one of these framed on the wall of Plague House when it's all set to rights. Whenever *that* may be,' he added with a laugh. 'There's a powerful lot of repairing to do. I must find out if there's any men in the village wants the work.'

'You won't have to look far,' Rosa said, again with a slight smile. 'I must go. Goodbye, Jed. I'm glad you — I'm glad you've got what you want.'

'Goodbye,' said Pierce. She gave him the same sort of subdued acknowledgement that was like shyness and yet like pride too, leaving them quickly with her purposeful stride.

There was silence between the two young men for a

time as they made their way back to the Grange. For Jed there was a powerful significance in his meeting Rosa Strickland on his first return to Heartsease. The events of thirteen years ago had touched the two of them, if not equally, then in the same way: the two of them alone, perhaps, now that Abel Jex was dead, still walked in the shadow of that time, and could be said to have been made the people they were by it. If he had seemed to sense some scepticism in Rosa, especially about his coming back here to live, then he felt he could understand it in the light of his own long-nurtured bitterness, which was only now beginning to dissolve in a glow of hope and vindication.

Pierce broke the silence. 'Well, I've refrained from asking you for long enough now. Tell me. No disappointment? Is it like a dream come true for you?'

They were returning down the village street. Outside the forge stood a great waggon of the East Anglian sort, so square and enormous and wonderfully carpentered that it looked as if, fitted with a sail, it might have safely gone to sea, or, turned upside down, made a comfortable dwelling – or done anything, in fact, except move fast and get out of the road when you were in a hurry. Jed noticed the quiet, and at the same time noticed the sound surrounding it, like a decorative border about a blank page: birdsong.

'No disappointment,' he said. 'I shan't have any more dreams, now.'

'I'm glad. Is that the Hall I see there?'

The Hall was visible only as a glimpse of parapet and pediments above trees, on the other side of a sheep-meadow and a fenced belt of parkland. 'Thass it,' said Jed shortly. The Hall was no part of Heartsease, not his Heartsease. He turned his face from it.

'I wonder if I would be allowed to sketch in the park,' said Pierce. 'There must be some noble views there.'

'As long as you mind the man-traps and spring-guns,' Jed said grimly, then looked at his friend and laughed. 'You must finish that one first.'

'Oh . . .' Pierce glanced down at his sketchbook with a frown. 'I'm not sure about this. It's not quite right. It needs a figure, I think.'

It had been a long day; and what with country air, and the good dinner Mr Ringrose had given them at the Grange, Pierce should have been tired when he got back to his lodgings in Pottergate that evening.

But he was not. Pierce's body tended to follow curious rhythms of its own, and often in the small hours he would be working, or reading, and he would look out at the darkened city with puzzlement, and wonder how anyone could sleep. Possibly the influence of his father, the captain – who instead of gravy poured cream on his mutton-chops, and would have bristled with indignation had anyone suggested there was anything odd about it – was responsible for this: whatever, Pierce was restless in his studio, and at last lit another candle and sat down with his sketchbook.

It certainly was an attractive place to the eye, this Heartsease; he had gone out of loyalty to Jed, and because he wanted to begin some landscape studies, rather than in any expectation of finding in the village anything out of the common. It was impossible, after all, that he could see the place as Jed saw it – refracted with burning intensity through the longing of exile. He well knew how that sad past of Jed's determined everything about him – all the wariness, the pride, the strong affection, the troubled aspiration that made up the character of the man he had come to know. One could not like and understand Jed Wintergreen without entering into those tortured private feelings that sprang from the public events of 1830, when a small footnote of history had crushed his family; and Pierce did like and understand Jed. If at first he had kept his promise to call on Jed at Abel Jex's gaunt house, and help him adjust to his new world, out of a simple readiness to help, he had soon come to respond more directly to the unaffected integrity of the man, and to value the friendship in itself. But Jed's desire to return to Heartsease he had seen as no more than a hobby-horse, the sort of personal obsession that his upbringing with the captain had led him to look tolerantly on. He had been half-prepared for Jed to be disappointed today, for his friend to find the reality sadly paler than the cherished dream. The fact that he had not done so led Pierce to think that he had underestimated Jed's passionate single-mindedness. He knew Jed was a man of deep feelings: just how deep he had not guessed until he had seen Jed walking about that decrepit Plague House with a visionary look in his unquiet eyes, transforming, creating.

But more than that: Pierce had seen the attraction himself. In the village and its environs – the gentle distances, the little islets of copse and hedge that broke up the broad, sea-like prospects of cultivation, the epic sky – he had beheld the East Anglia of his own dreams which, standing before the paintings of Cotman and Constable and Gainsborough, he had longed to enter. He had found what he was looking for there without expecting it.

Pierce looked at the face he had drawn, then tore the leaf from the sketchbook and tossed it into the cold grate. There was no executing a really good likeness from memory. Least of all from one meeting. Least of all when the face was so beautiful that the slightest inaccuracy of the pencil would glare out as a flagrant insult to it.

Unexpected too! Not the least part of the impression made upon him by Heartsease was the beauty of that young woman, who had seemed not only to share in all its picturesque qualities but to stand out as a superb picture in herself. Dazzlingly handsome country maidens were common enough in genre pictures at the Academy – perhaps they were common enough in life: all Pierce knew was that he could not have been more dumbfounded at meeting one of Signor Gardini's large-armed classical heroines in the flesh than he had been at coming face to face with Rosa Strickland. An ideal — yet how real too: how uncompromising her gaze when she did look at him; how her skin suggested the sun and rain and wind that touched it, unlike the coddled hothouse complexions of the young ladies who sat to him for miniatures! He had made no remark to Jed on how arrested he had been by her — Jed had seemed to see nothing out of the ordinary; though he had known her before, of course. And what, after all, was there to say?

Pierce put the sketchbook away and went downstairs to see Mr Trunch; the mourning-stationer kept late hours and was always glad to welcome him into his parlour for a glass of negus.

'You've been out to the country today, I think, Mr Coppinger?' said Mr Trunch. 'I thought so — I thought I detected the scent on your clothes. Oh! dear me, no, sir, I don't mean anything like that — a pleasant smell it is — just like fresh washing just come off the clothes line. I'm uncommonly sensitive to it, on account of living a rather indoor life here.' He waved a genial hand at the snug parlour; and certainly with its long drawn curtains and wallpaper all writhing with dense patterns, and perennially blazing fire, and obtrusive fire-screens that seemed to press forward to warm themselves, and its pervasive smell of tobacco, the place was Indoor enough for anything. 'I couldn't positively engage to say,' pursued Mr Trunch, 'that I've been out of the city these five years, except to coach over to Yarmouth, where I've an aunt who's a little infirm — not in her mind, no, I don't know her equal as far as power of mind goes; but she has set light to herself more than once, it can't be denied, and the servant-girl has to keep a tub of water to hand in case she should go up again — so I visit her, and it's quite as much a pleasure as a duty, for her conversation would reflect credit on, dear me, a Bluestocking almost, and if it wasn't for a little matter of keeping the candles out of her reach, and discouraging her from picking up live coals out of the fire, you might almost suppose yourself in a Salon. So you see I live quite an indoor life altogether.'

'You're not a lover of the country, Mr Trunch?' said Pierce.

'I adore it, sir!' said Mr Trunch, lifting his greased forelock like a crest, for emphasis. 'It's my greatest weakness. In my sleep, as the poet has it, I babble of green fields. In my younger days you could have taken me in a post-chaise to the remotest rural spot, and there dropped me, and said, "Nahum Trunch, there are no glasses of hot negus for miles – no tobacco, no warm firesides, no upholstered chairs, no newspapers, and no company as far as the eye can see. Shall I leave you here, or will you come back to the city with me?" – and my reply would have been, without hesitation: "Go, Mr Coppinger! Leave me! Leave me here in these flowery meads, with the birds for my music, the grassy bank for my pillow, and the limpid brook for my drink, and you leave me in the happiest condition a man can know this side of the tomb!" That's how I would have answered you, Mr Coppinger (politely I hope). But if you were to take me to such a spot now, and threaten to leave me, I couldn't answer for my feelings, and I fear I would beg and plead with you to take me back – take me back!'

Mr Trunch showing signs of agitation, Pierce reassured him that he did not have it in mind to spirit him away on any such expedition.

'This change in me, sir,' went on Mr Trunch, 'is directly referrable to that period of my life in which my affections were blighted by that trifler who, if I were ever to write my memoirs, would of tender necessity appear upon the page only as Miss Blank. There was a picnic, Mr Coppinger, in just such a rustic spot as I have described to you: She was there and so, alas, was the law-clerk you have heard me mention before. A river ran gurgling by, there was some capital smoked tongue, and I bathed in the light of my enchantress' eyes, with no thought of the calamity soon to befall me. It was then that the law-clerk

— a man of low, vulgar humour: I never understood why everyone thought him amusing — seized my hat from my head and tossed it into the water. "I say, Trunch," said he, "the wind's taken your hat, you know." There was a certain amount of laughter — I believe I took that in good part; but in attempting to retrieve my hat by means of an overhanging branch, I lost my balance somewhat. I maintain to this day that I swam back to the bank with a certain dignity, liable to excite at least a lively respect in the mind of a sensible observer, but the law-clerk (who else!) broke into the most ungentlemanly laugh you ever heard — really a donkey could have done no worse. I cared nothing for that, nor for the fact that I was uncomfortably wound about with weed, nor for the fact that my best clothes were ruined. ("Pop 'em in your vats, Trunch, if they run," were the law-clerk's words — I leave you to judge his character from that alone.) No — this was nothing: it was She who thrust the sword into my vitals and inflicted the wound which aches to this day, by bursting into a peal of laughter — Silver bells, sir, I always thought till then! She laughed, Mr Coppinger, immoderately: not to conceal anything from you, she lay on her back and drummed her heels on the turf, and gave the final twist to the blade by declaring that I was better than a play.' Mr Trunch sighed and drank deep. 'I date from that day the blight that has prevented my ever smiling with my whole face, Mr Coppinger, and which has among its other aspects, rendered the countryside too fraught with painful association to be borne.'

'I quite understand your feelings, Mr Trunch,' said Pierce. 'And I would have quite understood too if you'd thrown the law-clerk in the river, though it does honour to your self-possession that you didn't.' He spoke with exceptional feeling, perhaps, because it occurred to him to wonder what it would be like to be laughed at by Rosa Strickland.

'Well, there was the party to consider,' said Mr Trunch. 'It's best that a man hide his hurt, except before his particular friends. Speaking of which, Mr Coppinger – a little low in spirits tonight, sir?'

Pierce stirred and blinked at the fire. 'Not low exactly,' he said. 'I hardly know what it is, Mr Trunch. Do you – do you believe in that rather romantic idea of love at first sight?'

Mr Trunch merely raised his eyes with tremendous expression, as if to say 'Do I!'

'Only – only it's rather an illogical notion when you come to think of it,' said Pierce, leaning his elbows on his long thighs, and frowning at the fire. 'What's sight after all? It's all very well to be struck by someone's beauty – as, for example, I'm sure you were struck by that of – the lady we do not name.'

Mr Trunch murmured that a Thunderbolt wasn't in it.

'And yet for all the charms that you've described to me so well, Mr Trunch, she proved – well—'

'False!' sighed Mr Trunch. 'Say false!'

'I'm sorry – I distress you – what I'm trying to say is, what can one know of a person at first sight? Only the most superficial externals, surely. It's like – it's like falling in love with a portrait.' Pierce in fact had very romantic notions about life altogether, and did not know why he was trying to argue himself into scepticism.

'True – true – you're in the right of it, Mr Coppinger,' said Mr Trunch. 'I've no arguments to advance against that, sir – except that of experience. Illogical it may be, but when you are struck, sir – if ever it should happen to you, and if it does I sincerely hope the fair Striker won't be a trifler, and given to immoderate laughter – if it should happen to you, sir, I speak as a friend when I warn you that you won't be in a position to be logical – inasmuch as it will floor you, and settle your business.'

Pierce thanked Mr Trunch cordially; and did not say that he was afraid his warning was too late.

Chapter Six

Rosa's Dreams

Weary, though in her pride she does not care to show it,
Rosa comes home from weeding in the fields.

This is just one of the many jobs she performs in the
perpetual battle to keep alive. There is also Mr Ringrose's
poultry-farm, where she cleans out and feeds and plucks;
there are also, in their season, potato-setting, turnip-
trimming, pea-picking, hay-raking, and peeling osiers for
basket-making. And, if nothing else offers, there is
Pitchford a couple of miles away — Pitchford, which is a
straggle of beer-shops and slop-shops, with no big house
or resident clergy, where gang-masters will recruit a
needy platoon of women and children and carry them in a
cart to some more or less distant farm requiring cheap
labour for a day or so.

Once — and that time is perhaps longer ago, and more
difficult to bring back than Jed Wintergreen thinks — a
girl like Rosa might have lived in as a farm servant,
and eaten at the farmer's table; or at least been hired
by the year instead of having to go in search of a week's,
a day's, even an hour's work where she can get it; and
might have brought home, instead of a meagre wage of
shillings and sixpences, some of the rich Norfolk produce
that she helps to raise, and which is now sent out of the
village at such a rate that one might suppose the
inhabitants to resemble so many mayflies, and have
no mouths. But times have changed. The big farmers
find the new methods cheaper, whilst Mrs Hemstock, for
one, would as soon think of dining with the cattle, as
allowing Hands to sit down at her gorgeous rosewood
dinner-table; and as for the small farmers, they have

enough to do to feed themselves.

Rosa knows all this. She has, indeed, faint memories of a better time, which mingle with the spoken memories of older people in the village, and throw into relief the harsh outlines of the labouring life in Heartsease now. But Rosa is not interested in the past. It is dead and gone. There is enough to think of in the present: whether, for instance, she can put another patch in her petticoat — which is already more patch than petticoat — and if not, where she will find the money for some material to make up a new one. If she has dreams, like Jed — and she would be loath to admit that she does, for she believes they do more harm than good — they concern the future, not the past. They concern a time when she will escape from Heartsease — she does not know how, or where to; only that she will be free as she can never be here. But to escape is not easy. To leave the parish is to lose your entitlement to parish relief — which is your only cushion against starvation when you are looking for work — and so it goes round in a circle. She will go, one day, but it is hard to look up at the road ahead when you must concentrate on every step.

Rosa is thinking, of course, as she makes her way home, of her meeting with Jed Wintergreen. She did not fully reveal how much this affected her; but she has grown accustomed to smothering her feelings. How strange, that meeting in the lane! A gentleman called her name: 'Rosa!' just, it seemed at first, in the way all the masters of the village addressed you. Not rudely — casually, as you call an obedient dog to heel. Even Mr Ringrose has that way, kindly as he is. And then to see the playfellow of her childhood, in his grown and altered shape — but with that same look in his eyes, both defensive and defenceless — tall, well-dressed, transfigured. Transfigured chiefly by hope, she thinks.

Well, well. Her thoughts have often been with the Wintergreens over the years, for all her dislike of harking back to the past, and for all her carefully avoiding too much reminiscence with Jed that day. She could, for instance, have told him more of her own story − of how as a child she had scarcely recognized as her father the crushed and haggard man who was released at last from Norwich gaol; of how, like many others in the hard workless winter, he had gone to take temporary work with the Yarmouth herring fleet − unfit for it, and soon falling prey to pneumonia; of how her mother's hands, cracked by cold and labour in the struggle to support them, used to bleed. Her mother, reaching over to stroke Rosa's head, and leaving blood on her hair.

Well, well. Gone now.

A cart, delivering coals, stands before the Rectory. Rosa, who can read, though not with ease, notices that the cart has a Dereham address on its backboard. There was a time, too, when Heartsease had its own higglers to do such work, when various trades − draper, carpenter, grocer, tinner, druggist, plumber, mason − flourished in the village street as in any town. Many are gone now; the land has taken over. Townsmen, passing through this countryside with poetic ideas in their heads and Wordsworth in their hands, find this idea of a whole community dependent on the soil rather charming. 'Immemorial,' they say, and 'bonds of ancient custom', of a way of life newer than the steam-engine, and as artificial in its way as a cotton plantation. For the soil is a hard master, as Rosa knows − hardest of all when there are no other masters to turn to; and it does not pay a retainer nowadays, but only rewards its servants with cash when it needs them.

Rosa wonders how much of this Jed Wintergreen sees, in his hopeful return to Heartsease; wonders what picture of the village he carried about in his head during the years in Norwich, and wonders whether it most resembles the place of his boyhood, or the place as it is now, or some place quite imaginary, unwittingly conjured up by the sorrows of exile. And she wonders too, briefly, uneasily, how much of what she sees is the real Heartsease, and how much her own bitterness. Uneasily − for Rosa does not like to think she is bitter. No, no: realistic is what she is, clear-sighted, unsentimental. It just shows, she thinks, how much that meeting with Jed did affect her, that she should begin to suspect herself of bitterness; that memories of the riot, and of her poor father and mother, should come pouring back and make her eyes smart . . . But that way lies weakness, and the entrapment of dreams, and life is too hard for that. Something − perhaps it was the sight of that blood on her mother's hands − turned a key in Rosa's soul at a young age, and made her resolve that the only way to face life down was to meet hardness with hardness, be strong, never to look back, never to cry for the moon; and she has kept to her resolve. Is it, perhaps, written on her face somehow? Did Jed Wintergreen see it, and was it that that made him look perplexed on her, as if he missed something?

Rosa reaches home, or at least the place where she lodges. This is the cottage of the Widow Thorne, who gets a bare living by dressmaking and laundering. The Widow Thorne is a little woman with a pouchy, seamed face, and narrow eyes, and a tight slit of a mouth − as if, during the long years bent over her needle in candlelight, she came to sew herself up by mistake. The cottage, where Rosa has an oat-flight bed beneath the thatch, is a clean place but very bare, even by the standards of its neighbours, the poorest of which are given a semblance of homeliness by a valance over the fireplace, a sampler on the wall, a birdcage, or a piece or two of Staffordshire pottery. But the Widow Thorne does not have her heart set on worldly things. Methodism has placed her feet on the rock of salvation. There is to be an open-air meeting that evening at Pitchford: an itinerant preacher is coming to revive the faith. The Widow Thorne is very anxious to go to the meeting, and Rosa has already promised to accompany her − not willingly, for religious revivalism repels her, and as she eats a meal of bread and cheese at the scrubbed deal table she wishes she could stay in and rest; but Rosa, besides being insistent on keeping her word, has never refused to do anyone a kindness, and her heart is forever betraying the hardness and self-sufficiency she presents to the world.

So she and the widow set out in the cool thin dusk of early spring. Others are making the journey from Heartsease — not as many, perhaps, as would have done so a few years ago. It was after the riots of 1830, and their grim aftermath, that Methodism began to engage the hearts of local people. Rosa remembers well the bitterness of that time: men in gaol, soldiers still in evidence about the villages, and over all a smouldering sense of defeat and resentment. For sceptical as she is of any ideas of a lost golden age, Rosa recognizes that a sort of innocence was destroyed then. The men who ruled the countryside, from hall and farm and parsonage, from magistrates' bench and poor-law union, had shown themselves as the enemies of the ruled, and it had been a shock to find that enmity so nakedly stated; a shock to find that the village community, which the men had risen up with some confused idea of re-establishing, was in fact past saving. And in their bewilderment, people turned to another form of salvation. They gave up on this world, and fastened their hopes on the next, set out for them in glowing terms by the Primitive Methodist preachers who proliferated in East Anglia during those years. The passion with which they embraced this emotional religion has died down somewhat, as memories of the riots fade, as life settles down, but it is always susceptible to revival.

As they go along together, Rosa looks at the Widow Thorne, whose tight lips are already murmuring fragments of psalms and hymns. Does it, Rosa wonders, make all the hardship worthwhile, the bread and cheese and the cold grate and the worrying and pinching and scraping from day to comfortless day? Does the Spirit really make the desires of the flesh as naught, as the Widow Thorne says?

Rosa thinks again — she cannot stop thinking — of the

young man whom Jed introduced as his friend. She has never known a gentleman to doff his hat to her before — or at least, a gentlemanly sort of man, which he plainly was, though Dick Freshwater says these artists are a mixed lot and a lot of them only own the clothes they stand up in. The young man behaved to her as if — well — as if they were on the same footing; and it was perhaps that, she thinks, that made her so perplexed and awkward with him. He challenged her expectations, and that made her want to challenge him somehow. And the picture he drew: it was good (beautiful, she thought) but it wasn't true. If you are going to draw pictures, she thinks, you must make them true. There are already enough people ready to believe — longing to believe — what isn't so, without that.

Rosa and the Widow Thorne come to Pitchford. Not a place to catch the artist's eye: a shabby gathering of cottages where two roads meet, with a sort of muddy slope like a chute for a street, and shabby old clothes hanging outside shabby old-clothes' shops, and a seedy store where you can get a pennyworth of opium to keep the baby quiet or smother the world's ills for a space, and men lounging: some, in bright stocking-caps and neckerchiefs, are navvies working on the building of the new railway a few miles away, and have chosen to lodge here rather than in the navvies' temporary encampments. Their women are with them — different from Heartsease women, Rosa sees: they lounge too, and stare, and laugh loudly in the twilight; they are not afraid.

For it is no accident that the meeting is here, on the muddy space that passes for a green, and not at Heartsease, or some other village that makes a nice picture. For the rector of Heartsease, the Rev. Bouverie, would not care to have an open-air gathering of Methodies on his doorstep; neither would Squire Ingamells, or Farmer Hemstock for that matter. It smacks too much of independence. Deference is wanted there, and Rosa hates it — the bitterest labour would still only be labour were it not for that grain of deference that turns it to poison. The inhabitants of Heartsease live under a scrutiny as complete as if they were sheep in a pen: here in shabby, dirty, rackety Pitchford, there is no one watching you.

And yet how harmless this meeting is, thinks Rosa as they take their places in the circle of people around the preacher standing on his cart, how completely devoid of any of that spirit that rose up in 1830, the memory of which still makes Farmer Hemstock build higher and stronger fences. No dangerous discontent can grow from these unworldly seeds. The preacher, an elderly man with a high keening voice full of pain, is speaking of death; and his audience, some of whom have walked for many miles to hear him and are covered in dust, keep their eyes fixed on his face, as if at the unfolding of a great secret.

' . . . And you think of death as your enemy — a terrible, cruel, ruthless enemy, forever a-waiting for you. And yet here is the comfort I come to offer you on behalf of my Saviour — a comfort to heal your smart, and set your heart a-leaping at what the living God can do with a touch of His hand. For death is not your enemy. Death is your friend — take Jesus into you, and death become your friend, the sweetest of friends, dearer than the dearest beloved of your heart who you long to see from waking to sleep. And do you ask, what have I done, what can I do to deserve such a friend? Oh! ask that question of yourself, and you come near the answer. Be but convinced of your sins — look into yourself and see them — there! — seize 'em, pluck 'em out, offer 'em up in the sight of your Saviour! Oh, show Him your sins, in sorrowful humbleness of heart, and He will show you everlasting glory in return. He will make death your sweet friend: He holds in His hand a key, a key to a world that makes this one so much dust and rags; only reach out to His merciful hand — don't fear! Bear a repentant heart, and He will not turn you aside, oh no — He beckons you now!'

'Forgive me,' the Widow Thorne is murmuring. 'Oh, forgive me.' There are other murmurings from the small crowd: a man wipes tears with the heel of his hand. Rosa is touched yet annoyed. What has poor Widow Thorne ever done that she should have to beg for forgiveness? What have any of them ever done except work, and strive, and struggle for existence as best they can? Do they have to apologize even for living?

She withdraws a little from the lamplit ring into the shadows: she feels herself an impostor here. She does not believe − at least, not this sort of belief. She is not ready to give up on this world for a promise of the next. For that is what makes her feel sad, and a little scornful, as she watches those murmuring, twitching faces, marked with so much disappointment, and hope deferred, and lit now with a light as artificial as that of the storm-lantern on the preacher's cart. They expect so little of life they might as well be dead already. They are resigned to the injustices of the here and now, to being poor, disregarded, despised, cheated: they are resigned to it all, and will not complain; it will all be made up for in the next world.

But what could ever make up for the blood seeping from her mother's hands? thinks Rosa. What could ever atone for that?

It is long since she has dwelt on that calamitous past so much. It is the return of Jed Wintergreen that has stirred it up in her mind; she wonders what else his return to Heartsease may stir up. She retreats a little further into the thickening darkness, for emotion must be showing on her face, and she does not choose to let it be seen. Her feelings have been knocked out of kilter. Since her orphaned childhood she has set herself on a firm and straightforward course, not looking back, nursing no extravagant hopes, sustained by a mixture of pride and practicality. And now there is a bruised feeling about her heart as she listens to the over-charged and wandering words of a revivalist preacher for whose creed she has only disdain.

But the feeling is not religious. Rosa has in her own way made a habit of subduing the flesh — not for God, but as a means of self-preservation; life is all too ready to hurt you, without you offering it targets in the shape of longings and fancies. Such has always been her reasoning till now. Perhaps that meeting with Jed, all radiant aspiration, reaching forward to something better and brighter in life, has momentarily given her own cautious creed a hollow ring in her ears. And perhaps the memory of the fair young man who snatched off his hat and was — how strange to think of! — *respectful* of her, has something to do with it too. Certainly the memory of him haunts her as she stands in the darkness, outside the ring of the faithful, yet joined to them too by the unruly swelling of emotion that brings tears to her eyes, and transforms her downturned face as it transforms their uplifted ones.

Dearer than the dearest beloved of your heart who you long to see from waking to sleep . . . From the endless skein of the preacher's discourse Rosa has plucked this thread, and the words, like the fair young face, haunt her.

And yet they are only words, after all; and the preacher may well travel on to another village and use much the same words again. And the fair young man, the artist, has gone back to his own world, a world of which she knows little — as little as he knows of hers. He spoke to her as if nothing separated them — instead of everything, everything that has made her the woman she is. She must remember that: to win back her clear-eyed peace of mind, she must remember that. Not the fact that he is the most beautiful young man she has ever seen. That has nothing to do with anything. And besides, the child thinks the fire beautiful, until it stretches out its hand to it.

There is greater agitation amongst the listeners as the preacher reaches his peroration. A couple are kneeling with their hands clutched at their breasts; a woman is sobbing, and another is rocking and swaying as if she will fall; there is a continual muttering in which the word 'sin' is prominent, like a rustle through foliage.

' . . . The Spirit have moved here tonight – I've felt it washing me clean. Oh, friends, don't turn away that love that knocks at the gates of your hearts. Have you sinned, and gone astray, and back-slid, and been a-caught in the snares of the flesh? Confess it, then – let it out in the sight of the Lord – humble yourself before Him, and He will raise you up again! Thass how merciful He is – thass true, friends, the truest thing as ever was. I feel His mercy shining on us now!'

. . . The preaching is over, and the crowd is breaking up. Rosa sees the Widow Thorne moving away in a daze, almost stumbling in the darkness. She goes over and gives her her arm.

'Oh! There you are, Rosa,' says the widow. 'I hardly know where I am . . .' Her cheeks are wet. 'Did you feel it, Rosa? Why – why, I think you did, a little, from your face. Oh, I've wrestled with myself this night, Rosa: my soul saw such beauty – beauty that might be mine!'

Rosa does not speak for a moment. Then she pats the widow's hand. 'Come you on, mawther,' she said. 'Let's go home.'

Chapter Seven

The Farmer's Daughter

Marianne Hemstock, the eldest child of Farmer Hemstock of Heartsease, had come to the end of her education at a boarding-school for young ladies in Clapham, and was packed, and ready for her father to come and collect her and take her home.

She had spent the morning saying sad goodbyes to her fellow-boarders, a few of whom were leaving like herself, and would soon be scattered over the breadth of the country, and lost to her. Her sorrow was very real; not only at parting from the friends she had made, but at the prospect of leaving the school, which for all its little limitations seemed to stand in the very heart of the great rushing world, compared with the quiet home to which she must return.

The school was inconvenient enough, and dear enough, in all conscience; but it promised gentility. Her father had sent her there to learn ladylike accomplishments, and the school was good at teaching those. Initially there had been a vague idea of Marianne's training to be a governess, as many of the boarders did; but as time went on, and Elias Hemstock's substance continued to increase, along with his opinion of his own consequence, he decided that he did not care to have his own daughter go as a dependant to other people's families, and the project was abandoned. Marianne's feelings about this were mixed. She had not relished the idea of becoming a sort of servant, however elevated; but one of her fellow-pupils was going as governess to the children of a baronet, who spent the season in London, and regularly made trips to Paris and even Italy, in all of which the governess was a sharer – and Marianne, listening to this with wistful excitement, felt that her own promised independence was not an unmitigated boon.

The school was a tall squeezed house behind a box hedge, renowned for its airy situation – which meant that it caught the wind off the Common like a broadside, and ascending the endless stairs to the howling bedchambers in the roof was like climbing aloft to the crow's nest. Here the young women – daughters of stock-jobbers, of wholesalers, of aspiring farmers like Marianne's father – were taught to write letters in very curly calligraphy on very small pieces of paper, to speak French but not to understand it, to play the piano with a lot of right-hand tinkling, to draw each other sitting beneath serpentine trees, and to blind themselves with petit-point.

Some worthwhile knowledge was however bound to get through this screen of gentility, and Marianne Hemstock, who was quick and intelligent if not persevering, had picked up some history and geography and light literature, which might have whetted her appetite for more substantial learning, had not the whole tone of the establishment discouraged 'cleverness' in young ladies. Doors had been briefly opened on wider views of experience, only to be closed again: Marianne's mind had been stimulated but never satisfied; and as a result her healthy propensity to curiosity – rather like the girls' posture which was modified by stays and backboards – had been trained a little out of shape, and was liable to become fascination. For Marianne had a strong imagination, which took off on flights more soaring than the proprietress would have liked. She was proficient in French, and the very idea of that country held a magic for her; the word Paris, with all its associations, acted on her like a charm, and she was not content merely with the knowledge that it was the capital of France, and famous for its luxury manufactures. And there was besides the situation of the school, secluded yet close to all the dazzle and novelty of London. From the high window of her shared bedroom at night she fancied she could hear its music like the sound of the seashore – the hum of theatres, carriages, street-singers, receptions, Horse Guards, markets, docks, Opera: it was all glamour to her. She had sometimes drawn a little closer to it – staying during vacations with a schoolfellow whose father was a tea-dealer in the City, and who had taken them to Astley's, and driven them about in a post-chaise – but never close enough. It was all glimpses – all tantalizing – all frustration.

Her father had given her a handsome dress allowance, and her clothes had been made after the London fashion. Just the other day, when she was walking in crocodile with the other young ladies on the Common, a couple of mounted soldiers had interrupted their exercise to cast an admiring glance; but two ladies in an open barouche had demonstrated a very different way of looking at and through her, which intensified a feeling she often had of falling short, of being betwixt and between, of being neither one thing nor another. The school boasted in its prospectus of providing all the Finish proper to young ladies, but Marianne Hemstock, on preparing to leave it, had a lurking consciousness of not being finished at all, and of crucially lacking something. She watched for the arrival of her father at the window of the proprietress' little parlour, and her mind restlessly roamed over the years spent here, with all their piecemeal widenings of her horizons – roamed over the stories of Miss Ralph, the possessor of a fabulously rich uncle in India who sent her exotic presents and regularly shot tigers from the back of an elephant (though Miss Ralph had a hazy idea that it was the other way round); roamed over the anecdotes of the French mistress, whose family had been émigrés from the Terror, and who still had a claim (mysteriously unproven) on a ruined chateau and an estate of vineyards in Burgundy; roamed over the late nights, when in illicit candlelight she and her friends had pored over the society

novels of Mr Theodore Hook, or thrilled to Byron's
Corsair; roamed over the figures, glimpsed in the world
beyond the box hedge, whom her fancy had invested with
histories both plausible and romantic, roamed over a
thousand places, real and imagined, but was forced
always to return to one place: Heartsease, the home to
which her father was to carry her — and always with
misgiving and dissatisfaction.

Her father was here. The proprietress was greeting him
in the hall.

'Well, Mr Hemstock, it is always a pleasure to see you,
though I confess to a little sadness on this occasion, for I
shall be sorry, exceedingly sorry, to lose Miss Hemstock,
whom I humbly venture to hope you will find a credit to
my poor teaching . . . Ah! here she is.'

'Hello, Papa,' said Marianne, going to him.

She had learned to use the word Papa, instead of
Father, as more genteel; and in that there was perhaps a
small measure of the awkwardness between them, which
had grown up from the daughter's education, and the
father's aspirations, and had come to overshadow the
considerable natural affection that joined them. Mr
Hemstock kissed his daughter, looking at her with pride,
but also a certain perplexity — as he might look at a field
of his wheat that was almost too well grown — and even a
little humility too; and she looked at him with fondness,
and a little irritation that he should so plainly show,
before the proprietress, his surprise at his own daughter's
being so ladylike, and a little shame for thinking such a
thing. So that between them they were pretty glad to cut
short the proprietress's compliments (which as she had
had several hundred pounds out of Mr Hemstock, and
always promptly paid too, were sincere enough — though
over a private glass of port-wine with a friend she had
been known to refer to him as Mr Hayseed of Moneybags
Farm), and to make their departure.

Elias Hemstock in his fiftieth year was a tall, stocky,
upright man, with a bull-like strength still in evidence

about his neck and thighs, in spite of the stiff collar and trousers which he had exchanged for country stock and breeches. He had a large leonine head, the hair just thinning on top but thickly curling about his ears, and a face too stern and harsh to be handsome, but well-made, with a strong Roman nose and jutting underlip. He was always very close-shaven, his linen always very crisp and white, his thick-fingered hands always very clean; his voice, just softened at the edges with Norfolk intonations, was seldom raised, seeming always to have a sort of curb or restraint on it, like a well-trained but powerful dog. There was a certain measured and subdued quality too about his gait and his gestures, as if he had schooled them hard in one narrow compass, and allowed them no latitude. There was a good deal of alertness and keenness in him, but not spontaneity; and if he had feeling – and from the proud way in which he gave his daughter his arm, there was no reason to suppose he had not – then he handled it rather like his money, thinking perhaps a little too closely of its worth, and of laying it out only in the right places.

A hackney-coach, with Marianne's luggage up behind, conveyed father and daughter to the Black Bull in Bishopsgate Street, where Mr Hemstock had slept, and the Norwich coach was presently to depart. They had a meal together in the coffee-room, Marianne telling her father all her news – every now and then falling silent of a sudden, because she had been taught that it was ill-bred to gush. Her father listened, and nodded his great strong head, and steadily ate his way through his beef and capers; and Marianne felt her love for him kindling as he sat there so massive and reliable, for her feelings, in spite of petit-point and deportment, were naturally warm and affectionate – and though her father's manner was uniformly unyielding, she was well aware that she had always been a favourite of his, and that she could be sure of his indulgence. If she could not help finding something embarrassingly cumbrous about him in spite of his gentlemanly clothes, the same warmth of heart pricked her to conceal it; and certainly he tipped the waiter confidently enough, though her cheeks burned a little at the way in which he stared round the coffee-room, studying everyone who came in and went out, just as if he were amongst the farmers in a corn-exchange. At last the coach was ready, and they took their places inside; and were borne jolting into one of the main thoroughfares of the City, and did terrible battle with a tight squadron of hackneys, and a milling infantry of tall-hatted gentlemen going on 'Change, before they could make any speed. Marianne was absorbed in making a mental farewell of all that seemed to offer a chance of the excitement and passion and mystery that she felt she would die if she did not get soon; and it was only as London turned gradually into a wilderness of brickyards and brand-new railway-cuttings that she came to herself and, finding her father watching her, attempted a smile.

'You're sorry to be leaving, Marianne?' Mr Hemstock said.

'A little,' said Marianne. 'But I shall be glad to see home too.'

'Well: I think a change of air won't hurt you,' said her father, with his heavy lip judiciously jutting. 'You're a little pale, I reckon — well-looking though: yes, aside from that, very fair.'

Marianne stopped herself saying that a lady was meant to be pale, and that nothing was so countrified as colour, and contented herself with another smile: for it was pleasing, after all, to be complimented.

The girl that Elias Hemstock was thus proudly owning to be his daughter presented a forcible contrast to the rugged man opposite her in the coach. Marianne at eighteen was slender, very blonde, very clear-skinned; her features were on a small though not delicate scale, and her brown long-lashed eyes were full of expression — unguarded to precisely the same degree that her father's were cautious. From the fashionable ringlets framing her face to her neat well-shod feet there was not a sharp or discordant angle about her: she had something of the grace of a cat, that can sit on a rough gatepost and look comfortable, notwithstanding the constrictions of the tight sprigged muslin dress with its narrow waist and great dome of skirts. She united all the freshest aspects of youth with the first gleams of a lustrous maturity, whilst somehow giving the impression of a person who found herself less than the sum of her parts. That element of constraint in her father appeared in her too, with the difference that where Mr Hemstock seemed to have disciplined himself into a single inflexible manner, braced and hard, and never deviated from it, Marianne Hemstock seemed uncertain quite who Marianne Hemstock was — whether she was lively or languid, sunny or sulky, cheerful or discontented, or quite possibly all at once.

'Are they all well at home?' asked Marianne.

'Your mother's been a little out of sorts,' said Mr Hemstock, in a casual way that suggested this was far from uncommon. 'Wade and Margery are thriving. I let Wade handle his first gun the other day. The boy's got a steady eye and safe hands — I reckon he'll do well.'

Marianne suffered a little clouding of the spirits at the mention of guns, and the associated thoughts of dead rabbits, and boots, and barns. 'And Herbert?'

'Oh, he's home.' Mr Hemstock spoke in the curt tone he reserved for his eldest son, who was a year or two younger than Marianne. 'I'm in two minds whether he should have any more schooling. He don't appear to me to benefit. He'd be better helping me.'

'And everything's the same, I suppose, in Heartsease?' said Marianne, listlessly.

'Much the same. Summer's been a little too dry for the wheat if anything. I doubt I'll get last year's price . . . I knew there was something else. Young Mr Roland Bouverie paid us another call the other day. He's staying with his father for a while. Asked after you particularly

— very civil. He lent you some books when you were home at Christmas, apparently.'

'Oh! yes, those,' Marianne said, guiltily remembering that she had not even opened them. Roland Bouverie, the son of the rector of Heartsease, was a young man of earnest interests; as far as she could remember one of the books had borne the alluring title *Ogden's Sermons on Prayer.*

'Aye — a very civil young man. I think I shall ask him to sup with us next week.'

Her father seemed to expect a reply. 'Oh, will you, Papa? That'll be nice,' she said.

Mr Hemstock seemed satisfied. 'Whether the rector will come too I don't know: I don't think he dines out much — but he's always shown us very polite attention, you know; I believe he might come. I reckon the house is quite fit for any company, now.' Mr Hemstock thrust out his chin above his snowy collar, as if facing down an invisible doubter; an habitual gesture, which was both arrogantly assertive and — it seemed to Marianne now — faintly defensive.

'It'll be nice to have some company,' she said; but her heart sank.

Roland Bouverie! — was that all she had to look forward to?

Elias Hemstock farmed four hundred acres of prime arable land in the vicinity of Heartsease. It was high farming of the sort that had long brought admiring observers to Norfolk from the Continent: modern, scientific and immensely profitable. Mr Hemstock came from a long line of tenant farmers, mostly small men who were content to raise their crops, drive to market in a gig, and glance at the Agricultural Reports over a pipe by the kitchen fireside. Elias Hemstock's father had been somewhat of this kind, but he had also been alive to the new developments in farming, to the new potential offered by enclosure and four-course rotation, and it was he who had urged the Hemstock fortunes from a jog to a trot. His son had done more, for to energy and capital he added ambition. He not only wanted to be a wealthy man; he wanted the indefinables that went with wealth. He wanted to be respected or − what came to the same thing for him − feared. There was no sentimentality in Elias Hemstock − and if there was any pity, he had never shown it. Hence his reaction to the Swing Riots of 1830, when many Norfolk farmers had had some sympathy for the plight of the men who had broken machines and burnt ricks. He had nailed his colours to the mast for all to see on that occasion, with uncompromising defiance: he was of the squire's party. His determined bid for respect bore a mixed return, insofar as the labouring people hated him, and Squire Ingamells patronized him.

But he was not daunted. There was nothing fitful about Mr Hemstock's ambition; it ran through every vein of him. He had married at thirty a Swaffham woman only a little younger, who was beginning to count the years, and to look about her a little less fastidiously. She was considered a good match for a farmer, even so prosperous a one: she thought so too, and was good enough to remind him of it frequently. Her father had been a major in a line regiment, and Mrs Hemstock peppered her conversation with references to 'My late Papa − the Major', like a Masonic sign of gentility. She brought with her from Swaffham, which was an elegantly built little town much used as a winter residence for Norfolk gentry, a definite cachet. She did not bring much money, but Mr Hemstock could get that for himself. What she did bring was the knowledge of how to make money tell. It was she who advised on the furnishing of the handsome new house, built away from the village and adorned with stucco and curved roof-tiles, and on how to maintain the carpeted and pier-glassed rooms in separate state from the 'offices' necessary to the business of farming; and Mr Hemstock was a quick learner. He had an almost religious faith in thrift −

especially for the poor, to whom he sternly recommended it — but wherever money could enhance his status, he spent it. If he was spoken of in the village as proud and grasping, he did not mind it, for he was as dismissive of the people he saw below him as he was eager for the favour of those he saw above him. It was not solely the influence of a genteel wife that made him widen the distance between himself and the labourers who tilled his acres: his pride was his own. Lesser men might invite the Hands into their kitchen, and ply them with meat and drink until the fellows looked on the farmer as a charity instead of an employer — so thought Mr Hemstock; as for him, he had seen what stuff the labourers were made of back in 'thirty — and he did not intend forgetting it.

As for Elias Hemstock's children, they were the very limbs of his hope and desire. From the cradle they were never to work with their hands: they were only to direct and command. The boys must handle a gun, of course, and know how to oversee the smooth running of the farm, and the girls learn such housewifely accomplishments as their husbands would expect. But they were to be the gold coin of the Hemstock credit, acceptable everywhere and carrying his stamp. It was with that in view that he had had his eldest daughter educated so expensively, and in a sphere so removed from that of the farm. Marianne had always seemed to him to promise much; he detected in her something of his own spirit, and sought to develop it. It did not occur to him that that spirit might develop so far as to look with impatient contempt on the household of which it was meant to be an ornament — but then, in his hopes for Marianne, Mr Hemstock was thinking chiefly of himself.

So father and daughter arrived in Heartsease, having been met at Norwich by two farm-servants with the trap and a cart for Marianne's luggage. They rode into the village in the trap, Mr Hemstock at the reins, the cart following behind; and of the villagers who touched their hats or nodded in greeting, every one conveyed the impression that they would rather have had a tooth pulled.

Marianne looked about her with a certain inward confusion. It was home, of course, which in itself gave her a tender feeling — and to Marianne all feelings tended to be a conscious source of enjoyment, a sweet indulgence like bonbons. And yet its very familiarity contained dire foreshadowings, for now there was no other life to go back to, and to throw this slowness and quietness into picturesque contrast; and every warped cottage door and bulging wall and smooth-worn field-path seemed to her to say, 'Look how old we are! Think how many drab, passionless lifetimes we have seen plod by here, how many pink cheeks fade, and bright eyes dim, how many ardent hearts that once meant to do something, and make a stir in the world, sink unsatisfied to the grave!' It was all so completely unchanged — whilst within herself there were such dawnings, and shiftings, and disquiets, that sometimes she hardly knew what it was she felt, or what she wanted. All un-changed . . .

'Papa,' she said, turning her head as they passed Splash Lane, 'has Plague House got a tenant now?' For she had seen new thatch on the decayed roof, and a quantity of lumber turned out into the road.

'There's someone moving in, I believe,' Mr Hemstock said shortly.

'You never told me. Have you met him?'

'No.'

Mr Hemstock smartened the pony's pace. He had in fact met the new tenant of Plague House. He had been passing down the lane with his dogs one day and had seen the young man outside the house, looking up at the thatcher at work on the roof. He had seemed respectable enough, so Mr Hemstock had decided it was worth investing a greeting in him.

'Mr Hemstock, I believe,' the young man had said. Mr

Hemstock's gratification at being known had not lasted long: the young man had stepped out into the road, so as to face him directly, and had looked him up and down in a way the big farmer was far from accustomed to nowadays. 'My name's Jed Wintergreen,' the young man had said. 'You might remember my father. Name of Jacob Wintergreen.'

'I remember him well,' Mr Hemstock had said; and with no further word, had passed on his way. But just for a moment there he had been caught by surprise: had felt himself challenged, his bull-like power despised, his whole thrustful being questioned by the contempt in those light blue eyes. And so, that was the son of one of those insolent malcontents to whom he had stood up back in 'thirty! – well-dressed, and tenant of a fair little property! Of course, he shouldn't have been surprised at this evidence of scum rising to the top: the authorities were so soft on criminals these days the young pup had probably been given a government pension. And Plague House belonged to the Grange, after all – it was typical of Mr Ringrose and his liberal notions. Well, he did not intend telling Marianne of that meeting. It had been unsettling. And his family could have nothing to do with a chip off the Wintergreen block, jumped-up to prosperity or not.

'The house must be badly in need of repair,' Marianne said. 'I wonder who's taken it on.'

'Dismal, inconvenient place,' said her father, who was dismissive of anything old-fashioned. 'Look – we've turned part of the east closes over to barley this year. It's turning out well . . .'

A long neat drive brought them to the house, standing in all the naked smartness of sash windows and hipped roof amongst a few forlornly young trees. The two young children, Wade and Margery, eleven and nine respectively, came running out to greet them.

'Marianne, I'm learning the piano and I can nearly play a Valse in C flat!' cried Margery.

'There's no such key as C flat,' laughed Marianne, kissing her.

'Father, did you bring me the pocket-knife like you promised?' said Wade. He was a strong stout apple-cheeked boy who liked killing things.

'Aye, aye, I brought it,' said Mr Hemstock, indulgently. 'You shall have it presently. But you must learn how to take care of it, mind.'

Marianne allowed herself to be led into the house by a chattering Margery. The familiar atmosphere of home invaded her through all her senses. It had done so on many occasions when she had come home for the holidays, but never before bringing such complex emotions with it. The house was claiming her – for good it seemed – swallowing her up.

She went through to the carpeted parlour, which looked out on to her mother's flower-garden. (It was her mother's flower-garden inasmuch as it was her mother who gave the orders to the gardener who cultivated it.) Mrs Hemstock was seated in her usual place – as if she had never moved all the time Marianne had been away: a high-backed chair near the hearth. Though it was high summer and no fire burnt, there was a round fire-screen set close by her, as if to shield her tender nerves from life in general. 'My dear child,' she murmured, and gave Marianne her net-mittened fingertips; and then, with a sort of conspicuous resignation: 'I have one of my heads, but kiss me!'

'How have you been, Mama?' said Marianne.

'Not *so* bad,' Mrs Hemstock said after an habitual pause, in which she seemed mentally to review a hundred pains, and self-denyingly decide not to mention them out of consideration for her interlocutor's feelings. 'I must ask you not to draw back the curtain, my dear,' she added, as Marianne, dismayed by the dim light, was about to do so. 'I am a very great nuisance, I know; but when I have one of my heads, I really cannot bear this powerful sun. I am sorry to be such a trouble to you.'

'It doesn't matter, Mama,' said Marianne. 'I was just having a peep at your garden. How pretty it looks!'

Mrs Hemstock waved a hand. 'I do what I can. We are rather too exposed here for the tenderest blooms; the east wind comes straight across the fields.' Mrs Hemstock pronounced the word fields — as she did any word connected with farming — with a certain disdainful air of quotation-marks. 'Well, my dear, how do *you* bloom? Let me look at you.'

Her daughter stood smiling before her; and Mrs Hemstock gently shook her head. This was a sign with her that she approved of what she saw, but could not help sadly comparing it with her own situation. There were in fact strong resemblances between Marianne and her mother, for Mrs Hemstock had been good-looking; and her looks were not so much faded as mummified. There was a certain dewy preservation about her pale, fine-boned face and spare figure — perhaps attributable to her breeding, but surely not unrelated to the fact that she never did anything, and was thus unlikely to suffer much wear and tear. Even her clothes — the mittens, the frail lace cap, the black net shawl — had something gossamer and spidery about them, as if she had spun a web of gentility around herself, and would be suspended in it for ever.

'A child no more!' sighed Mrs Hemstock. 'If only your late grandpapa, the Major, could have lived to see you now. I well remember when you were born, he remarked that he looked forward to taking the floor with you at your coming-out, should his gout permit. There is so little society here, that one can scarcely talk about your coming-out — but such as there is, I believe you are equipped for, my dear. Well, you'll wish to change after your journey. Perhaps you're thirsty — will you have some tea first? I won't take any myself, but I can ring the bell for tea, my dear, if you would like.' Mrs Hemstock said this with as much noble self-sacrifice as if she were not only going to make the tea herself, but trudge to a plantation and pick it as well.

'It's all right, Mama, I want to change first— Oh, Herbert, there you are!'

Her brother had appeared in the parlour doorway. He gave her a faint smile and kissed her. 'So here's the young miss, come back to teach us all Lunnon ways. That's what they're wearing down Rotten Row, is it?'

'Come back to teach my brother manners,' said Marianne, giving him a hug. 'How are you, Herbert?'

'Ah, I'm a-dewing, mawther,' said Herbert, mimicking broad Norfolk, 'I'm a-dewing.'

'I must ask you not to affect that mode of speech, Herbert,' said Mrs Hemstock. 'There is nothing so ill-bred as flippancy.'

'As you say, Mother,' said Herbert, grimacing at Marianne. She sometimes suspected him of doing that dialect trick specifically to tease – for it annoyed their father too. And Herbert was far from a favourite with Mr Hemstock. He was the odd one out in a good-looking family: his stooped shoulders and pinched face gave him the look of an old man in a youth's body; and there was nothing in him that harmonized with his father's demanding character – everything grated. He was not sturdy; he was subtle and sardonic; he disliked farming; and worst of all he seemed, somehow, to look upon the stuccoed house and the embroidered bell-pulls and his father's silk waistcoat with a suppressed laugh in his throat. Marianne was very fond of Herbert, and she tried to be his ally in the various battles that blew up. But one crucial factor separated them, and limited the extent to which she could make common cause with him. Her father thought well of her, and not of him: in Herbert he saw disappointment, in Marianne hopes to be fulfilled.

'Clear the way, boy,' said his father now, brushing him aside as he entered the parlour with Wade in his wake. 'Well, my dear, here she is, you see: we're all complete.'

'I'm glad you had a safe journey, Mr Hemstock,' said his wife, offering her cheek to be kissed as a stoical

151

schoolboy might submit his palm to the cane. 'I'm sorry I did not come out to meet you when I heard the trap: I'm afraid my nerves aren't equal to it; the pony is inclined to stamp, I think.'

'Never mind, my dear,' said Mr Hemstock. He was in fact far from disapproving of his wife's immobility and general sickliness; he rather valued it: it seemed to him that there was something authentically refined in it. And certainly an unsympathetic observer might have judged Mrs Hemstock's illnesses to be pretty well refined out of existence.

'Thompson came to me this morning,' Mrs Hemstock said, 'to ask about the cutting of the hay — ' there were the quotation marks again — 'so I told him to begin cutting directly. I hope I did right. I did my best.'

'Quite right, my dear. I'm sorry you were troubled.'

'Marianne, can those *all* be clothes?' said Herbert, looking at her luggage in the hall. 'Who are you going to wear them for? The cows?'

'You wouldn't want your own sister turned out like a cottager, I hope,' said Mr Hemstock, with a glance of displeasure at Herbert.

Marianne went upstairs. Her brother's words, lightly spoken — they always were — went straight to her heart.

Her old room; unchanged too. On these whitewashed walls, framed samplers, wicker chairs, she had looked with the contented eyes of a child: now, fresh and pleasant as the place was, it wore something of the aspect of a prison . . . Yet had the child really been contented? she wondered. It seemed to her, as she curled herself into the chair by the window and looked out over the fields, that this restless, cramped feeling had always been with her, that the eyes of her younger self had scanned the level horizons with the same longing to see something that was never there, and the same uncertainty about what it was she sought.

The evening came: pleasant enough too, but doleful in suggesting to her mind the long succession of exactly

identical evenings it bore in its train. Her father came in
late from going over the farm on horseback, going
upstairs to change out of his riding-clothes. Margery was
allowed to stay up a little later in honour of her sister's
coming home, Wade whittled pieces of wood with his
new penknife, Herbert played backgammon with
Marianne and gnawed his nails. As for Mrs Hemstock,
she marked the change in the time of day by having the
needlework-box taken away from beside her chair and a
little pile of books placed there instead. For she was a
great reader: or she would have been, if literature had
been equal to her; as it was, her usual practice was to pick
up a book with a sigh, open it, read the title-page, read
perhaps half the first paragraph, sigh again, close the
book, lay it down, and say, 'There are no books I like
nowadays,' and meekly fold her hands in her lap, as if,
though life offered her so very little, she wouldn't dream
of complaining.

On this evening, however, Mr Hemstock, instead of
turning over the progressive pages of the *Farmer and
Stockbreeder* or working on his accounts, took a glass of
brandy-and-water and looked on his family, in particular
Marianne, in contemplative mood.

'I was telling Marianne, my dear,' he said at last to his
wife, 'that young Mr Roland Bouverie was good enough
to call on us again; and that we ought to have him here to
sup with us some time, while he's staying with his father.'

'As you say, Mr Hemstock,' said his wife. 'I have no
objection. Young Mr Bouverie is a very agreeable man,
and if he will honour us with his presence, I – ' she
seemed to contemplate Herculean efforts, and bravely
accept them – 'I shall do my best to entertain him.'

'The rector too, you know. I think I can say I'm on
pretty good terms with the rector,' said Mr Hemstock,
jingling the change in his pockets, and thrusting out his
chin with his look of facing down an invisible adversary.
'Martha can wait at table pretty well, and we have some
very good beef – and as to the ordering of the dinner, of

course, my dear, you know all about such things, and the right way to do them.'

(Mrs Hemstock closed her eyes in humility.)

'As for drink, I've some good port, and I can get in some burnt claret—'

'You needn't for Roland Bouverie,' put in Herbert. 'He don't touch drink.'

'Oh?' Mr Hemstock was surprised. 'Oh, well, after all, he's in orders, so—'

'That don't signify,' said Herbert. 'The rector's clergy too, and he drinks like a fish. Roland Bouverie's a prig, is what it is.'

'Herbert,' said Mrs Hemstock, 'I must ask you, in consideration of my nerves, not to make free with such expressions. Your late grandpapa, the Major, would have been shocked to hear you.'

'Well, ain't young Mr Bouverie a prig, Mother? Have him to dinner if you like, but don't expect *me* to suck up to him.'

'You hold your tongue, sir!' stormed his father, who had the ability of going from cool to white heat in a moment. 'You'll show a decent respect to our guests, or you'll not eat with us!'

'Oh − they'll get plenty of respect all right,' muttered Herbert.

'Young Mr Bouverie is, I understand, of an Evangelical persuasion, and I am very far from thinking the worse of him for that,' said Mrs Hemstock, who was herself so pious that of a Sunday she would sometimes sit for an hour at a time with a bible on the floor next to her chair. 'Probably he keeps no cellar, as maintaining a bachelor establishment at present. He is currently undertaking the curacy of Wingham, near Thetford, my dear,' she said to Marianne, 'but expects to be presented to a highly desirable living quite soon, the Bouveries being a distinguished family with connections among the great, you know.'

Marianne was aware of her father watching her: whilst

he listened to his wife with complacency, and tapped his hand upon his thick thigh as if her words were lively music, and he was beating out the tune: 'Conn-ect-ions am-ong the great, you-know!'

Full, bright summer. Marianne took her morning walk, bonneted and parasoled against the sun, and reacquainted herself — with no very cordial feelings — with Heartsease.

It was not that she disliked the village itself; and for the people of the little community, too, her breast entertained a fondness, though she found it increasingly difficult of expression. As a very small girl she could remember going out to prattle to the men who worked her father's fields, and even being lifted up by them and given a ride on the waggons; but her father had discouraged that and, as time went by and the new house was built, the distance grew between the family and the labourers, who only came to the house for their wages, and were paid through a rear office window by the bailiff. She lent a hand in the cool brick dairy occasionally, and rather enjoyed it, as she enjoyed all novelties; but the deference sternly insisted on by her father, and her own so different upbringing and education, meant that no common ground existed between her and the work-people; and there seemed no middle course between lowering herself, as her father saw it, and adopting the squirish tone, which came naturally to the likes of Mr Ingamells and the Bouveries, but which in her case she was afraid would seem affectation.

Thus Marianne picked a path through the wheel-ruts, and looked with a confused mingling of distaste and affection on the little narrow cottage-windows with the dormers above, some so low that but for the bristly brow of thatch one might reach up and tap at them; on the fragments of mossy wall that here and there enclosed the catty-cornered garden-plots of the larger dwellings; on open doorways that revealed scrubbed flagstoned house-places so bare of all colour that looking in was like beholding a steel engraving; on the old barns and storehouses dating from the days when all the farms were in the village street, and presenting to the view odd blind gables dotted with rusty studs, and nonsensical doors without handles six feet above the ground. And all the time her footsteps were taking her, almost independently of her will, towards Plague House, where there was at least something new going on.

Something new! The place was indeed changed, she saw as she approached, half-dazzled by the dapples filtering through the high hedges. The roof was all new-thatched, the plaster was new, the windows were new-glazed and all stood open to air new-painted sills. An old cart with its shafts pointing to the sky stood outside in the lane, filled with the dusty disembowellings of the house, and a man was coming round from the yard at the side with his arms full of more lumber.

Marianne did not recognize him as a local workman, and that somehow gave her more confidence to stop, and giving him good day, ask him: 'Has the new family moved in to the house yet?'

'Aye — though there's just the one man, at present — no family,' the young man returned.

Marianne thought — or at least her education did — that there was something too familiar about his manner; but she lacked the security — or she was too unspoilt at heart — to stare him down in the approved fashion. She hesitated, and then as the young man tipped the lumber into the cart and brushed himself down, she became aware that his clothes, though dusty from his work, were those of a gentleman.

He seemed to take pity on her perplexity. 'I beg your pardon,' he said, 'I should have made it clear — I'm the new tenant. Jed Wintergreen. How d'you do.'

His voice had the soft burrs of rural Norfolk in it. Marianne inclined her head in the flower-like way she had been taught, not knowing quite what to make of him.

'What a job you must have had, repairing it!' she said — speaking with her own native impulsiveness, even as she twirled the parasol in the prescribed manner.

'It was in a sad state,' he said, looking up at the house. 'But thass all put to rights now, barring a morsel of cleaning-up. I haven't done it all myself, of course,' he said with a slight smile at her. 'Then there's the land. I was too late to sow this season, but I've made a start at ploughing and clearing it ready for the next.'

'I always thought it a pity it was so neglected,' Marianne said.

'It won't be no more,' the young man said. His eyes, a remarkable light blue with faint shadows of sweat beneath them, regarded her with politeness but candour. 'Would you like to see over the place? I'm proud to show her off, to tell the truth.'

'Oh, I couldn't possibly,' said Marianne, in a rush of remembered proprieties.

He raised an eyebrow at that; but said with the same frankness, 'It's no trouble.'

'Thank you,' she said, 'but I mustn't stop.' How ridiculous it was, when she had all day ahead, and nothing to do in it! She felt herself caught between her natural curiosity and the genteel formalities she had learned, said 'Good day,' hurriedly and awkwardly enough, and went on her way with a burning sense of a pair of blue eyes watching the back of her neck, and a disconcerted wonder at what the owner of them could be thinking of her, and most of all a feeling, more intense than ever, of not knowing who she was, or where she belonged.

The only consolation was that she had seemed to discern something similarly betwixt-and-between in the young man himself — the well-dressed tenant of Plague House working with his own hands, and addressing her in his soft frank country voice; and as she walked away from Plague House she found that the curiosity which had taken her there was very far from satisfied.

* * *

'What are your feelings on the conversion of the Maoris?' asked Mr Roland Bouverie.

He had been placed next to Marianne at the dinner-table, and he addressed this question to her during a lull in the general conversation, so that her reply must take on an unnatural prominence. Her mind groped helplessly back over her geography lessons, in an effort to fix precisely where the Maoris came from, as if that might help.

'They are a very heathen sort of people, I suppose?' she said.

'Very fierce and warlike,' young Mr Bouverie said. 'And, Hum! inclined to cannibalism.'

'Oh dear,' said Marianne.

'They have shown an encouraging receptiveness to Christian teaching,' pursued young Mr Bouverie, 'but this in itself presents formidable dangers; for it is surely our duty above all to ensure that they are not exposed to the corruptions of Romanism. That is our paramount duty to them, would you not agree?'

'Oh! well – as long as somebody stops them eating each other, I dare say that's the main thing,' said Marianne.

'Ha ha! You're like me, Miss Hemstock,' said the rector, the elder Mr Bouverie, from the other end of the table, laughing with all his horsey teeth on show. 'These savages are all very well in their way, and of course they must be converted, but it doesn't do to expect too much of them, you know. Teach them how to behave, by all means, but don't coddle them, for upon my word, sir – ' he turned his teeth on Mr Hemstock – 'they won't thank you for it!'

The Bouveries, as Mrs Hemstock had said, were well-connected, and it was understood that a coronet was to be found on one of the more distant branches of the family tree. Rather a withered branch, as it happened, its sole sprig being a sort of idiot boy of fifty who was put to bed every night in a Scottish hunting lodge full of antlers; but for many years the healthier boughs had brought forth a distinguished crop of clergymen, who were to be found all over the eastern counties, collecting rich livings and making good marriages and serving as magistrates, and prescribing a strict observance of the letter of the scriptures – except perhaps that injunction to sell off your possessions and give the money to the poor. The rector of Heartsease, a widower of close on sixty, was a fair representative of the Bouverie clan. He was a vigorous florid man, very conspicuous in having all his own white hair and teeth, very much at home with the squire but at home too, as he thought, with the humble, whom he addressed in a sort of generalized argot which he thought was dialect; and regarding the latter it was a point of principle with him, as he often said, never to expect too much of them. He laid it down as a rule that it was no good being soft on them, for they wouldn't thank you for it – not they! And he was certainly true to his creed in that there was nobody in Heartsease who had anything to thank him for.

His son Roland, having followed his father into orders, had been some years at Oxford before taking up his present curacy. It had been rather a shock at first to Marianne to find that someone connected with the Church should be so good-looking. Roland Bouverie was very tall, and wore his hair swept back in long glossy locks like the poet Tennyson, and had a fine aquiline face with soft fledgling whiskers. Marianne had indeed idly wondered what it would be like to be kissed with those whiskers in attendance, and whether they would tickle, but it required an effort to imagine Roland Bouverie doing any such thing as kissing. There was such gravitas in his manner, such a terrible earnestness in his slow precise voice, and in the way he fixed his eyes on her, and in the way those eyes blinked, as if even a blink were to be weighed and considered, such a stiff, solemn attentiveness, such a literal-minded way of fastening on her every lightest word, that altogether he made her want to scream.

'D'you have it in mind to be a missionary, then, Mr Bouverie?' said Herbert.

'It is a noble avocation,' intoned Roland, as if he were reading off a tombstone, 'and I have looked long and hard into myself, before concluding that I am not fitted for it.'

'Roland can do better work here,' said his father. 'It takes a certain type to go out to these forsaken places. It would never have done for me. And Roland inclines to the scholarly side, you know. I wouldn't be surprised if we saw him in print in a few years.'

'Oh, what do you write, Mr Bouverie?' said Marianne.

'Prose of a devotional character has been the chief exercise of my poor pen,' said Roland. 'But I have also ventured to set my foot on the lower slopes of Parnassus, and, Hum! to try my hand at poetry.'

'Oh! I dote on poetry,' said Mrs Hemstock. 'My few little volumes of verse are exceedingly precious to me.' They must have been precious indeed, for she had never even cut the pages. 'I believe I inherited the taste from my poor papa, the Major, who carried Shakespeare in his tunic all through the Peninsula, and was known as the Scholar of the 43rd.'

'Well, now, as to writing poetry,' said Mr Hemstock heavily, 'you should see the album that Marianne brought home from the ladies' academy: all manner of verses, written out on hot-pressed paper, and very nicely bound – quite a thing to see.'

'Those were extracts, Papa,' Marianne said hastily – hating herself for feeling so embarrassed by him. 'Extracts from the poets, you know,' she said to young Mr Bouverie, who had looked interested, 'copied out in a fair hand – not my own work.'

'Extracts, to be sure,' said her father, still plunging on. 'Very prettily done. You should see the book, Mr

Bouverie. Marianne's well up in all that sort of thing — poetry, and so forth.'

'She can lack no accomplishments, I feel sure,' said Roland, with a dreadful blink, while Marianne cringed.

'Your children do you credit, Hemstock,' said the rector, who whatever else he was, was no fool, and considered suffering the farmer's occasional gaucheries a fair price to pay for getting the run of his teeth at such a well-stocked table. 'And you, Mrs Hemstock.'

'I have always considered motherhood — if I may properly say so in such distinguished clerical company — as a sacred office,' said Mrs Hemstock. 'A woman can hope for none higher — so my poor papa, the Major, used to say. He was no friend to those distortions of the character of the tender sex, which result from educating it out of its proper sphere. It has always been my especial care to ensure that Marianne is complete in those domestic arts which form a woman's chief duty and glory.'

'Oh! surely, surely,' Mr Hemstock said. 'We didn't want her turning out a bluestocking. She's the lightest hand with pastry and such — wait till we have the currant tarts in; those are Marianne's, you know.'

Marianne generally was not averse to being the centre of attention, but she had an increasing feeling of the calf being led around the ring. She had a respite from Roland Bouverie's blinks after dinner, when the men were left to drink at the littered table; but they were not long about it, young Mr Bouverie taking no liquor, Herbert being allowed only one glass, her father being fairly temperate — such was his constant tight control over himself — and the rector having already made so free with the burnt claret that his strawberry complexion had deepened to ripe plum; his resemblance to that fruit being further developed in that he seemed ready to drop off at any moment. Then she was called upon by her father to do the honours with the tea, and then to bring forth her sketchbooks and needlework and the dreaded album of extracts to show to young Mr Bouverie, whose ponderous attention made Marianne very uncomfortable — aware that such talents as she had, she had only exerted herself very fitfully in improving.

'I know very little of drawing,' Roland Bouverie said gravely. 'But it is a very elegant accomplishment, and perfectly capable, I believe, of improving the mind, no less than other branches of study. I observe that the faces of the sitters are but lightly delineated. This is, I take it, because in productions of this kind, likenesses are less sought than a free and spirited rendering of the disposition of the figure?'

'Well — partly that,' said Marianne, with a nervous laugh. 'In the main I — I am afraid that I don't draw faces very well.'

'Ah. Ah. Well, I am sure, Miss Hemstock, Hum! that if the faces of the sitters were as fair as that of the author of these admirable sketches, it can hardly have been in the power even of her skilful pencil to do justice to them,' said Roland; and this compliment seemed to take so much out of him, that he could do nothing but blink and breathe through his nose for some time afterward.

Soon her father called on Marianne to go to the piano — an acquisition of which he was very proud, and which, highly polished, took a prominent place in the parlour; and she was glad enough to escape for a while from Roland Bouverie's exclusive attention. She played through the little sonatinas and bagatelles that she had learned at the ladies' academy — tinglingly conscious again that she had never really worked hard enough at these things, and that what was remarkable to her father must appear terribly commonplace to people like the Bouveries. If only she had had the patience to learn those wonderfully dark, difficult, passionate pieces the music mistress used to play sometimes! And if only there was someone dark, difficult and passionate to listen to her! And if only her father would stop boasting about her and making such a thrustful fool of himself!

'Yes, I laid out a pretty penny on her education – a pretty penny,' Mr Hemstock was saying. 'But I wanted the best. I didn't think thirty guineas a term excessive for my daughter. French, music, all the rest.'

'Miss Hemstock plays charmingly,' said young Mr Bouverie, sitting at attention; whilst in a corner the rector, having taken on board all the food and drink he could hold, cut his moorings, and gently floated off.

'We are of course a little remote from society here,' said Mrs Hemstock. 'But then there are advantages too, in a country situation – not least for the health; though I am afraid my own is constitutionally too weak to admit of much improvement. There is no doing anything with my heads. My heads are indescribable. My poor papa, the Major, was convinced that one of my heads would carry me off in the end. But Marianne, I am happy to say, is quite strong – a splendid constitution – the same, I believe, that carried my papa the Major all through the Peninsula, and earned him the nickname of the Iron Man of the 43rd.'

'I am a firm believer in the salubrity of country life,' said Roland. 'My own current establishment at Wingham is in a retired, though eligible spot. The house is a little closer to the road than one could desire, but there is an extensive garden at the rear.'

'Oh! I dote on a garden,' said Mrs Hemstock. 'Marianne is like me in that. She is never happier than when in a garden.'

'Except when at an instrument, I perceive,' said Roland, addressing Marianne with starched gallantry, 'and then, Hum! the happiness is equally the privileged listener's.'

Young Mr Bouverie, who said he did not keep late hours, was soon ready to go; and the rector was roused, puffing and staring, and inclined to champ his great teeth together as if he tasted something nasty. Roland was very particular in taking leave of Marianne; and after much throat-clearing, asked if he might call on them next day.

When the visitors were gone Mr Hemstock took a brandy-and-water and strode about, his big harsh face not so much lit up as hardened even more by satisfaction.

'Well, that went off pretty well. I don't think the gentlemen can complain of the entertainment they had at Hemstock's place, I really don't; not to anyone.' He kicked at the logs in the grate.

'Mr Hemstock, it is very troublesome of me I know, but I must ask you not to do that − it has been an exhausting evening, and I fear my nerves are not equal to it,' said Mrs Hemstock. His wife had a way thus of making him feel coarse when he was feeling most pleased with himself; but nothing could deflate him tonight.

'Young Mr Bouverie certainly distinguished you with his attention, Marianne,' her father went on. 'Not that I don't think you worthy of it: not at all; and that was a good thought of mine about the album. Gentlemen like to see such things, you know, my dear.'

'They ought to,' said Herbert, with a sly glance at her, 'they see enough of them − all identical.'

'If you've nothing better to do than bring your own family down, you'd better go to bed, sir,' Mr Hemstock snapped.

Marianne soon escaped to bed too, in no very easy state of feeling. It was nice, of course, in a way, that her father was so proud of her; yet as she lay staring into the phosphorescence of the warm summer night, she knew the bitter poisonous sting of feeling ashamed of her own parent. And her heart sank again at the thought of having to meet Roland Bouverie tomorrow. Oh, there had to be something different − something better!

Young Mr Bouverie walked over quite early the next morning. Mr Hemstock was out about the farm, and Marianne and her mother received the visitor in the parlour. Roland was full of compliments about the delightful evening he had spent, and when he had exhausted those, he turned his blinks on to the flower-garden, and was complimentary about that.

'You would like to see my poor essay at cultivation, Mr Bouverie?' said Mrs Hemstock. 'Marianne will show you. I regret that my nerves are not equal to the full sunlight at this hour of the day: it would simply be inviting one of my heads. It is a great nuisance that I am forced to be inactive in this way, and never able to do anything but rest.'

'You bear it with fortitude, ma'am,' said Roland. Which she certainly did.

So Marianne showed Roland Bouverie the flower-garden, which though it adjoined the kitchen-garden, was cleverly separated and concealed from it by a long pergola trained with climbing plants. Mr Bouverie, bending at the waist like a pocket-ruler, solemnly stooped to examine each flower as if he were asking it its catechism.

'The Latin names of the various common flora make an interesting subject – as a refreshment for the mind in the intervals of more serious study,' said Roland. 'Though, Hum! the Latin is frequently not such as a classical scholar could look upon without a blush.'

Marianne, alerted to the fact that this was a joke by a sort of puffing noise issuing from Roland's arched nostrils, gave the broadest smile she could manage.

'I was reminded on coming here to visit my father,' he went on, proceeding with his hands behind his back, 'of that most musical botanical name, *Viola tricolour* – the wild pansy, or heartsease.'

'Is that the name? Oh, I like that!' said Marianne, really interested. '*Viola tricolour*. You can almost see that as a woman's name – a comic name in a play – Viola Tricolour, a republican lady.'

'I'm afraid I don't know the play to which you are referring, Miss Hemstock,' said Roland in his blandest manner; and before she could try to explain, he continued, 'The drama has not been my particular study. Not that I have any religious objection to play-going, I hasten to add, as long as the piece is calculated to effect a, Hum! a moral improvement in the spectator's breast. And such is my criterion for poetry likewise.'

'What sort of subjects do you write poetry on, Mr Bouverie?' asked Marianne, who dared not even guess.

'My verses are on the theme of the Paths to the Grave,' said Roland readily, 'and whether we choose the flowery one of pleasure, or the stony one of awful Duty.' He looked at her as if gratified by her interest. 'Those are the lighter specimens, at any rate.'

She was afraid he was going to ask her what poetry she liked — none of it seemed likely to effect a moral improvement in anybody's breast — but instead he said, 'I shall be returning to Wingham tomorrow, Miss Hemstock.'

'Oh, will you?' she said, trying to keep the relief out of her voice.

'A diocesan visitation impends,' said Roland, making it sound like the plague, 'and I would rather be accused of anything than neglect of my pastoral duties. We are such feeble and sinful creatures that to make a brag of anything is sheer impudence before the Creator — still, I will claim to myself, if nothing else, diligence. I am serious about my responsibilities.'

Marianne said she was sure of it. And she meant it; there was nothing worldly or hypocritical about him . . . Oh, but that didn't mean she had to *like* him — not in the way his talk seemed to be tending, and in the way her father obviously had planned for them. It wasn't fair, it wasn't fair she had to go through this . . .

'I shall of course be returning to Heartsease to visit my father frequently,' Roland went on. 'I shall take the liberty of asking your worthy father, who has given me such an amiable welcome, whether that welcome may be renewed, and whether I, Hum! may call upon the family, and not least their charming daughter, again.'

Roland breathed and blinked very hard; and Marianne, taking advantage of the fashionable drooping

side-ringlets to escape looking at him, said she was sure
her father would be glad to see him. That was a bit of an
evasion — or would he take that as an encouragement, a
signal to approach her father with his suit, and . . .?
That was a terrible thought! For it was painfully clear
that her father was very keen indeed to match his
daughter with a Bouverie. Really she ought simply to tell
Roland right now that she was flattered, but that what he
hoped was out of the question, she was sorry but that was
that . . . Consistency, however, was not Marianne's
strong point: the trouble was, she *was* flattered; and in
spite of all her training at the ladies' academy at
Clapham, she was far from possessing the adroit self-
confidence that the heroines of the silver-fork novels
would show in such a situation. So, awkwardly, she said
that perhaps they ought to go in now and see how her
mother was; and tried to steal a glance at Roland's face as
they returned, to see what he was thinking. He looked
contented enough, and said, 'It occurs to me that I have
neglected to ask you how you have liked the books I lent
you, Miss Hemstock.' Before she could answer he went
on: 'That is a most unfair question, of course, for there
was such an abundance of deep matter in the volumes
that you can hardly be called upon to give an opinion so
swiftly — forgive me. Perhaps you will do me the honour
of retaining them in your possession until such time as I
have the, Hum! even greater honour of waiting upon you
again, when I greatly look forward to hearing your views
upon the same.'

He was gone at last: gone, leaving Mrs Hemstock
paying tribute to his qualities, and affirming that, as her
poor papa the Major always maintained, blood will tell;
leaving Marianne staring more impatiently into the
enigma of what it was that she wanted in life, and sure
only of one thing, that it was definitely not the marriage
to Roland Bouverie which her father had in mind.

With so much to think of — and a contrary feeling that

she had nothing worthwhile to think of, and that only dead-ends and blank walls of dullness would present themselves to her mind for ever — Marianne took her regular walk in a listless abstraction, which she presently found had guided her steps once again towards Splash Lane, and Plague House.

The rubbish-cart had gone, and the windows were closed, and there was no one about. Marianne paused to look up at the renovated house. The name, and the great age of the main part of the building, gave it a rather romantic aspect to her fancy — so very different from the neat stuccoed convenience of her father's house. With a quick glance down the lane, she turned and rounded the gable-end, entering the cobbled yard formed by the L-shape of the house. All was repaired here too: there was a new panelled door in the other wing of the L, which extended back to a block of outhouses forming another L with an ancient barn.

Inquisitive as a cat, she went forward to peep into one of the little windows, and became aware of a male blackbird screeching at her from a gatepost, and then of a female on the thatch above, making the same piercing noise, like a chipping on slate.

'They think you're after poor old faint-heart,' said a voice.

She looked round, startled, and saw the dark young man with the blue eyes, leaning out of an upper window. In confusion and embarrassment she could only gaze up at him, and did not know what to say.

The young man smiled. 'There's a nest there, in the eaves — see? They've raised four young, and they've all flown this morning — I watched 'em — all except one. He's still sitting in the nest and can't make up his mind to follow. The door's open — come up and see.'

Marianne was about to say, as she had before, that she couldn't possibly; but after a moment's consideration, she didn't see why not. With the beady eyes of the blackbirds fixed on her, she opened the door and went in.

It was dim in the hall. The young man was standing at the top of a fine old wooden staircase.

'I – I'm sorry, I didn't know – you must think—' she faltered.

'Oh, never mind that,' said Jed. 'Come and see. It's comic to watch the poor fellow.'

Hardly knowing what she did, Marianne went up the stairs and followed him into a room new-whitewashed but empty of furniture, where he beckoned her to the window.

'See – there he is. All on his ownsome.'

The nest was built in a crook of rambler rose just below the window. Downy feathers still clung about its smooth interior, but only one fat, pudding-brown, bewildered fledgling remained, hesitating on the edge, fluffing out his immature feathers, and every now and then giving a forlorn chirp.

'Oh, poor thing! They've gone and left him!' said Marianne.

'The other three ventured out wi' no trouble,' said Jed. 'But this one don't take to the idea. The parents have been trying to lead him out all morning.'

The fledgling cocked an eye up at the window and gave another chirp.

'Oh, dear – you've got to go, you know,' said Marianne to the bird. 'You can't stay there. It's late in the season now.'

'This is their second brood this year,' said Jed. 'Hullo! There's Ma. I reckon she've had enough of this.'

The mother bird had appeared on a twig of the rambler, lower down, and was calling metallically, giving a sort of stiff clockwork twitch of her wings at each cry.

'I suppose you can't blame him,' Marianne said. 'Look how cosy that nest looks – and how terribly big the world is outside it.'

'Aye, there's a cold hard world waiting for him,' said Jed. 'Full of snares, and lime, and cats, and guns, and bitter winters—'

'Oh, hush, he never will go now!' Marianne said. 'Don't listen to him, faint-heart – you'll like it really, there are all sorts of things – oh, worms, and grubs, and puddles to bathe in— Oh!'

The fledgling had made a sudden clumsy plunge from the nest, scattering rose-petals, and was presently to be seen clinging desperately to a rambler twig a few feet down.

'Hooray! He flew! Well, he jumped, anyway,' said Marianne.

'That was your doing,' laughed Jed. 'Telling him about the worms – you tempted him. Go on, tell him some more.'

With a serious face, Marianne said: 'Well, there's being able to fly wherever you like – up in the blue, with all the land set out underneath you, and no one to stop you, just you and the sun and the wind, free as – well, free as a bird, you know. Just think of that – waking in the morning and knowing you're free, and the world's yours, and you've only to flap your wings and leave the earth behind . . .'

Jed was watching her with a faint smile. 'You're making me want to be a bird now,' he said.

She looked at him, looked away again. 'And then there's – well, those dull feathers will go, and you'll be all sleek and black and – and then you'll build a nest, and raise fledglings of your own—'

'There he goes!' said Jed.

After an agony of bobbing, twitching hesitation, the fledgling suddenly launched itself. Bumpily, heavily, losing height, but flying nonetheless, it took off in a straight line towards the outhouse roof where the parent birds were waiting.

'Oh, thank goodness! Oh, I'm glad I saw that!' said Marianne. They grinned at each other: for there was a kernel of miracle in the little commonplace that they had witnessed – a creature becoming itself before their eyes. 'I wonder if he'll come back

170

here to nest, when he's grown.'

'He might be a she. No telling at that age.'

The bird was not in sight now; and Marianne could not do anything but face the young man. 'I don't know what you must think of me,' she said, 'prying round—'

'Flattered by your interest,' said Jed, not politely, but as if he meant it. 'Well, now you're here, you've no excuse not to look over the place.'

'Well – if you would like—'

'I would like.'

It wasn't, of course, 'proper'; but after her encounter with Roland Bouverie, Marianne was for the moment in full flight from the proper. And to the curiosity that had brought her here in the first place was added the whiff of novelty, of the unconventional and faintly mysterious, in finding herself alone with the young stranger; so that altogether she felt more alive than she had since coming home.

Proudly Jed Wintergreen led his visitor through all the rooms, with their creaking floorboards, low sloping rafters, and great knotty beams obtruding in unexpected places as if the timbered house were in a state of growth, and putting forth wood like a grove that had somehow got itself indoors. Jed was like a father with his first child – or, indeed, a man with the first true home of his own, as, in a rush of candour, he confided to Marianne that he was.

'This is like a dream for me,' he said, as they stood in the hall. 'And I suppose I just need to show it to someone to prove to myself it's real. Sorry – that *someone* don't sound very nice, I didn't mean that, Miss—'

'Hemstock,' she said. 'Marianne Hemstock.'

The blue eyes were fastened on her, and the lean restless figure was still for a moment. 'Hemstock.'

'Yes, I—' She was puzzled by his look. 'My father has the farm just outside the village, off the west road – perhaps you know him . . .?'

He turned and looked up at the high lancet windows of

the hall. 'Yes, I — well, I know of him. These windows don't let in much light, and they're the devil to keep clean. Now through here is the parlour . . .'

Prominent in the parlour was a case of new books, which Jed touched affectionately. Marianne, scanning the titles, saw tales and poetry, accounts of voyages and far-off lands — the sort of books she liked, that appealed to the fancy and set off waking dreams.

'I've hardly even begun to do the reading I planned, when I — well, when I came into my good fortune,' said Jed. 'But it's all the business of moving in that's been occupying me: and there'll be time enough soon,' he said with satisfaction.

'What was your good fortune, Mr Wintergreen?' She did not mean to sound so baldly inquisitive; it was just that there was something enticingly mysterious in the idea.

'Oh! I came into an inheritance,' he said, a little shortly it seemed.

'You must think I'm prying again.'

'There's no secret about it,' he said, though still with a certain constraint. 'It come very unexpected: made a great change in my life.'

She watched him covertly under her long lashes as he paced about the room. He was an unusual sort of man. There was something high-strung about him, something suggestive of a dog on a slightly too short leash. His eyes, though they were so attractive and penetrating, gave the impression of being focused on something far off, different, elsewhere.

'A change for the better?' she said.

'Oh! yes. A million times. Not that my old life could have been much worse. But never mind that: it's all come right now.'

'But whatever made you decide to settle in Heartsease?' she said, with a sudden querulousness in her voice, for his words about everything coming right reawakened her own dissatisfaction.

'Why? There's no other place for me,' he said simply.
'I was born here.'

'Were you? Well – so was I, but . . .'

'You don't care for it?'

'Oh, it's not that so much . . . I don't know,' she burst
out, giving way to all the smothered and contradictory
feeling caused by her return, 'when I was away being
educated, I saw other places, and felt and thought
different things, and now it just feels as if I'm going
backwards somehow, and life has gone all mild and small
and ordinary, and life *shouldn't* be like that – should it?
– it's surely meant to be bigger and grander, and to
make you feel each day that you're *living*, and that you
weren't given a heart just to grind it and wear it away
against little dull trivialities . . .'

She stopped as abruptly as she had begun. Her
outburst had brought her back to a remembrance of who
she was and where – of the proprieties, in fact.

'I don't know why I'm telling you this,' she murmured,
confusedly; for he had listened very attentively.

'Because I'm here,' he said. 'And why not, after all?'

'I shouldn't even be here,' she said, with a little frown
at him as if he had detained her, 'it really isn't right.'

'Well, you are here,' said he, 'and I'm glad of it; and
thass nobody else's business, after all. So why don't you
sit down.'

She did so, in her perplexity of mind forgetting the
elaborate descent she had been taught at the academy,
and sitting with her own native grace. The furnishings of
the parlour were old-fashioned and simple: Windsor
chairs, a long dark oak table, a bright rug, pewter.

Still pacing, Jed said: 'What you said, you know –
those feelings – I do understand. Why, that was like
hearing my own voice – I thought nobody but me felt
that way.'

'And yet you choose to come and live in Heartsease!'
she said.

'Well, thass different for me. There's special reasons

173

why.' As she gazed at him he said: 'I can't really tell you them. I suppose you wouldn't know—'

'What wouldn't I know?' she said, with her impatient curiosity.

'My name don't mean anything to you?' he said with a frown. 'The name Wintergreen?'

She shook her head.

'You'd be too young, I dare say. Well, as I told you, I was born here: my father worked on the land here. For your father, once.'

'Oh!' She was surprised, though not greatly so: if a man worked in Heartsease, he would very likely work for Farmer Hemstock.

He stopped in his pacing and regarded her very soberly. 'You don't remember the riots of 'thirty?'

'I was very small. I've heard about them, of course. Some men . . .'

'Aye,' he said grimly. 'One of 'em was my father. He was transported.'

'Oh,' she said weakly. She did not know what to say: this was far removed from the little tattling refinements of Clapham. Yet the young man's revelation rather enhanced the aura of mystery about him.

'I'm afraid your father was — well, more than a little involved,' Jed continued. 'Putting the men down. I was a boy at the time, but I knew what happened. I knew. I never forgot.'

Broodingly he leant his arm on the mantelshelf, beating softly on it with his clenched fist. There was such a swift darkening of his manner, and such a smothered violence, that Marianne said in distress, starting up: 'Oh, but I didn't know ! It's so long ago . . . I'm so sorry, truly — but you surely can't hold *me* responsible!'

'No, no, no.' He made a pacifying gesture, and there was such renewed sweetness in his expression that she sat again. 'It isn't that. Don't think that. I'm just trying to explain to you why it mean so much to me to come back here — the place I left in sorrow. What you were saying about wanting to feel that you're really alive — thass what brought me here.' He suddenly smiled: it transformed his face, making it much younger. 'D'you dream, Miss Hemstock?'

'Waking or sleeping?' she said, with a wistful laugh. 'For I do both.'

'So do I,' he said. 'Oh, so do I: only thass the sleeping ones that are deepest and truest, I reckon. And in those, there's a place that you go to, a wonderful place, where your heart melts, and knows it's home. D'you understand?'

She nodded, eyes sparkling. Her own dream-place was something like Paris, except that she belonged there, and everyone recognized the fact.

'Well, Heartsease is that place to me,' said Jed, very quiet but distinct; and for a moment Marianne was quiet too. His words had stirred her profoundly: for while the two of them saw Heartsease so differently, she had seemed to glimpse a spirit that chafed like her own, and to hear an echo of her own restless longing.

'I'm sorry about your father,' she said timidly. 'Is he . . .?'

'He died,' Jed said. 'Mother too. It was a bad time . . . But, as you say, it was long ago. And, as I said, everything's come right now.'

'How terrible!' she murmured. That the young man had cause for bitterness against her father she saw clearly, but it did not impress her deeply: she well knew that Elias Hemstock was a man who did not mind making enemies. 'I'm sorry there should be — bad feeling,' she said.

'Nay,' he said gently. 'I'm concerned wi' good feeling now — the feeling of having my own place, and working a bit of land on my own account, and breathing this free air again.'

'Have you met my father since you came back?' she said, remembering the short way her father had replied when she had asked him about the new tenant of Plague House.

'Briefly. We — we can keep out of each other's way, I dare say.' His brow contracted again as he spoke. 'I don't suppose he cares to meet me, any more than I care to meet him.'

It occurred to Marianne then that her father would not approve of her being here; but then the whole idea of coming here like this was highly unconventional, and had something clandestine about it which appealed to her sense of the romantic. Jed seemed to be thinking of the same things, and said, 'As for you, Miss Hemstock — shall you be telling your father you met up with Jed Wintergreen?'

'I really don't see as it matters,' she said loftily, for he spoke as if she were the daughter of some brutish two-horse farmer who would strap her if she went against his will.

'True: you've better things to think of, I dare say,' said Jed, without irony, and with a glance at her fine clothes; and it occurred to her that to Jed Wintergreen, whose own place in the scheme of things was so ambiguous, she was an unknown quantity. He could not know how uncertain she was of her own identity; perhaps he imagined glamorous nights for her, instead of young Mr Bouverie and the conversion of the Maoris. That was a funny thought! — that was a depressing thought.

'Have I?' she said in bitterness. 'I wish I had. Just now I might as well be — that bird still in the nest, and never peeping over the top.' She began to walk about in her agitation, her skirts making a crisp frou-frou. 'And never flying — never even trying its wings.'

'But wanting to?'

'Oh, yes!'

There was admiration in his eyes. 'What would you do?'

'Something. I don't know. How *can* one know?' she answered fretfully. 'It's enough that there's this feeling like a slow fire inside that will burn you up if you don't let it out. D'you see?'

He nodded. 'I see very well. But you're letting it out a little now, here, and I'm glad of that. Nay, I'm honoured and proud.'

'You're joking with me,' she said, with an attempt at disdain.

'No, I'm not. Not I. Folk who only laugh — don't take things serious — skim along the surface of life — they're missing so much. Don't I know the feeling of that slow fire inside? But thass not a curse, you know — thass a blessing. It mean you're really alive. Why, all them years when I was poor, and life was just a-grinding from day to day, would it have been better if I'd just bowed my head and forgot Heartsease, and the life I'd lost, and put my dreams away for ever and resigned myself to going on like a man of clockwork? Never! Mebbe that would have been peace of mind, but that would have been death, too — living death. Better the burning inside, even if thass never satisfied — better, a thousand times.'

'I want to believe you,' she said, her eyes fastened on his face. 'No, I do believe you. But it's hard when you're alone — I mean when no one else thinks that way — when you look about you at other people, and they all seem so much more contented—'

'Don't believe it,' he said with energy. 'You're lost if you do. And besides, you're not alone now. Are you?'

Marianne faintly smiled, but looked away from him. She was not used to such candour. She felt herself in a new region of frankness: it was as if the two of them had gone on a long walk, and she only now raised her eyes to see that the country was unfamiliar, and she did not know the road back.

'Perhaps everyone feels this way, inside,' she said, falling back on a conversational tone. 'They just don't make a fuss about it.'

He looked at her as if disappointed. 'Now you're putting the flame out,' he said.

'Well, really, what else is there to do?' she said passionately. 'What's the good of crying for the moon, after all?'

'Why,' he said, slightly smiling, but very earnest, 'some day, somebody may fetch it for you.'

They were both very still.

'And the stars too?' she said, a little short-breathed.

'And the stars too.'

All at once they could not meet each other's eyes, and Jed went to the window and said hurriedly, 'I cried for the moon often when I was poor, in a way: I lived in a room high up in the city, and I used to see the moon there up above the chimney tops, looking so pure and white, and so near, it seemed. I never expected to get it, but then I never expected to come into my legacy, either.'

'Were you very poor?' said Marianne – with pity, but with only a very vague idea of what it meant; for though she could have learned about poverty by stepping into any cottage in Heartsease, that was one area of education from which her father had carefully excluded her.

Jed shrugged. 'Poor enough. Thass gone now. Sometimes – sometimes I do wake in the night, and in the darkness I wonder if my good fortune was mebbe all a dream, and when the light comes I shall see that dismal old room all about me . . .' He gestured at his clothes. 'After all, you can surely tell I weren't born to this.'

That was plain, especially to her eye, made sensitive to such things as it was by her own insecurities; but it did not diminish his interest for her. Far from it: it was part of that atmosphere of the unusual that enveloped him. 'We weren't born to anything, surely,' she said. 'I should hate that thought. That there's no escape . . .'

'There ain't, for a lot of folk,' said he. 'Not for my mother and father – not for many others.'

'Oh, but I couldn't help that,' she cried, for she felt he reproached her. 'It's not fair, just because my name's Hemstock—'

'Hush, hush. I didn't mean that. Only that there's

many who are still as poor as I was, who might have had my stroke of luck, and mebbe deserved it more.'

'Well, but it came to you, not them,' said Marianne, to whom this was not a congenial line of reasoning. 'And you must be glad of it.'

'I'm glad of it. After all, how else would I have met you?'

He spoke jestingly – yet not quite, for in the glance they exchanged great chasms seemed to yawn, and she was disturbed. 'Well, I shouldn't be here, at any rate,' she said, making ready to go.

'Why, who says so?' said Jed, not moving.

Marianne could only shrug.

'I thought from what you said that you didn't care for them what was it? – little dull trivialities.'

'So I don't,' she said, bridling, 'But I – oh, I don't know.' She looked at him with genuine appeal. 'You do take a person up so! And I really *have* got to go, you know, simply because I'm late.'

'Well, thass different,' he smiled. 'If it's because you're late that you've got to go, and not because you're thinking of some footling etiquette – no, don't be cross! – I say if it's because of that, then there's nothing to stop you coming again – is there?'

She paused, trifling with her gloves, which fitted her like a second skin. 'I suppose not,' she said.

'If you would like, I mean.'

She smiled then, at that little courtly touch; and meeting her eyes, he smiled back.

Chapter Eight

A Corner of Old England

Pierce had a standing invitation to stay with Jed at Plague House, and took it up that summer. Ben Catbush was there now, serving Jed as loyally as he had 'Mr Childs', and taking readily to farm work, for he had been born in the country; and Jed had engaged a poor local girl to come and work in the kitchen, paying a wage that might have made Mr Hemstock snort in disgust, and the Rev. Bouverie say she wouldn't thank him for it (which, strangely enough, she did). Jed and Pierce spent convivial evenings together, but Pierce's days were taken up with sketching, and he was apologetic for being such an absent guest.

'Oh, we don't need to stand on ceremony, ole friend,' Jed said; and he added, with a certain unease as it seemed to Pierce, that he was busy himself during the day, and not to worry about him.

Pierce, however, had other things on his mind. Painting — of course, painting, for he was loving it at Heartsease, he was absorbed, he sketched with a sort of exhilarated irritability, never content, convinced at each successive view that this was the one above all that he must capture and that would satisfy him; and it was the special fascination of this part of the world that there were so many views, continually changing with the intimate contours of the landscape. He felt that he had taken possession of his identity as an artist at last. He was learning to forget that high degree of finish that he had been taught at Signor Gardini's, and to be bold, loose, to think in blocks instead of lines. He was learning that clouds were masses, not aimless patterns in the sky; that

181

fields of barley and fields of wheat had their own different textures, tints, characters; that the shadiest copse was full of light, made of light.

All this engaged and extended his mental faculties so much that Pierce, in that quiet spot where great-wheeled waggons moved so slowly that wagtails walked rather than flew out of their way, felt himself to be living twice as fast as ever before. And yet he was aware of being divided also, divided against himself − disturbing to a young man who had always enjoyed ease of mind, and who in growing those extra inches above common height seemed to have grown a little above trouble and fret, and to breathe a saner air. He was relishing his artistic discoveries, yet he was not giving them his whole attention: he wanted to be wedded to his work, but his heart cheated on its vows. He could not stop thinking of Rosa Strickland.

How much it was the thought of her that brought him here he could not say: it seemed a nonsense to try and separate elements from such a subtle alloy of feeling. The place made him think of Rosa and Rosa made him think of the place. And they both seemed to have got into his blood. And from only one meeting! − he told himself that again and again, to try and impress on himself how nonsensical his fascination was − but the effect instead was to make that one meeting seem many, its modest details repeated in his mind like reflections in a hall of mirrors, and so to thrust the beautiful uncompromising girl further into the foreground of his consciousness.

He longed to draw her, certainly − but then that was Pierce's instinctive reaction to whatever impressed his eye and heart, and always had been. And it was more than that; somehow it seemed to him wrong, unthinkable, impossible, that the one brief meeting in the lane that had affected him so deeply could be an isolated incident, leading nowhere, an end not a beginning. He could not have said why without falling back on cloudy notions of fate or destiny that seemed to him altogether too dark for his own prevailingly light attitude to life. Too foolish also, perhaps: though they seemed less so, here in Heartsease.

Even to Jed, Pierce could have given no very lucid account of his feelings. Jed had known Rosa from childhood, had re-established his friendship with her since his return to Heartsease, spoke her name with a casualness Pierce could not manage. For Jed she was a part of life. For Pierce she stood startlingly outside it.

There was only one thing, of course, to do: see her again. And so he would, in spite of a curious trepidation about the prospect. Pierce had no less a sense of his own merits than the rest of us; but he had had a sensation, on meeting Rosa, of being seen through and through by her rich dark eyes, and it disquieted as well as attracted him. It was as if she recognized no formal steps and gradations in between seeing and knowing people, and Pierce, frank and open as he was by nature, had led too urbane a life to find that other than rather alarming.

Yet see her he must, and knowing that she worked at Mr Ringrose's poultry-farm and came away at the same time each afternoon, he decided to try and meet her in the road from the Grange – at least to give her good day, and submit himself to the scrutiny and, if need be, contempt of those eyes. With this in mind he spent the morning tramping far afield – bare-headed, sketchbook under his arm, short pea-jacket thrown over his shoulder in the high summer heat, stout boots on his feet – already a familiar figure to the labourers in the fields who saw from afar the glint of his fair hair turned Norse by bleaching sun.

He tramped through a tawny landscape almost ripe for harvest, until he was far south of Heartsease, and found, all at once, that he had come upon the building of the new railway. It was an even greater shock than when he had glimpsed it from the gig with Jed. The cutting that scored its way willy-nilly through fields and closes, leaving little forlorn amputations of them on either side and making disjointed nonsense of old roads and paths; the dull gleam of the iron rails, like taut nerves or veins in some vast and living dissection; the heaps of cinder and gravel, some being carted in great Norfolk waggons as if they were a dismal new sort of crop freshly reaped; the straggling shanty of sheds and lean-tos, with smoke rising from cooking-fires and ragged strings of washing; the raised walkways of narrow planks, along which the navvies steered their barrows as surely as if they themselves were so many trains on rails; and most of all the appearance of those navvies, oakum-whiskered and clad in brightly coloured stocking-caps and striped waistcoats, colourful as pirates — wonderful subjects for the pencil, if one were brave or foolhardy enough to ask them to pose: all this confounded Pierce quite as much as if he had happened upon a shipyard in the middle of the countryside, with a first-rater on the stocks. He wondered greatly at the impact these men must make on the quiet places through which they passed, with their free spending, their doughty independence, and their two-fisted manner, so different in every respect from that of the people who laboured on the land beneath the eye of the farmer and the squire; and in wondering, recalled to mind Rosa's comment on his sketch, with the pond missed out so as not to spoil the composition. Was he turning his back on truth in turning his back on this chaotic ugliness and resuming his sketches of the untouched fields? Was that what Rosa would say?

Rosa, Rosa . . . He tramped back to Heartsease in the mellow cloudless afternoon, dwelling on her still — with such concentration, that when she appeared coming down the road beside which he sat with his sketchbook, quite unchanged from their last meeting, it was merely as if his thoughts of her had taken on a single extra degree of vividness.

He was on his feet in a moment; and as she drew near, he was assailed with a consciousness of being a sweat-damp, dusty, and generally abject individual, and that it was practically certain that she would walk straight past him. Rosa did not, however; she paused and gave him good afternoon, and glancing down at the sketchbook, said, 'You've come to draw us again, Mr Coppinger?'

'Yes indeed — I've been half over the county today, I think.'

'I can see that,' said she, with a faint smile. 'You've caught the sun, I fear.'

'Have I?' he said, putting a hand — foolishly enough, he realized — to his face. 'I didn't think of that — my nose must be awfully red.'

'Not very,' she said, still faintly smiling. 'But you'd perhaps best wear a hat next time. You can be ill with the sun, you know.'

'Yes — of course — thank you kindly for reminding me.'

She was about to move on. Pierce, with no idea of what he was going to say, blurted out: 'By the by, I — I—'

She stopped to look at him. The sun was low, and its searching beams showed him that to call Rosa's eyes brown was to say nothing about them. The warmest, richest palette he had ever mixed was insipid compared to them: the tiny flecks of green and amber in the depths of them would have been beyond the power of the finest brush.

'I was going to say I — went over as far as the new railway today,' he said. 'Quite a sight . . . I wondered if you'd seen it.'

She shook her head. 'Not I. I've heard a good deal about it. One or two young fellows from Heartsease have left the village and gone to join the navvies.'

'Have they?' He was surprised. 'It's very dangerous work, I hear.'

'There are terrible accidents,' Rosa said, steadily regarding him. 'And the work's fearful hard, and the navvies are lawless folk, forever falling into fights, and doing hurt to each other. But it pay well; and it's a free sort of life. There'll be others follow, I reckon.'

'It's a pity,' Pierce said.

'Why so?' There was the challenge again.

Pierce shrugged. 'A pity they have to do it — leave their homes, and everything.'

She looked as if she were about to say something; then made a sort of nod of goodbye, and was about to pass him again.

'Will you — will you allow me to walk home with you?' Pierce said, starting after her.

'I'm not going home, Mr Coppinger — I've hay-bonds to make at Farmer Hemstock's before my day's done, so I'm going there.'

'I'll walk that way with you then — if I may?'

She glanced sidelong at him, and seemed to frown, and was silent, so he said, wretchedly enough: 'I beg your pardon — I'm bothering you, I'm very sorry,' and had started away in agitation before she could say: 'No, Mr Coppinger, really, I — tisn't that . . .' She gave the faint smile as he came back. 'Thass just strange to — to be asked such things, in that way . . . Of course I don't mind if you walk with me — as you like.'

He walked beside her, his mind all random confusion shot through with mad joy. He carried his big folio sketchbook under one arm, and his hinged wooden case of pencils, charcoal, and watercolour pastilles under the other — and both were aching. Somehow Rosa must have divined this, for she said, 'Shall I carry one of those?'

'Oh! no, I — I wouldn't dream of it,' he said, for it seemed to him that he ought to be carrying something of hers, if she had had anything.

'Well, that make no sense you carryen 'em both, and me empty-handed,' said Rosa, taking the wooden case from him without fuss. 'You staying at Plague House?'

'Yes — Jed's very kindly putting me up while I work on my landscapes.'

'He's a kind man, I think. Thass caused quite a stir, him coming back to Heartsease. You know the story, I suppose? 'Course thass a long time ago, but people's memories are long. Though I wonder if they're as long as Jed's, or if they remember quite the way he do.'

'He's a man of very deep feelings, I believe . . . He's been a very good friend to me.'

'Aye . . . It seem strange.'

'Why so?'

'Well, because I still think of Jed as he was — and as he still is, I reckon, spite of his money — and you're a gentleman.'

Pierce was discomfited, for she had touched upon the very thing that seemed above all to separate him from Rosa herself, but he said lightly, 'I'm flattered you should think so. As far as a lot of people are concerned, there's not much to choose between a painter and a chimney-sweep except the size of the brushes.'

'But you know what I mean.'

'I suppose . . . Though I really can't see what difference it makes to anything.'

'It's because you're a gentleman that you can say that. To you it don't matter. But it do make a difference, a powerful difference, all the difference in the world.'

He did not enjoy hearing this, and because of that he said with something of her own harshness: 'You mean I can't be sincere in being friends with Jed?'

It was her turn to be put out now. 'No — no, I never meant that, Mr Coppinger, at all—'

'There you go,' he said impatiently, 'Mr Coppinger again. I wish you'd call me Pierce. Look, I don't give a hang for whatever I am and whatever Jed is and whatever you are. And maybe that is a luxury I can afford, but I don't care about that either. Rosa — why do you suppose I waited for you today?'

She stopped and faced him. 'Why?'

Her gaze was so uncompromising that he faltered. 'Well — because I wanted to see you. I wanted to ask whether — whether you'd sit for me. Let me paint you.'

'You want to make a picture of me?' Rosa said slowly,

in a tone in which a certain wonder melted into her usual scepticism.

'I would love to. Just a sketch, anything, if you'd allow me.'

'But why?'

He felt himself mentally tensed for a leap in the void — but then made a timid sideways jump in answering: 'Why do I paint this countryside?'

'Because you're a painter,' Rosa said. 'And painters make pictures of such things.'

'Well, they make portraits too.'

'But thass for people who pay you for them. People who want likenesses. I—' She hesitated and her gaze, unusually, wavered. 'I want no likeness of myself.'

'I know it's an impertinent thing to ask,' Pierce said, and went on impetuously, 'but ever since I met you I've longed to try and draw you. You might tear it up or do what you liked with it when it was finished — or never look at it. I know it perhaps seems odd — but in London, you know, lots of people find artists want to draw them, and they sit for a fee — for their time, you know — and—'

'Because the artists reckon they look quaint, I suppose,' Rosa said.

There was truth in that: Pierce had done such fancy pictures himself, studies of flower-girls and bird-sellers. He coloured. 'But I didn't mean—'

She stopped him with a curious little smile, and said, 'Will you give me your hand?'

Startled, he did so. She held his long-fingered hand in her own brown one for a few moments, then released it.

'There,' she said. 'D'you feel how rough and hard it is? Can you paint that? Can you put that in a pretty picture of a country girl?'

'I—' It was no use equivocating, not with Rosa. He shook his head.

'Then it wouldn't be a picture of me,' she said, quite gently. 'D'you see?'

He was still all a-tingle from the touch of her hand; and its roughness and hardness was the last thing that concerned him, though he could find no way of saying so that would not seem mere compliment.

'It would be a lie, you see,' she said. 'I'm sorry, Mr Coppinger.'

'Not Pierce?' he said with a wistful smile.

She hesitated. 'Pierce then.' She handed him the paint-box. 'I must leave you here.'

'Not everything we artists do is a lie, you know,' Pierce said earnestly. 'I – oh, well, never mind. There was no harm in asking – was there?'

'No harm. Goodbye.'

Such turmoil as Pierce was feeling could not help but show on his face; and though Jed in his turn seemed curiously abstracted, he did say to Pierce that night, 'Are you feeling quite well, ole friend?'

'Capital,' Pierce said. 'Never better. Tired, though.' So he was, but he was afield with his sketchbook again at dawn. The energy that possessed him, like so much in his life all of a sudden, seemed a strange importation: the domains of self were being exotically colonized. He had told Jed that he felt well, but well and ill were irrelevances. He had a feeling of being emotionally fattened, though he could not tell what would be the culminating slaughter.

He had a fancy to try a view of the Hall and park, and he found a gentle rise in a sheep-meadow to the south, close to the park fence, which gave a fair prospect, though he wished he could get nearer. He sketched, was dissatisfied, changed his position, was dissatisfied again, and was about to throw himself on his back and give himself up to the visions which had been intervening between him and the landscape when a red setter appeared out of nowhere, frisking round him and attempting to taste his watercolour blocks.

'Goldie, go down!' said a voice sharply. 'Wretched animal.'

Pierce sprang to his feet and came face to face with a woman in a watered-silk walking-dress and Kashmir shawl. Face to face, for she was nearly as tall as he – though she wore her height with unease, and with a round-shouldered stoop that only made it more conspicuous. The face that regarded him from the shadow of the tubular bonnet was strong-boned and sallow, and though the lady was probably only in her late twenties there was no freshness about her except in the penetrating grey eyes – penetrating yet curiously vulnerable, weak points in a shell.

'The brute doesn't obey me but then why should they? It's all very well for us to lord it over them but after all if Goldie and I were lost in a forest she would surely survive better than I or you for that matter. Rabbits and so forth. One might make shift with a few berries I suppose but really I don't know I'm sure.'

All this came out in a rapid staccato voice that seemed curiously pitched a little higher than was natural to it, while the lady's glance flickered back and forth between Pierce and the dog and the point of her closed parasol swished restlessly over the long grass.

'She's a very handsome animal,' Pierce said.

'Goldie, leave! Handsome yes, you're quite right I'm sure though Goldie is hardly the most appropriate name for a dog the colour of a chestnut and not in the least gold at all, you must be wondering terribly and thinking me quite mad and I don't blame you I'm sure!'

'Not at all,' said Pierce uncomfortably.

'Good of you to say so but you needn't trouble on my account, especially when I've interrupted your sketching and a very spirited likeness of the old place it is though why you should care anything for my opinion heaven only knows, but I may at least speak familiarly of the Hall having been born there and destined to die there in all probability, we Ingamells tend to, beastly sort of tradition, you know.'

'Oh! Miss Ingamells – how do you do. My name is Pierce Coppinger. Dear me, I hope I'm not trespassing . . .'

'Oh! not on this side of the fence, though no doubt if you were to wander into the park without permission Papa would kick up a horrid fuss but then as he says what can one expect in these revolutionary times with the mob at the door and out for our blood, I declare I never prepare myself for sleep without the certain expectation that we shall be burnt in our beds by men with torches and I dare say we deserve it I'm sure! Would you like to sketch in the park, Mr Coppinger?'

'I would, very much, Miss Ingamells,' said Pierce. 'I've often admired it from a distance. Though I shouldn't wish to make a nuisance of myself—'

'Oh! don't speak of it I beg you, not to me, you could hardly be a greater nuisance to the world in general than me, it's rather a pity the world isn't one great picture for then I could be rubbed out or painted over and a much better composition that would make of it, however that's of no consequence, the point is you would like to sketch in the park – well, if it were up to me there would be no further ado, but I suppose you'd best ask Papa's permission, he's at Norwich at some horrid magistrates' meeting but he'll be home later this afternoon.'

'You're very good – but really, if it's any trouble—'

'Oh! quite a formality, I assure you, Mr Coppinger, Papa will be pleased I know, he has quite a taste for things artistic, we had a fellow here a couple of years ago making a series of views of the old place but he was a fearful charlatan, perspective all nonsensical and trees like so many cabbages on sticks, you're a professional, I think?'

'Well, I like to think so. I live by my pencil, at any rate.'

'Charming notion and I'm sure we all ought to live by our toil, when Adam delved and Eve span who was then the and so forth, though where that would leave me I don't know as I'm pretty well the most useless creature in existence, oh don't trouble to contradict, I beg you. There are some rather pleasant prospects from the north of the house, near the great cedar, I think you'll find a fine view from there.'

'You draw yourself, Miss Ingamells?' said Pierce with quickened interest.

'Oh! I call it drawing, I must do something to make a pretence of justifying my existence you know, but I dare say the sight of my horrid daubs would just send you into a screaming fit, and I wouldn't blame you, Mr Coppinger, I'm sure!'

'I would be very honoured to see your work, if you would care to let me see it,' said Pierce. 'And I would very much like to sketch in the park, if you think Mr Ingamells would be agreeable to my asking his permission.'

'Oh! I couldn't think of your seeing my scribbles, it would sink me further in your estimation if such a thing were possible, but come up to the house later and see Papa anyway and I can positively engage that he will see you.'

'You're very kind – I'm greatly obliged.'

'Not at all I'm sure I'm such a perfectly useless creature it's positively a relief to me to be of the slightest service, Goldie, come here, good day to you!'

Miss Ingamells stalked suddenly away, leaving Pierce staring after her rather dazed in his mind, and with a feeling of having been hit over the head with a sort of verbal truncheon. He was grateful for the offer, however, and not incurious to see the Hall which kept itself so aloof from Heartsease; and so he found himself walking down the carriage-drive in the warm afternoon, with the park about him all heavy with greenness and scent and slow drowsy sounds of wood-doves among the trees.

Architecture had never thrilled Pierce as did landscape, and his mouth tended to fill with a yawn at the mention of volutes and capitals; but there was no denying the beauty of Heartsease Hall with the westering sun on its red brick. It was an H-shaped building two hundred years old, with bay-windowed wings on either side of a central block, sash windows of classical symmetry, and a balustraded roof with a cupola. Though he was expected, Pierce's instinctive reaction on seeing the house was a feeling of being a trespasser. The beauty of the Hall was remote and unfriendly, the purdah beauty of a veiled and jealous lady, screened from the glance of common eyes. The very length of the drive seemed to reproach him for being on foot: the pediment over the door, crowned by a monstrous cannonball of an urn, seemed ready to crash down on him for his presumption in knocking. A footman in white gloves let him in, took his hat as if it were a small sick animal, and led him with a sort of stately creeping across a cool hall that could have had no earthly reason for being so big except to make people feel small, and into a library filled with folio volumes and adorned with the sort of ornate plaster ceiling that always made Pierce want to duck his head.

'Mr Coppinger – I must ask you to excuse me just for the merest moment – a single sentence is all that remains,' said the gentleman writing a letter at the desk, without looking up, so Pierce inhaled the odour of vellum and calfskin and listened to the scratching of the pen, whilst the footman disappeared quite as silently and mysteriously as if he were a spirit conjured out of a bottle.

'I hope I don't inconvenience you, sir,' Pierce said when the gentleman at last finished the letter and rose to greet him.

'Not at all – a morsel of business connected with the Bench,' said Mr Ingamells, shaking his hand. 'A tiresome duty, but a duty, I have always believed, to be embraced, not shirked. My daughter tells me you are an artist, sir.'

'Yes – I was sketching close to the park, and Miss

Ingamells happening on me there was good enough to suggest—'

'She did quite right,' Mr Ingamells said, 'I am happy to see you. You are a stranger to this part of the world, sir?'

Pierce gave an account of himself.

'Ah, the artist's life!' said Mr Ingamells with a sigh. 'I must confess to a pang of envy at your freedom, Mr Coppinger. I sometimes long for a taste of freedom myself, but — ' he gestured about at the book-lined room, and by implication at the whole estate — 'mine is the sparse diet of responsibility. And yet — here is the curious thing — I would not have it any other way! Well, my dear sir, I would be glad to think of our modest little grounds — they are scarcely worth the name of park — engaging your painter's eye. If it were just up to me, I would have them thrown open so that all might enjoy them; such would be my ideal, I assure you — but we are only mortal, and fall sadly short of the ideal, more than ever in these declining times! And I must never forget my duty to this place. This pleasant corner of old England, Mr Coppinger, cannot be considered in the light of a *possession*. I merely hold it in trust: I am only the custodian for a posterity that may or may not be grateful for my efforts — I wish I could be more hopeful on that score. But it is not for me to complain of my burden. I try to emulate the stoicism of the ancients. You are familiar, Mr Coppinger, with the works of Epictetus and Marcus Aurelius?'

Pierce, suppressing a reminiscent shudder at the thought of Latin grammar, confessed that he knew very little of them.

'My especial study,' said Mr Ingamells, going and taking down a volume and turning its pages fondly. 'You might place me naked on a desert island, and as long as I had this — the *Meditations* — I would consider myself rich. Ah, we are sadly decayed,' he said with an air of quiet resignation. 'I am afraid I do not understand the modern world. The spirit of progress, of which we hear

so much, is alien to me — I dare say that is my fault.
Nothing would please me better than to be a Roman
gentleman of the Antonine period, farming my own few
acres, and drinking spring water and eating wheaten
bread at my plain board. Or failing that, to have borne
crusading arms beneath the standards of Christendom —
my only possessions my sword and my faith. I am a lost
soul in these worldly times. Forgive me — you must think
me a dreamer.'

Pierce — who was very sensible of the modern benefits
of gaslight and steam, and entertained strong misgivings
as to the idea of his legs in a toga — said not at all, he was
inclined to dreaming himself.

'Ah? We are few, Mr Coppinger — we are few!' said
Mr Ingamells. 'But speaking of the plain board — let me
invite you to stay to dinner. No trouble at all! We dine
early here in the country — how greatly I prefer these
simple manners! — though in town one must, I am
afraid, sacrifice them. I would be glad to have a little talk
on painting, and so, I know, would Beatrice — my
daughter — who draws a little herself. She mentioned to
you, I think, that we had a man here to execute some
topographical views? Not a happy experiment. I must
show you such efforts as he finished. There is also a
portfolio of drawings made of the house at the time of its
building you might like to see — ah, the honest craftsmen
of those days! Where are they now . . .?'

Pierce's experience as a portrait-painter had
accustomed him to searching out family likenesses, and
even as he talked with Mr Ingamells his eye had been
unconsciously noting and comparing the features of
father and daughter. His conclusion was a strong feeling
of pity for Miss Ingamells, for she had inherited nothing
but the grey, cool, intelligent eyes from a father who was
undeniably a handsome man. Mr Ingamells, the squire of
Heartsease, was a soft-spoken, soft-handed, soft-footed
patrician who was approaching fifty with only as many
grey hairs at his sleek temples and lines at the corner of

his mouth as would lend the finishing touch of distinction to a smooth, square, reposeful face, pale of complexion and bland of expression. A feline poise was in all his movements, a feline neatness characterized his dress, from his spotless white linen to his highly polished boots. He was a man whom it was impossible to imagine falling over, getting drunk, suffering from a cold in the head, or sitting in a bath; a man who appeared as well-made, glossy, and utterly invulnerable as the lustrous articles of silver and mahogany in the great dining-room; a man who seemed, in his serenely urbane way, to have as little to fear from the world as a tiger prowling his own unpenetrated jungle. And all this, incidentally, threw into the very worst light the plainness, awkwardness, and constraint of his daughter Beatrice, who at dinner renewed her acquaintance with Pierce by declaring in her tight breathless manner that she must have quite ruined his drawing that morning and he must think her a perfect Harpy and she didn't blame him for it one bit.

'You find us very retired here, Mr Coppinger,' said Mr Ingamells. 'For myself I revel in the sweet simplicity of a country retreat, and would quite do without the sophistications of a town establishment, if the world allowed it to me. But some might find it dull: it is fortunate that Beatrice has resources in her talents and employments, her sketchbook and her music.'

'Oh good heavens Papa I'm sure it's me who's dull I declare having to put up with my company for days on end must send you into screaming fits sometimes and I don't blame you I'm sure,' said Miss Ingamells.

'She rallies me, you see, sir,' said Mr Ingamells, who seemed to adopt towards his daughter an attitude of indulgent condescension, as if she were a well-meaning poor relation whom he would not hurt for the world. 'As for company, I had forgot to tell you, my dear, that there was a letter from our cousin Mr Deacon this morning. He promises a visit very soon, though he is characteristically vague as to the exact date.'

'Happy to see him I'm sure,' said Miss Ingamells, with something more than the usual tension in her pinched smile, 'though it's like him to simply invite himself in that manner and why you should be happy to see him here I really can't think when it's like having the bailiffs in pricing the furniture or even the grim reaper with his scythe or is it his sickle some sort of horrid sharp instrument I'm sure.'

'Now, my dear, Mr Deacon is always very agreeable, you know,' said Mr Ingamells blandly. 'Not the steadiest young man in the world, perhaps — though that's none of our concern — but always agreeable.'

'Agreeable I'm sure he ought to be,' said Miss Ingamells, 'with his beastly expectations forever hanging over our heads like a sword of Damocles, my mind seems to be quite running on blades of various descriptions Mr Coppinger I don't know what your idea of me must be you must think me a perfect butcher or Ghoul.'

'Mr Alexander Deacon is a young relation of ours,' said Mr Ingamells in explanation to Pierce, 'quite a distant relation, and it is unlikely that we would have had much to do with him were it not for the fact of the entail. This estate is entailed in the male line, you see, Mr Coppinger, and my late wife and I were blessed only with the issue who graces this table — no male heirs. And as the Ingamells have never been a prolific family, it transpires that the nearest male relation is young Mr Deacon, who is — is there such a thing as a third cousin? No matter. It is he who will inherit this house and land on my death — which places us in a rather peculiar position when we meet, as we do from time to time. And in very friendly fashion too — he is a most cordial young gentleman, though I mean no disrespect when I add that he does not seem to be applying himself *very* diligently to his studies at the Bar, and perhaps considers that his expectations from this quarter render unnecessary any settled effort on his part to get on in the world.'

It crossed Pierce's mind that the most uncomfortable

position in such a situation must be Miss Ingamells', for unless she married she would be dependent on this distant cousin when her father died; his glance fell on her ungainly figure and taut expression for a moment, and he was assailed by a sudden vision of her as an intelligent woman who was daily faced with the knowledge of her own utter powerlessness in the world. But she caught his glance with a sharp look, as if she defied his pity, and said, 'Well after all who knows there may be nothing left for Mr Alexander precious Deacon to inherit for as I was saying to Mr Coppinger just the other day we may all be burned in our beds before long what with Chartists and engineers and radicals and goodness knows what — you know I was looking at the house from a distance today when Mr Coppinger was drawing it and the thought flew into my head, will it always stand? Or will it be brought down in some ghastly way with fire and who knows blood perhaps but there I'm being a Ghoul again what do you think Mr Coppinger?'

'Heartsease seems such a quiet spot,' said Pierce, though from his association with Jed and Rosa he knew something of its deeper disquiet, 'and I cannot think that anything is likely to disturb it to the degree you mention. Certainly I hope not.'

'Alas, one cannot be sanguine about these times,' said Mr Ingamells. 'All this mania for profit, for change, for hurry, this absorption in selfish material ends and gratifications.' He motioned for his crystal wine-glass to be filled again. 'I can only stand and watch in bemusement. Oh, to be a Cincinnatus, anxious only to serve his country and return to the plough when his duty was done! We are quiet here, certainly, but a monster is near at hand. You have seen the new railway being built to the south, Mr Coppinger? The modern world, alas! I dare say I am very old-fashioned, but I cannot help but regret the passing of those days when the humble Englishman was content to know and love his own spot of native ground, and never yearned to go racing about the country. I am thankful that this corner of old England will remain inviolate, at any rate, and will not be traversed by railways and their myrmidons — a rootless set of people, I fear, divorced from all ties of duty and station — and can they really be the happier for it? No, I shall remain here with my books, my few possessions marked with tender associations, and let such things as railways pass me by. The world will laugh at me for it, I dare say, and remark that old Ingamells is a quaint unworldly sort of fellow, but I don't mind that.'

'You bought those shares in the railway, though, Papa, after all, and did pretty well by them,' said Miss Ingamells.

'Yes, alas,' said Mr Ingamells, with a brief laugh, 'such was my surrender to the modern world. My lawyer advised me to invest, Mr Coppinger — he understands such things — and I am such an innocent in these matters I could only meekly follow him. And so it goes. You were saying, Mr Coppinger, you hope to exhibit with the Norwich Society . . .?'

When Miss Ingamells left them to the port Mr Ingamells settled back more comfortably in his chair — not that he ever looked uncomfortable, or capable of being so — and said: 'You observe the silhouette above the mantelpiece, Mr Coppinger? The late Mrs Ingamells.'

Pierce hoped it was not a recent loss?

'It seems so,' said Mr Ingamells, 'though in fact I lost her quite young. You share my distaste, I feel sure, for those who make a parade of their devotion: I will only say that my life since that day has been but a half-life. I buried my hopes with Euphemia — I buried my capacity for joy, and resigned myself to waiting to join her. People often tell me that, though she is gone, pleasures and comforts remain: so they may do, but I am indifferent to them,' he said, pouring himself more port.

'Miss Ingamells cannot remember her mother?'

'Barely. A father's care has been her chief portion. She has her books — her drawing and her piano — her little cares and employments,' Mr Ingamells said, his voice again lined with kindly condescension. 'They can do much, Mr Coppinger: no better resources against solitude, no better provision against the long night of old age. And really she draws admirably in her way: it is impossible of course that a lady should seek to develop her talents in any *professional* way – old-fashioned I may be, no doubt, but I hope to close my eyes on the world for ever before I see the tender sex step down into the dusty forum where we men contend, and blight that sanctity with which we surround them, as the radicals would seem to want. However, her skill was much praised by her last instructor – that was during our last residence in town. If her modesty will permit, you shall see some specimens of her work.'

It was with reluctance that Miss Ingamells, when they joined her in the drawing-room, produced some of her drawings, and she said in a sort of suppressed scream: 'I declare Mr Coppinger I'm almost ready to sink through the floor at the idea of your seeing such things I vow I would rather die upon the spot any death almost not even excepting burning at the stake and I assure you I have such a horror of fire I always have to withdraw at Christmas when the plum-pudding comes in.' But Pierce did not need to feign interest in the landscapes in pencil and wash which she at last produced. What they lacked in technical sophistication and finish they made up for in forcefulness; and what struck him above all was the peculiar character she gave to these simple views of Norfolk countryside. Choked skies loomed, trees were jagged and agonized, tiny figures looked lost and menaced. Pierce wondered again at the mind of the awkward sandy woman in the unbecoming silk dress – wondered how much of it was reflected in the brittle garrulousness, or whether that was merely presented, like a carnival vizard waved before the face. And as he talked to her of her work, he detected through the flurry of self-deprecating words a genuine feeling for what her father clearly regarded as no more than a genteel accomplishment.

'Have you never worked in pastel, Miss Ingamells?' he asked her. 'I feel it would suit your particular style.'

'Good heavens to speak of my having a style as if I were a Raphael or a who is that man who seems to have delighted in very large ladies a Rubens obliged I'm sure but really you needn't perjure yourself on my account Mr Coppinger I'm sure,' said Miss Ingamells, flushing.

'And here is a sketch for a half-length portrait, I see,' said Pierce. 'This has great dash too. A pity it wasn't finished.'

'Oh, that!' Miss Ingamells' flush deepened. 'Our cousin Mr Alexander Deacon sat for that on his last visit though when I say sat I mean was prevailed upon to sit still for two minutes and even that was irksome to him not that it was any great loss as the fellow is a perfect fright to look at and I swear I would rather make a crocodile's portrait or a what is that unlikely mythical beast that lives in fire not a phoenix a Salamander I'm sure.'

'Mr Deacon promised to sit for you again on his next visit, I seem to remember, my dear,' said Mr Ingamells.

'Very good of Mr Alexander Deacon I'm sure,' said Miss Ingamells, whose smile grew more fixed and glassy at each mention of the absent cousin, 'much obliged to him for putting himself out so but he needn't trouble on my account not that he seems accustomed to putting himself to a great deal of trouble generally and why should he when he is practically ready to move his bags in here and start rearranging the furniture as he seems to think he owns the place already.'

'It is a rather ticklish situation,' said Mr Ingamells smoothly, 'but we can hardly refuse him our hospitality, my dear. He is family, though distant, and a gentleman. We must bear with him.'

'Well really it's of no consequence to me I never think of Mr Alexander precious Deacon from one year to the next I'm sure!' said Miss Ingamells, closing her portfolio with a snap.

Pierce's introduction thus to the Ingamells at Heartsease Hall was quite unplanned; and it was quite unplanned too that in a few days he should find himself employed there. His job was to be two-fold: to act as drawing-instructor to Miss Ingamells, and to complete the projected series of topographical views of the house and grounds that had been abandoned by the disappointing previous artist. Mr Ingamells had invited Pierce to call again, after the evening of the dinner, and show him some of his work: had seemed highly satisfied with it, and made his proposition. He was anxious, he said, that Beatrice should not be bored – adding in his blandest manner that not everyone was by nature fitted for the social life that was the chief occupation of many young ladies of her station. Pierce, having produced his testimonials from the Royal Academy schools, Signor Gardini and others, was engaged till the end of the year, and was to have a room at the Hall, to eat with the family, and to be furnished with materials for his work. He was to be paid a stipend that was small enough, but no less than he had been earning as a portrait-painter, and he hoped to be able to keep up the rent on his little studio in Norwich.

He had never envisaged doing such work. It lacked the freedom that he relished. Mr Ingamells, though he was unfailingly courteous, was separated from him by the widest gulf of beliefs and sympathies, and Pierce could find nothing to respond to in the cool grey eyes; and Beatrice Ingamells, though she interested him, was no easy companion. The formalities of life at the Hall irked him. His father, he was sure, would be surprised at his decision when he heard of it. But then his father did not know Heartsease. His father did not know Rosa.

For there was the heart of the matter. Traversing the fields prior to his second visit to the Hall, Pierce had caught sight of a woman's figure in the distance, carrying a basket; and though for a moment he reproached himself with the telling folly of supposing every woman he saw was Rosa, a further moment convinced him he was not mistaken. No one else carried themselves in quite that erect, proud way, to no one else belonged that set of the strong head and neck and shoulders. And as he looked at her figure seeming to shimmer in the dusty-gold heat haze of the harvest fields, Pierce knew that he must be here, in Heartsease; that he could no more leave this place than he could lift himself off the earth with his own hands, and that because of Rosa he must stay even if it was only to subject himself to the rebuffs of those shrewd eyes and that sturdy spirit. And he was quite ready for that, not in any luxurious self-pitying way, but because there was no alternative: that he stay here and be near her was a simple imperative, and such simple imperatives now ruled him in a way that he could not have conceived in his old supple wayward life before Heartsease.

And so the offer of work at the Hall was not to be refused. Jed was surprised, but pleased that his friend would still be near at hand, and pleased too that Pierce had been so taken with the place he himself loved so consumedly. That it was because of Rosa was something Pierce could not tell him somehow. He could not have put into words to anyone what he was feeling: how it was that he found himself living in a gracious seventeenth-century manor, eating off silver, having his coats brushed by a solemn manservant, and wandering at will about the groves and ponds of a landscaped park — and all the time seeing all of this as no more than an indistinct and insignificant background to a figure with bare brown arms and a patched apron and a look of quiet defiance.

The Hall was a little world, self-sufficient. It was paid for, of course, by rents — Mr Ingamells owned a good deal of land — but for all an observer standing in the cupola on the roof could tell, the wealth that sustained the big house might have been drawn up in buckets from a well. For the village of Heartsease could not be seen from the Hall. A plantation of young trees had been laid out with the express intention of shutting out the sight of it. And other cunning dispositions of trees and hedges and artificial banks had ensured that the eye should never alight upon a farmhouse or a haystack or a ploughed field. Here, in the middle of the richest agricultural county in the land, there was no more evidence of cultivation to be seen than on the bleakest Highland crag.

Mr Ingamells personally considered this, he told Pierce, a pity. For himself there was nothing he loved better than to see the great waggons rumbling home at dusk, or to have a little plain chat with the farmers on a market day. But the world, alas, was changing. Farming was a great enterprise now, and he no longer pretended to understand it. There was his tenant Mr Hemstock – a sterling fellow, at the very head and front of progress, he had nothing but respect for him – but where was the charming homespun simplicity of the old days? Let Mr Hemstock have his spanking new gig and his pianoforte – for was this not, thank heaven, a free country, the freest in the world, where there was nothing to stop a man rising to high estate? – but for himself, let him indulge a little regret for the passing of the old times, when men's eyes were not so fixed on material gain.

Mr Ingamells was indifferent to material things. He often said so. Nothing disgusted him more than the sight of pretty young girls of the labouring classes wearing those Manchester print frocks, or the sight of humble cottages hung about with knick-knacks made by the score in Staffordshire or some such place. Such a sad dereliction of peasant simplicity! No, nothing disgusted him more than this acquisitive materialism – not even a stain on his new Turkey carpet, or a film of dust on his china cabinets. And certainly that disgusted him so much, that the housemaids' life was a burden to them,

and they visibly trembled at the sound of Mr Ingamells'
squeaking shoes.

It was a measure of the unlimited self-assurance that
Mr Ingamells exuded that there seemed nothing
ridiculous about his squeaking shoes. The squeaks
actually seemed to enhance his authority. His shoes were
made for him, he once happened to remark to Pierce, by
a little man in the Strand, and he would have no other.
Why the only worthwhile shoes in the country should
come from so remote and specific a location Pierce could
not guess: it was one of those serene certainties that made
up the world of Mr Ingamells – who also had his saddles
made for him by a little man in Leicester, his hats made
for him by a little man in Bedford, and his shirts made
for him by a little man in Dublin, so that Pierce had a
curious vision of an army of obliging gnomes scattered
over the kingdom, busily occupied in producing goods
exclusively tailored to Mr Ingamells, and never doing
anything else.

Pierce's own room was in a lofty, draughty part of the
house, close to some peculiar little cells with iron
bedsteads and bare floorboards where the maids slept –
Mr Ingamells apparently admiring peasant simplicity so
much that he was sure his domestics could not be happy
without it; but he was given a tour of the Hall by Mr
Ingamells himself. Venerable as it was, it was in good
repair, with no signs of worm in the dark panelling that
made the gallery like one prodigious coffin; and greatly
as he deplored modern luxury, Mr Ingamells had been
forced to sacrifice his principles to such an extent that
there was no comfort or convenience that the house
lacked.

'I am glad you admire it, Mr Coppinger,' Mr Ingamells
said as Pierce gazed wonderingly at the North Drawing-
Room, which was always shut up and never entered, and
was full of hunting-scene tapestries that were never
looked at, and gilt chairs that were never sat in, and
japanned fire-screens that never screened a fire, so that

the whole sumptuous futility might as well have been at the bottom of the sea. 'It is a heavy responsibility to be charged with; and for myself, I would be happy to retire to some plain cottage on the estate, with a few volumes of the ancients to bear me company, and await the happy day when I can rejoin my beloved Euphemia, who took all my joys with her into the tomb. But, I have been entrusted with the care of this corner of old England, as was my father before me, and I may not lay down the burden, but must bear up under it.' And true to his Stoic philosophy, Mr Ingamells did seem to bear up pretty well, and no one seeing him drink his fine brandy, mount his thoroughbred hunter, or step into his well-upholstered carriage, would have guessed that it all meant nothing to him.

'The name of the mason who did that is lost to us,' said Mr Ingamells, pointing out the carved pediment over the front door. 'A humble craftsman, labouring with joy and pride in his work. Did he think of gain, any more than the anonymous toilers who raised our great cathedrals? Ah, where are such craftsmen now? Pursuing the new god Mammon in these frightful mills or manufactories or whatever they are called — I do not pretend to understand such things. I am very old-fashioned no doubt, but I cannot disguise my regret that I was not born in a past age of faith, when our society was bound together by sacred ties of obligation and duty. However, I must leave you now, and get ready for the magistrates' meeting. Duty still! The Bench is a hard place, Mr Coppinger; but someone must do it.' And certainly Mr Ingamells' sense of duty was so strong, that he went off to the court with every appearance of cheerfulness, and stood up to the strain of sentencing his fellow-men to prison with such fortitude that he never appeared to tackle his dinner with any less appetite after doing it.

Much of the time Mr Ingamells was occupied with his own affairs; and it was soon borne in upon Pierce that he had been engaged partly in order to keep Miss Ingamells out of her father's hair. He and his pupil were left to pursue their studies undisturbed, and her father made only the vaguest enquiries as to their progress. And so – as Miss Ingamells was no stranger to moods in which the very idea of drawing was unbearable to her and she was absolutely fit for nothing she was sure – Pierce had plenty of time to himself, and to seek out Rosa.

They were sitting on a stile, Pierce having met Rosa returning from a tramp far afield in search of a little gleaning after the harvest. Pierce had carried her small sack of gleaned corn for her, and had at last persuaded her to sit and rest, knowing she would never admit to weariness.

'How much flour will it make?' Pierce said, looking into the sack with a sense of his own innocence.

'Well . . . that'll last us into the cold weather,' said Rosa. 'Good years you can get enough to see the winter through. But there's not so much gleaning nowadays. Farmer Hemstock don't allow it.'

'Jed tells me that when he gets his first harvest in, he'll throw the fields open to the village.'

Rosa smiled. 'Thass like Jed. There's a lot of little kindnesses been felt since Jed came back to Heartsease. He always trade local, always find little bits of work for men who need it bad. A lot of the young village fellows look up to him, and make a bit of a hero of him.'

'I'm glad. He did the right thing, then, coming back here,' Pierce said. As Rosa looked doubtful he added: 'Didn't he? He seems happy.'

'Oh! aye, I b'lieve he is. Happy, yes . . . Only he ain't popular with everyone. Mr Coppinger – may I trust you?'

Pierce gave a mock frown. 'Not if you call me Mr Coppinger.'

Rosa smiled. 'Pierce then. Only I've heard something, and I wondered if you knew what the truth of it was.

Something about Jed carryen on with Marianne Hemstock.'

'Farmer Hemstock's daughter? Good Lord — I had no idea . . .' As he spoke he remembered the something secretive in Jed's manner when he had stayed with him, and his readiness to have Pierce out of the house.

'Mebbe thass all so much talk. I hope so, anyway.'

'It must be. With Jed's past history . . . he used to hate the very name of Hemstock.'

'I don't reckon Farmer Hemstock like the taste of the name Wintergreen either,' said Rosa. 'And Miss Hemstock — she's the apple of his eye. Dresses her up like a lady complete — treats her like she's made of chiney. Hoping to marry her to young Mr Bouverie, they say, and be up alongside the parsons and justices before he's done. D'you see?'

Pierce pondered. 'Jed's said nothing of it to me . . . Perhaps I should speak to him about it, discreetly.'

'Oh! no — don't do that.'

'Why not?'

'It never do no good, getting involved like that,' Rosa said. 'Keep out of it — let people run their own lives, and ruin 'em if they will.'

He regarded her quizzically, perplexed again at the mingling of softness and hardness in her personality — as if one substance should be both diamond and down. 'I wonder if you really mean that,' he said.

'Why should I say anything I don't mean?' she said.

'I don't know . . . Perhaps I put it badly. All I mean is, you speak as if you have no heart — and I know you have.'

Rosa ran her hand thoughtfully back and forth on the gnarled bar of the stile. 'D'you remember being a very little child, Pierce? Such a little child that all the world seemed new to you, and all the people in it giants, and the end of the road outside your door like some far-off country? Thass the time when you never expect anything to hurt you. And then one day you put your hand into the fire, because it's so pretty, and you want to touch it. And it don't just hurt you — it shock you, and dismay you, like you been betrayed; and suddenly then the world's different, and you know you can't trust the fire any more. It seem to me that people are like that with their hearts — like children reaching into the fire. A heart's a thing just waiting to be hurt — to be bruised, and torn, and broken; and yet people go on being surprised when it is, and never learning to bury it out of harm's way as a child learns not to touch the fire. D'you understand?'

'I think so. But would it really have been better if we had never been given hearts at all?'

'Mebbe it would. If you've seen the faces of a poor man and woman, watching their child die in want with no arm to save, you begin to think it might be better.'

He looked at her soberly. 'Why do you say this to me, Rosa?'

After a few moments her gaze shifted under his. 'Perhaps because I want you to see me true — as I really am.'

'And then I won't — won't like you so much?'

'I don't see how anyone could.'

'You might be surprised,' said Pierce.

All at once he could not look at her any more. He ran his hand through the corn in the sack and said: 'I had free time today — I should have come and helped you with your gleaning.'

'You? Have you ever worked in the field?' she said, with a certain wry amusement.

'No,' he said, flushing, a little stung, 'and no doubt I wouldn't make much of a fist at it — but I would like to try, all the same.'

She touched his arm with a quick movement. 'Twas a kind thought,' she said, 'and I take it so. But I can manage. And you've your own living to make, without worrying about mine.'

'But I wish I could help you,' he said. 'I know your life is a struggle. I want to help. If I were a farmer I could offer you work; but as I'm a painter, all I can do is ask you to sit for me. And that's no charity — as I said before, in London there are many people who earn a little extra money that way, and the artists are happy to pay it—'

'Poor Pierce,' she said with a light laugh, 'you try to put it so kindly. And I know — you mean it kindly too. And I say again, I'll manage. If I was to let you make a picture of me, I wouldn't ask money — twould be between friends. But I shan't: and thass not just for you — for anybody. Oh, I'm not a pretty picture, Pierce,' she added as he seemed about to protest. 'Thass not me.'

'I can't help thinking you beautiful,' said Pierce. 'I just do. But it's more than that, Rosa. Yes, I would love to paint you — but it isn't just because of that that I keep meeting you. You mean so much more—'

'Oh, Pierce, you don't *know* me,' she said, striking her hand hard on the stile. 'You've got this idea of me in your head, but you don't know anything of my life and how it is — that ain't possible you ever *could* know — no more than I know anything of yourn.'

'Well, that's easily remedied,' he said. 'I'm nearly twenty-six years old. I'm an only child and my mother is dead. My father's a retired sea-captain who lives in Torbay with two cats named Hawkins and Frobisher and thinks all doctors and parsons fools and sometimes has his dinner in the middle of the night because he believes it's better for the digestion. I learnt Latin as a boy and forgot it all as a man, I have never wanted to do anything but paint since I was breeched, and I have bad dreams if I eat shellfish. I have never been able to ride a horse with ease but I can balance a spoon on the end of my nose and consider this an ample compensation — shall I go on?'

She was laughing and it warmed his heart to see it. He laughed too, and gave her his handkerchief to wipe her eyes.

'Hawkins and Frobisher,' she said, 'whyever did your father call his cats Hawkins and Frobisher?'

'Oh! they were famous admirals or captains or something. Like Nelson — that's my middle name.'

'I didn't know.' Her face was sober again. 'I don't know about such things, you see. I was never taught. That shows how different we are.'

'You know a great deal more useful things than me.' She shook her head. 'Thass not the same.'

'My father has always had nothing but contempt for book-learning. And I know he would have nothing but admiration for you.'

Rosa's face clouded, and but for the fact that he believed her incapable of it, Pierce would have called the expression in her eyes fear. Abruptly she shook her head. 'You're a sweet man, Pierce,' she said. 'There — thass so seldom you hear any but hard words from my lips, that I'll say it again. You're a sweet man — but you live in dreams.' She got down from the stile and picked up the sack. 'In dreams!'

'Some of the time, true enough, I do,' he admitted. 'What about you, Rosa? Don't you, ever?'

She faced him, very straight, glowingly dark. 'Dreams don't do any good, Pierce. They only do harm — they only lead to pain. I killed mine, long ago, before they could kill me.' She left him.

Dear Father [wrote Pierce]
I have settled pretty well in my temporary and
alarmingly grand home. My pupil tho' whimsical
is certainly not lacking in talent; and Mr
Ingamells is quite as polite to me as he is to his
horses, tho' I remain terrified of the manservant
who brings my shaving-water and puts away my
clothes with a very forbidding expression.

I am able still to continue my landscape
studies, and pursue ever harder the beauties of
this place which are so elusive of capture. I
almost feel as if I never want to see any other
place. Perhaps it is something in the air. I don't

know what it is, or I cannot say. I only feel that I have found something here — or will find something — I cannot be certain. I feel certain of nothing any more. I know that you, with your strong belief in the open mind, will not blame me for that — though you may blame me very fairly for writing such an incoherent scribble of a letter as this — for which my apologies, and my assurance that, though I hardly know what I am any more, I remain ever

your loving son
Pierce.

In his tobacco-filled sitting-room in Torbay Captain Coppinger re-read this letter for the fifth or sixth time, while his old friend Captain Beeny, who was spending a pleasant evening of grog and argument with him, opened the window and took a reading of the stars.

'From your boy, Coppinger?' Captain Beeny said, out of the back of his bald head.

'From my boy,' said Captain Coppinger, with a sigh; then, 'Why, how did you know?'

'Didn't know. Guessed,' said his friend, turning from the window with the long pipe in his mouth swinging in an arc like a jib-boom. 'Why, man, you've been picking it up and laying it down and sighing and frowning over it all night.'

'Devil take it, Beeny,' said Captain Coppinger, 'I won't be spied on in this way!'

'Talk of spying! A man must be a fool not to see it,' said Captain Beeny. 'But I dare say you think me a fool, Coppinger — or else an ass. I dare say it's all one to you.'

'Beeny,' said Captain Coppinger hotly, 'I resent that.'

'Coppinger,' said Captain Beeny, 'you may do as you please!'

'So I think I may, in my own quarters, sir,' said Captain Coppinger, red to the roots of his white hair. 'And in my own quarters, Beeny, I say to you that you are *not* a fool. I won't hear of it.'

'Ass, then,' said Captain Beeny.

'Beeny, I won't have it! I didn't take a pound of shot in the left knee off Finisterre to be told such stuff in my own quarters. I'm a little too fly, Beeny, after that, not to know a man of sense when I see one. And I see one now, sir!'

'Coppinger,' said Captain Beeny, 'your hand.'

'Gladly, sir.'

They shook hands; and Captain Beeny sat down opposite his friend by the hearth. 'If there's bad news in that letter,' he said, 'and I've pained you in alluding to it, Coppinger, I'll take poison. A man must be an unfeeling brute to do less.'

'No, no – not bad news,' said Captain Coppinger, gazing thoughtfully into his glass of grog. 'The boy's well enough, I think.'

'Coppinger, how long have we known each other?'

'What do you mean, sir?'

'I mean what I say, sir. And I repeat, how long have we known each other? Is it forty years, sir, since we were tender midshipmen in the gunroom of the *Puissant*, and you punched the head of that Welsh imp who was tormenting me with the name of String-Beeny, or is it not?'

'You know it is, sir!' barked Captain Coppinger.

'Very well, sir! And I say to you, out of those forty years of friendship, that you are troubled, Coppinger, and I don't like it; and out of those same forty years of friendship, tell me to mind my own business, and I will not be offended – not by so much as a hair, sir!'

'Beeny,' said Captain Coppinger. 'Your hand again. Perhaps I am a little troubled. I don't know why: nothing amiss with this post the boy's taken. He just doesn't sound like himself, somehow, and it makes me wonder if all's well with him. I can't account for it.'

'Coppinger,' said Captain Beeny. 'You know my sentiments. A man must be a weakling who won't stand by what he believes. And my sentiments are that you were too soft on the boy. Beat a boy hard — I don't say every day, but pretty frequently — and he won't go far wrong.'

'Do you suggest my boy has gone wrong, sir?'

'I see your old sword on the wall, Coppinger; and I'd cut off my own head with it before I'd suggest any such thing. No,' said Captain Beeny, drawing on his pipe with an air of calm sagacity, 'I'll tell you what it is, sir. There's a woman in the case.'

'Why, confound you, Beeny, he says nothing of the kind!' exploded Captain Coppinger, waving the letter about. 'Not a word!'

'That makes it more likely than ever. Depend upon it, Coppinger. There's a woman in the case.'

Captain Coppinger gave his friend a volcanic stare; blew out a long breath, and said, 'You may be in the right of it, Beeny. If there *is* a lady, then I'm glad for the boy. But I've a devilish strange feeling . . . Look here, Beeny! You know the feeling, when you're on the watch, and all's set fair, yet there's a taste to the wind that you don't quite like, and something about the swell on the sea that disturbs you, and your bones seem to tell you there's heavy weather ahead. You know it?'

'To a hair, sir!'

'Well, that's the feeling I have when I think of my boy now,' said Captain Coppinger, his voice dropping. 'I hope I may be wrong.'

Chapter Nine

Love In The Shadows

'There's a visitor here to see you,' said Ben Catbush, coming into the outhouse where Jed was chopping wood.

'A visitor?' said Jed absently: he could not think of any of the old and new friends he had amongst the villagers who would announce themselves in that way.

'He's waiting in the yard,' said Ben, his expressionless face quite as grainy as the timber beneath Jed's axe. 'I'll tell him you're on your way.'

Jed dusted himself down. It was nearly dusk, and he had been at work since soon after dawn – but he never seemed to feel tired nowadays, not that bone-jarring, life-sapping tiredness he used to feel after a day at the mill in Norwich. He went whistling out to the yard, his eye falling appreciatively on the new stable-roof, the hencoops and pig-pen. The work he and Ben had put in showed: it was all coming right; there was life here at Plague House.

A big-boned, well-groomed chestnut horse was tethered to a fence-post in the yard; and Jed's visitor, big-boned and well-groomed likewise, was standing near the back door of the house looking about him, his hands clasped beneath his coat-tails, riding-crop tucked in his boot. It was Elias Hemstock.

'Day to ye,' said Jed.

The farmer turned about to face him. The two men were roughly of a height, but Hemstock's way of thrusting his chin over his stiff collar gave him an air of looking down on Jed from above.

Hemstock said, 'I'll only take a few minutes of your time.'

'It's no matter,' said Jed. 'Will you step into the house?'

Hemstock shook his head. 'No need . . . You've got this place well set on its feet, it seems.'

'I reckon it'll do, with a bit more work.'

The two men regarded each other. So different as they were — Hemstock with his braced, unyielding look of stone-hewn pride, Jed with the quickness and vulnerability of his young mobile face — there was some resemblance between them at that moment: each was guarded to the ultimate degree.

'Well, I'll say it straight out,' said Hemstock. 'You've taken a lad on to work your fields, I hear.'

'Aye. Name of Tom Plummer, keenly lad.'

Hemstock dismissed the name with a curt wave of his hand. 'Whoever. Fact is, he used to work for me.'

'So I understand.'

'The whelp had the face to come to my bailiff and say he was leaving because he was going to work for Mr Wintergreen, where he could get two shillings a day,' said Hemstock. 'Is that right?'

'No,' said Jed with composure. 'I don't pay those starve-acre day-rates, where a man don't know whether he'll have work from one day to the next. Tom gets thirteen shilling a week, and extra in kind when I reap my first crop; and I shall hire him by the half-year do he take to the work.'

Elias Hemstock stared, hitching his great head higher: for the moment he seemed more startled than anything. 'Why, you're a fool!' he exclaimed.

'I don't see why,' said Jed. 'If a man's to work, he must eat well, and have a good fire at nights, and feel he's fairly done by. Ain't that so, Mr Hemstock?'

Hemstock did not answer for some moments: he was a man for whom heavy silences held no discomfort. At last he said: 'Now look you here, Wintergreen. You're new to this, otherwise you'd know better than to go luring away other men's hands. I'll pass that this time. But I'll tell you this — and I'm speaking to you now without regard to the past, and as one man of property to another — you'll do nothing but mischief paying this sort of wages. You'll make the labourers discontented: before you know it they'll be wanting a king's ransom before they'll lift a finger. Lord knows, it's difficult enough to get them to do a hand's turn as it is, without you coddling them and making them think they're born to feather beds and venison. We're a well-ordered little community here in Heartsease, nowadays; and I'm telling you, as a man of some influence here, that you'll make mischief, and people won't stand for it. I know Mr Ingamells, up at the Hall, would say the same.'

'I don't give a tinker's damn what Mr Ingamells would say,' said Jed. 'In the first place, it's no business of his. And in the second place, I'm not likely to forget the way he forced my mother out of her home, and had the cottage pulled down lest more poor folk should dare to want a roof over their heads. You say you're speaking without regard to the past, Mr Hemstock; but I'm not. That past made me: I can no more tear it out of my life than I can tear my own heart out of my breast. Just because I've come into property don't mean I forget what happened in Heartsease when I was a younker; and it don't mean I forget, or ever can forget, the part you played in it.' He had begun speaking quite coolly, but the memory of his mother with her sick wasted face, imploring him to remember, burned afresh in his mind, and his voice was not quite steady as he went on. 'You say you're a man of influence here: mebbe so, as far as wealth and power to bend folk to your will goes; but I mean to be a man of influence in Heartsease, too, in my way, Mr Hemstock. Mebbe you think you've got the people of this village so ground down as nothing'll ever raise 'em up again — paupers in all but name, picked like taters out of the pile when you've the need of 'em. Well, if I can rouse one crushed spirit, or remind one poor downtrodden hind that he's a free man with as much right to live as the next, then I'll do it. And as for luring workers away — aren't they free to sell their labour to whoever they will? Freedom of labour, thass the cant, isn't it? Though I dare say you'd take that freedom from them too, if you could.'

Elias Hemstock's big face was unmoved: only the quickness of his breathing showed how unused he was to being spoken to in this way.

'Well, I was prepared to give you a chance,' he said. 'I remember the past too, Wintergreen. I remember that father of yours, who thought himself too good for the laws of this country; and you don't know me, sir, if you think I've ever had a single moment of regret for turning him over to justice. Aye, justice,' he repeated as Jed was about to flare out, 'there's a deal too much of this silly-softness in the world, and talk of mercy and clemency: I don't believe in it; a man must take the consequences of his own actions. But like I say, I was quite prepared to give you a chance. That's why I came to speak to you today, man to man, rather than sending my bailiff. But I find that I've wasted my time — that you're Jacob Wintergreen's son all over.'

'You'll find, too, that I'm proud to be so,' said Jed; and added, with a sense of making a clean stroke, 'not everyone is ashamed of their forebears, Mr Hemstock.'

The farmer's face turned a livid red: the swift transformation to fury was the more alarming in that his actual expression did not alter. 'I say again, Wintergreen,' he said, his voice a soft rasp, 'you're a fool. It almost excuses your damned impudence, you're such a fool. Why, you're dooming yourself! Set yourself up as the champion of these shiftless villagers, and they'll rob you blind. They'll break you. But as you like — it will save me the trouble of doing so.' He struck his booted leg smartly, once, with his riding-crop, and went to his horse.

Jed watched him ride away. Then he returned to the outhouse, and resumed chopping wood. After a few minutes he gave it up: his hands were trembling wildly.

In the failing light he took a turn about his fields, cleared and drained now and ready for winter sowing. A great mass of unruly feeling was upon him, and he was trying to reason it away. There was nothing so very unexpected in what had just happened, after all. When he had come back to Heartsease he had brought with him a hatred of Hemstock: what he had seen and heard since his return had confirmed that hatred; and it was inevitable, given Hemstock's prominence in the village and his own declared sympathies, that they would come into conflict. In a way he had desired it. He had certainly never intended meeting in a forgiving spirit the man who had taken a reward for consigning his father to his death. The sword had always been half out of the sheath: now it was drawn. That was all.

Ah, but that was not all! Jed watched the dying day's sun make blazing crowns of the ancient pollards that bounded the field, and felt his life gliding into unknown regions, and penned about with ambiguous shapes. For even as the bitter words spoken between him and Hemstock re-echoed in his ears, as if to tune his hatred to highest pitch – even then, his heart was leaping forth to tomorrow, when he would hold Hemstock's daughter Marianne in his arms again.

Jed Wintergreen was a man who had taken possession of his dreams – long-cherished dreams, that reflected in their depths the very profile of his selfhood.

For some time after he had moved into Plague House and reclaimed his lost past he had not really seen Heartsease at all. So concrete was his treasured vision of the place that the reality had seemed almost insubstantial beside it. He moved about the village as if expecting to wake up any moment. Little by little, however, it was borne in on him that he was really here: little by little he had begun to compare the vision with the reality.

Physical changes there were: his parents' and the

Stricklands' cottages pulled down, several houses that had formerly contained the shops and workshops of small tradesmen reduced to the common cottage fate, and bearing now no boot-upper nailed to the doorpost or druggist's jars in the window to proclaim the modest independence of the inhabitants. There were continuities, too: faces familiar to him from his boyhood, some so changed with the years that they seemed to have caught Time like some disfiguring disease, others not altered in the least — such as that of Dick Freshwater, who still kept the Wheatsheaf public-house and acted as the village undertaker, so that beer-barrels stood alongside coffins in his yard, like two embodied views of the human condition; and whose phlegmatic greeting to Jed, after thirteen years, was, 'How dew, bor: you're back, then.'

But the important changes were those which would not be apparent to a traveller passing through the village — those which slowly and subtly impressed themselves on Jed through the days and weeks and months of residence in Heartsease, beginning to hear the special note of the little community, the timbre of its unique voice. He noticed the thread of religious fatalism that ran through their talk: they spoke of 'here below' and 'this side of the grave', as if life were a thing only to be endured; and he did not need to attend one of the Methodist revival meetings to understand the depths of feeling that the preachers stirred, and which was in such contrast to the indifference exhibited towards the parish church — that grey-white loveliness of flint and limestone, so typical of Norfolk, so admired by strangers, and so alien to many of the inhabitants of Heartsease in all it stood for that it might as well have been a mosque hoisting an exotic minaret above the chestnut trees. He noticed the dull inward look of men without work, as if they were resigned to a peripheral existence, looking in at the world from outside as if through a barred window. He noticed the unease and constraint that his own gentlemanly clothes elicited, before people knew who he was — the reluctant lowering look of a dog expecting a blow and knowing itself unable to resist. He noticed the neutral references to the slum-village of Pitchford — that place of gangmasters and pawn-shops that in his mind had always represented the inverse of Heartsease, the Bad Place where pride and self-respect perished. He noticed the frequent references among older inhabitants to sons and daughters who were gone — gone to the towns, gone to join the railway-builders, gone on the tramp looking for work. And he heard in all this a note of quietism, of inexpectation, of defeat — just as if the men who had stood up for their rights in 1830 had never existed.

But he heard another note, too — a harsh discord, though muted. It came chiefly from the youths and the young unmarried men of the village — the rootless ones, illiterate, thin-faced, hard-eyed, who saw nothing ahead of them but three or four days' work a week in Farmer Hemstock's fields when they could get it, and if they married only a cramped corner of their parents' cottage to make a home in. Jed was surprised to find, when his name and history became known, that these young men treated him with a respect he did not look for — that whereas the elder villagers, in their chastened, passive way, seemed to wish to forget the events of 1830, that time for their juniors assumed something of the heroic quality of legend. A tense resentment crackled around these young men like static electricity, and Jed began to understand the form it took when he heard two of them refer approvingly to a man of a neighbouring parish who had been charged with killing a gamekeeper. His own efforts to give these men work were rewarded with a fierce sort of loyalty, and with disturbing tokens of his acceptance by them — anonymous gifts of poached game left at his back door by night. Once or twice he tried to suggest, discreetly, that grateful as he was, he didn't like to think of the risk they were running — everyone knew how severe Mr Ingamells was on poaching. 'Risk?' said one, a violent glitter in his eyes. 'Why, friend, thass part of the pleasure. They'd have us all just as meek as lambs – not men at all – as you well know; and when I take the risk, thass when I feel properly alive-like – thass when I feel like a man for once, 'stead of yes-sir no-sir beggen-your-pardon-for-living-sir to ole Hemstock and Ingamells and every last bastard of 'em. I'd risk it to have meat in the pot once in a way – but I'll risk it twice over just for the pleasure of't – just for very hate of the bastards.'

This saddened Jed: saddened him particularly because sometimes he could see a little of himself in these young men – the aspiration and energy all turned to a taut frustration. There was much, indeed, about Heartsease that might have saddened him, and curdled the sweet triumph of his return into a sour disillusionment. Yet it was not so. The righting of his own wrongs had given him access to wells of hope so deep as to seem inexhaustible: the sight of so much apathy and resignation only increased his buoyancy. For he remembered all that his mother had bidden him remember – not just the injustices of 1830, but the fact that better, fairer times had existed once. And so for Jed there was no question of merely savouring the satisfaction of his establishment at Plague House; the light of a crusade was shed over Heartsease, and he sought to change things in the village for the better.

The sheer fact of his presence was a start in awakening people's minds. The Wintergreens had been ploughed up like so many weeds: yet here was a Wintergreen returned, a visible defiance of powers that had seemed beyond resisting. And he soon made it clear that he had not put on the attitudes of the masters along with his new suit of clothes. The raising of wages and reversion to long-hire that had scandalized Elias Hemstock were innovations naturally limited in their scope by the number of people he could employ on his own small farm; but as Hemstock had foreseen the effect would spread outward like ripples in a pond. And Jed made his influence felt in a score of other ways. He was no lawyer himself, but he had a very capable one – Mr Veazey at Norwich – whom he consulted on the villagers' behalf on plentiful occasions; and he overcame with his energy their doubts about having recourse to a law which had always appeared to them, with some reason, as their enemy. He made no purchases from Norwich, but relied for supplies exclusively on village dealers and craftsmen, so many of whom were slipping down the slope towards becoming just another element of the under-employed workforce dependent on the fields. And he sought too to further his ends through his friendship with Mr Ringrose of the Grange. That easy-going gentleman often ambled over to Plague House to take an absent-minded view of the property and whistlingly reminisce about the old rakish days when Beau Brummell boasted of having once eaten a pea; and Jed was quick to take advantage of Mr Ringrose's, as he said, 'inclining to the liberal side of the question'. He encouraged his landlord to oppose his weight to that of Mr Ingamells and Farmer Hemstock in parish matters, and to press for more clemency and generosity at meetings of the Poor Law Guardians. Dearest to Jed's heart was a scheme, which Mr Ringrose cautiously promised to look into, of letting small allotments of Grange land to cottagers, so that they might keep a cow or grow vegetables; and he engaged to subsidize the first year's rents, until they should begin to pay their way. 'A very taking suggestion, indeed,' said Mr Ringrose. 'I'm all in favour of that sort of thing, you know – gives a man self-respect, and so forth. Yes, I shall certainly look into it.' And though Jed sometimes despaired of Mr Ringrose's ever moving on from looking to doing, the core of vibrant hope within him remained untouched. Nor was he put off by the scepticism of Rosa who, whenever he spoke of changing Heartsease, seemed carefully to refrain from comment whilst being unable to banish a sort of admiring pity from her dark eyes.

No, nothing could daunt or discourage him: he stood

in a new relation to a world that had often seemed to him a vast refined engine of cruelty in which men struggled to a slow destruction. He appreciated the very sensation of being alive, the beat of his own heart and the pulse of his own moving blood. And as if this were not enough Jed was, besides, in love for the first time in his life.

He had never meant it to happen: had, indeed, resisted it. His new life was already full enough; and if, in the old dreams he had dreamt in the Norwich weaver's garret, the longed-for scenes of Heartsease had often been made yet sweeter by the presence of a vague figure to which his heart was yoked like the tide to the moon, still once established in the reality he had been conscious of no lack or longing. And then – how had it happened? He had met Marianne Hemstock, and at some point had crossed over into love, like stepping over an invisible border between two countries.

No, he had never meant it to happen; though looking back to the day Marianne had come to Plague House, when together they had watched the last fledgling fly the nest beneath the eaves, he seemed to see an inevitability about it. Yet that was the same day of the revelation – the revelation that should surely have nipped love in the bud. Her name was Hemstock. Elias Hemstock was her father. To the man whose callous hand had shaped so much of his life's unhappy course Marianne owed love and duty; in the pretentious house of that man, founded and built on the impoverishment of better men, Marianne had been brought up. His reaction when she had casually told him her name in the hall of Plague House had been swiftly covered up, he thought – a stare, a few moments' silence, and he had recovered himself – but inside he was in turmoil: he seemed to feel his very soul flinch.

And yet that in itself told his tale. Had he thought nothing of the girl, he would have thought nothing of her being a Hemstock. Instead, the revelation brought him smartly to an awareness of how drawn he was to her, how bewitched he was by the quick uncertain tones of her voice, how the glint in her eye reminded him of dew on branches and morning rain and everything that was fresh. His own recent resurrection – he thought of it as no less – had brought to Jed a vivid appreciation of vitality, and in Marianne he saw above all an abundance of life, transparent as the veins in a mayfly's wing.

And as he had talked with her in the new-paint-smelling parlour of Plague House that day – and when she returned on subsequent days, staying longer each time – Jed had experienced a sensation of recognition. Marianne's life had been one long cosseting, his a browbeaten struggle, yet there was a fundamental resemblance between them: they were unsure of their own identities. Abel Jex's legacy had transported Jed from poverty to comfort at one blow, and an awkward discordance persisted between the raw self-taught man and the circumstances in which he found himself; and it was obvious to Jed – and somehow it quickened his love for her to see it – that Marianne was not quite at home with her own gentility, and that she walked an insecure path of self-doubt through a world in which her place was uncertain.

Most baffling and wonderful of all, Jed found mirrored in her his own pervasive sense of aloneness, of having been set down on earth lacking some crucial capacity that every other mortal was safely in possession of. Something she said reminded him piercingly of his own nocturnal walks about Norwich, seeing the lit windows excluding him. 'When I was at Clapham, I sometimes had the strangest fancy,' she told him, 'that if I was to walk into those houses about the Common – those houses where I saw ordinary people going to and fro about their business – and begin to speak to them, and tell who I was, and what I did from day to day, and what was in my heart by way of little wants and wishes – if I was simply to say that, they would look at me with no more understanding than if I were a Chinaman, gabbling away in a foreign tongue – and I would go on from house to house and person to person, and meet the same look from everyone, for ever and ever!' So transfixed was he that, hardly knowing what he did, he seized her hand and kissed her for the first time; and feeling the tiny ticking pulse of the blood in her fingertips pressed against his own, he marvelled again. Mirrored: they were mirrored.

And so Marianne came to Plague House almost every day; and she and Jed unwound from themselves an endless twine of talk. They were romantics, and there was a sort of rapt, holy seriousness about them: neither smiled nor scoffed when the other spoke of rising at midnight and going out from sheer aching pressure of the heart to feel the starlit silence surround and dwarf them, or of gazing at a beautiful picture and longing with the clenched intensity of a child to step into it.

'I've always wished — no, felt — that someone existed, somewhere in the world, who understood,' she said, 'almost as if we were together before we were born, and then we were separated, and now I must hope somehow to find that person again amongst all the people of the world . . . And then at school old Miss Dobie said that Plato or somebody had thought of that, hundreds and hundreds of years ago — and I said to myself, I don't care what those old dead Greeks thought. It's what *you* feel in your own heart that matters — you can't look at the world through any eyes but your own . . . Oh, you do see, don't you, Jed?'

He scarcely needed to answer, so closely did this gospel of pure Romanticism, though he did not know it as such, correspond with his own. But he poured out his own dreams to her, and hardly noticed how different they were in matter from her own — her visions of travel, of Paris and glitter and gaiety, sharing with his own devotion to his spot of native ground only their spirit of longing and intensity; and so day succeeded day, and their hours together seemed to compress themselves into so many minutes, and they would come dazed out of their

226

talk to throw wild disbelieving glances at the clock.

It was not difficult for Marianne to visit Jed. Her father's insistence on her gentility meant she had whole days with nothing to do except go, ostensibly, for long walks. They could rely entirely on the discretion of faithful Ben Catbush, who was not, as the local saying went, fond of gape-seed, and who would not have twitched a muscle of his ship's-figurehead of a face if his master had been entertaining the Queen and all her ladies-in-waiting in his parlour; but in a village as ridden with gossip as a cheese with mites, it was necessary that Marianne approach the house via the fields at the rear, so as not to be seen entering it from the lane. Usually she rather relished this secrecy, which had the cardinal attraction in her eyes of not being humdrum; but one rainy day found a mood of despondency upon her, and she sighed, pouted, walked restlessly about the parlour, and at last burst out: 'How I hate creeping about, and forever being so furtive, as if I were a criminal! Really, it's not fair!'

'Never mind, my dear,' said Jed, taking her hand. 'You're here now.'

'Oh, I know I'm here now,' she said, withdrawing her hand, and shaking out her skirts, 'but my dress is a foot deep in mud from those wretched fields, and probably ruined, and will no doubt get ruined twice over when I walk back.'

'Why, thass only a dress,' he said soothingly, with an unerring masculine instinct for saying precisely the wrong thing at the wrong time; and a quarrel swiftly took shape between them, over nothing at all, and terminated in her leaving in a sort of seething coolness, with no indication of her ever returning again.

She did, the very next day — but in the interim Jed knew agonies of an intensity such as he had thought only physical pain could achieve. He paced and paced the fields, feeling that to be still was death, until his muscles cried out: he tortured himself with a thousand conjectures as to what she was thinking, all of which seemed appallingly to open on to a barren tract of future without her. And then the profound joy of their reunion and reconciliation — in which they both said a hundred ardent variations of sorry in the breathless interstices of as many kisses — was enough almost to make quarrels desirable, and more than enough to confirm to Jed that he was in love — deeply in love, in over his head — and wanting never to get out.

So, the day following his clash with Mr Hemstock, Jed waited impatiently as usual for his tryst with Mr Hemstock's daughter Marianne. The terrible discordance of such a state of affairs was not lost on him — but then it never had been, right from the start. When he held her in his arms, and inhaled the scent of her hair, he had no thought of who her father was, and the bitter history that both joined and severed them. But when he was apart from her, his mind sometimes stood back, and saw the situation in all its aspects, and he would come across a wry little twist in feelings that were passionately straightforward.

Why, for instance, could he not confide the fact of his being marvellously in love to his good friend Pierce, of whose discretion there was no doubt? Was it because Pierce knew his history too well, knew his hatred of Elias Hemstock and the vengeful resentment he had carried, preserved with pristine freshness, for fourteen years?

It was almost as if he were ashamed, and he had nothing to be ashamed of. He loved Marianne, loved the individual girl irrespective of any of the threads that joined her to the great web of the world. There was not an atom of falsehood in that. Yet there was, undeniably, a grain of something else. Jed had retained a curious sort of innocence through a very hard passage in life, and as a consequence was utterly unskilled at lying to himself. And so he could not deny the existence of that little contaminating grain in the pure substance of his love for Marianne Hemstock — the knowledge that through her he could revenge himself on her father.

The grain had not been present from the beginning — that he honestly believed. But coming to know Marianne, coming to know of her through the common talk of the village, coming to know Hemstock again likewise, Jed had begun to see the outlines of a wonderful retribution forming before him — a retribution of such superbly ironic fitness that it almost seemed that an amused Fate was admiring its handiwork as it shaped it. Hemstock's ambitions for Marianne were well known: the education he had given her, the money he lavished on her, the sedulous attention he paid to the high-born Bouveries with whom she might connect him — all proclaimed the drift of his hopes, and signified to the world that Elias Hemstock was not content to rest on the heights to which he had so ruthlessly climbed, but meant to mount higher by means of the lovely daughter whom he had made into a lady. Hemstock, in his pride and his disdain for the vulgar, did not care who knew this; and it was plain too in the person of Marianne, in her slightly self-conscious poise, her air of being on show and of anxiety to make the correct impression. All this Jed saw with a keen eye and, even as his very soul was gripped by love for Marianne, he was aware that the opportunity of a grim triumph had been placed in his hand: that their every kiss was a dent to Elias Hemstock's pride; that he might thwart the man he detested, and bring all his vain ambitions tumbling to the ground.

For Jed could not destroy Hemstock as Hemstock had destroyed his poor father, could not oppose power and wealth to his. The man was as firmly fixed in the world as a deep-rooted oak in heavy soil. Yet his daughter was his weak spot. There he could be struck, and struck hard. He had placed so much of his aspirations in her alone: a prestigious marriage was the very thing to consolidate his status. And Jed saw that for Hemstock to lose her to the son of Jacob Wintergreen — to the upstart son of a lawless incendiary, as he would have it — to the man who was determined on opposing everything he stood for in Heartsease − would be a blow that would shake the arrogant man to the depths of his being.

The fitness of it − that was what was so mesmerically appealing! And that fitness might be seen, too, as part of a chain of vindication. Abel Jex's legacy had righted the Wintergreens' wrong − now came the chance to punish the wrongdoer. It was like the turning of a great slow wheel of justice. So Jed told himself, at moments when some new account of Hemstock's insolent harshness reached his ears. Yet at other times he tried to quash the revengeful voice within him. He suspected there was poison in it. After all he was well-fed, happy, in love. His beloved sister Charlotte, though she still insisted she could not leave Shipden and the Skeels yet and join him, was comfortable and free from want. Life was good. If he could not forgive, he might at least forget.

But forget was what Jed could not do. He was blessed and burdened with a peculiar vividness of mental conception. He could not forget his mother's haggard eyes, he could not forget the workhouse and Charlotte's bewildered face beneath her cropped hair as she was marched off in file with other little girls away from him; he could not forget the last, resigned, uncomplaining letter from his father in the hulks before they had taken him away to die unmourned upon an alien shore. Because he could not forget these things, he could not remove that tiny grain from his feelings for Marianne Hemstock. The thought of thwarting her father's plans lined his mind like fur on the inside of a kettle.

It was all the more confusing in that he could see nothing of Hemstock in her. She had her vanities, certainly, but they seemed to proceed from diffidence rather than pride; her little affectations likewise, but they were thrown off as easily as her bonnet, and then the spontaneity of her nature shone through like sunlight between leaves. And it was this element that came to the fore when she arrived at Plague House the day after Jed's altercation with her father. There was a playfully devilish look about her. She found him in the still-room, checking some casks of home-brewed table-beer, and as he stood up from replacing the bung he felt a movement in his waistcoat pocket.

'Marianne,' he said, 'have you got my keys?'

'What would I want with your old keys?'

'Show me your hand.'

'I will not, sir.'

He made a dart at her. She skipped away, laughing, then caught him to her with her arms round his neck.

'Are you sure you don't have your keys somewhere about you?' she said with her lips brushing his face. 'Sure?'

'Now how — Oh!' he cried, as something cold and hard slid down his neck and slithered down his spine — she had slipped the bunch of keys down the back of his collar.

'There — that'll cure your hiccoughs,' she said, laughing as he wriggled to extricate the keys from his shirt.

'I haven't got hiccoughs!'

'Your sore nose then.'

'I haven't got a sore nose neither!'

'Now you have,' she said, giving his nose a sharp tweak and dancing away from him.

'You are a plaguey woman!' said Jed, as the keys fell out. ''Tis worse than a ped o' kittens!'

'Plaguey old woman of Plague House,' Marianne sang.

Jed caught her and kissed her. 'Plaguey — but not old. Fresh as a daisy. Fresher,' he said, sniffing her skin.

'Well, have a care for my petals, sir!' she said as he squeezed her tight. 'Good heavens, what brutes you men are. And now I suppose you want another kiss. There's two for you then. Oh, Jed, do your dance again!'

'What dance?'

'When the keys were down your shirt. You did such a

funny jig. Just like a Highland fling. Oh, Jed, let's dance! I feel like dancing.'

'I've never danced in my life.'

'Oh, it's easy. I'll teach you. Come on — all we need is a clear floor. That big spare room of yours.'

She sprang up the stairs, he following, to a bare-boarded room at the back of the house that he had recently cleared of lumber. A beam of sunlight, entering at the narrow window, lay athwart the dusty room with as clear a definition as if it were a fallen column.

'Not much of a ballroom,' he said.

'Oh, you must use your imagination. Picture the chandeliers, and the pier-glasses, and all the silk and satin — can't you just? And smell the perfumes and the flowers—'

'I can smell something,' he said, 'but I think it's mildew.'

'Now, Jed, behave! Look — these are the steps of the waltz. Triple time, one two-two one two-two. You place your left hand in mine, so, and your right hand here—'

'Hm, I like this dance already.'

'You are provoking! Now watch my feet. One two-two, one two-two, turn this way—'

'We've no music. There need to be music playing.'

'You must hear it in your head. I'm always doing that. Oh, sometimes at school, when the music-mistress would play some specially lovely piece on the piano, I used to hear it still in my head for days afterwards . . . And then I would try to play the same music myself, but it would never, never come out as beautiful as the music I heard in my head . . . Oh, Jed, why is that always so? Why do our dreams always fall short? Why does the real world never quite measure up to them?'

'It can, you know,' he said earnestly. 'It must. We must *make* it do so, Marianne — else why are we alive?'

'I believe it when you say it,' said she. 'When I'm with you, I believe it . . . Ah, but when I'm alone . . .!'

He studied her eyes; and abruptly said, with a feeling

of a cloud passing across the sun, 'Marianne, your father came to see me yesterday.'

'Oh?' she said dreamily, then, 'Oh!'

'No – twasn't about us. He don't know, I'm sure of that. He was mardy about me taking on one of his labourers to work here, and paying a higher wage and all . . . We quarrelled.'

'Oh dear,' said Marianne, soberly enough, but with a light about her face that suggested that the idea of her lover and her father quarrelling, considered in the light of a dramatic tableau without bearing on current actuality, was not unappealing.

'I felt I should tell you,' Jed said. 'Especially as – well, we never mention him, do we?'

'Why should we?'

'You know why.' He suddenly wanted to face the situation in all its ambiguities, perhaps disentangle the mixed knot of his own feelings in the matter. 'You know why I – I can never think well of him. The things that happened in the past.'

'But, Jed, I can't help that! You surely can't blame me – I would undo it if I could, but how can I—'

'No, no,' he said, kissing her. 'Tisn't that. All I'm saying is, your father and I are – well, enemies is the only word for it. D'you see?'

Her eyes were fixed very solemnly on his for a moment; then she closed them, and leaning her smooth brow on his shoulder began swaying in a waltzing motion again. 'Well,' she said, 'it was always so, wasn't it? Our meeting like this – it was never proper, never a right thing to do. Oh, let's not think about it, Jed. My father and you with your quarrels – what has that got to do with the two of us? We're safe here – let the whole world go to blazes.'

'I wish it could,' he said.

'So it can. Close your eyes, Jed, and it does. Try it. Close your eyes with me now, and feel it all go away.'

He closed his eyes, his arms around her, feeling himself surrender. When he opened them again he found her regarding him with a slight smile.

'You peeped,' she said.

'So did you.'

She laughed with a flicker of warm lips against his face, and he laughed too. 'That's better,' she said. 'Don't be an old grave-airs, Jed. Not today. Feel how warm that sunshine is.' She was in her most feline mood, turning her face up to the shaft of sun exactly like a cat: she seemed to savour existence through her very pores. He gazed at her, and the sunlight on her pure blonde hair and her lazy glinting smile made of her an uncomplicated being, clear-eyed and aglow, all delight; and all his shadowy doubts and misgivings seemed to dissolve.

'It isn't the sunshine,' he said. 'It's you. Those rays shine out of you, Marianne. All golden.'

He felt the beat of her eyelashes on his cheek.

'I wish we might sit down,' she murmured.

There was a palpable moment of silence, like a single translucent drop in the muddied stream of time.

'We could go into the next room,' he said.

She leaned against him. 'Yes, let's go into the next room.'

Elias Hemstock's modern Norfolk farm was an enterprise of so large a scale that many an urban manufactory was modest in comparison with it. The stables were large enough for a coaching inn, and the farm had as many wheeled vehicles as the rest of the village put together. There were several broad Anglian waggons, the first-raters of the fleet, a dozen or so carts that tug-like performed the smaller offices of the farm, a market-cart of slightly more suavity of design, and a smart gig in which the family made social journeys. It was in this gig, one crisp nut-brown morning in early autumn, that Marianne found herself feeling so sick that there was no possibility of disguising it any longer.

The sickness had been occurring rather frequently of late. It was unusual for Marianne, who enjoyed the strongest of health. But she had thought little of it for the simple reason that her whole equilibrium had been shaken since the early summer: she had been living all this time like a person in a low fever, with that peculiar cottony feeling of separation from the everyday world, and something disordered and hectic in her blood.

For the excitement that she craved had entered her life at last. Another girl might have mourned that love should come to her so fraught with secrecy and difficulty. But for Marianne the clandestine element of her romance with Jed Wintergreen intensified precisely that: the romance of it. Indeed, she could not conceive any worthwhile notion of love that was not lit with the flickering tapers of drama. And she was indeed consumedly in love with Jed: a huge potential for emotion seemed to have been fulfilled in her at last. As hers was a nature that did not acknowledge consistency as a desirable condition of mind, she found no difficulty in deceiving her father – no discomfort in passionately loving Jed and at the same time loving her father as of old. She had no sense of being pulled in contrary ways. Only occasionally, when young Mr Bouverie called to resume his ponderous courting of her, did she glimpse the true perilous nature of her position, and wonder at the headlong course on which she was blindly careering. For her father was exerting himself greatly to further the match he had set his heart on: she believed he had already spoken to the rector about it and had received a favourable response; and it seemed that it was only the monumental circumspection of Roland Bouverie that prevented Mr Hemstock from having the banns called at once, and driving the pair to church himself.

But these times when Marianne forced herself to stop and think about what was happening were few. For one thing, she did not believe in the virtues of stopping and thinking generally: the sudden inspiration, the unpremeditated impulse of the heart, were the articles of her faith. And for another, she was simply too hungry for experience to worry her head over moral niceties. She was well aware that she had always been impatient. Once when a child she had been promised as a birthday-treat a trip to Norwich to see a play at the theatre, and had been found early on the birthday morning in the coach-house, asleep on the strawy seat of the gig that was to take her. And this summer, in the cramped dissatisfaction and tedium of her life back at Heartsease, baulked of loftier dreams of conquest in opera-boxes and Parisian salons, her impatience had been such that she flew to Jed Wintergreen as if to slake a mortal thirst. In her impatience she had despaired of ever finding someone who shared her restless ache of soul and body, and finding in Jed Wintergreen precisely that focus for her longing which had been so elusive, she had impatiently clutched at him, and impatiently she counted the hours until they could be together again.

And the same impatience, she supposed, had led her to cross the threshold of Jed's bedroom, and make the irrevocable commitment that brought the temple of her genteel upbringing crashing down. She could not have precisely said why she did it, or how much her conscious will was involved, beyond a vague but ardent conviction that theirs must not be a love of half-measures, must be grander, wilder, more fateful. Perhaps too her ability to seal experience off into separate compartments came to her aid: that strange consummation in the quiet summer-soaked bedroom of Plague House was a thing of itself, without consequences . . . Except that now she feared, as she jogged along in the gig with her brother Herbert and knew she was going to be sick, that it did have consequences, and momentous ones indeed.

She made Herbert pull up the gig, and managed to jump down and get to the bushes at the side of the road just in time.

'Hmm,' Herbert said. 'They even taught you to be sick like a lady at Clapham, apparently.'

Marianne wiped her mouth with her handkerchief.

'Herbert,' she said, 'I don't think I feel up to going to Swaffham today.' They were supposed to be going there to get some shopping for Mrs Hemstock.

'I should think not,' Herbert said. 'You look as white as a lily. Feel any better for the, ahem, evacuation?'

'A little,' she said. 'Let's go home, please.'

'Perhaps it's something you ate. Though Lord knows you're a finicky enough eater. More than ever lately.'

She glanced at Herbert's ugly clever face. That ironical expression was so habitual with him it was hard to tell whether he was guessing at the truth.

Which she could no longer ignore, good as she was at doing so. It was no further use telling herself that missing her courses didn't mean anything as she had always been a little irregular . . . It was all too certain.

Herbert turned the gig about, and they headed home again. Home! There was the terrible core of her predicament. The alarm of finding herself pregnant, with all that it meant for her life in the long term, was a huge but ill-defined shape on the edge of her consciousness: her central fear, now that the unthinkable had been faced, was of the immediate reaction of her parents. Most of all, her father. All the many fond possessive attentions he had paid her seemed to pass in a rapid volley before her mind's eye; accompanied, haphazardly, by images of contempt and disgrace − a scene in a play in which a man threw a girl's portrait on the fire, haymakers singing a bawdy ballad about a farmer's daughter tumbled in the corn, herself and the other girls craning over the banisters at school to see a kitchen-maid turned out of the house for the ultimate crime . . .

She fought down another wave of sickness. What was she to do? Perhaps first of all she should tell Jed. Jed Wintergreen . . . She recalled his words about the enmity between himself and her father, and the way she had dismissed them. What has that to do with us . . .

'To the farmer's pretty daughter a-tumbled in the corn . . .' How did it go? The song tripped its mocking

237

measure round and round her head. Farmer Hemstock's daughter . . . How her father hated to be called Farmer Hemstock! He said it had a low sound.

She remembered her father reminding himself he must write a letter to young Mr Bouverie today . . .

'If you like,' Herbert said carefully, not looking at her, 'I could say we're coming back because the pony cast a shoe or something.'

She could not answer: only shook her head.

But when they drew up in the yard, and her mother, actually deserting her perennial seat in the parlour, came in surprise to the door, Marianne wished that she had accepted Herbert's suggestion and clothed herself even temporarily in a comfortable lie.

'Ill?' Mrs Hemstock said. 'Why, I cannot imagine what you can have to be ill about, child. If you were to endure one of my heads, even for the space of a minute, then you might talk of being ill. But, have it as you will. I declare the young girls nowadays make a great fuss about their health — my poor papa, the Major, always disliked that sort of sickliness extremely.'

Marianne escaped as quickly as she could to her own room; but Mrs Hemstock, apparently piqued at someone else poaching on the preserves of ill-health which she considered hers to enjoy alone, put herself to the unprecedented trouble of climbing the stairs, and walking straight into her daughter's room with a face expressive both of displeasure and of a meek resignation to the fact that pleasure was not her lot.

Marianne was lying down. Mrs Hemstock registered this with a lifting of the eyebrows, as if to say that lying down was very nice she was sure, and she only wished her many duties would allow her to do it once in a while.

'Well, my child, this is a sad turn,' Mrs Hemstock said, seating herself by the bed and folding her net-mittened hands together with a look of patiently awaiting her execution by, at the very least, breaking on the wheel. 'The inconvenience to myself in being denied those articles which I had hoped you would be good enough to purchase today is, of course, as nothing beside my concern for you — and as to the impossibility of my sleeping a wink tonight without the tonic wine you were to bring, I will not even allude to it.'

'I'm very sorry, Mama,' Marianne answered faintly. 'It will pass off, I dare say — I just didn't feel equal to the journey, really.'

'I am a great nuisance, I know, and no doubt it is quite right that I should be told so by my children,' said Mrs Hemstock, 'but I hope I may not be accused of utter indifference to their welfare — though if I am, of course, I must bear it.'

'Oh, Mama,' Marianne burst out, sitting up and taking her mother's bird-boned hand, 'don't be all stiff with me — please don't, not now, for I feel so very wretched, and — and—' All at once she was crying. She hadn't meant this to happen; but she longed for comfort, and though it was to her father that she had always looked for love, Mrs Hemstock generally considering her daughter a fit subject for tenderness only insofar as she was a sort of annex of her self, this was different.

'Well, my dear,' said her mother, 'no doubt I am a very harsh parent, and it's quite right I should be reproached in this fashion.'

'Oh, Mama, I don't reproach you!'

'No, Marianne: it is quite right that you do so; for a woman who suffers such heads as I do — and who is sometimes obliged to bite upon a handkerchief in order not to cry out with the pain of them, out of consideration for the feelings of her family — ought surely to sympathize with the sufferings of illness, however minor.' Mrs Hemstock absently stroked her daughter's head. 'Now I have a suspicion what is behind this. It was that veal we had yesterday. One would suppose, from the amount they eat, and the wages they demand, that kitchen domestics would take a little pride in their duties, and not send up ill-cooked meats, but I am afraid it is not so in these times, my dear. It must have been that: I myself have felt no symptoms beyond those which are so commonly my lot as to be barely worth mentioning, but then I ate very little of the veal, my constitution, as you know, forbidding me even the slightest enjoyment of the pleasures of the table.'

'It wasn't the veal, Mama.'

'No? Perhaps you are right, child — for you have a pleasingly small appetite yourself; that's the breed coming through; your grandpapa, the Major, always used to say there was nothing so ill-bred as gormandizing in a woman, and he was so abstemious himself that he went all through the Peninsula without tasting condiments, and was known as the Spartan Man of the 43rd. No — I know what it is — you have caught some sort of chill, from the draughts in the parlour. The servants will leave the back door open, not to mention treading all manner of unwholesome dirt into the house; a regrettable consequence, I am afraid, of living on a Farm — and really it is a wonder, surrounded by beasts, and soil, and so forth, as we are, that we do not all go down with something nasty every day — though your father, of course, is used to it.'

At the mention of her father Marianne gave a moan. 'It's not a chill, Mama,' she said. 'I — I know what it is.'

'Indeed? Well, Marianne, I dare say you may do, quite as well as Dr Bryant — he has never alleviated my sufferings in the slightest degree, and is apt to speak of them in quite a dismissive tone, scarcely appropriate, one would have thought, to a man whose father kept a livery stable—Why, child, whatever is the matter?'

Marianne was pressing her mother's hand to her face. 'I know what it is, Mama,' she repeated. 'I know what it is — and I can't say it . . .'

Mrs Hemstock was silent for several moments.

'That is not possible, child,' she said at last.

Marianne, unable to speak, shook her head.

'Marianne! Tell me at once it is not possible, or I am

afraid my nerves will give way altogether!'

'It's true, Mama. Oh, don't be angry, please—'

Mrs Hemstock withdrew her hand and, starting up, clasped it to her forehead. 'My constitution will not be equal to this,' she groaned. 'I can feel one of my megrims coming on already. Marianne, Marianne, how could you? Thank God your grandpapa, the Major, is not here to see this day! He received a piece of grapeshot the size of a muffin in the shoulder at the siege of Badajoz which would have killed a lesser man, and as a consequence was never able to open an umbrella with any degree of ease — but this! — this would have hastened him to the grave directly! And I fear I shall follow him — I know I shall!'

'Mama, I never meant it to happen . . . But it has.'

Mrs Hemstock interrupted another groan to regard Marianne steadily for a moment. 'Is there no possibility of a mistake, child?'

'No,' said Marianne.

Her mother closed her eyes. 'It is not for us to question the purposes of Providence, otherwise I might wonder what I have done to deserve so many cruel burdens. I am afraid I shall sink under this one, but I hope I shall not complain. I shall not even reproach you, Marianne, with being the probable murderer of a parent who believed, till now, that she had done her duty in bringing you up decently . . . I cannot say any more now — I must go to a dark room.'

'Mama! Wait, please! Are you going to tell Papa?'

'He will have to know, Marianne.' Mrs Hemstock looked at her daughter with a certain hard speculation glinting through the self-pity. 'And we will have to know the name of the man.'

'I — I am in love with him,' Marianne said. 'I just couldn't tell you—'

'His name, child.'

'Jed Wintergreen.'

The remainder of the day presented itself to Marianne as

a succession of splintered impressions, through all of which the bawdy song about the farmer's daughter circled in her head.

Soon after her mother left her Herbert came and tapped on the door to see how she was, and she scribbled a note and begged him to take it to Jed Wintergreen at Plague House. He lifted an eyebrow, and seemed, as so often, to see through and through her; but he made no comment, and did as she asked.

At some point in the day her father burst into her room. All the bull-like strength of his nature appeared, terribly, in the way he flung open the door so that it rebounded off the wall, and advanced so that his scarlet face was within a few inches of hers; yet curiously she was not afraid. Somehow she knew that not even this could lift that willed restraint from him. Perhaps too she knew that if he were to strike her, or rage at her, he would be destroying what it had been his life's ambition to build — he would be the boorish bumpkin farmer, belabouring the daughter tumbled in the corn. She saw the struggle in his face, and stepped outside herself sufficiently to pity him.

'I never meant to bring any disgrace on you, Papa,' she said, 'never, for a moment — how could I, when you've always done so much for me, when you've always been so dear to me? It wasn't like that. I fell in love, and I couldn't help it—'

'Say it's not true, Marianne,' said Mr Hemstock. His voice was quite quiet: in a less self-regarding man, the pain would have been audible in it. 'Say it isn't Wintergreen — just say that, and I'll be calm — say it isn't him, and I promise I won't be angry, and we can work something out together, and—'

He did not finish — did not need to. Her face said everything. A moment later he was gone.

And then — when from her window she could see the sun tucked into a fold of cloud on the horizon like a watch into a fob-pocket, and the humblest field-gates were throwing almighty shadows of themselves right across the stubble-fields, and the day seemed to have gone on for ever – her father was summoning her downstairs, and she found herself sitting like a stranger in the parlour, with her mother in her usual place behind the fire-screen, and her father glaring at her from the hearth.

'Marianne,' he said, 'it has occurred to your mother that you were forced.'

'Mr Hemstock,' said her mother, 'I am a great nuisance I know, but the present circumstances already being unbearable to such a degree that my head feels as if it were in a vice, I must ask you not to use expressions that only my wifely duty prevents me from calling coarse.'

Mr Hemstock bit his lip. 'Marianne,' he said, 'will you tell us the whole truth of the matter?'

'It wasn't like that at all,' said Marianne. A peculiar composure came over her: she felt as if she were talking in her sleep. 'I've been meeting Jed Wintergreen at Plague House: we met up quite by accident, and so I got into the habit of going there, and talking, and little by little we fell in love. I didn't want to deceive you – I didn't want to be underhand, and neither did Jed, but it had to be secret, because of – well, because of the way things are.'

Mr Hemstock was exerting so strenuous a control over himself that his very breathing was shallow. 'You know that man's history?'

'Yes.'

'And that makes no difference to you? Your father's feelings make no difference to you? The education you have had, the care that has been lavished on you so that you might go into any society with your head high – the attention of a gentleman such as young Mr Bouverie, that I was at such pains to engage on your behalf, and that promised fair to place you in a station that any other girl would have been proud of? All that makes no difference to you?'

'It isn't that, Papa. It's not that I love you and Mama any less. I am grateful, truly—'

'Ah, grateful! I'm glad!' said Mr Hemstock, his voice just beginning to rise, as though tight bonds were fraying. 'The sort of gratitude, apparently, that makes a girl who has lacked for nothing throw everything her father's done for her back in his face, and make him the laughing-stock of half a county, and undo everything he's worked for since he was no higher than that stool! I like that sort of gratitude, Marianne – the sort that makes a well-brought-up girl lift her skirts for any rabble-born upstart that asks her—'

'Mr Hemstock,' interposed his wife, in a voice remarkably sharp and crisp for an invalid, 'I must ask you finally to moderate your language, if you wish me to take any further part in an interview which is already so painful to my nerves as to render insensibility a likely prospect.'

Mr Hemstock breathed out a loud deep-chested breath, but did not protest: he was a little shocked by his own lapse, and he prowled about the room for a moment before going on in a lower tone: 'Does he know?'

Marianne swallowed. 'I wrote him – today.' She wondered what Jed was thinking.

'It's impossible, of course,' her father grunted.

'What's impossible?'

'Why, that you should see him any more.' Mr Hemstock resumed his pacing, his arms loose by his sides. He had often this look of being somewhat embarrassed about the hands, for he would never allow himself to put them in his pockets. 'God knows the fellow ought to be accountable for what he's done, but that's out of the question. If Ringrose wasn't such a soft-minded jelly of a man, I'd ask him to turn Wintergreen out, but there's no talking to him – he's got a tenderness for these troublemakers—'

'But Papa – don't you see?' cried Marianne. 'I love Jed—'

'Don't use that name to me! I won't hear it!' Mr Hemstock barely opened his lips for this: his fury, like so much about him, was not unruly − simply a sort of colourless extract of will. 'I can't undo what's done, God knows, but I'll see it goes no further!'

'My dear Mr Hemstock,' said her mother, again with great distinctness, 'I think it best that you consider what you are saying for a moment. As you say, what is done cannot be undone: Marianne has been deceiving us, and has formed an attachment of so improper a character, with so unsuitable a person, that I am obliged to have recourse to sal volatile every time I think of it, and to wonder how such madness could have entered her blood, as my own family had such a reputation for firm rectitude of conduct, that my poor papa the Major was known as the Steady Man of the 43rd. Be that as it may, we cannot retard what I am obliged to call the course of nature: shamed and dismayed as we are, I fear we must swallow this bitter pill down, and cast our minds forward to the future − and consider, in short, how much greater would be the shame and dismay of acknowledging an illegitimate grandchild.'

Mr Hemstock's colour deepened as his wife spoke; but he listened, and understood. Feeble as she seemed, Mrs Hemstock had at her command her birth and gentility, the very things to which Elias Hemstock deferred; and what was more, she did not see any less shrewdly and realistically for being wrapped in a nimbus of sickly snobberies. In some respects she was more hard-headed than her husband who, in acknowledging no limits to his ambition or the power of his will, was perhaps quite as much a romantic visionary as his daughter and her lover; whereas Mrs Hemstock, whose poor papa the Major had had scarcely a shilling to bless himself with, knew the value of keeping up appearances, and of covering up the unsatisfactory patches of life with the decorous valances of compromise.

'The alternative,' she went on, 'that is, the young

man's making Marianne his wife, is certainly so far short of the ideal, that I can only be thankful that my poor papa the Major became a companion of the seraphim before he could see it; but perfection is not to be found except among those bright beings, and I see no other solution. I would merely add,' she said, even more distinctly, as Mr Hemstock seemed about to speak, 'that in order to save such shreds of good name as remain to us, Mr Hemstock, a marriage — however repulsive to our feelings — cannot take place too soon. I speak of course as a wife — that is, I merely suggest, and do not presume to dictate.'

Mr Hemstock went over to his decanter of brandy. His hand was not quite steady, yet he poured only his usual temperate measure. 'All very well to talk of marriage,' he said, his eyes at their most heavy-lidded and brooding, 'but who says he'd marry her anyhow? I doubt that's ever been part of his plan—'

'Oh, no, Papa!' protested Marianne. 'That isn't Jed — though you don't like him, I won't hear you say that of him! He loves me very truly and dearly, and he will . . .' What, indeed, would he do? The note she had sent must have come as the greatest shock to him. All her anxiety thus far had been for her parents' reaction; now her mind turned gropingly and uncertainly towards the thought of Jed.

'Like him!' snapped her father. 'You might as well talk of liking a scavenging crow.'

'I quite share your aversion, Mr Hemstock, though I must object once again to your mode of expression,' said Mrs Hemstock. 'But I fear that our only course under the circumstances — I merely suggest, of course — is to have the young man here, and speak to him.'

'By God, Mrs Hemstock, I wish I could admire your coolness! To talk in that way of having him here — a fellow I'd never have allowed across my threshold even if he'd never been within a hundred miles of my daughter, let alone—'

Mr Hemstock was cut short by the timid entrance of the maid, who said that Mr Wintergreen had called; and a moment later Jed was there.

Marianne was so overjoyed to see him that she hardly noticed the awkwardness of the bow he made to her mother, or the general rough-hewn plainness of his bearing as he stood among the glossy furniture of that parlour. His eyes flickered a reassurance to her; but he addressed himself, openly and simply, to her father.

'Miss Hemstock wrote me,' he said. 'I came as soon as I could.'

Mr Hemstock withdrew a step or two, as if he dare not trust himself near him. 'You've the devil's own impudence, coming here,' he said.

'It would have been worse in me to stay away,' said Jed calmly.

'Quite so,' said Mrs Hemstock, addressing Jed as if she were seated on a lofty dais with a flight of steps up to it. 'But you do not appear to have been so scrupulous in your conduct on former occasions, Mr Wintergreen.'

'No, ma'am,' said Jed. 'I'm sorry. I – what has happened must appear to you in a very bad light.'

'You mean – ' Mr Hemstock was applying such overwhelming force in choking down his feelings that, but for the molten colour of his face, he appeared almost torpid – 'do you suggest that there's any *other* way of seeing this?'

Jed considered. 'I'm not looking out for no excuses,' he said. 'All I mean is, for two people to fall in love isn't such an unnatural thing, after all – nor a bad thing in itself, surely.'

'Don't speak of my daughter like that in my house, sir!' cried Hemstock, as a glance passed between Marianne and Jed. 'You ought to be horsewhipped, yes, by God, horsewhipped!'

'I'm sorry for this result,' said Jed, who was also at great pains to control himself, 'sorry because it seem to drag in the mud what's good and true and always have

247

been. But I'm not sorry for meeting Marianne, nor for falling in love wi' her, nor for her loving me − no man could be sorry for that. And if you horsewhip me, Mr Hemstock, you must horsewhip your son-in-law, for so I mean to be − not out of duty to you, not out of duty at all, for duty mean reluctance, and I *want* to be married to your daughter, to cherish and care for her with all my soul.' He smiled sadly at Marianne. 'This isn't the sort of proposal I could have hoped for, Marianne − but that come from the heart, just the same.'

'Wintergreen,' said Mr Hemstock, his words almost slurring in his smothered passion, 'stand further off − stand there, sir − or I shall knock you down.'

'Mr Hemstock,' said his wife, with a sharp motion of her hand, 'I must ask you for the last time either to consider the state of my nerves, or witness my complete collapse.' Turning her face to Jed, but closing her eyes, she said, 'I take it, sir, that you propose to shoulder your responsibilities?'

'Very willingly, ma'am.'

'I can scarcely be expected to rejoice in your willingness to do what under any circumstances would be highly unwelcome to me,' sighed Mrs Hemstock, 'but I can, I suppose, acquiesce in this lesser of two evils.'

'I thank you for that, ma'am,' said Jed, with a little combativeness entering his tone for the first time, 'I would rather have it so; but it don't signify, as I mean to wed Marianne in any case.'

'Do you indeed!' said Mr Hemstock. 'You know, of course, that she is not of age, and can be legally prevented? Or do the laws of the land mean as little to you as they did to your gallows-bird of a father?'

'Mr Hemstock, you will kill me!' cried his wife − but already Marianne had sprung to her feet and placed her hand on Jed's arm. 'Papa,' she said, 'if you speak in that way I shall leave the house with Jed this very moment, and not come back. I will! And I don't want it to be that way, Papa. I will marry Jed − I will indeed − but it needn't be like this. Oh, I don't love you any the less for what's happened – how could I? – it doesn't change who I am, it doesn't make me any less the daughter who loves you and wants to be married with your blessing. With your blessing, Papa.'

'You will wait for that,' said her father, 'until you and that ruffian are so much food for the worms.'

'And your permission, Mr Hemstock?' said Jed. 'Need we wait for that?'

Elias Hemstock made a lunge, and then checked himself – a movement in which forty years of both arrogance and self-restraint were equally expressed. He recovered himself with the characteristic hitch of his chin above his cravat, and spoke with chill conviction. 'I declare you planned this, Wintergreen – I swear you contrived the whole thing. I won't even say God forgive you for it, because I hope He won't. I never shall. Never.'

Jed had turned pale at this, and Marianne could feel the sinews of his arm stiffen like tightened reins. 'You'll take that back before I go,' he said hoarsely.

'Enough,' said Mrs Hemstock. 'Mr Wintergreen, leave us now. We will communicate with you shortly. Please, go.'

Jed gnawed his lips, his eyes balefully fixed on Mr Hemstock; then again gave his awkward bow to Mrs Hemstock. 'As you ask me, ma'am, I will. Marianne: I shall see you again soon, my dear. Ma'am.'

Marianne lay in bed that night gazing out through her open curtains. The moon was almost at the full, and from a cloudless sky shed that weird light that gives to the sublunary world the illusory look of a scene reflected in a pool.

She had shed tears, but they were dry now, and her mind was passing quite calmly through various stages of wonder and speculation at what was to come. A sort of forced marriage – though not an unwilling one; alienation from her father, who felt she had betrayed

him; motherhood . . . How different this was from the
dream-futures she had woven for herself in the idle hours
at school — and how suddenly her jog-trot life had
broken into a canter and then, Pegasus-like, taken wing!
— frighteningly sudden, the transformation!

And yet — disturbing as the encounter between her
father and Jed had been — Marianne could not deny
finding a certain savour in being the centre of attention,
in finding the spokes of the world converging so
dramatically upon her sole self. She had sighed for
weariness so often at the way events slowly unrolled
before her watching eyes, that the sensation of being
swept along by the tide of them was far from disagreeable
to her. The implacable hostility between Jed and her
father pained her deeply, but her own emotional nature
was of such quicksilver pliability, that she could not
conceive of such a state of affairs enduring long, any
more than a mayfly can envisage the passage of the
seasons; and while she recognized the unyielding fixity in
the characters of both her lover and her father, she
supposed it only the transient hardness of ice, not the
immutability of stone. For the moment all was change,
and change was life to Marianne; and even the coming
marriage presented itself to her consciousness as one
more attractive landmark upon a journey fraught with
exciting variety, and with no hint that a flat featureless
plain might lie beyond it.

Elias Hemstock was still awake. The groom had called
him to the byre where one of his prize heifers had been
taken sick, and he stayed there while the village farrier
was sent for.

He stayed there, too, after the farrier yawningly
arrived. He stood just beyond the circle of lamplight
which wove from the snorting breath of the heifer,
condensing in the cold air, a mockingly beautiful filigree.
The heifer was near death and there was nothing the
farrier could do. Hemstock looked silently on, his face in

the shadows a mere arrangement of harsh planes and surfaces, apparently no more susceptible to impression than the stone walls of the byre. He was not indifferent to the sufferings of animals insofar as they were useful and valuable to him; but he watched the slow death of the heifer with no more active emotion than a vague feeling that this was an apt enough rite to accompany the death of his own hopes.

For such seemed the business of that day to Elias Hemstock: a wrecking, ruining and destroying of his life's work that many a strong man, feeling it as acutely as he did, would have cried aloud to behold. Such another man, indeed, might have found some small relief in his cries − relief that was denied to Hemstock as he stood in the corner of the byre impassively watching one of nature's smaller and incidental cruelties, as it were a divertissement to the main drama. For if he had the strength of an oak, he likewise lacked suppleness: against trouble he could only pit the massive solidity of his egotism, and let it beat against him or break him if it would. He was a man of intense but narrow vision: he had poured his whole self into the channel of a single ambition, and allowed that self no minor tributaries of expression; he had no pastimes or amusements, no idiosyncratic interests or pursuits, no friendships or connections that were not cultivated as a means of advancing his status, no convictions religious, political or aesthetic that were not the merest reflexes. Everything was absorbed in his one fixed purpose of cutting a greater and greater figure in the world, and now that purpose had been thwarted in the most humiliating manner.

And he did not know quite how to react. He did not pity himself − indeed, so obstinate was his pride that he simply could not imagine himself as an object of pity, vulnerable and defeated. He could only stare into the face of his humiliation as if to stare down a living adversary. It would never occur to him to shift his ground, to reconsider, to reappraise. His disappointment lacerated him, but he merely hugged it closer to him, and drove its point deeper.

He kept thinking of the Bouveries, and what they would say. Would they laugh in derision? Young Mr Roland, of course, would not; but Hemstock had doubts of the rector, whom he had sometimes suspected of a little sly humour at the expense of his pretensions. And then there was Squire Ingamells, to whom Hemstock had virtually described the match as a settled thing. Would they pity him? He hated that thought more than anything: at the very suggestion of it his soul seemed to flinch and withdraw into its hard carapace of stubbornness.

Yet even if the match with Roland Bouverie had come to nothing, there would surely have been someone else. So much beauty, poise, cultivation in his daughter − so much, indeed, that he was half afraid of her − how could all that go to waste? And the money he had planned to settle on her (Wintergreen would get none of that − it was barely worth stating). He had invested so much, both financially and emotionally, in Marianne, that nothing seemed to remain to him now she was lost. The fine house, the trappings of wealth, had been a setting for a single jewel. Herbert was a milksop who would never elevate the Hemstock name; Wade and Margery promised well enough, but they were children, with a long perilous track of years to traverse before they could make any mark in the world. Only Marianne could lead him to the place where he dearly wanted to be, and now instead she had dragged him down into the dust.

His bitter thoughts brooded and hovered over her, lying asleep, as he thought, in the house: yet, half-afraid, half-possessive as he was of her, all his anger rebounded from her upon Wintergreen. That he could not attach any blame to her was the result not of tenderness but of a fixed habit of regarding her as a passive object rather than an active agent. All her life he had simply turned her about on the potter's wheel of his aspiration: her own feelings, wishes, ideas, desires, it had never occurred to him to speculate upon. 'She is my child still — I must love her, and try to understand' was a formula that would have sounded as alien in Hemstock's ears as a Greek theorem. He could not disentangle his love for her and his long-laid plans for her — the two were one.

It was Wintergreen who was responsible. The man had risen up in Heartsease like some terrible mocking spirit of opposition. Only the fact that his daughter was carrying the man's child — a maddening thought, like a tic in the brain! — prevented Hemstock from taking him and breaking him in pieces like a doll.

The last wisps of the heifer's breath thinned and gave out; and the animal departed life as it had entered it — unconsulted, and uncomplaining. The farrier shook his head and got to his feet. 'I'm afraid she've gone, Mester Hemstock,' he said.

'Aye.' Hemstock turned brusquely away. 'She's gone.'

The third party to a destiny whose interweaving none had sought was also awake that night. Jed, knowing he would not sleep, had put on stout gaiters and a muffler and gone for a walk about his fields.

Though the moon shone and the sky was clear, patches of fog clung about the lower closes, where the stream ran between rows of willows. The sound of Jed's footsteps in that profound silence was a palpable eruption. He was impressed by the quality of infinite stillness and endurance expressed in the trees on such a night: theirs was the possession of the earth at such a time, and man was a feeble intruder; old as the individual trees were, their shapes, precisely delineated in the moon-coloured mist, were immeasurably more ancient — their characteristic configurations of bole and bark, branch and twig, retained through millennia, with magnificent indifference to the human flux around them.

Jed's mood was solemn as the scene; for his was not a nature to take any of the vicissitudes of life lightly, and a great responsibility lay before him. He did not think of shirking it, or wish to in the least; the moment the news had come his heart had cleaved steadfastly to Marianne, and he had embraced his future on the spot. He loved her, she needed him, they would be married; he had reviewed this troop of imperatives in a twinkling, and it was this mood of settled resolution that had seen him through the interview with her parents, which had bristled with so much bitterness, spoken and unspoken, that at any other time he feared he could not have got through it.

Well, the coming child was a startling stroke, though he should perhaps have expected it. The loss of restraint had perhaps been inevitable in a liaison as secret, passionate and exclusive as theirs. And the sole prerequisite of a marriage, he thought, was surely love, and there was abundance of that. On her part there must be loss too − the loss possibly of a family, certainly of a father − but then that had been implicit from the moment of their first kiss.

But at the heart of this true, loyal and protective feeling, Jed recognized something else, and it was that that kept him from sleep. There was a wriggling maggot of triumph in the kernel of his better nature. For when he had faced Hemstock in that overfurnished parlour he had seen that the big man was hurt, beaten, wounded, as he had never been before; and Jed, who would not kill a mouse, had exulted in spite of himself, and silently called on the wronged shades of his mother and father to witness his victory, and mark the lines of pain in Elias Hemstock's face. Oh, it had been sweet.

Could there be poison in such sweetness? Was it wrong to enter marriage carrying such malice, however well-deserved, even as an additional motive beside the purer ones? He would not believe it. But he could not sleep.

Chapter Ten

Charlotte's Dreams

From the Crab Pot Inn Charlotte wrote her
congratulations to her brother Jed on his marriage.

Writing did not come easily to her, and this letter was
especially difficult. Jed had never had any secrets from
her, and so he made no bones about the reason for the
premature suddenness of the marriage, which prevented
her being invited to attend, and made it a quiet private
ceremony with only the necessary witnesses. Charlotte
was not in the least disposed to judge her brother: in spite
of the change in her circumstances caused by Abel Jex's
inheritance, she remained the down-to-earth girl brought
up in cottage, workhouse and kitchen, and sincerely
wished the couple happiness. But it was hard to express it
in the right way; particularly as the maiden name of her
new sister-in-law was Hemstock. The events of 1830 were
too dimly remembered to hold any bitterness for
Charlotte, but she knew it was not so with Jed, and
between the lines of his letter she discerned a world of
complexities.

She was invited to come and stay with the couple as
soon as they were settled in − but then Jed had wanted
her to come and be with him in Heartsease from the first
day of his return there. About that, too, Charlotte felt
uncomfortable, and feared he had grown impatient with
her continual postponements. It had been no surprise to
her that Jed should use his new fortune to return to the
village of their childhood and set up house there: she
knew how deeply he felt about it; but for herself she felt
no more than a mild nostalgic interest in Heartsease.
Still, she would have gone there immediately, simply for

255

love of Jed — were it not that something held her in Shipden.

That too was difficult to convey to him. She had made the excuse of wanting to see Mr and Mrs Skeels, who had come to depend on her, comfortably settled — but it was not that. Certainly she felt a fond obligation to them, but it was not that that made her continue to haunt Shipden like a spirit about its late home.

At Shipden, which faced north, you could watch the sun both rise and set in the sea. Charlotte had done so almost every day of her years here: had seen the sun dragged down into an agitated spume, while the sky above broke out in red weals as if from some cosmic scourging; had seen it crest the horizon as serene as a swan on a lake, and slowly flood the main with golden oil. She dearly loved these sights: dearly loved the cliffs, the dark wooded slopes that rose behind them, the pantiled roofs, the yawls and crab-boats drawn up on the flats, the long trestles with the nets laid out upon them to dry and looking in the sparkle of morning as if an almighty spider had passed that way; dearly loved the skyey sound of gulls, the long suspiration of endlessly turning shingle, the boom and cymbal crash of high waves against the sea wall; but it was not because of them that she stayed.

The unexpected inheritance had naturally made a difference to Charlotte's life at the Crab Pot. At first the Skeels drew back in horror at the idea of her continuing to help with the running of the inn; but, as she said to them, just because she had some money of her own all of a sudden didn't mean she wanted to do nothing but twiddle her toes. Their acceptance was reluctant: their happiness in her good fortune enormous and unaffected. As for Charlotte's reaction to her windfall, she veered between being simply delighted with it, and not being able to take it in. The lawyer Mr Veazey forwarded her the allowance monthly, together with a formal letter with all the long words abbreviated so that she could hardly understand it; but she always noted the phrase 'in possess. of an independ. income', and marvelled that it referred to her. Not that she could not find things to do with it. She laid out money liberally, in spite of the Skeels' protests, to add to the comforts of the Crab Pot, and engaged a man to do the heavy work and help Mr Skeels; and while she hardly knew when she would wear them, she bought new clothes, gratifying Mrs Skeels extremely by consulting her on pattern and cut, until that lady began to consider herself quite a connoisseur, and could not pass one of the town's wealthy visitors in the street without a critical glance, and a whispered exclamation such as 'Not with that lace bertha – whatever was she a-thinking on?' And then there were numerous poor families in Shipden – the sea being a terribly efficient widow-maker – whom Charlotte was able to help effectively at last, and who would accept from the ordinary girl they had known for years what they would refuse from the condescension of ladies-bountiful or the cold hand of the parish.

Still, wonderful as the change was, somehow it did not occupy the forefront of Charlotte's consciousness. Often she found herself darning or mending – and when she awoke to the realization, or was reminded by Mrs Skeels, that this was no longer necessary, she made the excuse of habit. But it was not that: something else was responsible for her absence of mind, and made her material circumstances seem to lie far off from her, and to leave a wide margin about her heart.

Almost daily, Charlotte and Toby met Loveday Ward, the beautiful invalid young woman, either on the clifftops or the beach.

Loveday's nurse, Mrs Vickers, after her initial indignation at her charge's preferring these companions to herself, soon resigned herself to it quite willingly – particularly as wintry winds were beginning to blow across Shipden's seafront; and she took to having tea in

the snug parlour of the Crab Pot with Mrs Skeels, and
regaling the landlady with accounts of the delinquencies
of the absconding Mr Vickers, who had last been heard
of in the East Indies, where he was living in a hut with a
native Concubine – Mrs Skeels, under the impression
that this was a species of vegetable, nodding very
solemnly, and declaring that nothing men could do would
surprise her. Toby, in the meantime, pushed Loveday's
wheeled chair, and Charlotte walked alongside, and the
sick girl talked to them, in bursts of candour and gloom
and gaiety, and regarded the changeful sea as if it held the
answer to a nagging question.

They were strange, these walks. A vivid picture of the
scene would remain before Charlotte's mind's eye long
after she had returned home, and would often appear,
bright and sharp in all its details, in her dreams at night:
Loveday reclining in the wheeled chair, her fingers
moodily tugging at the auburn ringlets which looked so
rich and living beside the whiteness of her skin, her eager
eyes seeming to reach out and hungrily seize the passing
world in default of her weakened body; the wind drawing
patterns in the clifftop grass, the movement of clouds like
a great scene-shifting in the sky, the crimped edges of the
waves beetling up the shore; and Toby, pushing his light
burden as if he wished he might do so for a thousand
miles, glancing down with a sort of painful wonder at the
slender neck, and his whole lithe frame seeming to tauten
again with wonder whenever Loveday got out of the chair
and took his arm to walk a little way.

There was something inward, hushed, and absorbed
about Toby at these times – Toby who had always been
so much quicker and more communicative than his
fellow-fishermen, his emotions playing over the surface
of him like breeze-ruffled down on a bird's back. If
Loveday wanted to talk, he talked: if, as not
uncommonly happened, she fell into an abrupt silence, he
was silent too; but always he watched her, as if he were
afraid that she might disappear into the ether if he took

his eyes off her for a moment. And in the watching, his face seemed to Charlotte to lose some of its old character. The elasticity of expression, with the fun always lurking at the corners of his eyes and mouth, seemed to leave it, and a light more intense, yet more remote, to take its place.

Loveday startled her one day by suddenly asking: 'Do you dream, Charlotte?'

'Not – not very often,' said Charlotte in confusion.

'But when you do,' Loveday persisted, 'what do you dream of?'

'Oh – just foolish little things.'

'And do they ever come true?'

'Sometimes, perhaps.'

'Such as? Oh! but of course – you and your brother came into an inheritance – that must have been a dream come true. So it does happen, after all!'

'What do you dream of, Miss Ward?' Toby asked.

Loveday drew in a deep breath; and Charlotte heard the whistling of it, and felt the girl's hand tighten around hers for a moment. 'I dream of so many things,' she said. 'Sometimes it feels as if the whole world had got into my head, and goes spinning round and round there all night, so that I wake more tired than when I lay down.' She abruptly tilted her oval face upward with her sharp, unhappy smile. 'That's no answer, is it? Very well. Out of all that crowd of dreams, waiting to pounce on me when I go to bed, the one that comes most often is the dream in which I am invisible. At least, I can see myself; but all the other people can't see me, and go about their business quite oblivious of my being amongst them – and they even walk right through me, just as if I wasn't there at all! Think of that!' she said, clutching Charlotte's hand, and rapidly tapping Toby's where it held the back of the chair. 'And every time, I wonder: is it because I am a ghost – or are the other people ghosts? Am I dead amongst the living, or living amongst the dead?'

'Miss Ward, thass not right for you to think of such things – that don't do you no good, talking that way,' said Toby solemnly.

'Doesn't it, Toby?' Loveday looked brightly up at him. 'But then it's different for you – you have so much life in you, and so you can have no doubt which one of the two you are. But it makes one think, doesn't it? Do ghosts know they are ghosts, for example? Or do they see us walking by, and wonder and tremble just as we do at them? What do you think, Toby?'

'I don't reckon I believe in ghosts at all, Miss Ward,' said Toby, with mingled trouble and respect in his tone. 'But I do reckon as thinking on cheerful things, not grim ones, make a body feel better.'

'So now here is someone else telling me what I can and cannot do!' said Loveday, tossing her head with irritation; but seeing how crushed Toby looked, she softened at once, and said, 'And I know it is because you care for me – both of you – how kind you both are to me, and what a cross, disagreeable baggage I am in return! I may torment Mrs Vickers, because she's paid for her trouble (besides being a witch), but I should not take out my temper on you, and you must simply tip me off the cliff next time. I want to walk now. Toby, will you give me your arm?'

She levered herself out of the chair – Charlotte noticed that she did not spring lightly out of it as she used to – and they walked along the cliff-path, the white scuts of rabbits whisking away in the long grass and heather.

'The trouble is, you see,' said Loveday, 'I have never had friends, and so I don't know how friends behave. Poor Charlotte, don't look so sad for me! I dare say I don't deserve them anyhow. But being always poorly, I never went away to school, and just had a succession of governesses, all I think from the same coven as Mrs Vickers – so no friends; and being of a horribly rich family, and brought up by horribly proud and proper grandparents, I never had other children come to play with me, except one or two little pampered beasts as frosty and tight-laced as I − so no friends; and then since I have grown up, I have been dragging on from place to place, trying this air and these waters and that climate, and never staying in one spot for five minutes together − and so no friends!'

She gave her most brilliant, beautifully transforming smile, but tears glistened in her eyes.

'You've friends now, Miss Ward,' said Toby, seeming to wrench the words out of himself. 'Good friends.'

'So I have! Oh, I should have come here years ago, shouldn't I, and met you two . . . I suppose you have been friends for a long time?'

'Oh! yes,' said Toby easily, 'Charlotte and me have been friends since we were younkers. We're like brother and sister, ain't we, Charlotte?'

'Very like,' said Charlotte faintly, with what she hoped was a smile.

'That's charming. I like that,' said Loveday, squeezing their arms. 'But how did you make friends? How does one go about it? I never learnt.'

'Why, I reckon twas through collecting shells on the beach, wasn't it, Charlotte?' said Toby. 'She'd come here all lost and lonely-like, to work at the Crab Pot, and she were trashen along the seashore one day, a little lorn mawther such as you never saw; and so I ask her do she want to look for shells wi' me, and so we went along together − and that was about the breadth of't.'

'Was that how it was, Charlotte?' said Loveday.

'Thass how it was,' said Charlotte, remembering the scene with something like the emotional equivalent of tickling − a sensation balanced between pleasure and pain. 'And I was ashamed to show I'd been crying − but then I soon forgot about my tears anyhow, and the wind dried them away.'

'Oh! I want to do it − just as you two did all those years ago!' said Loveday excitedly. 'Let's go and collect seashells − let's go down to the beach, now!'

'The tide's not long gone down,' Charlotte said. 'I'm afraid the sands will wet your feet.'

Loveday gave Charlotte a wry, straight, adult glance, with worlds of darkness behind it. 'Oh, my dear, I don't think wet feet will make much difference to me, you know,' she said; then, turning them both around: 'Come! You shall wheel me down to the beach, and then I shall be fresh to walk again.'

They descended to the beach, where the damp sand was the colour of brown sugar in the sun, and dimpled all over with the footprints of gulls and waders. Again it cost Loveday an effort to push herself out of the chair, but she set out to forage across the flats with energy.

'And is this the place where you and Toby met?' she said. 'Just here — this very place?'

'Round about here, I think,' said Charlotte. She remembered the precise spot very clearly, but she decided not to reveal it.

'Gloves, gloves, horrid gloves, I can feel nothing!' cried Loveday, snatching them off. 'Ah, there's one. How rough outside, and smooth inside! And look at the shape of this one — like a little Brighton pavilion! Why should such humble little molluscs or whatever they're called have such wonderful intricate things to live in? The parson would no doubt have some terribly pompous answer to that. And here are some that look just like razors, d'you see, Toby? Oh, I'm sorry, I keep forgetting — this must be terribly stale for you.'

'No, no,' said Toby. 'Thass like doing it for the first time.'

They came to a timber groyne, all ragged with barnacles and beach-wrack, and without thinking Charlotte scrambled over it. 'There's a little pool here,' she said, looking back, and saw Loveday standing helplessly on the other side.

'I don't think I can climb,' Loveday said. 'Not any more,' and as Charlotte beheld the sick girl, with the wind blowing her mantle about and the sun shining through it, she saw that the body beneath the bonneted head was like the stalk of a sunflower. She was lanced through with pity.

'Will you allow me, Miss Ward?' said Toby; and he gently lifted her in his arms and carried her over.

'You are quite a knight, Toby – you are!' Loveday said, laughing, as he set her down on the other side. 'You should have been born in another time, and lived in a castle, and ridden one of those horses with a tablecloth all over it.'

Toby did not seem to be listening. A dazed, blinded, almost blank look had been on his face as he had lifted the slight form in his arms. It was as if the force of that moment had driven out of him every prior thought and emotion, leaving him as mere a vessel of sensation as a new-born babe. And in that transfiguring moment Charlotte saw the culmination of these past months, in which Toby's interest in Loveday had deepened, in which his talk had been more and more of Loveday and how she was and how they must help her get better, in which his life had come to revolve around the figure of the beautiful girl on the seashore – a sun that seemed to shine more brightly even as it burnt lower.

Charlotte had seen it all happening, in her quietly observant way; and as Toby set Loveday down on the sand and came to himself, like a man awakening, she saw too that a final seal had been set on feelings that Toby, with his habit of believing what he wanted to believe, had surely been only half aware of. She saw, and knew: the knowledge would not be refused, it battered its way in. There was nothing very remarkable about this intuition of Charlotte's, when Toby Dane was its object – for, as he had said, were they not just like brother and sister?

The Danes' new boat, the *Heartsease*, was finished, and was to be launched on the morning tide with a little libation of rum. Charlotte and Mrs Skeels, among others, were to go down to the beach and see the launch; and on the great morning Mr Skeels, with the warranted superstition of the fisherman, was careful to avoid ill-omens. 'Do you be sure and crush the egg-shells, mawther,' he said to his wife at breakfast. 'They reckon half a shell's enough to make a boat for a witch, who'll follow 'em out to sea and tudd 'em. I dare say there's mebbe nothing in it, but thass better to be sure.'

'Well, now really, Skeels, I may not have a perfesser's head atween my shoulders, but I hope nobody could accuse me of being quite shanny when it comes to watching for o'ems,' said Mrs Skeels. 'Thass not fair I should be accused of not knowing great A from a bull's foot, when in all your years a-crabbing I never once wound wool after sunset in case I were making your shroud. I hope you don't mean I'm no better than her up at the King's Head, who'll look at a new moon through glass and think nothing of it. I'd put my head in the pickle-barrel and leave it there before that.'

'Oh, never mind, mawther − it's all according,' said Mr Skeels. 'Charlotte, give these halfpennies to Toby, will ye? They're to throw over the side to buy a good catch. And give my best to him and Skipper.'

Charlotte was able to give only half an ear to Mrs Skeels' conversation as they descended to the beach, for she was much preoccupied. The launching of the *Heartsease*, which she had named, was something she had greatly looked forward to, as had Toby; but his own pleasure in the event seemed quite swallowed up in anxiety that Loveday should be there to witness it. The other day he had secured her promise that she would come out early to see the launch, but Charlotte wondered whether Loveday had taken it quite as seriously as Toby did, and whether she would not turn up. And she did not know which of the two alternatives disturbed her more.

On the beach the familiar crab-boats, double-ended, brightly painted, had been joined by a brighter newcomer which had been hauled down by carthorse and still stood on its wheels, surrounded by a knot of fishermen casting critical eyes over the straight keel and massive beam and full bilges that gave the boat the look of a tubby basket. The *Heartsease* was ready for her maiden voyage.

'How do, Mrs Skeels. Hullo, Charlotte,' said Toby, who was fussing round the boat like a hen round a clutch. 'Handsome, ain't she? She took a bit of a scrape on the stern coming off the stocks. Hope that ain't a bad o'em.'

'Oh! I don't reckon so,' said Mrs Skeels. 'I reckon thass a good o'em − showing as she'll stand up to any treatment, and always stay upright.'

Toby's eyes impatiently scanned the path leading down from the sea-wall. 'You haven't seen her, have you, Charlotte?' he said aside.

'No,' Charlotte said. 'But that look like rain today − mebbe she thought it best not to turn out, or her grandparents said so—'

'Oh! she'll come. She said she'd come.' Toby ran his sleeve along the name *Heartsease* painted with abundant curlicues on the bow. 'She'll come do she say she'll come.'

'She's beautiful, Toby,' Charlotte said, examining the new boat.

'She is − she's the most—' Toby followed the direction of her gaze, and flushed as he said hurriedly, 'Aye! a handsome boat − we're right proud on her.'

In the meantime Toby's father Skipper Dane had cracked a bottle of rum and given tots to his fellow-fishermen, who stood about in their stiff canvas slops and deep boots like so many gnarled tree-stumps, and with as little apparent likelihood of ever being able to sit down. Toby, however, declined to taste the drink, and continued to pace about the boat and scan the seafront with puckered eyes.

'Well, bor,' said Skipper Dane at last, 'the tide won't wait for us, so we'd best hoist the ole girl, and give her a taste o' salt.'

'Oh! no, not yet,' said Toby, with agitation. 'We needn't shift yet − hold hard a few minutes more.'

He would not hear of their launching the boat; and the other fishermen, though no more given to expressing impatience than the weathered rocks of the cliff-face, began presently to lift their eyebrows, and shake their heads at each other.

'Blest if I know what's amiss wi' the boy,' Skipper Dane confided to Mrs Skeels. 'He've been as jumpy as a dab on a deck all mornen.'

'Thass his third cycle of seven – always a ticklish time,' said Mrs Skeels. 'Skeels was the same at his age, when we were courten. Always climbing up trees, I recall, and hallooing at me from atop of them. My mother didn't hold wi' such monkey doings, and said I'd finish with a crick in my neck as wouldn't go, and have to walk to the altar with my head back and my eyes on the roof-bosses like a Foxe's Martyr – but there, twasn't without its charm, took in moderation.'

Charlotte saw the approaching figures of Mrs Vickers and Loveday a few seconds before Toby; and thus she was able to see the reaction on his face, the sudden tension in his limber body, that made him look less like himself. He hurried forward to greet the girl.

'Hello, Toby, are we late?' said Loveday, who was thoroughly wrapped in pelisse and muff, and whose fair skin, Charlotte noticed, had an almost bluish tinge around the jaw and eyes. 'It's Mrs Vickers' fault – she's sluggish today; I think she was up late last night casting spells over her cauldron.'

Mrs Vickers, who already looked sufficiently affronted at the presence of so many whiskery fishermen, maintained a look of lofty abstraction, and merely permitted herself a nod to Mrs Skeels.

'Not late at all,' said Toby. 'We're going to launch her in a moment.'

'And so this is the new boat,' said Loveday, who sounded to Charlotte as if she were weary and trying not to show it. 'How prettily she's painted – very pretty.' Her eyes wandered from the boat to the watching fishermen, and to Skipper Dane, who somewhere among the seamed wrinkles of his face wore an expression of surprise.

'This is my father,' Toby said awkwardly. 'Father, this is Miss Ward, who — who specially wanted to see the launch.'

'Hullo, Mr Dane. Don't mind me, now: do go on,' said Loveday. 'Charlotte — where's Charlotte? Oh! there you are. Will you give me your hands, my dear? — you always warm me so.'

Charlotte did so; and whatever she had been feeling a moment before swiftly gave way to pity as she touched the thin cold fingers. 'The doctor said he did not like the look of me this morning,' Loveday whispered, 'but I don't like the look of him either, and so I insisted on coming out . . . The *Heartsease* — that's very singular. Why did Toby name her so?'

'Well — it was me who named her,' said Charlotte.

'Did you? What made you choose that name? Is it because that's what you hope to find — heart's ease? Oh! but it can't be — you already have that, Charlotte — you always seem so calm, and it always eases *my* heart to see you.'

Charlotte smiled a little, and said nothing.

'I suppose that's what everyone searches for, isn't it?' pursued Loveday. 'Where is it to be found? I wonder. And why did the Fates, or whoever, decide to hide it and make us spend our lives searching for it, instead of placing it near at hand? But perhaps if it were near at hand we shouldn't want it — simply because it *is* near at hand . . . Forgive me, my dear, I'm rambling today — I don't know why. I had such strange dreams last night!'

'So did I,' said Charlotte. 'I wish I could stop having them.'

Toby, his father, and a few others were preparing to carry the boat down to the sea by means of oars passed through ports in the gunwales. Suddenly Charlotte remembered something.

'Toby!' she said going to him. 'Wait — Mr Skeels sent these coppers, to throw over the side for a good catch.' She put the coins in Toby's hand, then added a few more. 'And those are from me,' she said.

'Why, Toby!' laughed Loveday, 'how very heathen! You surely wouldn't throw good money to the fishes, for a superstition?'

'Oh — I don't believe in it, really,' Toby said, laughing awkwardly.

The *Heartsease* was slung upon the oars, and transported down the beach to meet the tide. Charlotte returned to Loveday's side to watch the boat take to the waves. The figures of Skipper Dane and Toby were clearly visible aboard it, busying themselves with the sail; and it was plain to Charlotte's sight, too, that Toby did not throw the coins over the side into the water.

'How light the boat looks on that great grey sea,' said Loveday. 'There's Toby waving — Hulloo, Toby good sailing!' she called, waving her handkerchief. 'Charlotte, look he's waving to us.'

'Yes,' said Charlotte, after a moment waving too, 'I see.'

Charlotte sat up late in the parlour that night, after the Skeels had gone to bed. She intended to write to Jed and tell him that she would like to come and stay; but somehow she could not bring herself to do it, and the paper slipped from her lap, and the candles had burnt low before she came out of her reverie, alerted by a sound in the passage.

Taking up a candle, she went softly to the parlour door and looked out; and beheld the extraordinary sight of Silas Skeels making his way down the passage, as if some miracle had restored life to his legs. But in another moment she saw that, having laboriously dressed himself, he had hoisted his great body on to crutches, and had thus struggled his way a few paces from the downstairs room in which he slept. The candlelight showed his big smooth face contorted with effort and pain; and Charlotte flew to support him.

'Mr Skeels, whatever were you a-thinking of?' she said, taking his weight on to her shoulder. 'Didn't you ring the bell for Joseph? What's the matter?'

'Want to do summat for meself for once in a way,' gasped Mr Skeels. 'Got to go and see Skipper Dane — he'll still be astir at this hour — see him and sort things out . . .' He sagged and nearly fell.

'You can't, Mr Skeels, indeed you can't,' said Charlotte. 'Come — come and rest yourself in the parlour.'

Miserably, but at the end of his strength, Mr Skeels allowed himself to be led into the parlour. He lay back panting on the settle while Charlotte got him a glass of grog and a footstool to support his legs.

'I'm sorry, gel,' he said. 'I'm sorry. That was a scramble-brain thing to do. Should ha' known. Only I lay there a-thinken and a-wittlen, until I say to myself I got to go and see Skipper Dane and talk things over, do I go mad! . . . I must ha' give you quite a turn.'

'Never mind that,' Charlotte said. 'Drink up.' She knelt and massaged his wasted legs, in a way that she knew relieved the stabbing twinges he suffered, kindly nature having decided to deprive the paralysed limbs of all feeling except pain. 'Is that any better?'

'Tisn't the ache o' them that troubles me,' said Mr Skeels, 'though thass kind of you, gel, and that do ease 'em — but it's the trouble in my mind I wish I could settle.'

'Can't I help you settle it?' Charlotte said.

'I don't know, gel. Thass partly about you, you see.'

'Me?' said Charlotte. 'Why, Mr Skeels, I'm all right.'

Mr Skeels shook his head restively. 'Mebbe I fancy things, being forever stuck in one place, and looking on like an Aunt Sally at a fair. Only — only some mornings you come down and I reckon you don't look right. Like you been having bad dreams.'

269

Charlotte went and trimmed the candle to hide her flush. 'No, no,' she said. 'Nothing like that.'

'I know you've had this bit of good fortune, with that money coming your way and all,' said Mr Skeels. 'But there's some troubles money won't cure. I know that. And so I get to thinking . . . They told me about the launch o' the Danes' new boat today,' he said after a pause.

Charlotte turned and presented what she hoped was an easy smile. 'Yes. She went off as trim as you like.'

'I wisht I could ha' been there,' said Mr Skeels. 'And I wish I could see Skipper Dane, and talk over a pipe and a glass. I got some things to say to him. I know we was your master and mistress once, Charlotte; but for a long time now thass seemed more like we was your father and mother, and thass a father's part to − to look out for his darter, and see she ain't being made unhappy.'

Charlotte did not speak for some moments. Then she squeezed Mr Skeels' hand. 'I couldn't wish for a kinder father, real or no,' she said. 'But you don't want to worrit, Mr Skeels, truly, for there's nothing amiss with me.'

He looked at her with a wistful smile. 'Well, I hope so, gel,' he said. 'But if there was − couldn't you tell me it in my bad ear, mebbe? That wouldn't signify.'

Charlotte laughed gently and shook her head. 'The fire's out, and you'll take cold,' she said. 'Let me ring the bell for Joseph, and you go back to bed and rest easy.'

Mr Skeels sighed and said no more until the manservant came to help him back to bed; then, leaning on Joseph's brawny shoulder, he shook his head and said, 'Legs that won't walk, and an ear that won't hear! And yet I'm afraid there's summat much worse − and thass a man with eyes who won't see!'

The *Heartsease* had been in service a couple of weeks when Charlotte walked into Shipden one chill afternoon to visit a poor old woman.

Gammer Druce was a fisherman's widow who lived with her niece in a tiny flint cottage that gave straight on to the road, so that draught-horses looked in at Gammer's windows, and ladies brushed the leaded panes with their cloaks. Gammer kept her soul insecurely fixed in her bent body by taking in washing, when arthritis would allow her, which it would not do at present; so Charlotte, who knew her well, took her some calf's-foot jelly from Mrs Skeels, and some money from herself which she placed discreetly on the chimney-piece; and having made up the fire, swept the little house-place, and set the kettle to boil, she sat down to keep the old woman company a while.

'Ah, thass a treat to see a young face acrorst the hearth,' said Gammer Druce, who was all dressed in shades of tissuey grey from cap to stockings. 'Faces in the fire are all very well, but they're never so pretty as yourn; and I don't see my niece from one week to the next lately.'

'She's not left you, surely, Gammer?'

'Not properly, dair: she've gone over Stiffkey way to get work cockle-gathering and such. Thass poor hard work, and I've heared the women as do it aren't more than half decent, some of 'em, wi' their skirts hitched and their legs unkivered summat unnatural; but she've give up her job with the gentlefolks up the hill a-ways, and she say anything'll be a feather bed after the way they treated her.'

'Why, were they unkind to her?'

'Oh! bless you, I've seen her pipe her eye many a time, when she've come back from there. Not that they took a broomstick to her, or anything of that shape: twas the hardness, and coldness, and sneering and fleering she couldn't abide. I thought at first that would be a good place: two old gentlefolks, very staid-like, wi' a granddarter in a consumption who they brung here for the air, renting a house and wanting a day-servant. Oh! but they're terrible rich and proud: the sort of folks who

271

look at you like they make gold guineas in the chamber-pot 'stead of stales; and do my poor niece make the smallest mistake — for she's rather a haynish item, though no harm in her — then they'd call her afore 'em, and dress her down, and make her feel like no more than a piece of dirt under your thumbnail. Everything in the house had to be just so, for they were used to living high in Lunnun and such, and besides being ole frail bodies they couldn't hardly bear to go out-a-doors and be among such a lot of common folk as Shipden show; and though the granddarter spoke to her nice enough — not long for this world, they reckon — my poor niece couldn't put up wi' the ole bodies' high ways no longer, specially when they called her a trull for no more'n waving to her young man from the kitchen-window — and so she give notice, and they only put her wages on the table, and tole her to be off then and there athout another word.'

'What's the name of these people, Gammer?' asked Charlotte, with her eyes fixed on the fire.

'Ward's the name — though my poor niece called 'em by others I'll not repeat. My niece do say she feel sorry for the pretty granddarter — not only on account of her going into a decline, but because the young lady used to go out of her way to be kind, and talk to her — but whenever she did, there would be the ole bodies complaining, and saying that wasn't proper for a granddarter o' theirn to goo getting familiar wi' sarvants and the like. Hey, well! I've nothing agin gentlefolks as such; but I'd like to take such high sorts as them down to Shipden church crypt, where the sexton found a cache o' bones all mixed up like spillikins, and ax 'em if they can tell which bones belonged to a fine lady and which to a fishwife.'

After this Charlotte did her best to keep up a conversation with the old woman, but her mind was elsewhere; and at last she got up to say goodbye. Gammer Druce, allowing her glance to fall on the pile of coins on the chimney-piece, laid her hand on Charlotte's arm a moment and said, 'Thass good of you, dair, and I won't say no as that's from you; but let me give you summat in return.' She took something from the folds of her shawl and placed it in Charlotte's hand. 'My niece found that over Stiffkey ways, and brought it me. Thass a fairy-loaf, and that'll bring you luck all your life — and there's nobody desarve that better.'

In Charlotte's hand lay a sea-urchin shell, known locally as a fairy-loaf, and much prized by the superstitious. 'Oh, I can't take that from you, Gammer,' Charlotte said. 'I've had some luck, you know — and surely you'd like to keep it.'

'Oh, I've got one of my own,' Gammer said, pointing to a similar shell on the window-sill. 'And this here fairy-loaf's a special lucky one — see the crosses on't, there — that mean you'll find a good husband who'll never give you a day's grief. I dare say there are such husbands, though I've never seen one,' she added with a chuckle, 'but howsomever, the little Pharisee who lost this loaf will bring you a good man, and you'll have your heart's desire. Take that, dair: keep that safe!'

Charlotte thanked the old woman; and with the fairy-loaf tucked in her waistband, set out for home along the seafront in the gathering dusk. Winter was at hand, and the picture presented by the sun dying on the sea-horizon was a harsh etching, with hatches of coppery light on a metallic ground. The air was cold, but when Charlotte paused and leaned with her hands on the sea-wall, she found the stone of it as warm to the touch as the surface of an oven — the massy sea-wall having absorbed the sunshine of the earlier day, and retaining the heat yet.

There was comfort in the feel of it, but a comfort which did not extend from her senses to her mind, for Charlotte was troubled in thinking over what the old woman had told her. She had never seen Loveday's grandparents, who as Gammer had said kept themselves aloof from Shipden; and neither had Toby.

She found herself thinking of Toby's situation without reference to herself. It was no use trying to deny what Toby so plainly felt for the sick girl; and in that state of feeling, he would not see the dim shapes of foreboding that Gammer's words had called up before her. He would not see – or if he saw, would refuse to consider. Reason was the first casualty of love. Charlotte knew that well.

She went on her way, and passed within sight of the Danes' cottage, where a chink of light showed at the shuttered house-place window. Something – perhaps that touch of comfort imparted by the stored warmth of the sea-wall – made her steal close to the cottage in the deepening shadows, and lay her hands against the exterior surface of the chimney-breast. The smooth flint was warm too – almost like a living thing – from the fire within; and Charlotte, after glancing around and seeing no one by, laid her cheek against it, and with dully beating heart closed her eyes for some moments.

For though that apprehension of Toby's predicament had suddenly come upon her without reference to herself, it could not remain so. Her feelings were not disinterested; and her pitying dread of his being hurt was all the keener, because she knew that hurt herself.

They were on the clifftop one morning – Charlotte, Toby and Loveday – when, breaking a long brooding silence, Loveday said abruptly: 'Take me up there again, will you, Toby? Where we went that very first time I met you.'

She pointed to the high promontory; and was silent again as Toby pushed the chair up the steep path winding between ferns, with Charlotte following nimbly behind.

'Wouldn't you like to walk?' said Toby, after Loveday had gazed at the sea for some time.

'Not today,' Loveday said. She stayed in the chair more often of late. Toby resumed his station by her side, observing her with that watchful, suspended look, like a mortal arrested by the sight of a goddess in a glade.

'How far out to sea do those gulls fly?' Loveday said.

'Oh, a good ways,' Toby said. 'They're always about our boat when we're out of the bay, and they follow the Yarmouth herringers too.'

'Suppose they were to fly so far, and then get tired, and be unable to fly back to land?' Loveday said. 'What would happen to them?'

'Oh, I don't reckon that happen,' Toby said. 'They can glide on the wind, for one thing, for any amount of time, athout so much as a flap of their wings.'

Loveday gave a wry smile. 'You always see the bright side of things, don't you, Toby?'

It was characteristic of Toby's reverential attitude to Loveday — and so uncharacteristic of his former self — that he gave a serious attention to her lightest remarks. He pondered, and said: 'I suppose I do; but I reckon it's always there to be found, you know. A-thinking of a bad thing's half-way to inviting it in — same wi' good things.'

'If I think of my health, then, will that bring it back?' said Loveday, her smile now so wry it was not a smile at all and made Charlotte shiver.

'Twill bring it nearer,' Toby said earnestly. 'That I know.'

Loveday sighed. 'I'm not good company today. I don't know what to think . . . I wanted to come up here, and see this view again, because I might not see it any more.'

'There, you see,' said Toby, 'thass not the way to think—'

'Dear Toby,' Loveday said, touching his arm, 'I mean because we may be going away soon. My grandparents are talking of taking me somewhere else, to try a different air again. They say — they say I'm not getting any better here.'

'Thass not true!' cried Toby.

'Where do they think you should go?' asked Charlotte.

Loveday shrugged. 'Somewhere I haven't tried yet, if there is anywhere. One doctor says one thing, another says another: they hark to the music of my lungs, and one doctor hears one tune, and another hears another, and so it goes on.' She suddenly wiped tears from her face with an angry motion. 'I don't *wish* to leave here,' she said. 'Why shouldn't I stay, for all the difference it will make?'

Toby threw a wild glance at Charlotte; but before he could speak Loveday said, sitting up straight in her chair with effortful brightness, 'Here comes Mrs Vickers, to spare you any more of my dreary company. I'm sorry, my dears, I promise I will be livelier tomorrow. What a fright she looks, marching towards us like that! She says she only takes tea in the Crab Pot, but I believe she tipples.'

Mrs Vickers reclaimed her charge and took her away, Loveday waving a languid backward hand as she went. When Charlotte at last looked at Toby, she was startled to see his boyish face mottled with rage.

'They can't do it,' he said, speaking as if to himself. 'They just can't do that.'

'Well – they are her guardians,' said Charlotte helplessly.

'Fine guardians! To suddenly decide to take her away from the one place that's done her good, and where she's started to get better at last!'

Charlotte, thinking of the way her own smallish hand now completely encircled Loveday's arm, could say nothing.

'Charlotte,' Toby said, with urgent appeal, 'she *is* getting better, isn't she? You think so too, don't you?'

'She – she is certainly no worse,' lied Charlotte, the weakness of whose nature it was to prefer any untruth to the giving of pain.

Toby paced about the turf. 'They can't take her away,' he said, again in the self-communing tone. 'Not now. That'd be the worst thing of all – for her sake – aye, for her sake. Well, they're making a mistake: I know that – so I must tell 'em so.'

His eyes were bent on the wind-rippled grass, so he did not see Charlotte blench.

'I'll go see these grandparents of hers, and introduce myself, and say how I've been helping to push Miss Ward's chair, and showing her the pretty spots along the cliffs, and so forth,' Toby said, 'and I'll say how much this do seem to benefit her, and how I've heard as they might be moving on, and I've come to ax 'em to think again—'

'No, Toby!' said Charlotte: the vision in her mind of Toby in his fisherman's gansy approaching the haughty Wards, made her cry out with unusual emphasis. 'Toby, please – think what you're saying.'

Toby looked baffled. 'I'm saying no more'n the truth. If they love their granddarter, they'll surely listen; and I can say how being with us seems to help her—'

'Don't do it, Toby,' Charlotte said.

He frowned. 'Why, don't you care if Loveday leaves?'

She bit her lip. 'It isn't that.'

'Well, I reckon it sound like it. Thass not like you, Charlotte.' And as she again shook her head he went on with annoyance: 'If I didn't know you better, I'd say your turn of fortune's made you hard. You always used to care for folk so.'

'Thass because I care that I don't want you to go and see the Wards,' said she indistinctly.

Toby shook this off, as not even wishing to understand.

'Toby, please promise me you won't do it,' Charlotte said, struggling to master her emotion.

'Not athout a reason why.'

He was obdurate; and so, unable to bear giving him the pain of the real reason, and unable to bear the thought of him going to the Wards and suffering the pain of their disdainful dismissal, Charlotte used the one weapon she dreaded to use – the weapon that only hurt herself. 'Toby,' she said, 'do you remember when we first became friends, all those years ago? When you'd lost your sister Meggy that you loved so much? And you said to me that I was like another sister to you, a dear sister like poor dead

Meggy . . . I was − so proud and happy about that, and − I still am . . . So I'm saying, if Meggy had asked you, as a favour to her, not to go see the Wards − if Meggy had asked you to promise that, would you have give your promise?'

The anger had left Toby's face, and his voice was soft as he answered, 'Yes. Yes, I would.'

'Then, Toby, won't you give that promise to me?' She swallowed − it felt like swallowing knives. 'As your sister?'

Toby, with sudden weariness, sat down on the turf with his forearms on his knees. 'Of course, Charlotte,' he said. 'Of course I will. I'm sorry. You are a sister to me − how could I forget it? − a dear sister, and I'll do whatever you ask.'

She knelt beside him, determined not to show in her face the agony her own words had cost her. He inclined his head against her shoulder, and with a slightly trembling hand she smoothed the crisp black hair that the busy wind had twined and tangled.

'I think of her − so much,' he said.

'Of Meggy?'

He shook his head. 'Of Loveday.' He glanced up at her, his eyes with their arched brows no more than a hand's breadth from hers. 'But you've got my promise that I won't go see the Wards − a brother's promise.'

After a minute they descended the cliff path, and parted outside the Crab Pot. 'Sorry I was mardy, Charlotte,' Toby said as he left. 'I don't know . . . Thass like I don't quite know where I am lately.'

'Thass all right, Toby,' said Charlotte; and she went into the inn, and helped with the baking, forgetting as usual to put an apron over her fine new frock; talked a while with Mr Skeels, who was net-mending; and then made the excuse of her soiled frock to slip up to her room.

The inn-sign beneath her window gave its croon of welcome, but the sound fell on her ears like a screech;

and Charlotte, flinging herself down on the bed, longed to cry out too, to rend with screams the air of the peaceful little room that had seen her grow, and seen too the quiet growth of feelings that were now a source of profoundest anguish to her.

But Charlotte did not cry out. She was the sort of person whom no one expected to cry out, the sort of person who put up with things, and smoothed things over, and always had a good-humoured laugh that made other people wish they were as easy-going and down-to-earth as she. She was not framed for the expression of despair, and for that reason it afflicted her gentle body and patient soul with the tortures of the damned.

'A sister – oh, a sister! No, no, no!' she whispered, running one hand back and forth on the ragwork counterpane, which the tears in her eyes refracted to a swirl of mad colour. The hand that had touched Toby's hair she crammed into her mouth to stifle her sobs. Well, she had Toby's promise that he would not go to the Wards – that humiliation would not be his: she believed him, for he had promised her as a brother . . . But how much rather she would have had even the perfidy of a lover, than the faithfulness of a brother! How she could have borne even to watch him humiliated, if only it was upon her breast that he would seek to hide his burning face afterwards, and in her eyes look for the assurance that he was loved, and worthy of it!

She rose abruptly from the bed, and went to the trunk beneath the window to find writing-paper; for it suddenly came upon her that she should leave Shipden at once, and go to Jed in Heartsease. Although it was not in her power to stop loving Toby, she could at least put herself out of reach of him, and so not be forced to witness his progress to the end of the path on which he was set – an end of which nothing was certain but its ultimate darkness. If she could not help him, she could at least spare herself.

But she had barely set pen to paper before she desisted, and tore the sheet across. She could not go away: she must stay and see it through, even though it threatened to tear her heart in twain as surely as that paper. She did not think well of herself for the decision; but a compassionate observer must surely have granted that Charlotte Wintergreen was not the first mortal to embrace her pain, nor was likely to be the last. No observer, however, was on hand to see the marks of the suffering that she hastened to hide, no observer would see the tears that she quickly dried — the tears so secretly shed, so burningly felt, by those loyal natures that do not choose to parade their hurts.

Chapter Eleven

Love In The Light

One December day, two figures were to be seen pursuing a path through the wood that, straddling the road to Madhouse Heath, lay immediately to the south of Heartsease. A winter gale had lately shaken the wood, bringing down dry twigs and branches, and as Squire Ingamells had yet to find a way of preventing the villagers from picking up what the elements scattered on the ground, Rosa went stick-gathering for fuel, and Pierce went with her.

A bleak white sky showed through the interlacing of boughs, and seemed even to bleach the moss of colour, so that the wood formed a composition of severest monochrome; and there was a feeling of naked emptiness in the air that gave to the spot the atmosphere of some ruined work of man's hands, roofless and deserted, rather than a segment of nature at a customary stage of its cycle. The crackle of dead vegetation under the feet of the stick-gatherers sounded like the report of gunfire, and the occasional flight of a crow or pigeon disturbed in the upper branches was attended with such an almighty crashing and creaking that creatures of primeval wingspan might have been supposed to be roosting there among the homely beech and ash.

In this scene the human participants, the one so fair, the other so dark, exhibited all the glow, vitality and significance that leafless nature had resigned, and accordingly wore an aspect larger than life. There was a sufficient combination of urgency and harmony in their movements to make speech unnecessary and silence not uncomfortable, Rosa with her experienced eye doing most of the gathering, Pierce making up the bundles with twine and hoisting them on his shoulders; and when at length they sat down to rest on the ground where it sloped to form a small dell, the same companionable silence obtained for some time, until Pierce pulled a package from his pocket.

'Courtesy of Heartsease Hall,' he said, unwrapping bread, cold tongue, and cold beef. 'Only the best.'

'Fire me!' breathed Rosa, her eyes widening. 'Never tell me you're creeping down to the kitchens to fill your pockets.'

'No need. All this cold collation was set out this morning for the hunt that's meeting there. Miss Ingamells invited me to take some as I'd be going out sketching. It's because she and her father are with the hunt that I've got the day to myself. Eat up.'

Rosa did so, hardly bearing to swallow what tasted so wonderful, for she never had butcher's meat from one month to the next. 'That was thoughtful of her,' she said between mouthfuls. 'Have she got a taking for you, d'you reckon?'

'Good God, no,' said Pierce. 'We get along pretty well, but I'm only the drawing-master. I fancy Mr Ingamells would have me in Norwich Castle if there was the faintest suggestion of *that*.'

'Do she have admirers, then?'

'None that I've seen. She often says, in this self-mocking way she has, that she was born to be an old maid; and certainly her father treats her so. It's a pity: she's a clever woman, and talented; but she is awkward, and will never get less so living the way she does.'

'Plenty of fellows will put up wi' awkudness and plainness if there's money to go with 'em — so I've heard,' said Rosa.

'Well, she's no heiress — most of the Ingamells' wealth is tied up in the estate, and that will go to this distant cousin of theirs when Mr Ingamells dies . . . Why, Rosa, you don't think *I'm* one of those mercenary fellows?'

'I wouldn't blame you if you were,' Rosa said. 'If you can get a good living just by walking down a church-aisle, why not?'

He smiled at her but did not answer. She knew that she had a tendency to produce these hard and cynical remarks in his presence, as if to undermine his admiration of her; and she suspected that he realized it. She dropped her eyes.

'Anyway what's all this talk of admirers?' Pierce said. 'You know there's no one for me but you, Rosa — there'll never be anyone else.'

'Now, Pierce,' said she, holding up a warning finger, 'you promised me there'd be none of that nonsense today.'

'Very well,' he said easily, leaning back with his arms behind his head. 'I don't want to do anything to spoil such a day as this.'

'Yes,' said Rosa, regarding his keen profile through a fringe of lowered lashes. 'That've been a good day.'

'If there's anyone up there listening,' Pierce said, addressing the sky, 'send me a few more days like this, if you please.'

'I don't think there's anyone listening,' said Rosa. ''Tis we alone, I believe.'

'You needn't be alone, Rosa,' said Pierce, propping himself on his elbow in his loose-limbed way. 'Life needn't be so. If you would only accept me — yes, I know I said I wouldn't talk nonsense. And I'll stop now, on my solemn oath.' His face, so open and candid, was serious — too serious for her peace. 'But it isn't nonsense, Rosa — far from it.'

She tore her gaze from his, and stood up to brush the crumbs from her hessian apron. 'Have you seen Jed lately?' she said.

'I called at Plague House the other day, but he was out in his fields. Marianne entertained me a while. She looks well again, though a little subdued.'

'Thass a cruel thing to miscarry a child,' said Rosa.

'And yet even after that, that father of hern still won't see her. No one was surprised at him being set agin the wedden; but thass got to be a cold man who can still carry on as if she's no darter of his. They do say he've grown harder than ever since she left, and them of the workpeople who aren't frit to death on him hate him like the very devil.'

'I'm afraid none of them hate him more than Jed does,' said Pierce.

In the distance, where the edge of the open heath was visible through the tracery of trees, Rosa could see swatches of bright scarlet in rapid movement, and simultaneously a disturbance in the air that had been increasing during the last few minutes became identifiable as the baying of hounds. She and Pierce picked a path to the outskirts of the wood, and watched the hunt go streaming away across the heath. It was a familiar sight to Rosa, but it would have confirmed Mr Ingamells' view of the decline of the sturdy peasantry had he known that she saw nothing of lovable Old England in the sight. All she could think of was the grain that just one of those horses had eaten that morning, and how it was more solid food than the Widow Thorne had in a week.

'I'm glad you don't hunt, Pierce,' she said.

'Put me on one of those thundering great horses and I should be terrified out of my wits,' said Pierce. 'I only hunt views.'

'You're a gentle man,' she said, speaking her thoughts aloud, her caution slipping for a moment. 'Thass a different thing from a gentleman.'

'All too often, I'm afraid,' he said. 'D'you know, when I was working for Signor Gardini in London, there was a baronet who used to come to the studio — quite a patron of the arts, cultivated, and he once declined Signor Gardini's invitation to stay to supper, because he was going to Soho to a ratting-match — to see a pit full of rats mauled to death by terriers.'

These glimpses he gave her of his past, of that wider grander world in which he had been accustomed to move, afflicted Rosa both with curiosity and with a sort of shrinking within herself. The intimacy enhanced her sense of separation, for how could their two worlds touch?

'My father had a rough enough life of it as a sea-captain, as all sailors do,' Pierce said, 'but he is extraordinarily gentle, in a fierce sort of way. In Portsmouth once I saw him seize a man who was whipping an old underfed donkey and upend him in a horse-trough. He grasped the fellow by the legs and dunked him over and over. "Let us see how ill-treatment improves your temper, sir!" he kept saying. "Let us see!"'

She was always touched by the affection with which Pierce spoke of his father; but disturbed, too, by an image of this Captain Coppinger, and what he might think if a crystal ball should show him his son tramping the fields with a coarse-dressed village girl who could only just write her name. Her misgivings deepened as Pierce went on: 'I know you would like him, Rosa: he's so true and plain and warm-hearted.'

'I'm sure he is,' she said uneasily.

'He's the sort of man you can always speak openly to. That's why I wrote a letter this morning telling him about you, about the wonderful girl I've met at Heartsease, and how proud I am to know her—'

'How dare you! You had no right to do that!' she cried – so loud and sharply, and with such a violent flushing of her cheeks that Pierce stepped back in astonishment. 'Don't – don't do that any more, I tell you!'

'I never dreamed it would make you angry—'

'No? Well it do. Tisn't right . . .'

But her anger was a disguise for alarm – alarm at the thought of Pierce's gentlemanly father and what he must think of her. She was a proud girl, but pride and self-esteem do not necessarily go together, and often the first can be a cover for the lack of the second.

'Rosa — I would never have done it if I'd known you'd feel like this. And I give you my promise I won't post the letter if that's what you want,' Pierce said. 'But I just don't understand. It's because of you, after all, that I'm here. I wrote only the truth—'

'Don't speak of't any more, Pierce,' said she, shaking her head, and picking up one of the bundles of firewood.

'I've got to. Rosa, we've been so happy in each other's company today, haven't we? You said so yourself. How can I not wish for a lifetime of such days? Why can't that be?'

'Twould be very nice if the world wagged like that. But that don't. Thass folly to think so.'

He regarded her sombrely. 'You're hard, Rosa,' he said with an air of sorrowful discovery. 'I never realized how hard.'

Rosa's cheeks tingled, for the words stung her, but she answered doggedly, 'Because I have to be.'

'Even to me?'

'Especially to you. Because thass best, best for you. Oh, Pierce,' she said, 'why can't you find a girl of your own sort, and love her, and be happy?'

'Of my own sort.' It was his turn to be curt. He paced about, breathing hard. 'So, after meeting you, who have so much spirit and beauty and warmth and courage that every other girl looks like a shade beside you, I am to go into society and gaze into the little pink eyes of a pampered miss who believes that the bread on her tea-table grows on trees; and I'm to spend an eternity of evenings with her in a stuffy drawing-room, talking stale gossip and growing stout inside my sober waistcoat, and never once thinking of the time when I walked in the woods with Rosa, and heard Rosa's voice that thrilled me to the soul, and felt more alive through one touch of her hand than I shall ever feel again.' He was angry: she had never seen that before. 'And that is being *happy*, is it?'

The love of her expressed in these words struck to her heart, but so accustomed was she to little valuing herself that she fended them off. What chiefly afflicted her, as he stood balefully gazing into her eyes, was a sore realization that she was making him unhappy. He had lost his ease of mind because of her. She did not want that.

'I only meant — I only meant that you see too much in me,' she said. 'For your sake, it would be better if you didn't.'

He made a helpless gesture with open hands. 'Perhaps it would. But it's no good. I'm lost.'

'I wish you would think badly of me,' she said, but he only shook his head, seeming to sink into profound thought, and at last they picked up their bundles and resumed their way.

He left her at the door of the Widow Thorne's cottage, seeming at the last to try and recover his lightness of manner, as if he felt he had behaved badly. No such thought was in her mind: it was of her own conduct that she was thinking as she set to work in the yard behind the house, chopping up the wood and tying it into faggots.

Yes, it had been a good day until then: she had allowed the happiness of it to steal upon her, like sunshine warming the back. That was the trouble — she did enjoy his company: she enjoyed it more than was good for her peace of mind. The temptation was all too great just to let it continue, as you were tempted to bask a while in the sun when you were working in the field — until the farm-bailiff caught you, and you were turned home with no money for bread.

For she must not allow it: in very fairness to him, she must not allow it. He was too romantic: that was his nature. He could not see, as she could see, that real life did not admit of such a union as theirs, that he was sinking deeper and deeper into a fanciful dream from which the waking would be all the more disastrously disillusioning. She did not blame him for it: her own harsh experience of life had made her alert to the unstinting way in which fate doled out pain, and so she had mounted the necessary guard about herself. Pierce lacked such defences, and was all the more likely to be hurt.

She did not want him to be hurt − not he, of all people in the world! And she had seen today that she was hurting him. While refusing to countenance what could never be, she was continuing to see him, and talk with him, and so kindle in his breast a smouldering hope; and that was not fair. She had a hatred of flirts and coquettes: anything less than complete frankness in human relations she saw, in her blunt way, as a lie. To carry on would be to compromise her own nature, and to insult what she knew was a true, though misguided, feeling in his.

She rubbed her cold chafed hands together, and looked up at the thatch of the cottage, where tattered remnants of birds' nests spoke of a dead spring. She hoped the Widow Thorne would be able to manage here on her own, for she knew she must go away.

It must be quickly: a sharp amputation. That was best. He would come to see, in time, that it could never have worked.

She roused herself, and began to haul the faggots into the woodshed, straining her tired muscles so that she should not think of anything but the ache of them; for just for a moment there her heart had seemed to give out a moan at the prospect of never seeing him any more. Even as she toiled, an uncertainty momentarily settled on her − a suspicion that if Pierce erred on the side of romanticism, she erred on the side of scepticism, and that what she called self-preservation was cowardice.

But she brushed it aside. 'There's good land where there's a foul way' was a favourite local saying; and her way lay out of Heartsease, away from Pierce, away from the dangers of the unguarded heart.

The doctor from Swaffham had gone away again in his red-wheeled gig, and Jed and Marianne were left alone in the parlour of Plague House.

'He makes me feel rather a fraud,' Marianne said.

'No, no,' said Jed. 'No harm in sending for him if you don't feel quite right.'

'But that's just it. I feel perfectly all right. I have done for some time. I feel as strong as an ox. It's the mind, I suppose — a sort of listlessness . . . He calls it loss of tone, which makes me feel like a piano. He says exercise might help — riding, perhaps.'

'We don't have a horse fit for the saddle. I must see if anyone round about have got a gentle nag they want to sell . . . If you fancy the idea of riding, I mean.'

'I suppose it might be a novelty . . .' She raised one delicately shaped eyebrow, a quirk of hers that still charmed him. 'I wish we might go away somewhere.'

'Where?'

'Oh! I don't know. The doctor did say a change might benefit me. See new scenes, new people . . .'

'Tired of me already, eh?' he said, kissing her hair.

They both laughed, a little too heartily.

'A little tired of Heartsease, perhaps,' she said.

'Marianne, you know I can't leave the farm just now. This will be my first season of crops, and I want it to be a good one. Come harvest I want there to be plenty of work for people, and plenty of food that'll go to their tables and not straight to Norwich market. Twould be very nice to go jaunting, but it wouldn't be right, and I wouldn't be good company on account of worrying about the fields—' He made himself stop: he suspected that she grew irritated when he spoke in that dogged tone. 'You do see, my dear, don't you?'

'I was brought up on a farm myself, Jed,' said Marianne. 'I'm not quite ignorant.'

'I know you're not.'

He wasn't sure, but he couldn't remember their ever conducting conversations in these jerks, these odd cooling phases, before they were married.

'Do you still grieve that your father won't see you?' he said.

'Oh . . .' She shrugged. 'I suppose it's no different from living in another part of the country, say, and never seeing him because of that. It's just the thought of his hating me that troubles me.'

'It isn't you he hates. It's me,' said Jed grimly.

'Couldn't you — couldn't you try and make it up with him, Jed?'

Jed made an impatient gesture. 'Your father won't even greet me when we pass in the road. He'll only be reconciled to me when I'm under a tombstone.'

'Jed!'

'It's true, Marianne — you know it. And besides . . . It's not just a question of his being reconciled to me. I can't think of him with anything but — but hatred. D'you know last week he had a poor woman who'd come looking for work thrown out of the parish ? She could barely stand on her legs, and so she was thrown on a donkey-cart and driven out to Madhouse Heath and put down on the road and told she'd go before the magistrates if she come back. And the other overseers congratulated him on his firm stand against idle vagrancy.'

'That's not my fault.'

'I never said it was.'

'He's still my father. I don't expect you to like him — but things never will be any easier between us if you insist on keeping up this feud with him, and setting yourself in opposition to everything he does in Heartsease.'

'Am I to stand by and do nothing, then, while he takes his anger out on poor folks who've no power to hit back?'

'I notice your precious powerless poor folk still manage to bring you poached game,' said Marianne.

'I can't help that.'

'You needn't encourage them. You're like Guy Fawkes and his plotters with those young fellows — quite ruffians, some of them.'

'I dare say I should be something of a ruffian myself if

I was in their hopeless position,' said Jed. 'I give 'em work when I can; I help 'em when I can; I don't encourage 'em to poach, not because I've any tenderness for Mr Ingamells' game, but because I know Mr Ingamells would have 'em wear out their lives on the treadmill if they were caught.'

'Parson Wintergreen is preaching to me again,' said Marianne.

As she said this there rose in Jed an impatience so intense that he was alarmed by it; and he seemed to rebound to an anxious tenderness. 'Marianne,' he said, 'you know I love you, don't you?'

'Of course I do,' she said, looking up at him and finally smiling. 'I know you do, Jed.'

He knelt beside her and kissed her; and it did not occur to him that a few months ago such a thing would not have needed to have been said.

'And I'm sorry you're feeling dull.'

'Oh! well − life can't be all excitement, can it?' said she, with a laugh that was more wistful than careless.

A figure passed the parlour window.

'Thass Todd Gault coming to see me,' Jed said, rising.

'Oh, Jed, won't you go and meet him outside? He does make such a mess in the house with his great boots.'

He started to say something, then changed his mind and patted her hand. 'All right, my love.'

He went out to the yard to meet Todd Gault, his most frequent visitor. He had found Todd a good deal of work when he was renovating Plague House, and had helped him out in numerous small ways since; and he was repaid with a regard almost disconcerting in its loyalty. Todd was a young man not yet twenty, stocky as a terrier: his curly hair and fresh beardless face gave a peculiar poignancy to the haunted and troubled expression he habitually wore. Of all the dispossessed and discontented youths of the village, it was to Todd Gault that Jed felt closest, insofar as he saw in that struggle-marked face, expressive of hope searching for a toehold in the blank wall of circumstance, a reflection of his own younger self.

'Come in the kitchen and have some ale, Todd,' said Jed.

'No, no: I won't stay, thank ye,' said Todd. He was dressed in the neckscarf, short waistcoat, breeches and coarse woollen stockings of the poorest of the village labourers; and Jed perceived that he did not feel at ease entering Plague House in the presence of the mistress who had, since their marriage, considerably gentrified the old place. 'I just wondered if you'd heard about my cousin Clem. He've packed up and left, and gone for to work on the railway-builden.'

'Another, eh?' said Jed sadly. 'I thought Clem wasn't over-strong, Todd: will he be equal to navvy-work?'

'He say he will, if that mean he get a decent wage at last,' said Todd.

Jed sighed. 'I suppose I can't blame him, nor the others who've gone to join the navvies, but thass wrong they should have to do it. Come my first crop, I should be able to take on some more people here, but I've no more work for 'em just now . . .' He regarded Todd with misgiving. 'Why, Todd, you're not thinking of doing the same as Clem?'

The young man, whose unrestful air gave him the appearance of being perpetually nerved for flight, scuffed his boots upon the cobbles and said, 'That've crossed my mind more'n once. Thass not what I want in life: I feel like Heartsease is the place where I do belong. But you know what thass like here now, Jed: you know better'n anyone. There's hardly a hand's turn of work but what Farmer Hemstock offer; and he pay so low, and hire so short, thass no better living than a pauper; and no one dare lift their head to him, he've gone so short and hard and fierce. I'm sorry to say it – I mean, you wedden his daughter and all.'

Jed shook his head. 'You know there's no love lost between me and Farmer Hemstock, Todd; and you're only speaking true. But I don't like the thought of you going to join the navvies. Thass not the life for you.'

Earnestly Todd said: 'Me and some of the other ole boys . . . we talk a lot about what the men of Heartsease did all them years ago – your father and the others – how they stood up for theirselves. And how we ought to try and be like them. Oh, mebbe not in the way they did it,' he added hurriedly. 'I mean we should ask for what's right and fair, straight out. I reckon it's because folk in Heartsease have been so quiet and frit so long that men like Hemstock think they can do just as they like – we make it easy for him, you see, yet that'd make him blink his eyes a bit do we change our ways, and show him we're not about to be down-trod no more – d'you see?'

This was spoken in Todd's characteristic rapid, urgent fashion, his hands clasping and unclasping the air as if he were groping for the words.

'What do you think to do, exactly?' said Jed, musing.

'Why, ax Farmer Hemstock to set right what's wrong. Ax him to grant us a fair wage, like you do pay, and to hire by the week, at least, so's we know there'll be bread on the table come Saturday. Thass only fair dealing – ain't it?'

'Who's to do the asking?'

'I reckon I'll do it myself.' A sort of anxious defiance crossed Todd's young face. 'You don't think I'm afraid of Farmer Hemstock, do you, afraid to stand up for myself?'

'No, no,' said Jed. 'Nothing of the sort. What I'm thinking is you and the others who feel the same ought to stand together if you're to have any chance. Hemstock can just refuse to employ one man; but thass different if there's a group of you, all determined.'

'Right enough: I reckon there's plenty who'll stick by me. But I mean to do the speaking, all the same. I want to do something to show I'm made of the same stuff as the men of 'thirty. Thass since you've come back that I've started to see how things might be in Heartsease, and how there's other ways of living besides creeping along wi' your hat in your hand just because the big folks like to see you that way.'

It was a high satisfaction to Jed to hear these words, and to know that his hopes of working a change in Heartsease were beginning to be fulfilled. But one thing made him uneasy. 'I like your spirit, Todd,' he said. 'My father, and the others, would have been proud to know there was still Heartsease men to come after them who'd stand up for justice. But I don't think you'd better mention my name when you ask Farmer Hemstock for higher wages. There's such a world of hate between him and me, that if you was to use me as an example of the sort of terms you want, that'd be the very thing to make him more stubborn than before.'

'Well – all right – if thass what you think best,' said Todd. There was a mingling of respect and surprise in his tone; and it occurred to Jed that his own proviso had a cowardly sound. He believed that what he had said was true, that Todd's cause would not be helped by bringing in the name of Jed Wintergreen, but to Todd that must sound like an evasion. It was not right to encourage the young man to assert himself against Hemstock and then disclaim any involvement himself.

'Todd – forget what I just said,' he said emphatically. 'You go about it however you think best – I'll back you up.'

Todd gave one of his rare smiles and shook Jed's hand, and as he departed waved with something of the air, always embarrassing to Jed, of saluting a hero.

Jed waved back, then walked round to the stables. He experienced again a faint misgiving. He liked Todd, and felt a strong loyalty to him and his kind; but sometimes he had a sense almost of belonging to another generation, and wondered whether he quite had the measure of what went on in their heads, and whether he might not be playing with fire. But his heart revolted at the thought of any more of them drifting off to join the railway navvies — that was precisely the trend he sought to reverse in Heartsease; and his own enmity with Elias Hemstock was too powerful to subside into a passive opposition. He had been married to that man's daughter for several months, yet the purity of his hatred was undiminished.

And his love for Marianne? Had that been sustained so completely, so passionately?

He cast his eye over the stables. There should be room enough for a saddle-horse, if Marianne took to the idea.

Outside again he saw his wife's graceful form walking about the small flower-garden she had had laid out. It was one of those winter days of clear penetrating light, when shadows, whatever the colour of the surface they fall on, take the form of beautiful variations of indigo; and Marianne, fair-skinned and slender in her sky-coloured gown, seemed herself more of an optical impression than a creature of flesh and blood. Pity, tenderness and bafflement were only some of the constituents of Jed's emotion as he regarded her, an emotion he could not name or grasp. It was plain that she was quite well now in body: equally plain that in mind she was far from content.

She had miscarried only a matter of weeks after their marriage. The doctor was reassuring: there was no congenital disorder that would prevent her carrying a child to its full term next time; it was a sad mischance of nature. But nature could hardly have chosen its moment more mischievously. The coming child had hustled them into marriage: now that the child was no more, it was as if they were awakening, and looking about them at their situation, and wondering how they had got here.

Their courtship had grown up in a passionate rejection of external circumstance: it had gone forward as if in a material vacuum. Indeed, courtship was too conventional a name for what had flared up from the combustion of their two natures. But marriage was a mould in which the raw material of any love must assume a more or less prescribed shape; and so it was with theirs.

Perhaps it was foolish to expect an eternal satisfaction to reign once their union was settled, like a line drawn under their account. But it was being swiftly borne in on Jed that that dissatisfaction that had characterized Marianne when they first met was not like an arithmetical sum to which there was a single answer. Whatever she had found in him, it was not enough; and in the faint bitterness of this realization, he wondered if anything could ever be enough, and whether that restless aspiration which was one of the things he had loved about her was like an appetite that fed on itself, and was incapable of fulfilment.

Heartsease had brought them together: Heartsease divided them. To him this place was everything he valued and cherished. Plague House, the farm, the village, the people, the woods and fields and meadows, were to him not simply a way of living: they were the expression of an ideal which had long sustained his soul. But where he saw a visionary community, Marianne saw rural isolation and backwardness. The turning of the soil by the harrow, the sight of familiar faces and figures in lane and stackyard, the touch of the seasons transfiguring with leaf or snow or blossom a thousand spots already freighted with association, continued to fill him with that sense of glorious rightness missing through the lost years. For Marianne these were the wearisome incidentals of a world with which she had no connection beyond mere proximity. He knew she was bored with Heartsease: he did not yet believe she was bored with him, but the question was raised in his mind for the simple reason that he could not dissever his own identity from that of the village. And nor did he want to.

Yet it was not as if marriage had revealed them to be strangers to one another. They had seen and loved in each other the same warm impulsive temperaments they still possessed. But it was in the tendency to wishfulness, rather than in the wishes themselves, that they were well matched. Their dreams were like curves that intersected only to diverge again.

And would they go on diverging, travelling further and further apart? Dread thought, and Jed rejected it even as some stubborn part of him insistently embraced Heartsease and the life he had found here. No, there must be a way to common ground for himself and Marianne, even if it could never again be the enchanted ground they had trod in those wonderful vanished days before their love had come out into the light.

The next day seemed to bring opportunity. A letter arrived from Jed's lawyer Mr Veazey, chiefly consisting of business matters, but concluding with the news that Mr and Mrs Veazey had tickets for a charity ball at the Norwich Assembly Rooms next week, and cordially inviting Jed and Marianne to join them and to spend the night at their house.

Though it was a far from attractive prospect to Jed, he determined, in the spirit of yesterday's decision, that they would go. Marianne was delighted – though the delight was tempered with despair that she had nothing to wear.

'Why, what's wrong with that frock you've got on now?' said Jed.

'Oh, Jed, you are impossible! This is an *evening* occasion. I really must find something at least half-way tolerable else I shall hardly dare show my face. I suppose my pink shot silk is a remote possibility, if I could get a girl from the village to alter it for me . . .'

'You look lovely whatever you wear,' said Jed, experiencing a rush of affection at seeing her so excited, and kissing the nape of her neck.

'That's very sweet of you, and not at all true,' she said, absently kissing him back. 'If we're to stay with the Veazeys I'll need a decent morning-dress too. And you must try on your evening-clothes, and let me inspect you – you're too handsome to go walking in there looking like a two-horse farmer in a boiled shirt.'

'Well, I am a farmer, my dear.'

'Now you know what I mean, Jed Wintergreen, so don't be provoking.'

The week that saw the approach of the ball also saw Marianne in higher spirits than at any time for months. It was impossible for Jed not to be infected by them too; and they set out for Norwich in mutually sunny mood — even though in a humble spring-cart which Marianne deplored for the traces of cattle-fodder in its interior. They made the journey early, for there was a livestock-market in the city that day, and Jed intended looking out for a saddle-horse for Marianne; and when they arrived at the Veazeys' house in Tombland, Mrs Veazey alone welcomed them, her husband being engaged with business until four.

'I hope you had an easy journey — I fear the roads must be rather the worse for these sharp frosts. The railway terminus at Thorpe is all finished now, you know, and no doubt soon we shall all be flying about the county on the wings of steam,' said Mrs Veazey. 'Mr Veazey has ridden upon a train, and informs me that the sensation is delightful.'

Marianne, not wishing to trample about the market, said she trusted Jed's judgement, and let him go horse-hunting by himself; and she spent the afternoon with Mrs Veazey who, amiable, loquacious and eagle-nosed, entertained her in the parlour wearing, as a token of domesticity, an ornately embroidered apron (about as practical as a tutu) and so many beads and seed-pearls in her hair that they made reflected constellations in the polished rosewood and glass.

'Well! we shall see a fair sprinkling of good company tonight, I fancy,' Mrs Veazey said. 'The charity boasts several distinguished names among its patrons, though of course some of them winter abroad, and are not seen in the county at this time of year.'

Winter abroad! Marianne had to stop herself sighing aloud at that; for all her old yearnings for travel and glamour were fired anew at this temporary respite from country dullness, and from the cramped enervation of spirits that had possessed her these past months. She felt at ease with Mrs Veazey: the small arts and protocols that had formed the chief substance of her expensive education returned readily to her; and she began to wonder whether Jed might be persuaded to move to Norwich, for if the old city was not London or Paris, neither was it Heartsease, and she already felt more alive after a matter of hours here.

The shapes of her own discontent, thus thrown against the bright background of her desires, manifested themselves to Marianne's consciousness for the first time. The grief of the miscarriage and the sheer strangeness of being married had obscured those shapes, but now there was no longer any denying that married to Jed and living at Plague House she felt like a caught bird in a cage. The farmhouse domesticity irked her: she had no taste for the everyday tasks from which her father's ambition and wealth had protected her; and the strain of separation from her family had begun to tell on her, for though before her marriage she had often longed to be free of them, she was a person who craved love, and on whom the coldness of disapproval struck like a physical chill. She wondered whether the baby, had it lived, might have made a crucial difference; but it was no use dwelling on such conjectures when what oppressed her was the prospect of the future.

The future, of course, with Jed. Perhaps it would have been better if they had met in some conventional social manner! – for whilst she had fallen in love with the essence of him, felt that she dearly loved it still, she looked with dismay on the superficial aspects of him, those everyday ways and habits that married life forced into such prominence. Castaway on a desert island she could have loved him wholeheartedly: as a social being he afforded her frustration and disappointment. She felt herself buried in an earthy seclusion from all the alluring variety of the wider world, which to him was only so much distant chatter, but which called to her with enticing accents.

It was typical of Marianne that when Jed returned from the market, declaring he had found the very horse for her, her mood swung round from extreme impatience to affection on seeing him again; though she deprecated the awkwardness of his kissing her so heartily in front of Mrs Veazey even as she enjoyed the kiss. The old battle between the natural impulses of her heart and the demands of a learned decorum was, in fact, thoroughly resumed.

At four Mr Veazey bounced in from his office, breezily shook Marianne's hand, and expressed his great pleasure at meeting Mrs Wintergreen at last; and declared that he had been convinced that matrimony was the ideal state, ever since the day when the former Miss Brocklehurst had consented to change that distinguished name to his.

'That, Mrs Wintergreen, was a day to remember!' said Mr Veazey. 'Such quantities of lace and orange-blossom! Such an equipage! Such a cake! For this, you must remember, was a Brocklehurst wedding; and there were at the wedding-breakfast, if my memory serves me right, no less than eleven bearers of that notable name—'

'My dear — twelve!' said Mrs Veazey, complacently smiling. 'My great-uncle Horatio, down from Derbyshire.'

'How could I forget!' beamed the lawyer. 'Possibly most distinguished of all — seventy if a day, upright enough for forty, noble head like a bust of a philosopher—'

'Aristotle, was the general opinion,' said Mrs Veazey.

'Aristotle! You've hit it, my dear! Twelve Brocklehursts, gathered at that wedding-breakfast, Mrs Wintergreen; and if a thunderbolt had levelled the house at that moment, the loss to society would have been too awful to contemplate. As for the marriage-service — may I speak confidentially to you, Mrs Wintergreen?'

Marianne said she would be honoured.

'Honoured! I call that obliging! You're the incarnation of the graces, Mrs Wintergreen – that's what you are. Well, as I knelt at that altar, my dear madam, I confess to you that this thought crossed my mind: can I, a plain country solicitor, really dare to take the hand of a Miss Brocklehurst, in full view of her relatives, amongst whom may be counted, to take only one instance, the sister-in-law of a man who would have been certain to be the next Lord Chancellor, had not Providence intervened in the form of an attack of flying gout, and carried him aloft to sit on the heavenly Woolsack—? Can I presume to lift this veil of Isis? But my answering thought was: Do it quickly! Such an opportunity is not to be refused! And so I did; and Mrs Veazey's great-uncle Horatio was good enough to throw a shoe after our nuptial carriage – and this mark of regard from a man with such a head made me swear upon the spot: I will be worthy of her!'

Marianne said she was sure he had been so, thinking the while of her own hurried quiet wedding, which at the time had seemed rather romantic like an elopement, but which now appeared to her as an emblem of the unsatisfactory nature of her married life.

Came the time for the ball, and Marianne examined herself in the dressing-room mirror – if only they had such a mirror at Plague House! – bit her lips to redden them, and worried – for such vanity as she had consisted rather in an anxiety about her appearance than a conceited admiration of it.

'I wish my skin were whiter!' she said, looking at the low décolletage of the gown.

'It couldn't be,' said Jed, coming over and kissing her bare shoulder. 'H'm, I reckon I could grow to like these evening frocks.'

'Jed, dear, mind my flowers! Now let me look at you. Well – quite presentable. I only wish you would use a little oil on your hair.'

'Bah! no – I'd feel like a greased pig at a fair,' said

Jed, who cut a handsome enough figure in his tail-coat, but whose thick black locks remained defiantly unmanageable. He thought his wife looked beautiful, but then he thought she always did whatever she wore; and he looked merely to get through the evening − which promised nothing that he particularly enjoyed − for Marianne's sake, for it seemed to be working an improvement on her spirits already.

The Assembly House was an elegant Georgian building close to the great vaunting church of St Peter Mancroft. Brightly lit, welcoming, gracious, it presented an attractively civilized appearance in the dark winter night. But passing through the streets on the way there, Jed could not help privately dwelling on his own bitter years in this city, could not help thinking of the poor weavers going supperless to bed within half a mile of here, the shoemakers labouring on into the night till they fell asleep at their lasts for a pittance from a garret-master, the street-sellers returning to the filthy mattress in the corner of a lodging-house that was all they could call home. These things were recalled vividly to his mind by the plush contrast exhibited in the Assembly Rooms; and Mr Veazey, noticing his abstraction, asked if he were quite well.

'Aye! thank you, Mr Veazey: I was just thinking of the many poor wretches, who would look on this here scene like it was fairyland − for you know, I was one of them once.'

'True: melancholy thought − melancholy indeed,' returned Mr Veazey brightly. 'But recollect, Mr Wintergreen, that this very evening is a charity affair, which will raise funds for deserving causes.'

'Is charity enough, though?' mused Jed. 'Just because I am comfortably settled now, I tend to forget these things; but much is wrong in this world of ourn, Mr Veazey − much!'

'Come, my dear sir,' said Mr Veazey, 'you know I have the greatest respect for you: you're a true Samaritan, that's what you are; but if you will allow me to say so, you should not try to take the troubles of the whole world upon your shoulders. That is your weakness — dear me, such a very honourable one indeed, that it would hardly merit the word weakness at all, were it not that I fear it will lead, like most weaknesses, to unhappiness and sorrow.'

'Sorrow for whom?'

'For yourself, my friend. Dear me, such a theme for an evening party! Let me introduce you to a colleague of mine . . .'

The ballroom resembled a great aviary in which two species of bird, one of brilliant plumage, the other hedgerow drab, obstinately refused to mix. Around the walls the great domed skirts of the seated ladies presented variegated swathes of colour, whilst about the floor the men stalked in uniform black. At the top of the room members of the charitable committee preened themselves importantly, and looked as righteous as if they were going to spoon-feed the deserving poor themselves, while a master of ceremonies prowled possessively about his captives, and made little darts of introduction amongst them, as smartly as if he were administering the whip.

Marianne circulated with Mrs Veazey, greeting such people of local society as she knew, and being presented to others whom she did not, and who pierced her with glances of polite speculation. It was highly unlikely, of course, that any rumour of her enforced marriage had penetrated here from Heartsease; but she could not escape a feeling that the rows of ladies, their bare-shouldered busts projecting above the mass of gowns as if they were all taking a sociable bath of silk, were unpleasantly curious to know about her, and that only decorum prevented them from seizing her, carrying her off to a place of inquisition, and extracting all her secrets with rack and thumbscrew.

She was seated at last and, working her fan, regarded the contending shirt-fronts of the men, and noticed Jed amongst them very plainly wishing to put his hands in his pockets. Again she experienced a sensation of being betwixt and between. She knew it was an assembly of a thoroughly old-fashioned provincial sort, to which the people with old names came to snub the people with new money, at which bankers' daughters and manufacturers' sons made terrified peeps at each other from behind barricades of dancing-school proprieties, and at which pinched old maids who lived on pinched incomes in rooms above tailors' shops yawned over the card-tables; she knew all this, but could not find in herself any secure grounds for a feeling of superiority – she had neither the naïveté to admire it as the last word in sophistication, nor the self-assurance to dismiss it with amused indifference.

The dancing proceeded; and Marianne loved to dance. It was wonderful to hear music again; and by half-closing her eyes she could fancy that she was in a Parisian ballroom, and that glamorous creatures moved about her in the susurrus of skirts and wafting of scents . . . Yet she was dishearteningly conscious, too, of being a married woman: as different from the unattached girls, for whom the occasion teemed with possibility, as a cut flower from a living bloom; and she could only dance with Jed, who had no taste for the exercise, or with Mr Veazey and one or two other such known quantities. The draught of pleasure afforded by the evening, sweet as it was, was laced with frustration.

The second set of quadrilles over, and negus and lemonade circulating, she found herself seated alongside Mrs Veazey with a group of ladies more finely dressed than most, of whom the conspicuous suzerain was a Mrs Cozens: scion of one of the oldest Norwich families, whose hideous ancestors could be seen unctuously praying in stained-glass in several of the city's ancient churches. She was a woman with a huge head, creased eyelids like little window-blinds, a mouth that had no more appearance of lips than a seam in a pocket, and a slow soft drone of a voice that counted out the syllables like silver money.

'You have kept her at study too long,' she was informing a fellow-matron on the subject of her daughter. 'If you over-educate the girl, she will go about with a head full of nonsense that can be turned to no account, and can only inhibit her proper womanly qualities, and so she will be fit for nothing.'

'I am sure you are right,' murmured the other, 'but she does love reading so, that I have the greatest trouble making her leave off, and go and dress.'

'Reading in itself is no great harm,' pronounced Mrs Cozens. 'A woman's mind should be lightly furnished with literature, as long as it is of the right kind.'

'Mrs Wintergreen was telling me she is a great reader, were you not, my dear?' said Mrs Veazey, with some kindly idea of including her.

'Oh! yes, I quite lose myself in a book, if it is one I really like,' said Marianne.

'You reside in the country, I think, Mrs Wintergreen?' said Mrs Cozens, raising the blinds fully to take in every inch of Marianne, and then lowering them again. 'A book is, indeed, a solace in a retired situation. Let me see, where is your place?'

'At Heartsease,' said Marianne, 'the other side of Dereham.'

'Ah, you'll know the Ingamells, then.'

'Not − not well,' Marianne faltered. 'I have not been back in the county long.'

Mrs Cozens nodded distantly. 'And what reading do you enjoy, I wonder?'

'Oh . . .' Marianne was about to say that she had just read Dickens' new Christmas tale *The Chimes*, when she recollected that a few minutes ago she had heard the ladies agreeing that Boz was hopelessly vulgar: she floundered, and in her confusion could only think of the books that young Mr Bouverie had lent her. '*Ogden's Sermons On Prayer*, is one I was reading lately,' she said.

'How refreshing to find that young minds are not entirely closed to works of a devotional character in these sorry times!' said an abbreviated woman in drop-curls, who was quite dry and faded from forever lurking in the great shadow of Mrs Cozens, and who could not have been more plainly the wife of a clergyman if she had worn a sandwich-board announcing the fact.

'There are a few encouraging signs,' said Mrs Cozens. 'One is gratified to see the movement of opinion towards closing gardens and places of public resort on a Sunday in order to promote the observance of the Sabbath on the part of the lower classes. Not before time! Chapel Field has long been such a haunt of idleness, and brings so many people out into the streets till all hours, that going out to dinner becomes positively an ordeal.'

'Quite so – they will turn out for idle amusement, but not to church,' put in a much-dressed lady neither old nor young, dark nor fair, who merely hovered over the conversation like a lacy vulture, and made a sort of pounce of agreement upon any scraps that came her way.

'My husband says these railways are to blame,' offered the clergyman's wife, without venturing to explain why.

'Oh! it is all very well to parcel out blame,' said Mrs Cozens. 'A man steals, and we are told it is because he has no work; a woman becomes one of those fallen wretches to whom I need give no more explicit name, and we are told it is because she was dragged up in an indecent home. It is rather curious that the blame never seems to lie with these people themselves!'

It was at this time that Jed found himself growing bored, and though it seemed to be not the done thing to stick to one's wife at such an occasion, he elected to go back to Marianne. Taking his station by her, he was introduced to the other ladies; and Mrs Cozens, having raised the blinds for a comprehensive survey of him, resumed her thread.

'I was quite insistent with the charitable committee that the *deserving* only should be our object,' she said. 'And heaven knows that is difficult enough. It is well known that there are mendicants who will deliberately lame themselves, or scourge themselves with vitriol and vinegar to present a pitiful appearance; and I am of the opinion that if they can go to that trouble, they can quite as easily go to work.'

'So they can,' agreed the vulture, fluffing up her lace. 'And there's work enough to be had — we positively despair of getting anyone to clean our chimneys.'

'Now here is another difficulty,' pursued Mrs Cozens, unheedful of the hard gaze that Jed was directing at her. 'Helped the poor must be, no doubt, but how are they to be helped? I am afraid that in all too many cases, if you give them money they will *not lay it out in a sensible manner*, but spend it on gin.'

'Oh! dear,' absently squeaked the clergyman's wife in response to the word gin, rather like a cat prodded in sleep.

'Suppose then we give blankets,' went on Mrs Cozens. 'What is to prevent them selling the blankets, and spending the proceeds on gin? You see the difficulty. One may surely pity a man in want, but when he compounds that want by spending what little he has on intoxicating liquors, really one's pity turns to impatience.'

'And the gin they drink is such nasty poisonous stuff, I understand!' said the vulture.

'So it is, ma'am,' said Jed. 'And I reckon that alone shows what anyone must see who thinks about it for a minute — that they drink it not for pleasure, but for a little temporary escape from suffering.' Mrs Cozens' blinds went up, and an illusion of her actually having lips briefly appeared on her face; but she turned urbanely to the clergyman's wife and said, 'What does your husband say, my dear? How are the *deserving* poor to be identified?'

'Oh! well — he says we have the poor always with us, you know,' said the clergyman's wife, apparently so flustered at being directly addressed thus, that she went out like an ember, and presented but an ashy appearance thenceforth.

'You are in a different case in the country, of course, my dear,' Mrs Cozens said, turning to Marianne. 'You will not have those dreadful rookeries of poor we have in the city, but you are troubled with vagrants, no doubt?'

'Sometimes we see people on the tramp, looking for work,' said Marianne, who was naturally kind, and if she came across a beggar promptly gave him everything in her purse, but who greatly preferred not having to think about such things.

'Or looking for a free meal, no doubt − which in the goodness of your heart you give them, I'll wager!' said Mrs Cozens, with something like a jovial twinkle coming from behind the blinds; whilst the vulture, being occupied with sipping lemonade, gave a sort of moist squawk to signal her agreement.

'We do, certainly,' Marianne said, wishing no controversy, but only to keep up her part in the conversation, 'but we try to help them to some work if we can, for they are so much more grateful for that.'

'Oh, my dear, I am quite charmed with you!' Mrs Cozens said, with condescending archness. 'These rogues must impose on you terribly: when you have only half the knowledge of the world that I have, you'll see through them at once; but I wouldn't have you change, my dear − not a bit − you're quite a breath of country air!'

'I certainly hope we'll be spared this knowledge of the world,' put in Jed, 'when it looks so much like coldness of heart.'

Mrs Cozens turned to Jed with demonstrative serenity. 'You think me cold-hearted, Mr Wintergreen, to make a distinction between genuine indigence and designing extortion?'

'There's all too many cold-hearted folk about these days, Mrs Cozens,' said Jed, trying to control himself.

'But you think me one of them?' said Mrs Cozens,

adding to Marianne: 'Don't mind me teasing your husband, my dear.'

'I think you a very cold-hearted woman, since you ask, ma'am,' said Jed. 'As cold-hearted, puffed-up, stiff-necked a piece of selfishness as it's ever been my misfortune to meet.' He could not help himself: the woman's talk, coming fresh upon the memories of his own poverty, was like a goad on a sore; and the patronizing way she treated Marianne incensed him. 'The only excuse I can find for you is that you simply don't know what you are talking about − and in that case you ought to hold your tongue.'

Mrs Cozens' serenity had grown more and more tremendous: except for the convulsive tapping of one hand, she looked exactly as if she were inhaling some delicious scent. She waited, as if to be sure that Jed had finished, and then drawing the blinds right down said to Marianne: 'You have not been married long, I think, my dear, so you have not got him quite properly trained as yet. I'm rather afraid it will be quite a task for you, but I'm sure you'll manage it in time.'

The powdered shoulder which Mrs Cozens then presented to them was as effective as the slamming of a door, but Jed was now too heated for any further tolerance of the evening, and Marianne too embarrassed; and so Mrs Veazey had a few words in her husband's ear, and as soon as was feasible the four of them left.

Jed was apologetic to their hosts on their return to the house in Tombland; but Mrs Veazey, displaying a tact that might have come from the Brocklehurst blood but was more probably kindness of heart, said she was not sorry to leave so stuffy an affair. Mr Veazey's cheerfulness too was unimpaired; but before they retired he smilingly shook his head at Jed and murmured, 'You see, my friend − taking the troubles of the world on your shoulders! It's admirable − but it won't do!'

In their dressing-room Marianne brushed out her hair before the mirror and watched Jed moving about in the background of her reflection. She could not tell what he was thinking, and she did not care: she felt he had humiliated her. The disappointments of the assembly itself were forgotten: after all, it might not have been Paris, but it had at least been the sort of occasion for which she felt herself to be fitted, and for the lack of which her life was so dull – and he had wantonly ruined it, made her look like a clumsy farmer's wife unsuited to society.

As for Jed, he was not unaware that he had cause for contrition, at least as far as Marianne's feelings were concerned, but his mood was far from simple. The things he had said he could not wish unsaid; there had been truth in them, and his was a nature that prized truth above all, and believed it to be a universally valid currency. Out of this confusion of feeling he could not identify the motive that made him approach her and bend to kiss her, but her reaction was clear enough.

'Twas only a kiss,' he said, moving away, more annoyed by the rebuff than he liked to show.

'And it makes everything all right, I suppose?' she said tartly, inwardly acknowledging that there had been a time when it did, and that the time was gone.

'I never meant to spoil your evening, Marianne,' he said with difficulty. 'I'm sorry. But after all, it was only a tuppeny-ha'penny dance, with a lot of overdressed folk—'

'I know what it was,' said she, sharply. 'And perhaps if I saw a little more of life, I shouldn't care so much about it. But I never do see anything of life; and so when I get the chance at last to spend a moderately civilized evening, I think I'm entitled to feel aggrieved when my own husband deliberately humiliates me.'

'What?' he said. 'Because of what I said to that ole crow? The one who was patronizing you, and making you feel about two inches tall . . .?'

'*You* made me feel two inches tall, Jed,' she said, turning to face him. 'I'm quite well able to hold my own in that sort of society, or I *was* — God knows how I shall ever be able to face them again.'

'Anybody would think you agreed with her,' grunted Jed.

She glared at him. 'You *don't* begin a swearing-match with that sort of people,' she said. 'It just isn't done.'

'That sort of people,' he mimicked her. 'By God, you *are* your father's daughter, aren't you?'

They were silent then, and silently they retired, submitting to one of the absurder ordinances of marriage which decrees that two people who are at daggers drawn should lie in the same bed. It might have been better if the incongruity of this had struck them; but unhappily neither Jed nor Marianne was of the type to lighten the stormier passages of love with the grace-notes of laughter.

At length Jed sighed, and said, 'Thank God we shall be back at Heartsease tomorrow!'

After another moment or two he asked her if she minded him opening the bed-curtains for more air. She said no: he drew them back, and lay down again. Their hands touched briefly, but it meant nothing. There was between them that quietness, almost softness, that conceals deep division. Marianne lay awake a long time, her mind adrift in great echoing spaces of unrest. The choice she had made in marrying Jed appeared to her in stark colours. Bored and impatient, she had craved sensation and escape: with ready passion, she had sought them in the person of Jed Wintergreen. But a person was not a world. And she wanted to weep for the world that now could never be hers.

Chapter Twelve

A Gentleman In Waiting

'I'm afraid you're rather out of sorts for drawing today, Miss Ingamells,' said Pierce. 'Perhaps we should leave it and go in.'

'Really I don't know what's the matter with me, I declare you must think me worse than a bad-tempered child that won't eat its dinner and persists in making projectiles of the mashed potato.' Beatrice Ingamells tore her sketch in two. 'There that's about all it's fit for and a very shocking waste of good watercolour paper it is and typical of the wicked extravagance that will surely end in riot and flame and the guillotine as the radicals would have it and they're quite right I'm sure.'

'Never mind,' said Pierce, who was by now well accustomed to Miss Ingamells' self-disparagings, and did not trouble to contradict them. 'The nine Muses didn't include one of the graphic arts, as I remember, but certainly inspiration only visits the pencil when it feels like it, and won't be forced.'

'Good heavens, the idea of my possessing a Muse,' said Miss Ingamells as they returned across the park to the Hall, her red setter trotting at their heels, 'what a horrid fright she must be, I somehow imagine her in spectacles and a scratch wig and dirty draperies that don't fit her anywhere, really you know I fancy the whole of the ancient world must have had a permanent cold in the head what with those flimsy robes and open sandals, perhaps that accounts for the fall of the Roman Empire, the barbarians who overwhelmed it being all warmly dressed in furs and so on, perhaps I should put that theory to Papa as he's always got his nose buried in those

313

ghastly Latin bores with their ums and us-es, not that I could possibly know anything of such things being a mere woman — but there it's of no consequence as no doubt the modern barbarians will very soon overwhelm us with Charters and steam-engines and I dare say we deserve it I'm sure I don't know.'

Pierce had his suspicions as to the real cause of Miss Ingamells' distracted mood. The cousin who would be heir to the estate was due to arrive at the Hall that day to begin a long visit: Mr Ingamells had gone in the carriage to Norwich to meet him. Miss Ingamells had long been making sardonic references to the awaited guest, and when she and Pierce entered the Hall she exclaimed, 'Well, Mr Coppinger, we are in sole possession for the moment, at any rate — our heir-presumptive has yet to make his grand entrance, and begin ordering us about and making us feel like tenants who owe three quarters' rent, so I may offer you tea if you would like, we may as well drink it before Mr Alexander precious Deacon arrives to spoil the taste of it.'

Miss Ingamells remained as jumpy as a kitten while they took tea in the winter parlour, continually finding excuses to go to the window for a glimpse of the drive. At length, when she had resigned herself to remaining seated in gloomy suspense, Goldie the red setter, interrupting that gaze of drooling imbecility popularly supposed by dog-worshippers to represent devotion, sprang barking to the door, and a few moments later the sound of carriage-wheels reached their ears.

Even allowing for Miss Ingamells' habit of hyperbole, Pierce had begun to picture the young cousin as an idle fop insolently conscious of his expectations; and his cancelling this long-promised visit to take off suddenly on a jaunt to the Continent had done nothing to discourage the supposition. So on going out to the hall he was surprised to meet a handsome, well-made, intelligent-looking man in his late twenties, whose every gesture proclaimed a wish to make himself agreeable, and a tactful awareness of the sensitivity of his position.

'Mr Deacon, you have not met Mr Pierce Coppinger — engaged upon a portfolio of views of our little corner of old England, and drawing-instructor to my daughter,' said Mr Ingamells, who was at his most mild and magnanimous, like a Roman senator freeing a slave.

'Mr Coppinger, how d'you do. I've seen my cousin's drawings, sir — you have the ablest of pupils,' said Mr Deacon, shaking Pierce's hand.

'Oh! good of you I'm sure, but really you needn't endanger your soul on my account Mr Deacon I declare the recording angel must be quite blushing with shame at such an untruth,' rapped out Miss Ingamells, who had not so much given him her hand as dabbed his fingertips with her own for a fleeting moment. 'This is such a terribly conventional enquiry that you must be quite yawning inside but did you have a good journey?'

'Thank you, tolerable,' said Mr Deacon, 'though I must confess I shall be glad when the railway finally joins London to Norwich.'

'Ah, it will come soon enough, though I am such an old-fashioned fellow as to regret the change,' sighed Mr Ingamells. 'I am rather a helpless child in this modern world, Mr Deacon — forgive it. You'll want to change after your journey, sir. Watson, don't stand there, take Mr Deacon's baggage — ' Mr Ingamells, for a helpless child, did a very good imitation of a man who tyrannized his servants — 'we dine early, my dear sir — plain country manners, plain country fare, but I hope the sincere spirit behind it will make our modest hospitality acceptable!'

'It always has been in the past, Mr Ingamells — thank you.'

The young man went upstairs to dress, and Pierce presently did likewise. This did not take him long, and he occupied himself with preparing Bristol-board and cutting pencils for the last of his topographical views of the estate. This commission had taken longer than he expected; and as Miss Ingamells seemed to enjoy and benefit from such instruction as he could provide, he was to stay on at the Hall at least until the spring. He was glad of it; or at least, he thankfully registered the fact that it enabled him to stay in Heartsease, and continue searching for Rosa.

For the girl who had taken complete command of his life had disappeared from the village. She had told the Widow Thorne that she had found work elsewhere, and simply left: no one knew her whereabouts. Pierce knew that she had long wanted to leave Heartsease, for she had often spoken of it; but he feared that her flight had been impelled by nearer motives than the old aversion to a place that she had always found oppressive. It was inexact to say that he was hurt by her defection without a word: his pain was the simpler one of missing her and longing for her, the sheer fact of her absence as grindingly present to him throughout his days and nights as the dragging of toothache. He took comfort − or rather, was kept from despair − by his conviction that she could not have gone far. His friendship with Rosa had disabused him of at least some of his innocence about the lives of country working-people, and he knew that mobility was one of the many things they were denied: they could travel only as far as their legs, the kindness of carriers or waggoners, and the vigilance of poor-law unions would allow them. He was sure she must be somewhere in mid-Norfolk, and he spent all his free time in long tramps across country, asking for news of her. His first thought had been the slum-village of Pitchford; but though he had tried there several times, and had once narrowly escaped a beating from a group of railway-navvies lodging there who suspected he was an agent of the law, there was no word of her.

What he would say to her if he found her he did not know. He could not think rationally. Poor Pierce, for the first time in his life, was walking in the shadow, and in the workings of a world that he had always deemed to be at least neutral he now descried stealthy motions that had as their object the thwarting of human desires. He seemed to have found new, disturbing places in his heart. It was as if there were something in the very air of Heartsease, something that had produced not only that beauty of Rosa's – surely darker, richer, nobler than could be seen in the world beyond – but had worked an alchemistic transformation in him. His old self would not have recognized this haunted being he had become; or, recognizing it, would have smiled in amused compassion. Pierce was beginning to see that the general tolerance on which he had always rather prided himself had been based on a feeling of superiority. He had plumed himself on not being a self-tormentor, as so many other mortals appeared to be; even towards Jed Wintergreen, whom he dearly liked and respected, he had adopted an unconscious condescension, as to a man gripped by a pitiable obsession. Now he knew better. If Jed was obsessed with a vision of Heartsease, then Pierce was quite as obsessed with a vision of Rosa; but he was beginning to wonder whether obsession was not something everyone felt, in their heart of hearts, for something or someone – whether everyone was not driven by some passionate idea, be it towards fulfilment or destruction.

Thus he lived, the outer man going about his business at the Hall whilst the inner man brooded: in this state of dissociation he was heedless of the physical, and as he sharpened his pencils the knife slipped. The keen blade cut deeply into his thumb, and he had started to his feet, dripping blood, when there was a knock at the door.

'Hullo – all right if I come in?' It was Alexander Deacon, who began to say something about not disturbing him when he saw Pierce's hand. 'Good God, you're in a pickle – what happened?'

'Oh, it's nothing,' said Pierce, who felt rather foolish. 'Careless of me—' He began to fish awkwardly in his pocket with his other hand for his handkerchief.

'Here, let me — you'll never manage.' Alexander pressed him to sit down, took a basin of water from the nightstand and without fuss washed Pierce's thumb. 'Thought for a moment you'd despaired of life in this place and decided to end it all. Well, it's a clean cut. Not your painting hand, I hope? That's all right then. Handkerchiefs in this drawer?'

The young man bound up Pierce's hand quite as naturally as if they had known each other for years; and this proximity allowed Pierce to study the face of the distant cousin who stood in such a singular relation to Heartsease Hall. It was a rather boyish face, in spite of the faint suggestion of a widow's peak to be seen amongst the clusters of curling brown hair: fair of complexion, rounded rather than angular, with a notably well-shaped mouth and deep-set eyes; a face, indeed, Pierce thought, that might have served as a model for Alexander's great Macedonian namesake in one of Signor Gardini's vast historical paintings — though perhaps for Alexander as the lover of Roxane and Hephaestion rather than as the fearless warrior.

'This is very good of you,' Pierce said.

'Better than all the formalities of introduction, anyhow,' said Alexander. 'Feel easier? I hope you don't mind me barging in on you. Fact is I feel like a lost soul in that guest bedroom. I say, they've put you in pretty spartan quarters, haven't they? Don't they ever light a fire in here?'

'Oh, I'm pretty well used to it,' said Pierce.

'Painting don't pay, eh? So I've heard,' said Alexander, sitting on the bed. 'Rather like the law — at least, what I see of it.'

'You're reading for the bar, I think?'

'At the Inner Temple. Sounds rather Egyptian, doesn't it? Well it might. The old fellow in whose office I study is, to all intents and purposes, a mummy. And the mysteries of the law might as well be the mysteries of one of those gods with dogs' heads facing sideways —

whatever their names are – for all my penetration of them. Don't mind me asking – what made you choose your profession?'

'I suppose it chose me,' answered Pierce, 'if that doesn't sound too affected . . . You feel you made the wrong choice?'

'Oh! it does as well as any other, I suppose.' Alexander lay back on the bed, one leg idly waving, and said abruptly: 'Look here! What do you think of me, anyhow?'

'Well – really, I don't know you,' said Pierce simply.

'But you've been here a while. You must have heard my name brought up by my cousins, and you must know the peculiar position I'm in. And so you must have thought . . . Sorry, this is damned unfair on you; but you must surely have thought me a pretty lucky dog, with nothing to do but kill time until I come into the inheritance. Hm?'

The young man accompanied this with a look of such droll frankness that Pierce could not help but laugh. 'Something like that,' he said.

Alexander laughed too, and folded his hands behind his head. 'It's the most curious thing, isn't it? I mean, there's my uncle – or cousin or whatever he is – makes me thoroughly welcome whenever I visit: rub along with him very well, and can't say I wish him any harm – yet I know, and he knows, that my life will begin with his death. And most curious of all, we never mention it!'

'And Miss Ingamells knows, too, of course,' said Pierce.

'Ah, Beatrice! She's a whimsical creature, isn't she? You mustn't be surprised if she and I quarrel, Mr Coppinger: it's quite plain what she thinks of me, and I dare say she's right, but don't take any notice. We may squabble like two cats on a fence, but we're the best of friends really.' Alexander suddenly sat up, and became serious. 'I suppose whenever she looks at me, she is forcibly reminded of her father's mortality. Like one of those cheery tablets people used to put in churches — a little smiling death's-head saying As I Am, So Shall Ye Bee. De-da de-da, de-dee de-dee.'

'And I suppose she wonders what will become of her then,' said Pierce.

'Oh, she needn't worry,' said Alexander vaguely. 'There are disadvantages to my position as well, of course. One lives in a perpetual ante-room. It's so infernally difficult to settle to anything — such as the law — when at any moment my poor uncle may be removed from this terrestrial whatsname, and my prospects transformed by a dose of fever, a stray lightning-bolt, or a bad lobster . . . I mean a poisonous rather than a morally delinquent lobster, of course. Hard to see what a lobster can do in the way of transgression, really. I suppose it might have a crabbed disposition. A selfish shellfish. Where was I?'

'Your prospects,' laughed Pierce,

'Ah, those. You see, I *am* grateful: but I'm aware, too, of how awkward it is for them to entertain me here. Not that my uncle shows it, of course. It would take more than that to unsettle him . . . Then of course I must face the not unlikely possibility that he will simply live for ever.'

'Have you never thought of doing away with him?' said Pierce, to whose humour his present heartache had given a grim touch.

''Orrible Murder, eh?' said Alexander with a grin. 'I'm afraid the police wouldn't have to look far for a suspect. And I rather think that nothing less than silver bullets would do the trick — like those fellows they have on the Continent — werewolves. I suppose if you turned into a bear that would make you a were-bear. And if you turned into a house you'd be a warehouse. That reminds me, I've brought some presents for my hosts. Come along to my room and see. That guest bedroom is remarkable, you know. It's the only country-house bedroom in the land in which Queen Elizabeth did *not* sleep . . .'

In his room Alexander drew forth from a trunk a pair of chased goblets. 'For my uncle, of course. Paris made. And this for Beatrice.' It was a shawl of Lyons silk. 'I picked them up when I took off for the Continent before Christmas. Shouldn't have gone, I know − it's put me in deep water with the moneylenders; but I can't abide staying in the same place for very long.'

'Shall you be able to settle at Heartsease when the time comes?' Pierce asked.

'I wonder. It's a pretty spot, I suppose. Of course, you know I shan't run things in quite my uncle's way. He's one of the old guard − I've got different ideas. There's change in the wind, Pierce − I sensed it in France especially. I mean to get to know the people here − tenants and so forth. All those artificial barriers between man and man, man and woman, they're going to come down.'

'Are they?' said Pierce, thinking of Rosa.

'Aye, aye. "The dust of creeds outworn". That was Shelley, I think. I wish I could wear an open shirt-collar like Shelley. The age of gold, the age of bronze − and we live in the age of starch,' said Alexander, throwing on to the bed an array of coats and fancy waistcoats. 'Let me show you this Turkish garb I bought in Venice—'

'Good Lord,' Pierce interrupted him, 'there's a mouse in your clothes − look there.'

'Oh, there he is. I was wondering where he'd got to. This is Mordecai,' said Alexander, picking up the white mouse and allowing it to run up his arm. 'I named him after my moneylender. A very well-travelled mouse. I did have three, but Rachel had a contretemps with a ship's cat, and Ezra ran away in Paris, having had his head turned by stories of rodent *filles de joie*, and was last seen heading for the Faubourg St Germain with a flower in his buttonhole and a look of expectation.' Alexander deposited the mouse in a soap-dish and produced from his trunk an embroidered jerkin, sash and turban. 'Now look here − consider yourself at liberty to laugh, but I rather fancy myself in this outfit − probably about as authentically Turkish as Farmer Giles' smock, but never mind. Wasn't it Byron who had himself painted in this sort of costume? − a thunderously unsubtle hint, I do realize.'

There was great charm in the young man's smile, which was a little lopsided, a bit of upper lip projecting down over his teeth. 'I should be glad to do it, if Mr Ingamells permits me the time,' Pierce said.

'Don't worry about that,' said Alexander. 'You know, I call it damned hard on you having to live in that garret of a room. Suppose I suggested that you be given a better one—'

'Oh! no, please, don't trouble,' said Pierce, who did not wish to appear to be currying favour with the future heir.

'No? Well, I see what you mean. Might look as if I'm trying to take charge. Beatrice wouldn't like that.'

That the tension in the atmosphere proceeded from Beatrice was clear to Pierce at dinner. Mr Ingamells, whatever his private thoughts about the young cousin who would inherit his estate, was if anything more nerveless than ever, presenting his impeccable politeness to his guest rather as if he were tendering a five-pound note from an unbreakable bank. Miss Ingamells, by contrast, was all edge. In the drawing-room after dinner she acceded to Alexander's request that she play the piano with a shrill 'Oh! if it will amuse you, I suppose I must comply'; and she played − excellently − with such a stony, suppressedly savage expression on her face that it was as if music were a sort of bloodsport, and she were strangling the notes with her bare hands.

'Good of you I'm sure,' she said when Alexander complimented her on her playing, 'but of course you don't mean it, madness to suppose even for a moment that you could, you are wishing I would leave off − you are wishing I would go up in a puff of smoke this very moment, and I don't blame you I'm sure!'

'Injustice, Miss Ingamells,' said Alexander. 'I won't say to my sincerity, for that's of no account, but to your own accomplishment.'

'Good heavens Mr Deacon,' said Miss Ingamells stalking back to her seat, 'and you just returned from the Continent and from having your ears if the expression is not indecorous ravished no doubt in salons and such where the execution is surely such as makes me appear the excruciating amateur and general dead-weight upon the hands of the world that I undoubtedly am.'

'*Execution* was, indeed, what many of the musicians I heard fully deserved,' said Alexander. 'In Paris I even managed to squeeze myself into a concert-room to hear Liszt, but all I could see of the phenomenon was a pair of green gloves tossed into the air for the ladies to fight over, and all I could hear was a lot of rapid arpeggios that reminded me of running a stick along the railings when I was a child. I was glad to get out in the fresh air and have a cigar.'

'Dear me it must be mortifying indeed to live a life of idleness and pleasure and to find even that palling I declare I'm quite sorry for you Mr Deacon I'm sure,' said Miss Ingamells – smiling, not with her eyes, nor even with her mouth, but rather with the muscles of her neck.

Alexander seemed amused, and quite undaunted. 'You have yet to visit Europe, Miss Ingamells?'

'Circumstances have prevented it,' put in Mr Ingamells. 'Had my beloved Euphemia lived, things might have been different: travel would have been enlivened for Beatrice by the company of a mother, whereas there can be no pleasure for her in visiting foreign shores with her dull dog of a father. As for myself, though it is no doubt very foolish and old-fashioned of me, I consider myself bound by my duties and responsibilities here – unworldly, I know! forgive it! – and prefer to remain in this modest corner of my native land, and await that happy day when I can rejoin Euphemia.' And certainly Mr Ingamells seemed at such pains to spare his daughter the dullness of his company that he never took her anywhere with him if he could help it.

'What about you, Mr Coppinger?' said Alexander. 'Have your studies taken you abroad — Italy perhaps?'

'Well, I didn't like to impose on my father's purse any more, after I had been at the Academy schools,' said Pierce, 'and so I began as a painter on my own account quite early, and indefinitely postponed a visit to those places that artists are supposed to visit.'

'Mr Coppinger came to manhood in the peculiar position of having to do something for his living, Mr Deacon,' said Miss Ingamells, 'rather than merely following his inclinations in the knowledge that the world will provide for him in time, and no doubt he would have liked to go to Italy and study those what are the ones that sound like grottoes Giottos and so forth but curious as it may seem to you Mr Deacon there are people in the world who have to apply themselves to something other than leisure and profligacy.'

'Oh — well — I am doing what I enjoy, anyhow,' said Pierce hurriedly, very uneasy at being used as a bone of contention between Miss Ingamells and her cousin.

Alexander merely gave his pleasant laugh. 'You reprove me quite rightly, Miss Ingamells. But you must consider, cousin: I have no talents to which I can apply myself, unlike Mr Coppinger — and, I must add, unlike yourself.'

'Oh! to speak of my having talents I declare you will quite lie yourself into the seventh circle of hell or is it the eighth whichever is the most uncomfortable anyhow,' said Miss Ingamells.

'I don't think I'm endangering my soul. These are your work, I think?' said Alexander, going over to a work-table and turning over some of Miss Ingamells' recent sketches. 'They pay equal tribute to Mr Coppinger's teaching and your skill. Really they are admirable. Now this — I have seen pictures of this quality hung in exhibition-rooms.'

It was, Pierce judged, one of his pupil's best, a view in line and wash of the distant Hall on a bitter winter day, with a fine rendering of the cloud-masses and chasms of the East Anglian sky. He saw Miss Ingamells flush as Alexander went on: 'If I felt I had a little more of your good opinion, I would ask if I might take this, and have it framed, and have it on the wall of my lodgings in London . . . Indeed, though I know I don't have your good opinion at all, I'll ask it anyway.'

This was spoken still in Alexander's characteristic gently jesting tone, though the request seemed sincere: it occurred to Pierce that the young man was like an instrument that had no lower register, on which every tune that was played came out in the same light manner.

'Really I shouldn't be surprised at your mockery I'm sure as my dreadful scrawls are really fit for nothing but laughter and I do appreciate the joke I assure you,' Miss Ingamells said, almost in a whisper, her face averted.

'I shall carry the picture up to my room this very night, to prove I'm in earnest,' Alexander said. 'And I shall have it framed as soon as I return to London. Provided I have your permission, Miss Ingamells.'

The lady made a tense gesture. 'Good heavens it's such a little thing I can hardly refuse especially when the very idea of such a wretch as I presuming to grant or refuse anything is perfectly hilarious but there if you insist though I declare your friends in London of whom you have many I'm sure will think you quite a laughing-stock for possessing such a thing.' Miss Ingamells' blush was so fierce that Pierce pitied her; and though Alexander's liking of the picture seemed perfectly genuine, Pierce felt himself to be in the presence of such a complex and combustible freight of emotion that he was glad enough to follow Miss Ingamells' lead a few minutes later and retire early.

He rose likewise the next morning, long before the Ingamells' young cousin was stirring. Breakfast not being ready, he wandered into the drawing-room, and found Miss Ingamells there.

The disputed picture was still lying on the table where Alexander had left it. Miss Ingamells, with one long finger on the corner of the picture, turned at Pierce's footstep. Her face alarmed him. The sandy-lashed eyes that always appeared so vulnerable were terribly naked in expression: they seemed less like external features than internal organs from which the protective flesh had been flayed off.

'It is curious,' she said, her voice more forced in pitch than ever, 'how very different things can look in candlelight and daylight. It seems to me now that there is only one fit place for this.' She carried the picture over to the fireplace between finger and thumb. An excellent fire had just been laid, and as Miss Ingamells tossed her picture into it the flames appeared to reach out red claws to seize it, and to leap up in exultation as the stiff paper crumpled and smoked. She had turned on her heel and gone before Pierce could utter a word of protest, and before the painted image of the Hall was consumed.

Pierce found himself within the space of a couple of days the best of friends with Alexander Deacon — a circumstance that would have been more remarkable but for the fact that the young man made friends with everyone, Miss Ingamells always excepted. He was on good terms with all the servants at the Hall, from the stately housekeeper down to the undersized stable-boy. He walked and rode about Heartsease, mixing with everyone, presenting a strong contrast with Mr Ingamells, whose familiarity with the village was limited to those parts of it he had had enclosed or demolished. He was a frequent visitor at the Grange, where Mr Ringrose took rather a shine to him, perhaps seeing in the young man a trace of the Regency rake he longed to be: a sort of latter-day Byron without the scandal.

In Byronic pose, indeed, Alexander sat for his portrait

to Pierce: good-humouredly laughing at himself for his fancy of wearing Turkish garb, but determined on it too in his lightweight way. He laughed at himself very readily – about, for example, his taste for clothes, which Pierce soon found was as exacting and particular as that of Mr Ingamells; but he laughed in such a way as to suggest that he found nothing really reprehensible in this vanity, or indeed in anything he did. He had all the self-confidence of his elder cousin; but what was in Mr Ingamells too seamless for comfort became in Alexander, with his easy manner and his vein of fantastic humour, a capacity for making other people feel confident too. Painting someone's portrait, Pierce knew from experience, was a peculiarly effective way of getting to know them, but with Alexander the process was so swift as to be almost instantaneous. There was no gradual halting penetration of the layers of self: getting to know Alexander was like ploughing a light soil, there was no need to go deep. He was also one of those rare people, Pierce found, who looked different at every sitting: it was hard to capture a likeness of him, as if his appearance were as fluidly adaptable as his nature.

Between Alexander and Miss Ingamells there was a sort of constant fencing which, while it seemed good-humoured enough on Alexander's side at least, made Pierce uneasy. Miss Ingamells seemed to take an acid pleasure in drawing attention to the general aimlessness and lack of integrity in her cousin's life: Alexander's response was to laughingly admit that everything she said was true – at which Miss Ingamells grew more bonily affronted and sardonic than ever.

'I'm afraid it just shows the general unfairness of things, cousin,' he said. 'An accident of birth, and a worthless fellow like me finds himself heir to something he freely acknowledges he doesn't deserve in the least. But consider – I, as you've said, am surely destined for hell: whereas your place in heaven, I'm sure, is guaranteed.'

'Oh you must excuse me such blaspheming is I'm sure thought prodigiously amusing amongst your set but you must remember a hoyden like me has been brought up differently and even taught to believe that God is not mocked — terribly un-smart of me I know but then I'm only a provincial old maid and no more to be taken notice of than those fire-irons and really I don't expect it.'

'It would be a foolish man indeed who failed to take notice of you, cousin,' Alexander said. 'The one fault I can find in you is that one of not valuing yourself enough: otherwise I should be tempted to say you are the most sensible woman I ever met.'

These compliments seemed to make Miss Ingamells fairly quiver with anger, embarrassment, contempt, and Pierce could not tell what other emotions. Whether Alexander mischievously purposed this he could not tell. The trouble was the things he said were perfectly true, and in private with Pierce he echoed them. 'She has an infinitely better head on her than me,' Alexander said. 'Or even her father come to that. Yet she has scarcely more power in life than the kitchen-maid.'

'It's a disturbing thought,' said Pierce.

'It is, isn't it? Ah well, that's one of the things that'll be set to rights one day. I've a fancy for a brandy-and-water, what do you say to a drop . . .?'

Pierce and Alexander, out walking in the village one day, ran into Jed Wintergreen; and after Pierce had made the introductions, Alexander asked whether he might call at Plague House one morning, as he wished to be on good neighbourly terms with everyone in the village. Jed, seeming much preoccupied, said he would be glad to see him; and the young man made his call the very next day.

It was scarcely to be expected that Jed would welcome with open arms a relative of Mr Ingamells, and future squire of Heartsease; but he had already heard good reports in the village of Alexander Deacon, who seemed to be going out of his way to show that the new dispensation, when his time came, would be much more liberal than that of Mr Ingamells; and so he was prepared to be cordial to him on the strength of that alone. Marianne, moreover, was curious to meet him: it would aggravate her discontent if hers was the only household in the district not to receive the gentlemanly stranger. And her discontent was great: Jed knew that. In the hall fireplace, big as a pantry, of Plague House, a great wood fire blazed to keep off the cold of the lingering winter; but nothing could warm the emotional chill of that home in which the young husband and wife strained against each other like two wilful and mismatched horses placed in harness together.

He knew her discontent: and it was perhaps typical of their position that he sought to assuage it in small matters, such as the receiving of a call from Alexander Deacon, whilst setting his face against curing it at the root. Marianne openly longed to get away from this place: Jed embraced Heartsease all the more stubbornly. For one thing, he said, he was needed here — more than ever now, with her father growing increasingly tyrannical over the community. Marianne did not so much reject that reasoning as simply not acknowledge it, so great had the gulf between them become. And somewhere in that gulf floated dangerous unspoken accusations: from Marianne that he loved Heartsease more than her, from Jed that her impatience with Heartsease was really an impatience with him.

How much of this unhappy atmosphere Alexander Deacon perceived, Jed could not tell. Certainly their visitor had a way of putting them at their ease just as if he were the host rather than the guest: he made a tour of the farm with Jed, and took a lively interest in all he saw.

'Next week we'll sow beans and peas,' Jed told him. 'St David's and St Chad's days — thass the traditional time.'

'St David's and St Chad's — I must remember that,' Alexander said. 'It must be satisfying to raise crops — to see them grow and ripen, and harvest them at last, and know that that good food comes from your own efforts. Hard work I know, and it must have its disappointments and frustrations, but it goes towards feeding people's bellies, and that's more than can be said for most of the busy-business that goes on in the world and that people make such a great noise about.'

It was gratifying to Jed to hear this, which accorded so well with his own belief. He walked back to Plague House not displeased with his companion; and could not help saying, as they entered, 'Some people, I'm afraid, reckon this to be a tiresome sort of life.'

'There's more than one sort of tiresomeness,' replied Alexander readily. 'London often reminds me of Gibbon's description − crowds without company, and dissipation without pleasure. I've found company and pleasure in Heartsease, and I don't know what more one can ask.'

Marianne, Jed's eye saw, had in their absence been hurrying about making the homely parlour look more genteel. She had half-closed the window-curtains to give that subdued light that irritated him, but he resisted the urge to draw them back. As the three of them chatted he walked about in his restless way, scarcely aware that he was doing it.

'Well, I mustn't impose on my uncle's hospitality too long,' Alexander said when Marianne asked him how long he was staying. 'And of course the law beckons. It's a pity, because I'm greatly enjoying getting to know people here. No disrespect to my uncle, but being forever shut away behind the gates of the Hall like an ogre in a castle is not my notion of the way to live.'

Ben Catbush was there. 'Here's Todd Gault to see you,' he said to Jed.

Jed caught the annoyance in Marianne's eye. 'I'll come out to him,' he said. 'Excuse me, please, Mr Deacon.'

He found Todd Gault, not waiting for him in the yard, but at the woodpile behind the barn. The young man had

taken an axe and was chopping wood as if his life
depended on it.

'Thass savage amusement, Todd,' Jed said. 'Come in
the house and get warm.'

'I'll do as I am — make myself useful,' said Todd, with
another great heave at the axe. A splinter of wood struck
his face but he took no heed. 'I hope I ain't taking you
away from work.'

'Oh! no,' said Jed. He noticed, with pity, how red and
bony Todd's wrists were, despite the bulldog sturdiness
of his shoulders. 'Look, no need to go knocking yourself
out with that wood. Why don't you—'

'I feel better for it,' grunted Todd. Chop went the axe
again. 'It's the only work I shall get.' He raised the axe,
and then the strength seemed to go out of him all at once;
and with a stricken face he lowered it and said: 'He's
sacked us.'

'Hemstock,' said Jed, after a moment in which he was
shaken by a spasm of purest loathing.

Todd kicked suddenly at the wood. He looked like a
whipped boy, hurt and helpless. 'It weren't right,' he
said, 'I went to him respectful enough — didn't raise no
rumpus. Just went to him like I told you I would, and
said how we was all agreed we couldn't live on what he
was paying, and how I'd come to ask him to settle a new
wage rate, how we didn't want no favours, only fair
dealing same as from Mr Wintergreen, and I started to
say how much a loaf cost nowadays, and how much just
to have a yard o' thatch over your head, but I got the
feeling he weren't listening at all, and then he turns his
back to me and walks over to that toad-eating bailiff of
his — ' Todd spat on the ground — 'and tells him to pay
what's owed to every man as put his name to this and
then turn 'em all off the farm — and they're never to
work there again and do they so much as come up the
path asking for work he'll go to Squire Ingamells and
have 'em committed for trespass.'

As he came to the end of his story Todd seized the axe

and flung it against the barn door so that it hung there, the head buried in the timber and the haft vibrating like an arrow. But the violence of the act was at least partly a screen for the fact that he was near tears.

'Perhaps I done it wrong,' Todd said. 'Perhaps I should have gone about it different . . .'

'Twould have made no difference if you'd crawled to him on your hands and knees,' Jed said.

Todd surreptitiously wiped his face with his sleeve. 'Well, I shall never do that − never − not do I see my own mother starve first.' He glanced up with his look of vulnerable suspicion. 'D'you think I'm just saying that, Jed? 'Cos thass not so. I mean it − I mean it like death.'

'I know you do. And you didn't do no wrong,' Jed said. 'It's him who's in the wrong − and any man with a morsel of feeling would say so. You stood up for yourselves, and that's just what Hemstock can't abide.'

Todd, even defiant as he was, seemed to find reassurance in hearing this from Jed. A little more calmly he went on: 'There was more'n a dozen of us in it − young boy-chaps like me mostly, as have got nothing much to lose. But one or two married fellows come in too, saying they couldn't feed their families. Hemstock turned 'em all off. And then he went right round the farm asking do anybody there sympathize with us and anyone who said so much as a doubtful word he turned off as well. There'll be men out of work behind every second cottage-door in Heartsease tomorrow . . . Thass why I had to come and tell you, Jed − because I kept thinking mebbe I shouldn't have done it—'

'God damn the bastard to hell!' cried Jed. He so seldom swore or raised his voice that Todd, with his tendency to idolize Jed, looked startled. ''Tis him who should be stinging inside at what he's done, bor, not you. If he can live with himself after this . . .' He swallowed. 'How does he suppose he's going to run that great farm without workers ? He won't be able to keep his precious gig and his fancy carpets if the fields ain't tilled.'

'He said he'll find people who want to work instead of wanting everything handed 'em on a plate.'

Jed nodded. He could just hear Hemstock saying it. He felt sick.

'Listen, bor,' he said. 'I'll go see Mr Ringrose at the Grange. Between us I reckon we might find work for a few fellows as need it bad.' He made an irritable gesture. 'What am I saying – you all need it bad. Anyhow, I'll see what I can do. Tell 'em there's wood here for their fires while this cold weather keeps up – they've no need to ask; and I've a clamp of taters that want eating.'

'I'll do that,' said Todd. All that rather disquieting respect was in his eyes, together with a certain speculation, as he said: 'Is this how it was back in 'thirty, Jed? When your father—'

'Something like,' Jed said. 'I must leave you now, bor.'

He went back to the house, and as he entered the hall he heard Marianne laughing in the parlour. Her laugh was one of the many things about her that captivated him – still; but just then it irked him. It irked him that she was sitting there making polite chit-chat with the gentlemanly stranger when these grim events were unfolding, and when her father was the cause of them. He wanted to go and see Mr Ringrose straight away, and he did not fancy having to go into the parlour and make a lot of flowery excuses. No: he wouldn't bother. This was too important for delay, and besides the young man did not seem the sort to make a lot of fuss about ceremony. If only they were all as pleasant.

Marianne, vexed as she was by her husband's tedious conferences with Todd Gault and his like, had been somewhat relieved when he was called away. He had been pacing about in that highly strung way – she sometimes suspected he did it on purpose to annoy her – and she wanted to show their visitor that she had at least lived in the world a little, and knew how to entertain him in proper style. For the first time in an age she had put on her best afternoon gown (Jed of course hadn't noticed); and she could not help observing, as she sat in a sort of pleased poised nervousness, how Alexander Deacon sat at his ease in the Windsor chair, and showed no urge to roam about like a caged bear.

'The law must be a very hard study,' she said when they were alone.

'I'm afraid it is, for those poor fellows who actually apply themselves to it,' said Alexander with a rueful smile. 'I can't pretend to you, Mrs Wintergreen, that I work hard at it – or enjoy it – or even have the slightest genuine interest in it. I see the barristers go about the Temple with their wigs and gowns, and I feel rather like you do when you are a little child gazing up at an adult – firmly convinced, in spite of all you've been told, that you will never be that big, and so deciding never to think about it.'

'Shall you abandon it, then?'

'Well, my late father did lay out money to enter me in the profession, which makes me rather uncomfortable at the thought of throwing in my hand, but then he had the lowest opinion of lawyers himself. He said he never met one without being reminded of a crocodile. Where he had met a crocodile, and on what terms, I can't conceive, as he never went out of England in his life – except to cross to Boulogne once, where a cartwheel ran over his foot, and so he came back on the next packet with all his prejudices against foreigners confirmed. Whenever he saw someone with a limp after that he would say, "French, I should think – poor devil!"'

'Well, I'm sure your father wouldn't wish you to be unhappy in your profession,' Marianne said.

'I don't know. He was, bless him, rather a gloomy fellow. "We weren't put on this earth to be happy, you know!" he used to say; but he would never tell me what we *were* put on this earth for.'

'Oh, but we were!' said Marianne ardently. 'At least –

if not to be happy, for I suppose one can't always expect that, then at least to be fulfilled. It would be terrible to think otherwise!'

'I agree with you,' Alexander said. 'But suppose one person's happiness, or fulfilment, is another person's sorrow?'

Marianne considered, seriously: the young earnestness of her nature overcoming her education, which told her she ought only to keep the conversation moving. 'Perhaps that's always doomed to be so,' she said. 'After all, if you look at it in one way, every time you eat a slice of bread, you are preventing someone else from eating it.' She might have added that that was how Jed often made her feel – that everything had to be measured against some lofty moral yardstick, and that the slightest frivolity on her part was an insult to the poor people about whom he seemed to care so much more than he cared for her.

'True enough,' said Alexander, closely regarding her. 'But carry that philosophy into practice, and the only moral thing for everyone to do is commit suicide. And,' he laughed, 'though there have been wet Sundays in Heartsease when that has appealed to me as a very desirable alternative, I can't think it a helpful proposition for the world.'

Yes, Marianne thought, smiling, she would have to use that answer to Jed; then, the implication of his second remark arresting her, she said quickly, 'You don't care for Heartsease?'

'I see I must be careful with this one. Let's say there are people in Heartsease that I greatly care for, and that the place is very agreeable to look at for, say, a quarter of an hour.'

'You needn't fear offending me, Mr Deacon – not when it comes to criticizing Heartsease,' said Marianne, with both mournfulness and frustration rising to the surface.

'Well, my quarrel is not with Heartsease *per se*,'

Alexander said, 'but with the country in general. Was it Sydney Smith who said the country was a sort of healthy grave? I know it was Hazlitt who said that there is nothing good to be had in the country, or if there is they will not let you have it. I'm sure crops are all very well in their way, but I would much rather forgo the pleasure of seeing them until they are on the table, cooked, diced, refined, and generally unrecognizable. Forgive me, Mrs Wintergreen − I wouldn't say this to you if I didn't suspect that you share my feelings to a certain degree.'

'Does it show so very plainly?' said Marianne, her tone still mournful, though she smiled.

'Well, no,' said he judicially, 'but what does show is that you are no stranger to other modes of life . . . Is that someone tapping at the window?'

'Oh − no, no,' Marianne said, recovering from a flush of pleasure, 'it's that climbing rose-bush − it was dislodged during those terrible gales we had at Christmas. We could scarce step outside the door. Was it so in London?'

'I couldn't say, I was in Paris at Christmas. I'm afraid the season of goodwill in England has quite the opposite effect on me. I have a sneaking sympathy for Boz's Ebenezer Scrooge, and I must confess to a terrible urge to give Tiny Tim a good downright slap . . . Now you are going to reprove me, and send some ghosts to reform my character.'

'Not at all − I quite see what you mean,' said she. It was true that *A Christmas Carol* had made her cry dreadfully − but then for Marianne truth was relative rather than absolute, and besides, the word *Paris* had acted like a spell upon her, suspending all faculties but that of wonder. And he had spoken it, too, with the same casual intimacy with which she would have mentioned King's Lynn or Norwich. Whence came that ease, that brilliant confidence that was expressed in every lineament of the young man's body? Was it too late for her to find it too ? All the longings of her youth (which she half thought of as gone) returned upon her, and she experienced a sort of inward cry of protest at her situation, which could only find a vent in a wistful murmur of: 'I would dearly love to see Paris.'

'You have never been there?'

'Oh! no, not I.'

'Forgive me — I don't know why, I rather supposed you had.'

She shook her head, while his eyes lingered curiously on her face. 'I suppose it must be all terribly familiar to you — Paris, and so on,' she said.

'Well, I like to flatter myself that I'm as *blasé* as any native, but in truth I go about there stretching my neck and widening my eyes at everything like the greenest of unseasoned travellers,' said Alexander. 'I couldn't imagine ever growing tired of it — and if that makes me rather a goose, then I'm happy to be so.' Hearing the door, he said, 'I believe that's Mr Wintergreen again. I say, I hope I'm not interrupting his work. Perhaps I should go too—'

'No,' said Marianne quickly. 'At least — there's no need, Mr Deacon. My husband's always — always busy. Unless you have to go.'

He made an open-handed gesture. 'I'm at your disposal, Mrs Wintergreen.'

She smiled a little timidly. 'Then we'll have some tea; and perhaps, if it isn't dull for you—'

'Yes?' he gently encouraged.

'Perhaps you would tell me a little more about Paris . . . '

It was a dead grey morning at the dead grey end of winter, when even the cold seems listless rather than brisk, and the seasons seem to stand on the point of dissolution into nothingness rather than advancing towards spring. Elias Hemstock, having risen early as ever, went out on his sleek cob to watch the arrival in his fields of his new workforce.

They came in two large open carts that seemed more suitable to the transportation of the roughest fodder than the carriage of human beings; and they got down stiffly but uncomplainingly, shaking out ragged shawls, retying lappet-caps about their heads, and looking about with a sort of flat neutrality at the bleak ploughed spaces in which they had been set down. The curious thing about them was their almost complete silence, for there were children amongst them — many children: a few were mere infants, bundled in their mothers' arms or clinging to their skirts. The rest were mainly women, young and old, though in them distinctions of age had shrunk to a narrow compass, and appeared only as degrees of haggardness; and there were one or two tramping Irishmen, in the last stages of drink and debility. All were spectrally quiet.

The gang-master came over to Hemstock, poking a stubby finger to his hat-brim. 'All ready to set to, mairster,' he said.

'That woman has a baby at the breast,' said Hemstock. 'I hope she's not going to be fussing with that all the time, instead of working.'

'Oh! don't yew wittle yourself about that, mairster. She'll work. I'll see to that, don't yew fret,' said the gang-master — who would, indeed, see to it, for the more work he could wring out of his gang the better he was paid. He was a small spare fox-snouted man, who threw up at the mounted farmer a glance both ingratiating and speculative, and who carried with him the switch he used to urge on his horses.

'My God,' said Hemstock in disgust, 'you'd think they were poor enough already, without bringing these brats into the world, yet still they have 'em!'

'So they do, mairster: you're in the right of it. *I've* tried reasoning with 'em: I say to 'em, what do yew want to goo and dew it for? Yew don't reckon thass any pleasure to me, to see a whole boiling of babes in my carts, do you? But there, thass natur, when all's spoke.'

'You engage to return them to Pitchford tonight?' Hemstock said. 'They can't be put up here, you know — I'll have no quartering of folk overnight in my barns, as I know you fellows do sometimes: I'd be robbed twice over.'

'Yew can trust me, mairster: yew won't see hide nor hair of 'em once the work's done,' said the gang-master, whose face was smiling whenever Hemstock's eyes were on him, and scowling whenever they were averted.

'Very well. My bailiff will set them their tasks,' said Hemstock and, clicking his tongue to his mount, he drew off.

He remained a while at a short distance, however, watching from the back of his horse as the gang went about their work: a figure so massively proud, rooted, and stern that the toiling labourers with their bent backs and scrawny frames might almost have been another species. It was, indeed, some such thought that went through Hemstock's mind as he observed this mass of cheapest labour mechanically and apathetically weeding, stone-picking, setting potatoes, and singling turnips. They were, to him, a rabble; and the only emotion that accompanied this idea was a faint distaste at his having to resort to such dregs as these to do the work of a farm that was admired as a model enterprise all over mid-Norfolk. A pity, but necessary, for he would not employ this new breed of troublemakers — young Gault and his cronies — that had arisen in Heartsease: no, not for a single hour; and so he had turned to the gang-masters of Pitchford who gathered these sweepings of indigence, and transported them where they were wanted, and could guarantee that, if they were not ideally strong or skilled, they were certainly docile.

Hemstock's mood was dark. He was preoccupied with injustice — injustice towards himself. For it seemed to him that the Fates which had hitherto rewarded him, justly, for his industry and perseverance, were now conspiring against him. For not only had he lost

Marianne, the most prized of his possessions, but he need never have done so. The baby that had forced him to accept her marriage had miscarried. The pregnancy might never have happened, the hated marriage need never have happened. But now, of course, it could not be undone. It was as if a carefully laid trap had closed around him. And now, having been robbed of the daughter whose loss put an end to all his bright prospects, he found these village malcontents and agitators like young Gault coming and asking him for sky-high wages, and trying to rob him of what he had left . . . And behind it all, behind all his troubles, the same man — Wintergreen. It was Wintergreen who had stirred up his labourers, just as his impudent father had done back in 'thirty. But at least, he reflected with a sort of stony satisfaction, he had shown them that he hadn't gone soft in the intervening years. He wouldn't be dictated to by a set of alehouse troublemakers. If they didn't want to work, then he would employ people who did.

But his satisfaction was stony indeed, and as nothing beside his frustration, anger and resentment. Another man than Hemstock might have known himself to be, in fact, deeply unhappy; but Hemstock equated unhappiness with weakness, and so was doomed doubly to suffer what he would not acknowledge, like a man insisting on using a broken limb. Only a spirit of grim opposition sustained him — to Wintergreen, and to everything about Heartsease that was associated with him; but he was finding it a poor substitute for hope.

At last he turned his horse about, and proceeded through the village. But then ahead of him he saw a small crowd of people gathered in the middle of the village street, and with the habitual caution that made him assess every situation before committing himself to it he reined in, and observed from a distance.

The peep-show man had come to Heartsease. Whether he travelled a fixed itinerary, and where he started out from, if anywhere, and how long he had been doing it, no

one knew, for no garrulous showman was he, with a
budget of news from the places he had passed through
and a raconteur's flourish to part the villagers from their
pennies. He was a sere, dusty, blinking-eyed old man,
with great flat feet that gave him the appearance of a
tailor's dummy set walking; and he displayed his peep-
show, dusty likewise on its rickety donkey-cart, and
covered with mildewed black velvet like a disreputable
bier, as if it were something scarcely worth seeing at all.
In a village like Heartsease, where generations lived and
died without ever stirring beyond the parish boundaries,
this old wayfarer with the crusted dirt of a score of
counties on his boots was mobility personified, yet he
stood by his peep-show with the blank inward gaze of a
man who never left his chimney-corner.

Trumpery as the peep-show was, the villagers gathered
round it, some with eagerness, some with amused
tolerance, and those children whose parents had pennies
to give jostled to put their eyes to the lens. There were
adults, too, who took a turn with a sort of smiling
pensiveness, as if they were wistfully comparing that little
world within with the sorry world outside. Among the
onlookers were a couple of railway navvies, absent from
the site on a spree; Todd Gault, who was leaning with his
arms hooked around the cast-iron shaft of the village
pump, and to whose unfledged face his new misfortune
had given a look rawly bruised; Pierce Coppinger, who
had been drawn thither by a nose for the picturesque,
hoping he might work up a genre-picture from the scene;
Alexander Deacon, who had been riding through the
village, and had dismounted to see the diversion; and Jed
and Marianne, who had come out of Plague House to do
likewise.

Elias Hemstock urged his horse on and approached the
group. The peep-show proprietor took no heed of the
newcomer, or indeed of any of them: in his apparent
blindness, he might have been an emblem of that
conjunction of circumstances that had brought these

diverse people into fraught relation – a still centre to a brewing turbulence.

Hemstock, with a single cold glance at the company, passed by, the villagers instinctively moving aside to give his horse room. But he found that Todd Gault had moodily stepped away from the pump, and stood obstructing the gap between the house-wall and the peep-show cart.

'Stand out of my road, there,' Hemstock said.

Todd did not move, but stood glaring up at the farmer. 'Do the road belong to you now, along of everything else?' he said.

'Step aside, or I'll ride over you,' said Hemstock coolly, making a curt gesture with his riding-crop.

Todd went crimson. He made a lunge as if to grab the horse's bridle. 'Try it, then!' he cried. 'That'll be nothing new – you've ridden over folk hereabouts for years! Mebbe the time's coming when they'll fight back!'

Suddenly Jed was at Todd's side, and was gently but firmly holding his arms down and urging him away. 'Enough, bor, enough,' he said. 'That'll do no good, you know.'

'I'm interested to see that you claim responsibility for this ruffian, Wintergreen,' Hemstock said.

'The responsibility's yours,' said Jed. 'And I hope you'll be made to answer for it some day.'

Hemstock's hands tightened on the reins. 'Do you threaten me, sir?'

All at once it was as if neither man could bear any longer even to address the other; but the long gaze into each other's faces which abruptly closed the exchange was more expressive than words. With a snap of the reins Hemstock moved his horse on, passing away from the group without even a nod to his daughter, who had stood wretchedly looking on throughout.

'Come on, bor,' said Jed soothingly to Todd. 'You go on home – it's best. I'll walk with you.'

He guided the young man away, leaving a backwash of

excited chatter to die out amongst the villagers, who presently returned their attention to the peep-show. Marianne, meanwhile, stood as if paralysed — feeling no less of a public exhibition than the peep-show itself, with the final twist given to her mortification by her own father passing by her as if she were a stranger.

She turned to go home, tears of vexation standing in her eyes. She had not gone a score of yards down Splash Lane when the voice of Alexander Deacon hailed her.

He had followed her on foot, leading his horse. She turned her head again, quickly, to conceal her tears; but he had seen.

'Mrs Wintergreen, I — forgive me. My presence disturbs you.'

She shook her head, and tried to smile. She could only convey thus perfunctorily a feeling that smote her like a lightning-stroke — that his presence, with its gentlemanly lightness of touch, was the very thing that did not disturb her, and that gave her a sensation of being where she belonged.

'Will you allow me to walk with you as far as Plague House?' he said.

She signalled yes: still not able to look at him, and keeping her eyes fixed on the ground where his well-made highly polished boots flickered in and out of her circle of vision as he walked beside her.

'The name of this horse is Ebony,' Alexander said. 'It is, as you can see, a grey, so I can only suppose my cousin Miss Ingamells named it on the same principle that made her name her red setter Goldie. The Vikings even used to give names to their *swords*. I suppose the modern equivalent of that would be to give a name to one's umbrella. Or hat, perhaps. I wonder what name would be suitable for my hat? I rather see it as a Walter, or possibly an Arthur. Your own very charming bonnet must surely be an Emma or Louisa. Nightcaps I imagine should have gloomy Biblical names like Hepzebah and Ezekiel. Which reminds me that the jolly Puritans of Cromwell's time had a penchant for giving their offspring such pretty names as Sin, Death, and Corruption. Though it could be worse, as I've read somewhere that the Red Indians name their children after the first thing that the father sees after the birth – so only an accident of geography has saved me from rejoicing in the name Soda-Water Deacon. This exhausts all I can think of on the subject of names, and very tedious it was, but it has I hope allowed you to recover yourself, Mrs Wintergreen – one smile is all I ask, to set my mind at rest.'

She did smile at him, very brilliantly; for in her acutely vulnerable state the very fact of him ministered to her pain like a specific medicine. The sight of his face, blurred a little by the last of her tears, seemed to make Heartsease and all the material conditions in which she was trapped fall away. There was nothing *obvious* about that face, good-looking as it was: he was plainly a man of some intellect, but even that was incised subtly on his features; the sort of composure that usually goes with bovine stupidity he combined with quick intelligence, and the combination was attractive indeed.

'I don't know what you must think of me, Mr Deacon,' she said.

He only made a gentle interrogative murmur.

'I mean – I must seem one of those lent-lily females forever having the vapours.'

'Your resemblance to a flower I won't dispute,' he said deftly. 'As for the rest . . . I can't speak of the circumstances, except to say I'm convinced you would not be so upset without very good reason.'

This was very welcome to her ears, with her sense of grievance smarting within her. Her feelings, always volatile, were so close to the surface that she could not help bursting out: 'If our lives are doomed to disappointment, why are we given hearts to feel hope? It is cruel – cruel to taunt us with visions of what we can never have. It would be better if we were like the beasts, with no imagination to torture ourselves with.'

'Would it?' said he. 'Which is better off, the man in a closed dungeon, or the man in a prison-cell with a view from a window?'

Marianne shrugged. 'They are both in prison.'

'True.' He was so deeply absorbed in her that he only noticed with a start that they had arrived outside Plague House. 'But you know, Mrs Wintergreen, it is always possible to escape from prison.'

'Is it?' she said, with a listlessness that belied her.

He did not reply, but swung himself into the saddle; and then looking down at her said, 'Do you ride, Mrs Wintergreen?'

'Yes,' she said. 'Quite often. My doctor says the exercise is good for me.'

'I think he's right,' he said; and leant down to press her hand before riding away.

Marianne had not taken to her regimen of riding with any great enthusiasm, and the horse that Jed had bought in Norwich had spent much of its time in the stable. But the next morning she dressed herself with care in the riding-habit that gave her a silhouette as elegant as a wine-flute, and rode out directly after breakfast.

The countryside was leafless, and a light that was as cold as a reflection from sheet-metal fell from a lowering sky, braced across with dun rafters of cloud. All the elements of the scene, the trees, the flint-ribbed fields, the field-gates, the broken shapes of cottage roofs and chimneys, appeared like mere husks of themselves, as if the world that presented itself to the eye was a discarded chrysalis, from which a better world had risen and for ever departed. The sight of the labouring gangs of women and children – painful in itself, and a reminder to Marianne both of her estrangement from her father and her estrangement from Jed, who was so incensed by this development that he moved about in a trance of fury – caused her to turn her mare in the direction of the woods which Pierce and Rosa had roamed some weeks before.

The ground along that way was much cut up by horses' hooves, and a distant baying of hounds, brought to her ears on a rare breath of wind, confirmed that the hunt was meeting again and had passed that way shortly before. Marianne, who intensely disliked hunting, had no wish to follow it, and she had turned again to pursue the bridle-path skirting the edge of the woods when her attention was caught by a movement among the copsewood, which at this season appeared like a tracery of wrought-iron.

It was a horse, saddled but riderless, its coat steaming from a brisk ride: it gave a pleased grunt as she dismounted and approached along the rough path through the copsewood. Her first thought was that this must be the mount of a straggler from the hunt; her second, that the rider must have been thrown; her third took the form of a gasp as she saw a prostrate figure, in hunting-coat and breeches, stretched upon the leaf-mould and moss beside the path.

In a moment she was kneeling beside the motionless man – and stifling a cry as she recognized the face, smoothly beautiful in pale repose, of Alexander Deacon. The conviction that he was dead ran her through like a rapier, and in doing so released a gush of suppressed feeling that hitherto she had barely acknowledged. She dragged off her glove, so that it fell upon the leaves inside out, and put her hand to his face with a low moan.

She touched, not the coldness of marble, but the warmth of living flesh. Alexander opened his eyes with a start, and she sprang back, hiding her bare hand out of sight.

He sat up, seeming to behold her with as much surprise as if she had been a wood-sprite. 'Good God!' he said. 'Am I awake?'

'What happened? Are you hurt?' cried she.

Alexander blinked about him. 'I *am* awake – of course I am. I'd fallen behind the hunt, so I tried to take a short cut through the woods – which my mount didn't like at all, she shied at something in the trees — and I ended up on my back. So winded — felt as if I'd never be able to draw another breath, and didn't fancy the effort of standing — and then I must have drifted off a moment.'

'But are you sure there's nothing broke ?' said Marianne, as he began to climb to his feet. 'Oh, do take care . . . I thought you were dead!'

The vehement emotion with which she said this, together with the recollection of her touching his face, arrested them both. Alexander looked at her with a clearer apprehension than he had yet shown; then he bent to pick up her glove, and carefully put it on her bare hand, sliding it upward as if it were a stocking.

When a moment later he began kissing her, the knowledge that this was wrong existed only on the outermost verge of her consciousness, displaced as it was by so expansive a feeling of rightness. It seemed right that she who was so neglected should receive such a tribute; right that she should receive it from a man who inhabited the grander sphere beyond Heartsease, and who recognized that she did not belong here. The swift succession of emotions — alarm, shock, relief — had had an effect as of the throwing down of barriers; and she pressed her lips to his as eagerly as if she might suck forth from them all the sustenance that her unsatisfied soul craved, and in embracing him embrace London, Paris, Europe, and all the enticing world.

Pierce went up one morning to retrieve some brushes from the attic room of the Hall where he had been painting Alexander Deacon's portrait. It looked now as if the portrait would not be finished, for Alexander seemed to have lost interest, and most of his days lately were taken up with riding.

Flinging open the door of the attic room, Pierce was surprised to find Miss Ingamells within. She was standing before the portrait of Alexander on the easel, as if studying it, and she seemed to Pierce to have just drawn back a little as he entered.

'Mr Coppinger you must forgive me quite the Paul Pry am I not or perhaps the cat that curiosity killed though the proverb omits to mention precisely how the unfortunate animal met its end almost as nonsensical as the one about teaching one's grandmother to suck eggs which always seems to me an outstandingly undesirable occupation not to say impudent.'

She spoke with even more rapid inconsequence than usual. Her breast heaved, and Pierce's quick eye noticed, before she could hide it, that her fingertips were marked with oil-paint, and that the portrait on the easel was a little smudged about the lips.

He said something about the painting requiring a lot of work; and Miss Ingamells, fastening her unquiet eyes on him, brightly rejoined: 'But such a good likeness of the monster, Mr Coppinger, you are really to be congratulated for bearing to look at him for such an unconscionable length of time together I declare it would make me positively ill but at least you will be spared that any further at least I presume so as my cousin's interest in the matter seems quite to have evaporated even sitting still being apparently too tiresome for him but there it's not for me to pass judgement on the future heir of Heartsease Hall for after all who am I but a sort of corporeal ghost haunting its corridors I declare all I need to complete the resemblance is to carry my head under my arm and that you are thinking would be a considerable improvement on my appearance and I don't blame you I'm sure!'

'It does seem, I'm afraid, that Mr Deacon has tired of the project,' said Pierce.

'Supposing that to be so Mr Coppinger might I ask what you will do with the painting? I mean it seems a pity your work should be wasted and I wonder could you not varnish it as it stands, that would preserve it would it not?'

'Certainly, I could do that.'

'I would be obliged — for then this image would be preserved just as it is for years to come — and when Mr Alexander Deacon is old and worn and marked and hideous there it will be as a reminder of what is lost. I like that idea,' said Miss Ingamells, smiling a terrible smile, 'I like it extremely!'

Chapter Thirteen

Marianne's Dreams

Footsore but exulting, Pierce returns to the Hall after a long Sunday tramp across Madhouse Heath, away to the south of Heartsease, where at last he has heard word of Rosa.

Sheer good luck brought him this news that sets his heart capering. He stopped to refresh himself at a little ale-house that was no more than an open window with a board affixed to the sill, and overheard a higgler who was doing likewise talking of the load of besom-brooms he has in his cart: made, he said, by a curious old blind man who lives out on the heath, alone but for a beautiful young girl who helps him with his work and looks after his house. His eager enquiries left no room for doubt that the girl was Rosa; and the higgler gave him directions, too, to the place. It was too late in the day then for him to carry on to that remote spot; but that does not matter. He has found Rosa. He will see her again. As he approaches the Hall from the drive, colour that has been absent seems to glow again in the grass and the spring-tipped trees, and on the façade of the house it is as if a thousand brilliant details leap out to beguile his eye.

Over dinner he goes out of his way to be pleasant to Miss Ingamells, who has been in low spirits of late; thus by chance compensating for the silence of Alexander Deacon, who usually conducts the conversation down all sorts of amusing avenues, but who is rather reserved tonight, and retires early. Pierce too goes to bed in good time, but lies for an hour with his hands behind his head and his long legs aching from their exercise. He is surrounded by a cloud of hopes and fears which bite him like gnats all through his sleep; and on waking he is sensible of presenting a rather wild appearance to the terrifying manservant who brings his shaving-water and boots, and who seems able to endow this simple action with tremendous scorn and disdain.

This sleek persecutor, however, is late this morning – an unheard-of thing. He seems, moreover, to be a little agitated, and explains to Pierce that the morning routine has been rather upset, on account of Mr Deacon's sudden departure.

This is surprising to Pierce but, knowing as he does the quixotic character of Alexander, not unduly so. He thinks little of it until he reaches the dining-room. The many silver dishes are set out (Mr Ingamells always makes a hearty breakfast – presumably, since he is indifferent to material pleasures, out of mere habit) but no one is eating. Miss Ingamells is standing at the window staring out at a rainy spring morning; Mr Ingamells is questioning one of the maids.

'Mr Coppinger,' says Mr Ingamells at last, dismissing the maid, 'you must excuse this disturbance in our domestic arrangements. A most unexpected circumstance, and I – but please, sir – be seated: there is no need for *you* to be incommoded . . .' This with a melancholy smile, as if to say 'As for me, I am used to it!'

Pierce thanks him, and hesitates, looking at Miss Ingamells who remains fixed at the window.

'Beatrice, my dear,' says Mr Ingamells, 'will you do the honours of the table? It is a very perplexing business, I know, but duty, my dear – duty!'

Miss Ingamells comes without a word to the table, sits herself stiffly down, and stares about at the dishes of eggs and tongue and kidneys with as much frozen incomprehension as if it were an aboriginal banquet, with insect life prominent amongst its delicacies.

'I understand Mr Deacon has left,' says Pierce.

'At first light this morning,' says Mr Ingamells. 'He roused the servants himself, and had his luggage taken out to a hired conveyance, which he had stabled at the Wheatsheaf. He left a message begging our pardon for the unseemly haste, and saying he is called urgently back to London. This is not, in itself, untypical of my young cousin's habits: I fear he has caught a little of the modern contagion, that love of speed and change, that discontent that manifests itself so regrettably among the labouring classes. But now a message has arrived from Plague House in the village, which seems to throw rather a different complexion on the matter.'

'Plague House?' says Pierce with a start.

'Tea, Mr Coppinger?' enquires Miss Ingamells, with a sort of feverish urbanity of expression, very strange to see.

'I have not the honour of knowing the people there, beyond the fact that the lady is the daughter of my estimable tenant Mr Hemstock,' says Mr Ingamells, 'for I have led but a retired life since the irreplaceable loss of my Euphemia, and am out of touch with the times. However, their name, it appears, is Wintergreen; and I regret to say that it appears that Mrs Wintergreen also made a sudden and unannounced departure at first light this morning – that, in fact, Mrs Wintergreen and Mr Deacon left together, for what destination we know not.'

Pierce drops his knife with a clatter, transfixed not so much by the news as by the memories that rush upon him – little suspicions, little rumours, little hints that now appear as plain as day.

'Mr Wintergreen, it seems, found on rising his wife gone, and a letter acquainting him with the fact of her flight, and the name of her companion; and so he applied to us here to see if we knew any more.' Mr Ingamells' tone, as befits an admirer of Roman virtue, is quite unmoved as he goes on: 'Naturally I returned what information I possess; but I fear there is very little that can be done in such a case. It appears that the lady – such one must call her, out of respect for my worthy friend Mr Hemstock – is acting of her own free will in this matter. Time was when it would have been an absurdity to talk of the free will of the tender sex, for a dutiful submission to their husbands was something womankind prided itself on and gloried in − I need only instance my Euphemia; but we are decayed, sadly decayed! I make no secret of this distressing matter to you, Mr Coppinger. But it is of course very painful for me to contemplate a relative of mine engaging in such a rash and discreditable action, not to mention the deceptions that must have preceded it: though in such a case the woman is more to blame, man's nature being what it is. One can only stand amazed at − and yes, pity! − a creature who can thus sacrifice at a stroke all those qualities that render the fair sex an object of reverence, and condemn to perpetual oblivion her reputation and good name.'

Mr Ingamells, seeming to find consolation in these reflections, takes some more smoked ham; whilst Pierce, dumbfounded, and occupied with pitying thoughts about Jed, and wondering conjectures about Marianne and Alexander, stares at the cup of tea Miss Ingamells has handed him, as if he cannot imagine what he is meant to do with it.

'Well, we are fearfully solemn,' says Miss Ingamells, 'but as for me, I declare I find it prodigiously amusing, just to think of that poor creature eloping with Mr Alexander precious Deacon, just imagine it being with the monster all the time and dear me one must suppose actually in love with him really I find it so terribly amusing I can't help but laugh really I can't.' And she begins to laugh − a thin high screech of a sound, utterly mirthless, that is like the drawing of fingernails across a slate, and produces quite the same prickly effect at the back of Pierce's neck, the laugh going up and up, and seeming to circle about the ceiling like a bat, flittering and trapped. Tears start to her eyes as she rocks in her chair, with her bony arms wrapped about herself, and shrieks out: 'I can't help but laugh − actually in love with him no really I can't help but laugh I'm sure I can't help it!'

While Miss Ingamells laughs at her breakfast-table, Jed sits slumped at his with his face in his hands − old Ben Catbush standing over him the while, as if grief were like a fierce glare, and he were trying to shade Jed from it.

'How far d'you suppose they'll have got by now, Ben?' says Jed, muffled.

'They must have been gone three hours or more,' answers the stolid Ben. 'And it were a light post-chaise, according to Dick Freshwater's boy who saw it. A good way, I reckon. You're not thinking of trying to catch 'em, surely?'

Jed sighs and uncovers his face, which is as grey as wood-ash. 'There's no telling where they've gone; and even if there was . . .' He lays his hand upon a note lying on the table. 'She've left me, Ben: thass what I've got to take in. She've not been kidnapped or stole away. She've gone away with him, because . . . Because she want him and not me.'

'Thass a shame, that is,' says Ben, helplessly; and then, as if only repetition can convey his feelings: 'Thass a shame, that is − a shame, thass what it is.'

Jed stands, and irresolutely walks to the window, where rain and sun are contending for the dominion of the spring morning. 'I don't know what to do,' he says dully. 'What am I to do?'

'You want to eat something,' says Ben, 'thass what you want to do. You'll be ill else.'

Jed barely shakes his head; and glances round at the snug room, where every single thing that meets his eye is so eloquent of Marianne's presence that it seems the maddest of paradoxes that she is not there. 'I didn't know,' he says, in the same dull stunned tone. 'All this time she must have been . . . But I didn't know. How was it I didn't know?'

'You've been busy,' says Ben, in his loyalty setting

himself to answer every question.

'Aye — busy: thass what she say in the note,' says Jed. 'Busy with everything but her, it seem . . . But that wasn't as if I'd stopped loving her!' he cries, with a note of anxious denial in his protest. 'Surely she didn't think that . . .'

He watches through the window a blackbird gathering twigs; remembers a fledgling that would not leave the nest; turns and, patting Ben's shoulder, as if he were the one in need of consolation, goes upstairs. Most of Marianne's clothes remain still in the closets: she packed only one small bag. There is a peculiar pain for him in seeing her clothes thus abandoned: it is as if she wished to throw off every last vestige of the woman she had been, Jed Wintergreen's wife.

The note she left is short: it speaks of the death of what there had once been between the two of them, of his turning away from her and having no interest in her thoughts and wishes, of his disregard of her unhappiness in Heartsease. She implores him not to be hurt by her going away with someone else, for they would only go on making each other more wretched, and this puts an end to it. The note is hastily written — it recalls vividly to him her quick, mercurial speech — and hastily sealed, as if she sought thus to forestall second thoughts.

Jed cannot stop thinking of the fact that he was obliviously sleeping in his room — for they sleep apart now — when she was slipping out of the house and out of his life. He dwells on that, rather than reviewing with hindsight her behaviour in the last few weeks when she rode out so often, and was often abstracted. Perhaps he failed to notice anything amiss because of his own abstraction of mind, concerned with Todd Gault and the workless men of the village — perhaps, indeed, his failure, or refusal, to notice things is the crux of it all; but somehow that does not seem to matter beside the stark, unbearable fact that he lay asleep while Marianne stole out of the house to elope with a lover. He almost feels that had he only woken then, and confronted her, everything might have been different — and yet he shies, too, from a fearful suspicion that it would not have been, and that he would merely have seen written in her face what is written in the parting note.

For the moment he cannot think of the man, Alexander Deacon, with any clearly identifiable emotion. All he can think of is Marianne, and the fact that he has lost her — lost her as swiftly and unthinkingly as a pocket-book or handkerchief. But he hardly knows which is worse — that, or the suspicion that grows on him with each glance of retrospect over their life together, that he at least partly drove her away, that the yoke of sorrow he must bear henceforth was fashioned by his own hands.

There is a commotion in the hall below. Jed goes to the top of the stairs, and sees àt their foot Elias Hemstock glaring up at him.

The big man is wet from the rain; but that is not the only change in his appearance. Hemstock is, unthinkably, dishevelled, his mane of hair uncombed, his linen rumpled and soiled. He looks — and this too is scarcely believable — rough and coarse, unguarded, uncouth. It is as if his loss of self-command has also involved loss of self, and ancestry has displaced the individual.

'Where is she?' bellows Hemstock, grasping the carved newel-post in one great hand as if he would hurl himself upward at Jed.

'You've heard, then,' says Jed, surprising himself with the flatness of his voice.

'Tell me where my daughter is, sir!'

'I don't know where she is,' says Jed; and it is as if the articulation of these words breaks the numbness he has been feeling, and drives needles into his heart. 'She've left me. She've run away with that Deacon fellow, and she say she's not coming back.' He adds after a moment: 'She've left both of us.'

It is that association of the two of them that seems to incense Hemstock to the uttermost degree. He slams his open hand against the newel-post with such violence that the whole banister shivers and creaks again. 'Wintergreen,' he says, pointing a forefinger like a bludgeon, 'I hold you responsible for whatever happens to my daughter. Any harm that comes to her—'

'What's to happen?' says Jed. 'She've done nothing against her will. Besides . . .' A deathly feeling comes over him as the future seems to rear up before his eyes: a future empty of Marianne, empty of love. Only hate remains, and he clutches at it. 'Why should you care a jot for your daughter's disgrace, Hemstock? Where has been your care for her this past half-year, when you've treated her like she don't exist?'

'Disgrace. Talk to me of disgrace. Marrying *you* was the disgrace, Wintergreen – none worse. This is only finishing the work you started. It's you who ruined her, man, God damn you for it.'

'Ruined her,' says Jed carefully, 'or ruined you?'

With an ominous grunt, exactly like that of the bull he resembles, Hemstock places his foot on the bottom stair – but Jed in his turn begins to descend, saying: 'I've got nothing more to say to you, Hemstock. She've gone, and there's nothing you can do.' He pauses, and points to the front door. 'And what's more, you're trespassing,' he says coldly; and not until the farmer has stormed out does he realize that in using those words he sounded very like Hemstock himself.

The scene is a private supper-room at the York Hotel, Dover; the hour, late in the evening, with a strong night-wind blowing without, and echoing the boom of the sea about the cliffs; the actors, a young man and young woman, both good-looking, though the former has a far more easeful appearance than the latter, travelling as Mr and Mrs Sanderson.

Marianne, who seems to have left her country appetite

behind her along with much else that pertains to her old identity, finds herself scarcely able to touch the food that is set out on the cloth before her; and, though she is not used to it, drinks freely of the wine instead. The candlelit room is snug, panelled and secure, but what she finds a little disconcerting about it is the number of reflective surfaces it contains; for look where she will, at the silver covers, at the wineglasses and decanter, at the polished pewter and brass on the walls, she sees everywhere a little miniature of herself and Alexander sitting together at the table, as if the whole material world is peculiarly interested in their situation, and is breaking out in visible thoughts of them.

Alexander, who is admirably relaxed, and who bespoke the private room with that casual self-possession she so envies and wishes to acquire, reaches out more than once to caress her fingers, and reassure her. 'We've broken no law, my dear,' he says. 'No law in fact, and no unwritten law either – no law that the heart acknowledges, anyhow. And what other law is worth obeying? To anyone who says that what we're doing is wrong, I would simply say: how can it be *right* that you should go on being miserably trapped in that living-death of a life in Norfolk? Where is the good in that – for anyone?'

'I'm sure you would have made a brilliant lawyer, after all,' she says, 'for you are so persuasive . . . But are you sure you won't regret abandoning the law? Won't there be – I don't know, consequences?'

'None at all. And I don't have the slightest regret. Truth to tell, my love, I've been dithering on the brink of giving the whole dreary business up for some time, and it was meetingyou that gave me the fillip in the right direction. Let them all go and hang themselves with their ridiculous wigs, and choke to death on all that dismal dust of precedents and arraigns. I'm a free man, hooray!' As she blenches a little he adds, in the nearest thing he has to an earnest voice: 'We're *all* free, Marianne – if we did but know it. You as well as I. There are only the chains of convention to bind us – paper chains, easily broken. There are no gods to hurl thunderbolts at us, that I know. We wish to be together: I have a little money, or can get some – and as for the future, well, we'll see. I shall come into property sooner or later. And you want to see Paris – and tomorrow you shall!'

She smiles, for it is impossible not to when Alexander fixes her with that look, half-tender, half-raffish, all gaiety; and in truth her troubled doubts are only the shady side of a great noontide glow of excitement. The consequences of what she has done seem only marginal notes to the tremendous fact that she has done it – *she*; it is as if she has found herself living out the plot of a romance. She has never thought of herself as a courageous person, and now the surprising spectacle of her own courage shuts out from her sight all other aspects of her action.

Which is not to say that Marianne has not thought, over and over, of the home in Heartsease she has forsaken, and the man there who is her husband. Is, or was, for Marianne sustained herself through her secret preparations for flight with a formula of reproach that was partly 'This will make him care!' and partly 'Nothing will make him care!' He was, she told herself, so distant from her in sympathies that physical distance could make it no worse: the estrangement was already virtually complete. Thus she tells herself again, as she toys with a supper she cannot eat, with her luggage awaiting her upstairs in a room with a double bed. The elegant man whose fingertips delicately brush hers values her, she feels, as her husband does not; and it is perhaps because she has so insecure a sense of her own worth that Marianne needs, constantly and consumingly, to feel herself valued.

Thus she turned to Alexander, meeting him by means of her daily rides about the fields and woods; thus the personality of Alexander, who from her first meeting with him impressed her as the sum of all that was desirable in human cultivation, wound its coils about her heart; thus she experienced what she thought of as the burgeoning of her true self, opening out in response to his charm, his genial assurance, his knowledge of the world. And thus he asked her – in his light way that makes everything seem possible, and nothing hedged about with fateful shades as in Heartsease – to come away with him. And it is, as he promised it would be, quite easy. It is as if he possesses a master-key that enables him to pass at will through the incarcerating complexities of life. And Marianne is quite swallowed up in him. A person can be a world after all.

'I learnt French at school,' says she – her mind skipping over the prospect of the night ahead, and fixing itself on the crossing tomorrow of that sea which is making a sound like an almighty groaning and sighing about the cliffs – 'but I'm afraid I'm rusty – I hope I shall be able to make myself understood.'

'You'll get on much better than me, my love – my education being of that useful sort that equips a man to talk to poets who died two thousand years ago, but not to anyone living at all. I only get by in French by waving my arms about.' He pushes away his plate, having made a good meal, and raises his glass to hers. 'If Paris fails to be as enchanted with you as I am, I shall be very surprised.'

She clinks her glass to his, smiling into his eyes, with a stronger consciousness than ever of being like the heroine of a romance; thinking, too, of the school at Clapham, and the other girls who seemed destined for futures so much more glamorous than hers, and what they would think if they could see her now. All her old dreams are within reach, held out to her in Alexander's white hands, and they are as vivid as ever – so vivid that the interval between her dreaming them in the school dormitory and this moment of their realization appears a mere momentary blur, and the events that happened in that interval so trifling that the very ring on her third finger seems insubstantial, instead of a band of unyielding metal.

At a distance from Heartsease sufficiently short to be covered by a sturdy walker in a morning, but far enough from that place to be as untouched by events there as by events on the moon, Rosa lived in the cottage of Christmas Hubbert, the broom-tier.

To a young woman who had lived all her life in a village, with the eyes of a tightly knit community always upon her, it was strange to reside in a house so isolated that the eye could travel from horizon to horizon without alighting on the smoke of a single chimney. Others might have felt uneasy, but Rosa had her own reasons for seeking solitude, and she liked it.

The broom-tier's cottage stood on the southern side of Madhouse Heath, which was itself a sort of outrider to the large uncultivated area, reaching down to the Suffolk border, known as the Brecks. This was country in which an authentic breath of the ancient was exhaled from the very soil, and beside which the neat enclosed acres of Farmer Hemstock appeared as artificial and evanescent as hothouse blooms under glass. Bare, poor, infertile, sparsely populated, it was yet a place so powerful in presence, so pure in its severity, that it seemed less a passive relic than a latent potency, choosing to bide its time in the certain knowledge that it would triumph at last as it had triumphed over the ancient hunting-tribes whose flint arrowheads could be seen lying about the great hedgeless fields, and over the Roman occupiers whose broken pottery crunched beneath the soles of Rosa's boots as she walked the sandy tracks.

Sand was everywhere — as pervasive in this landscape as if it were a fifth element. It drifted in hollows and pits, there to be pocked by the nests of sand-martins; it was borne by the gusty wind in lazy flails like smoke; it peppered the fleeces of the thin sheep that eked a living from the heath, and clung always to the hairy feet of the rabbits that abounded in the region, inhabiting ancestral warrens that exceeded in size the hamlets of their human neighbours. The sand added its dun tint to the prevailing sombreness of colour, which was relieved only in late summer by the purple blooming of the heather and the yellow of gorse; for the most part the face of the heathland, bracken and lichen and furze and mosses and tough wiry turf wore a subdued secretive aspect more typical of plant life that never sees the sun, even though it was entirely exposed to that brilliant overarching Anglian sky. There was something curiously primeval too about the resilient feel of this vegetation beneath the foot, which in treading upon it left a print as clear as that formed in fresh snow. Scattered pine trees were the chief verticals of the scene, but verticals of such twisted and tortured shape that they seemed rather to have agonizingly clawed themselves up from the horizontal than to have grown shootwise. They appeared to express in their writhing distortions all the enmity of the elements, an eternity of scourging and buffeting. But they embodied too what was so profoundly impressive about the heath. It was not facile and flowery. Even on the balmiest summer day the wintry, storm-driven shapes of the pines testified to the fact that bleak November is not so much a transient time of year as an enduring condition of existence.

Rosa, roaming long distances to gather the heather that was used in the making of the brooms, became intimately acquainted with the heath, so that its characteristic music, the call of stone-curlews and lapwings and the scurry of wind through thorn-bushes, soon grew as familiar to her ears as the jingling plough-teams and clicking pattens of Heartsease. The sound of humanity was entirely absent from this new music; for whole mornings together she was as distinctively alone as if the prehistoric flint-diggers whose burial-barrows dotted the landscape represented the last generation of man. She was utterly removed from the busy fret of human life, from its disappointments and its desires alike; and if she had not come here precisely with the idea of escaping those things, she found an unexpected pleasure in being free of them. Sitting to rest in the shadow of one of the many ruined buildings of the breckland — where even man-made dwellings seemed too little hardy for the thin soil — Rosa was a prey to that flattering idea that seduces the hermit: that rejection as a principle is somehow nobler than acceptance.

An observer watching Rosa toil along those tracks might have found a sad incongruity between the austerity of the scene and the beauty of the woman, whose tall straight figure seemed to brim with life to the very ends of her wind-whipped hair. But there was no one to see, for the only companion of her days was Christmas Hubbert, and he was blind.

He had been born on the day of the nativity some sixty or seventy years ago. That it was impossible to be more precise was typical of the element of mystery that attached to him — a mystery, however, that derived not from any hint of secrets in his past, but from the peculiar stillness and self-possession of his nature. Likewise, in a region with a long and dishonourable history of belief in witchcraft, there were occasional whisperings among the breck-dwellers that Christmas Hubbert was a 'toadman', with magical powers; but though he had a rare rapport with animals, the curious respect accorded him proceeded less from fear than awe — at his patience, his gentleness, the way in which he seemed to move above the pettinesses of humankind. He had been blind for some years, and had carried on his work with the help of a youth who had a bad name in the district, and who had at last confirmed it by making off with all the money his employer had made in a month. Yet just as Christmas had taken the youth in with a quiet refusal to listen to the warnings about him, so he quietly refused to hear of prosecuting him. That was his way.

He was a smallish, square-hewn man with long hair

and a spade beard as white and soft as the hanks of rain-washed wool that the sheep left on the thorn-bushes. His open eyes were transparent and colourless, and were turned upward to give him that alert listening look often seen in blind people; but in Christmas the listening seemed to be directed towards something within himself. His invariable dress consisted of an embroidered smock, billycock hat, and leather gaiters into which the creases of long wear had so established themselves that they were more like a second hide than an article of clothing. The cottage in which he lived was of flint and thatch, sparely furnished, though much room was taken up downstairs by an abandoned loom; for Christmas in his younger days had been a weaver, until the concentration of the trade in the mills of Norwich had silenced such country looms for ever. It was not difficult to imagine his hands plying the shuttle, for they were hands in which intelligence was as clearly manifest as in the domed pate of the scholar; and wherever one fixed the eye in that cottage one saw something that he had made with them or mended with them, or which took its particular moulded or polished form from the touch of them as he guided himself sightlessly about. Indeed it was as if inanimate objects took on life in his hands: his very walking-stick had a sentient look, and seemed to fit its beaked head into his hand like a complaisant pet.

He remained wonderfully skilful at making the besom-brooms that were his livelihood; and they kept him, if not richly, at least decently above poverty, for higglers were very ready to make the lonely journey to his cottage for a supply so reliable and so obviously the genuine article. Apart from gathering the heather and collecting the timber and twine that formed the raw material of the brooms, Rosa's job was to see to the domestic tasks of the cottage for which Christmas's blindness incapacitated him. Quite incidentally, she acted as a companion for the old man; but though she very soon established a candid friendship with Christmas, there was a sense in which she knew this to be the least part of their association. He would have remained just as mild and forbearing, she felt, had she been unable to find a civil word for him: she was as welcome as anyone else to draw near to his peculiar simplicity and complexity of soul, and as welcome to go away again; he would remain unchanged. And this was in turn to Rosa a very welcome way of living – no dearth of kindness, but the heart could remain aloof and untrammelled, unengaged, invulnerable.

That was how she wanted it and that was why she had left Heartsease – to escape the man who in misguidedly loving her was putting his own heart in jeopardy. Much as she hoped, however, to effect a cure by thus withdrawing herself from his view, she had a foreboding that Pierce would still seek her out – and this was not a recognition of her own attractions, which she did not believe in, but a recognition of the strength of purpose which lay at the root of his apparently flexible nature. And so when one spring day she heard Pierce's voice at the open door of the cottage, the double beat her heart gave was not of surprise.

She had been raking the furze from the oven, and Christmas had gone to the door to greet the visitor. When she came out from the kitchen into the house-place she found Pierce, having doffed his hat, shaking the old man's hand and courteously introducing himself. She wished she could see that as calculation, insincerity – but the trouble was she knew it was not. He was simply like that. That was what made it so hard.

'Hullo, Rosa,' he said; and the look he gave her showed that he had not changed.

'Will you come in and sit down, Mester Coppinger?' Christmas said. The subtlest moods were as plainly perceptible to him as the smell of new bread, and he added simply: 'I've got coneys and hens to see to, and I can go out and do that now.'

Pierce however would not hear of the old man going out of his cottage on his account; and so Rosa said, picking up her shawl: 'Let's go walk, Pierce. Thass fine out. Christmas, I shan't be long.'

They set out across the heath. That stern place had made a few concessions to spring in the form of soft fronds of new bracken, and white blossom on the whitlow-grass; but Rosa noticed that Pierce, whose painter's eye was normally so responsive, scarcely glanced at the scene. Looking at the ground, he asked various desultory questions about her work and her life here, nodding at her halting replies. It struck her, like a light blow to the chest, that he did not look quite as well as he had used to: there was something worn about the fairness, and a smoky look about the eyes that reminded her a little of Jed Wintergreen.

That name soon came up, as Pierce told her the news from Heartsease: Marianne's elopement with a lover, the grim state of the village in which Jed and Hemstock faced up to each other like two angry rams.

'Poor Jed,' said she softly. 'And poor Heartsease . . . There was bad feeling growing when I left − that was part of the reason—'

'But not the whole of it,' said Pierce, stopping and facing her. 'Was it?'

She avoided his eyes, though even such a slight evasion rubbed like a burr against the truthfulness of her nature. 'No,' she said, 'twasn't only that. I thought that'd be best all ways. Being near you − that wasn't doing neither of us any good and never would, and so I decided that I should go away. Then you wouldn't see me any more and soon—'

'Oh, Rosa, for pity's sake,' said Pierce brokenly, 'I've searched high and low for you. You left no word, nothing—'

'I did it for the best,' she said, turning herself about with a wrench and plunging onward. 'I thought you'd see that.'

He paced beside her. 'It was a way, then,' he said in a compressed voice, 'of telling me there's no hope.'

'Not hope in the way you mean. Not hope in this world as it stand. Oh, Pierce, ain't that enough for you? I could tell you I hate you if you like but that wouldn't be true – and I can't find no easy road atween kind and true—'

She broke off with a cry of pain and stumbled on the sandy track. A thorn like a needle had gone into her foot straight through the sole of her boot, which was worn down to the thinness of pasteboard. Pierce helped her to sit down on a ferny bank in the lee of two twisted pines, the scaly limbs of which were intertwined as in a wrestler's hold. Kneeling before her, and waving away her protests, he took off the boot and gently removed the thorn from her bare foot. She saw a troubled tenderness come into his eyes at the sight of the grazes and abrasions, born of constant walking, that marked the white skin.

'My God,' he said, 'I might buy you a new pair of boots with the money I get for a week of that nonsense I practise at the Hall.'

'I'm sure you could,' she said stiffening, 'but I don't want that.'

'Still proud, eh, Rosa?' he said with a sort of desperate harshness. 'Let's throw it in the dust then. Let me get rid of it.' Feverishly he began yanking handfuls of coins from his pockets and scattering them broadcast on the ground. 'Perhaps if I divest myself of this rubbish you will see me for what I am – and the gentleman's hat too, there it goes – and now the coat—'

He had dragged his coat half-way down his arms when she stopped him, seizing his shoulders with her strong hands. 'Pierce, don't,' she cried, 'think what you're doing – only think, for God's sake . . . Pick up your money.' She fastened her eyes on his. 'Pick it up, Pierce, else I shall do so and give it back to you.'

After a moment he bowed his head and gathered up the coins, Rosa putting on her boot the while. Above their heads the wrestling pines were shaken by an easterly gust, which produced such a deep and haggard moan that the twain both started in alarm. For a moment it was as if Grima, the ghastly pagan spirit whose name was recalled in the flint-mines of Grimes Graves across the other side of the brecks, was at large upon the heath.

'This is a forbidding place,' said Pierce. 'Am I wrong for wishing to take you away from it?'

'For what?'

'To love you, Rosa. To marry you — be with you always—'

'Not wrong,' said she. 'Foolish. And that can come to the same as wrong. Shall I tell you why? D'you want to hear it, Pierce — my dear sweet Pierce, for so I reckon I may call you this last time of our meeting? Because I am rough and not educated and know nothing more of the world you live in than the bottom of the sea. And you say that don't signify and mebbe at first that wouldn't. And then your father would meet me and he'd try to be kind but he wouldn't be able to help wondering what on earth you'd done — and little by little you'd begin to wonder too. And so that would go on, wi' the impatience and the unhappiness creeping up on you; and then when one day you are a famous painter, as I know you will be, and great gentlemen invite you to their tables, won't you sicken at heart when you turn to see me by your side, and won't I sicken too to see the hate in your eyes, and so begin to hate in turn? Twenty years of different ways o' living, different ways o' thinking, dressing, eating, speaking, everything — thass what separates us, Pierce, and sooner or later that'd come out, like a doom waiting for us. And I don't ever want to see that hate in your eyes, Pierce. Thass why we must part now, while the light's still in them — so that when you see what a trick they played you, it won't be too late.'

The pines shuddered again, and Pierce seemed to shudder too, as if a blackness overcame his spirit. 'Dear God, why were we two made to meet, only to be thwarted like this?' he said.

Rosa shook her head. 'There's no answering such questions.'

With a hopeless gesture, as if he admitted the triteness of his words, Pierce said: 'The answer — the answer lies in our hearts!'

'Aye — lies,' said Rosa. 'For our hearts lie too. Even they set themselves against us!'

Pierce dug his hands in his pockets, and studying the ground at her feet said, 'I am not to see you again, then.'

She was about to say that she could not stop him, but that was not fair, it sounded like coquetry. 'Yes,' she said. 'It's best.'

After a long still silence he stirred and looked about him. 'Where is my way back to the high road?'

She pointed out the way. At the last she touched his hand and said, 'Forgive me.'

He smiled a little then. 'No need,' said he. 'Perhaps we should talk of forgiving the maker of a world that does this to us.'

She could not watch him go. She sat and concentrated her gaze on some stems of chickweed, vibrating in the wind, until her eyes ached.

Rosa was glad of the heath as she made her slow way back to Christmas Hubbert's cottage: glad of its impartiality, its freedom from association, its aloof solitude. There were snakes on the heath, cold winds blew, the earth yielded poisonous fungi, but these were impersonal dangers, and the chief thought it suggested to Rosa's throbbing mind was: 'I am safe here!'

Safe, and alone. There was no one to suggest that the bleakness she had chosen to live in had its counterpart in her heart, and that her withdrawal here was more than just a withdrawal from a village and from the man who pursued her. There was no one to suggest that in retreating, self-protectively, from the hurts of life she was denying life altogether, and that what she called wisdom was fear. There was only Christmas Hubbert, and he was not a man to pass judgement.

He was sitting at the open door of the cottage when she returned, his hands busy with a bundle of heather, his face turned up to catch the thin sunshine. 'Have your friend gone, Rosa?' he said.

'Yes, he've gone.'

'Thass a pity. We could have give him a bite of dinner. We must ask him next time.'

'He won't be coming again,' Rosa said.

'Ah. Do he love you?' said Christmas, in his usual neutral tone.

'No!' said Rosa, with a start. 'No, he—Whatever make you say that?'

'He came a long way to see you,' said Christmas with a shrug.

She groped for an excuse, but somehow it was impossible to lie to Christmas. 'Oh, Christmas, he – he think he love me, mebbe, but he can't really – how could he? Not as I really am. You, with your poor blinded eyes, you see me as he can't.'

'Mebbe.' Christmas calmly went on with his broom-tying. 'But thass sweet to be looked at wi' love, I reckon, do the eye see false or true. Sweet, but frightening, mebbe.'

Rosa stirred uneasily. 'I'm only afraid for him.'

'Why?'

'Because – because he'll be unhappy.'

'With you, or without you, d'you mean?'

'I mean – oh! I don't know what I mean.' She picked up the pail to fetch water from the butt. 'He'll forget in time.'

'Yes, he'll forget in time,' said Christmas. 'And mebbe you will too.'

The old man's hands worked on, and his transparent eyes gazed upward; and Rosa was thankful that, though he seemed to discern much about her, he surely could not see her tears.

For Jed the spring was a hollow mockery. His soul lived a

dark winter. There was no word from Marianne, and any faint twinkle of hope that her flight might have been an ill-considered freak, recoiled against as soon as accomplished, was extinguished. Even had it not been, he felt his position could scarcely have been different. There were no degrees of betrayal: the thing was done. Marianne had left him for another man, and he must daily live with the consciousness of it. There had been but one love in his life, and though it had soured, Jed could no more dismiss the loss of it than he could have dismissed the loss of a hand; and to be bitterly indignant, stung, sore, vengeful, and disenchanted with his wife was, he found, not quite the same as to cease loving her.

His first crops were green in his fields; but this, for which he had worked so hard and waited so eagerly, was no satisfaction to him. The relish was gone. Occasionally he was caught out, and found himself starting towards the house to tell Marianne some piece of encouraging news about the farm, or looking forward to seeing her as he rode home from Norwich: his mind thus continuing to prepare itself for happiness, when the fundamental conditions for it no longer existed. He continued to exert himself about the farm partly because it tired him sufficiently to ensure sleep, partly because it provided work for at least a few of the men of the village. The effect of Hemstock's wholesale sackings and use of cheap labour-gangs instead had been profound, and there was much distress in Heartsease. Jed did what he could; Mr Ringrose likewise, at Jed's repeated promptings − which brought their own pain, for whenever he called at the Grange he had to endure the absent-minded gentleman's enquiries after his wife. But they could only furnish so much work, and the village was haunted by unemployed men with nothing to do but loiter in lean baleful-eyed groups, and with nothing to say to each other because of the sameness of the days, except the odd furtive whisper that had poaching as its theme.

Todd Gault, Jed knew, was taking it especially hard.

But he did not know how hard until one day Ben Catbush brought him some news that temporarily shook him out of his bitter self-absorption.

Todd had been caught taking a handful of turnips from a clamp in Elias Hemstock's yard. The farm-bailiff had caught him, and had merely sent him off with a flea in his ear; but when he mentioned this to his employer, Hemstock had violently reproved him for his folly, threatened his dismissal, and gone straight to Mr Ingamells to request Todd's arrest for theft. Mr Ingamells, as examining magistrate, had taken the bailiff's deposition, and committed Todd to trial at the Easter quarter sessions in Norwich, a couple of weeks hence.

Horribly familiar to Jed, that pitiless promptness of the authorities! Hardly knowing what he would say, but so tipful of rage that to be still was intolerable, he went to see Hemstock. He knew he would not be admitted to the house, and chose a time when he knew the farmer would be making a tour of the fields with his bailiff. Hemstock, on seeing Jed approach, motioned the bailiff away like a dog and then took out his watch.

'Two minutes,' he said, 'and then I have you thrown off this land.'

Jed ignored this. 'Todd Gault,' he said. 'You can't really mean to prosecute him for a handful of turnips.'

'Oh, no,' said Hemstock acidly, 'I mean to let him go free, so that he can steal from me again, of course.' He kept his eyes on his watch. 'You're a fool, Wintergreen.'

Jed considered a moment, trying to think of Todd and not of his own boiling feelings. 'Suppose I was to stand surety for him? — my word that he won't do anything of the sort again.'

'Your word?' grunted Hemstock. 'You really think that's worth anything? The word of one rogue for his jackal?' He snapped the watch shut and regarded Jed with an expression of disdainful puzzlement. 'In the name of God, man, what do you stand to gain from defending this ne'er-do-well? What's it to you whether he walks free or goes to the treadmill, as I hope he will?'

'For a handful of turnips,' said Jed whitely. 'Think of it.'

'I've thought of it well,' said Hemstock. 'And I shall make sure I attend the sessions and see him get the punishment he deserves. I stood up to your father and his cronies when they tried to threaten me, Wintergreen; I stood up to Gault and his cronies when they came to me with their insolent demands about wages. I don't change – I never will, even though the whole world goes soft, as it seems to be doing.' He turned his back. 'You've had your two minutes.'

Hemstock remained staring into the distance after Jed had gone; and only he knew how his words, though true, had contained an element of desperate bravado. For the elopement of Marianne had dented that massive self-assurance; and within his unconquerably strong body, behind the ever more arrogant exterior that he felt it necessary to present to the world, Hemstock's soul howled its outrage. Strangely enough, it was the receipt of a letter from Marianne that had brought his wretchedness to its present extremity: a brief page sent from abroad, assuring him she was well, begging him not to think badly of her, giving her love to her family. That was all: but it thrust her presence powerfully upon him. Till now he had found an opiate for his affliction in thinking of her as if she were, to all intents and purposes, dead. The letter brought her back to life, and with it the consciousness of his shame and humiliation. He had already noticed a subtle change in the elder Mr Bouverie's attitude to him – was there not a faintly amused scorn in the rector's bluff manner? – whilst young Mr Roland Bouverie had coolly declined an invitation to call. And even Mr Ingamells, polite as ever and offering bemused apologies for the behaviour of his young cousin – over which, he smoothly emphasized, he could not be expected to exercise any influence – had regarded Hemstock with a certain lofty speculation in his glance, as if he were curious to see how the farmer was reacting to the final ruin of his social ambitions.

Well, he could take that. He could take anything but their infernal pity. No, fate might deal him what blows it chose, but he would never show the world that he flinched. He had lost his daughter, lost his name, lost his dreams; but he still had the pride that had always been his staff, and now it must serve as a weapon too against a universe at war with him.

Jed rode to Norwich, and with the help of his lawyer Mr Veazey was able to see Todd for a few minutes in the Castle prison.

'I'm not here to reproach you, Todd,' Jed said. 'But I don't understand. You know what a double-dyed bastard Hemstock is: why didn't you come to me if you were hungry, 'stead of running that risk?'

'I've come to you for help enough times,' said Todd sullenly. After only a short time in the deep cells of the Castle he looked as bloodless and pale as a mushroom. 'I couldn't take no more from you, Jed, not and keep my pride. Why should it always have to be you who helps folk? You're feeding half the village already. And there's Hemstock all awash wi' money, and it's on account of him that folk are hungry in the first place . . . twas only justice, that when I needed food I took it from him! And so I shall tell the magistrates — tell 'em what he's like!'

Jed knew the boy would get no very sympathetic ear from that quarter, but he bid Todd keep in good heart, promised to see his mother all right, and said he would be present at the sessions to testify to his good character.

'Caught in the act — not a hopeful look-out, I'm afraid!' said Mr Veazey, when they were back in his office. 'One must trust to the leniency of the presiding magistrates.'

'I'd as soon trust a cat in a pigeon-loft,' said Jed.

'In a pigeon-loft! Ha ha ha! I call that pithy! You're a

born satirist — that's what you are,' said Mr Veazey, then went on, as it were dousing his cheerfulness with businesslike snuffers, 'Now, my dear sir, let us return to the matter you wished to discuss with me . . .'

The matter was the legal aspect of Marianne's desertion of Jed, which he had forced himself to turn his mind to. He listened gloomily to Mr Veazey setting out a disclaimer whereby he denied responsibility for future debts incurred by his wife: it seemed like the final murder of love to hear it travestied in these cold ceremonious phrases. He watched from the window a carter in the street whipping an old bony horse till the blood streamed, while the lawyer talked on.

'Come, my dear sir,' said Mr Veazey when he had done, observing Jed's black mood, 'I have never seen you quite downhearted before — I hope I may speak to you thus as a friend and not a client. Events do appear to unfold themselves somewhat distressingly at times, but much may be hidden. I rather stray from the legitimate ground of my profession here, and poach on the preserves of the clergyman, ha ha ha! but permit me to remind you of Providence — Providence, sir.'

'I don't deny Providence, Mr Veazey,' said Jed grimly, turning his unquiet eyes on the lawyer. 'My quarrel is with what Providence sees fit to provide.' He thanked Mr Veazey, shook his hand and took his leave.

The next day a letter arrived that brought a warm light to Jed's face for the first time since Marianne's flight. He put the letter in his breast pocket, and was just about to go out with a brisker step when Ben announced that Rosa Strickland was here.

She was wet from a spring shower, her skirts muddy: Jed placed her before the kitchen fire and gave her some warm spiced ale. It had been a good while since he had seen her, and he thought she looked thinner.

'I heard about what happened,' she said. 'So I thought I'd come see you, and say—well, that I'm sorry. It is true, then?'

Jed nodded. The shared childhood experiences of these two meant there was no awkwardness between them, and it was natural for Rosa to say: 'Are you hurting deep, Jed?'

'I still keep trying to understand, and make sense of't — as if that might make some difference,' said he. 'That won't bring her back.'

'You want her back, then?'

'I don't know what I want . . . My mind's all scatten abroad like broken chiney. If I could have her back as she was before — but thass just it. We can never be the same . . . Well, Rosa — tell me where you've been to all this while. You seemed to vanish like a wisp o' smoke.'

She told him where she was living and what she was doing. 'You know I've always dreamed of leaving Heartsease,' she said. 'And now I've done it.' But there was no gladness in her tone.

'Fresh start, eh?' said Jed. 'Any chance of that for me, d'you reckon?'

'You're still married to Marianne,' said Rosa. 'I'm afraid that can't be undone.'

'Aye — I know it. And so it seem we must pay for ever for our mistakes — never allowed to settle the bill and be quits till we die! Do God laugh, d'you reckon, to see men and women struggle wi' these puzzles he set us? To see us caught like birds on a limed twig?'

Rosa shook her head. 'I know you're bitter, Jed. Could you not mebbe leave Heartsease? Break free of the memories, at least.'

'Nay, I'm needed here. I couldn't leave. I'd really be an empty shell then . . . Besides,' he said freshening, 'I've got some fine news today. Things are going to be all right. There's some good coming to Heartsease.'

'Thass about time,' Rosa said. 'Why, what's afoot?'

Jed took the letter from his breast pocket. 'It's from my sister,' he said, and all the bitterness left his voice: it became tender in a moment, and Rosa smiled too. 'It's from Charlotte. She's coming to live here with me —

she'll be here at the end of the week,' Jed said.
'Everything'll be all right. Charlotte's coming.'

Chapter Fourteen

Sister and Brother

Charlotte had made a start on packing up her possessions, a process which wrought a melancholy change in the beloved face of the old room above the inn-sign, when Mrs Skeels called up to tell her that Miss Ward had come to see her.

The bath-chair was outside the door, and Loveday was leaning on the arm of Mrs Vickers.

'We didn't see you in the usual place this morning, Charlotte,' Loveday said. 'Are you not well?'

'I'm well, thank you,' Charlotte said. 'I'm sorry I wasn't there. I've been packing. I'm leaving Shipden very soon.'

'And how we shall get on without her I can't think,' Mrs Skeels put in. 'Skeels have quite got the maunge over it.'

Loveday regarded Charlotte for some moments. 'Mrs Skeels,' she said at length, 'may I talk with Charlotte in your parlour? Mrs Vickers, you go and have a nip of whatever it is you tipple. Don't get drunk.' The two young women seated themselves in the private parlour, Loveday continuing intently to study Charlotte's face.

'Where are you going?' she said.

'I'm going to live with my brother,' Charlotte said. 'He've had a bad turn of luck, and he's all alone, and he need me.' It was a simple statement of the simple facts of the case. As soon as she had heard from Jed of his desertion by his wife, Charlotte had known she must go to him: she had written at once that she was coming to Heartsease to be beside him. Instinctive loyalty had spoken. Grieved as she was for her brother, this had

379

come partly as a relief: his need for her forced the decision she had so long been unable to make. It was for the best.

'Then you're not coming back?' Loveday said.

Charlotte shook her head: then saw with surprise that tears stood in Loveday's eyes.

'Oh, Charlotte,' Loveday said, 'this is dreadful . . . I shall miss you so!'

This could not fail to move a heart like Charlotte's. 'I shall miss you too,' she said; and then, her guard slipping a little in her confusion: 'But I would have had to leave, anyhow.'

Loveday caught her up sharp. 'Why?'

Charlotte could not answer: she was afraid she had already said too much. She rose. 'Let me get you some tea—'

'No.' Loveday caught at her arm. 'Charlotte, sit down. Something's wrong. I'm not a fool. Tell me. It doesn't matter what you say to me. As long as it's the truth I don't care — I'm past that.' The day was warm, but Loveday ran her hands up and down the wasted flesh of her upper arms, as if she carried her own creeping chill about with her. 'It's something to do with me, isn't it?'

'No, Miss Ward — 'tisn't that—'

'Don't Miss-Ward me. I'm Loveday — I'm your friend, Charlotte, or I hope I am. You've been the sweetest of friends to me, you and Toby . . .' She paused. 'Does Toby know you're going?'

'No . . . I haven't told him yet.'

'Why haven't you?'

Charlotte could not meet Loveday's eyes: their beautiful, unnatural brightness seemed to burn through and through her.

'Charlotte Wintergreen,' Loveday said, seizing Charlotte's hand and mournfully beating it against her own, 'I've begun to have the most terrible feeling. I've begun to think I've not been a good friend to you at all—'

'Oh, but you mustn't say that,' Charlotte said. 'You've never done anything wrong—'

'You mean I haven't meant to,' said Loveday. 'But that's not the same . . .' She suddenly said in a curious conversational tone: 'I've just seen Toby on the cliff, by the way. He was wondering where you were. "Where's Charlotte?" he kept saying.'

'Was he?' said Charlotte, with such a determined, doomed effort at lightness that her words came out almost as a gasp.

'Ah, my dear, I'm sorry — I did that on purpose, and your face told its tale just as I thought it would!' said Loveday, gentle now. 'So I'm right. Toby Dane. You're going to leave Shipden because of Toby Dane — or what he's become. Oh, my poor Charlotte, I haven't been a friend to you — indeed I haven't!'

'You've done nothing wrong,' said Charlotte, whose feelings at that moment seemed all merged in one universal ache. She tried to smile. 'Unless being beautiful is wrong.'

Loveday ran a finger along her own cheekbone, indicating its waxen pallor, its hollowness. 'Is this beauty?' she said.

'Yes,' Charlotte said; for it was true. It was as if in the progress of her illness Loveday's striking looks were being refined to an essence of themselves, pure line without distracting detail.

'You ought to hate me,' Loveday said.

'I have wanted to, often,' Charlotte said. 'But it couldn't have made any difference.'

'Oh, dear God, I've been a fool!' said Loveday, tugging with irritable fingers at her bonnet-strings. 'Charlotte, how long have you loved Toby? Well — no need to answer that one. Women love deep and long, while men write pretty poems about it. You've been painfully in love with Toby all this time — haven't you?'

'Yes,' said Charlotte. There was a sort of relief, at last, in having it spoken, though it no longer mattered.

'Here – let me.' She untied the strings of Loveday's bonnet for her, and went on quietly: 'Yes, I've loved Toby – I don't know how long. We were friends when we were younkers, and then – well, thass hard to tell when you cross over, like, from friends to love.'

'But once you've crossed over there's no going back,' Loveday said.

'I'm afraid so,' Charlotte said; and, managing to keep her voice steady, 'I'm afraid that go for Toby too.'

Loveday was slowly shaking her head. 'I like Toby,' she said, 'but I shall never forgive him this piece of folly – at least, I may do if he wakes out of it . . . Charlotte. Look at me. First of all, I must know that you sincerely believe that I never meant this to happen – that it never for a moment entered my head that Toby could – well, *imagine* that he felt anything for me.' She was severe, a little fierce. 'Don't lie. I want truth, now, Charlotte. Nothing else will do for me.'

'I know it's not your fault,' Charlotte said. 'It just happened. But I'm afraid thass not just a matter of Toby imagining it—'

'Of course it is,' said Loveday briskly. 'Because, in the first place, I'm not at all a nice person, so anyone who thinks otherwise must be deluded – and in the second place, Toby loves you, Charlotte – you!'

Charlotte folded her hands in her lap, and perhaps even Loveday's piercing glance could not see to the turbulent depths of her agitation. 'He love me like a sister,' she said. 'That I know. No more.'

'But you are not his sister!' cried Loveday. 'And he is a fool to think so – and a fool to go chasing after a vision that only really exists in his head! I ought to tell him so.'

'Toby isn't a fool,' Charlotte said firmly. 'Please, don't speak of him like that. And don't tell him – don't say anything to hurt him.'

Loveday was silent a moment. Then she took Charlotte's two hands in hers. 'Dear God,' the sick girl said, 'what a world this is, where such a loving loyal heart as yours bleeds itself away in silence! There is something wrong somewhere — I have always thought so; and I have some pretty hard questions ready to ask whoever is responsible, when the time comes.' She thought for a minute. 'Charlotte, you do genuinely have to go to your brother?'

'Yes,' she said. 'He need me. Often I've thought of going to him before; but somehow I kept hanging on here, because—'

'Because you could not leave Toby! Ah, Charlotte . . .' Still pensive, still retaining Charlotte's hands in her own, Loveday went on: 'I have not done much good in my life, you know, my dear. No, let me speak. I have not done much good, for I have never felt the world deserved it. I have been selfish and spoilt because anything else would seem like going against my nature — and it still does. But I can and will do something. I shall leave Shipden directly. My grandparents have been talking of our moving on — Brighton, perhaps; but I hung on too, because I like it here, because I like you and Toby, and — and because, in short, this seems as good a place to die in as any. No, Charlotte — don't speak! You have seen much, with your quiet eyes — not blinded like poor Toby's; and you know I am not going to get better. Do you know what arterial blood is, my dear? Well, never mind — I do, and my pillow knows its garish colour, every night. So you see. I am not framed to be a heroine — I would much rather stay selfish for the little time that remains to me; and I certainly don't expect any reward for any good I do, when I go to meet this almighty tormentor of creatures that never did him any harm, who seems to expect in return a devotion I shan't give; but I can try to set something right while I'm here, at any rate — doing his job for him, if you like. And I can do that by leaving Shipden, straight away. I can't be cured, my dear, but Toby can! And the best way to do that, it seems, is for him not to see me any more. And that *will* be a good thing, for though he is foolish enough — yes, I say foolish — to fancy himself smitten with me, I know he is sensible enough to love you as you deserve, if he would only look into himself — for I've seen the two of you together often, remember, and I know how well you match, how you fit as neatly as the two halves of a shell. Perhaps Toby will be hurt and bewildered at first, as I shall go quickly, and leave perhaps just a note saying goodbye to both of you — but that's a good thing in its way. And I won't say it breaks my heart to go, because my going will be the means of making you happy — and there's nothing heartbreaking about that — nothing at all . . .'

Charlotte had bowed her head upon the sick girl's hands, and was weeping.

'There, my dear,' said Loveday, 'this is a new experience for me, to be comforting someone else . . . And you won't forget me quite, Charlotte? — but that's a vain question — just like when people say they look a fright, and are only fishing to be told the opposite.'

'I shall never forget you,' Charlotte said in a low voice, clasping Loveday's hands. 'Whatever happens — I shall never forget.'

'Well,' said Loveday, with her old transfixing smile unsteadily breaking through, 'somehow when you say it, one believes it. Now, Charlotte, wipe your eyes, for you have nothing to cry for, you know — and I must go and fetch Mrs Vickers from the gin-bottle and be off, for there is no time to lose.'

'I have much to cry for,' said Charlotte, on whom a new perspective of the world had suddenly broken, revealing configurations of light and shadow hitherto unknown to her young soul. 'I have you to cry for.'

'No, no, I won't have it!' said Loveday. 'That is just what the old tormentor-in-the-sky wants, and I won't let him have that satisfaction. If you think I blaspheme, my dear, then ignore it — it's just my whim. But if you must think of me, then laugh when you do — or smile at any rate — and that will baffle and dismay the old tormentor, to look down and see that one of his creatures, at least, is not in pain!'

Charlotte nodded, unable to speak; and rising, gave Loveday her arm to see her out, and say goodbye to her for the last time.

Just two days later the note addressed to Charlotte and Toby was brought to the Crab Pot, announcing, in offhand phrases that only Charlotte knew the reason for, that Loveday was leaving Shipden, and bidding goodbye to both of them.

The spring had been marked by brash winds that in the woodland behind the town had stripped the blossom as soon as it appeared, and left bluebell and primrose scattered forlornly about the spinneys; and a strong north-easterly was blowing as Charlotte ascended the cliff-path to meet Toby at their usual place. Since last night there had been a heavy ground-swell on the sea, but now its dark surface was swept with confused eddies. Here and there plumes of spray went up. The gulls were numerous and noisy, and were moving inland in high wheeling flocks.

'Something blowing up,' Toby said when she met him. 'Wonder if that'll break here or miss us like the other week. Loveday's late: mebbe she won't stir in this wind.'

Charlotte, touched with misgiving, produced the letter. Toby could read pretty well, but he was a long time poring over the paper that the wind tugged and tweaked and tried to tear from his fingers.

'Toby,' Charlotte said, watching him anxiously, 'we knew — we knew she wouldn't be staying always . . .'

'This isn't her,' said Toby, who had gone white. 'She wouldn't just go like this, without a word. Thass not Loveday. Thass those grandparents of hern. Just because she's weak they reckon to haul her about from pillar to post, without so much as a thought of what she want. She don't want to leave here — she said so. She liked it here.

Thass wrong to take her away — all wrong!'

'But we got no power over her, Toby — thass not our affair.'

Toby was not listening. 'This is writ last night — she say they're going early this mornen. They surely can't travel fast even in their carriage, not wi' Loveday sick as she is. I can catch 'em up on the road. There'll be a waggon or something going out from Shipden — I'll catch 'em up, and tell 'em thass wrong, they can't take Loveday away like that—'

'Loveday, Loveday, always Loveday!' cried Charlotte. 'Oh, Toby, hark to yourself, can't you? You're all swallowed up in her so you hardly know what you're about, and that grieve me so to see you . . . Don't do it, Toby — it's madness — don't go after them.'

'Why, what can they do to me? They're not ogres, surely. I don't understand you, Charlotte. I thought you'd be sad to see her go—'

'So I am.' She gazed at his infuriatingly beautiful, distracted, lost face. She had been feeling guilty and uneasy that all this had been put in train just for her sake; but now for the first time she felt angry with him — an anger that only profound love could have brought to stir the calm surface of her nature. 'I don't want you to go, Toby — and I can't stop you. All I can say is — if you do, I reckon I shan't be here when you come back.'

He looked stunned. 'What?'

'I'm going to my brother in Heartsease,' she said. 'Soon. And that might as well be today.'

'Charlotte . . .' His stricken manner was swiftly followed by a flush that covered him from throat to scalp. 'Why didn't you tell me?'

'Why?' She dropped her head in sadness: the unaccustomed anger had died as soon as it flared. 'If you have to ask, you'll never know.'

There was a moment of silence from Toby, filled by the sibilance of the seething sea. 'It seem like I'm never to be told anything,' he said with boyish hurt. 'First Loveday

— now you . . . It's all wrong . . .'

Presently, when she looked up, Toby was descending the cliff-path.

'Where are you going?' she cried.

'Like I told you,' he said. 'To see them grandparents of hern.'

She did not leave that day. She had spoken out of pique, and was ashamed: that she had behaved badly afflicted her far more than the fact that Toby had done so. She obeyed the command of a heart in which patience was an active principle, and waited.

Come twilight she went down to the town and knocked at the door of the Danes' cottage. No, Skipper Dane said, there was no sign of him. 'Be blamed if I know what's amiss wi' the boy — he was never one for such freaks afore. Mebbe yew can drive some sense into him, Charlotte; I'll swear you're the one to dew it. We'd reckoned to goo out on the night tide, an' all — but there, thass as well not to stir tonight, wi' this gret ole storm a-whipping up. I reckon the yow-yows'll be calling later, do they're not already!'

The yow-yows were the ghosts of drowned sailors, locally supposed to cry out across the waves as a warning of an approaching gale. Charlotte could not suppress a shiver at the name. Seeing this, Skipper Dane invited her in to feel the fire for a bit, but she refused with thanks, saying she must be getting home.

Instead, however, she lingered at the top end of the street overlooking the little town, with the thundering sea below and the murmuring masses of the woods above, the lights of Shipden in between appearing as the frailest assertion of human endurance, and seeming rather to survive narrowly the gathering darkness than to combat it. She sat down on the edge of a horse-trough, gathering her cloak about her. Several foot-passengers had passed her, briefly lifting their heads, bent against the wind, to bestow a surprised glance upon her, and the afterglow had quite faded from the sky when she was rewarded with the sound of a light footstep that she knew better than any in the world.

The light from a cottage window was enough to show her Toby's face, pale and drawn, and quite blank of expression. For a moment it seemed he would pass her without recognition; but then his eyes softened.

'Charlotte . . . what are you doing here?'

'Waiting for you,' said she.

Something like pain seemed to flit across his face then; but he said gently, 'You shouldn't be out on a night like this. You'll catch your death.'

She glanced down at his legs, which were coated in dust and mud up to the knee. 'Toby — how far have you walked?'

'Hm?' He glanced down at himself, without interest. 'Oh, I got a ride back on a farm-cart as far as Ingworth — had to walk the rest of the way.' He slowly sat down beside her, leaving a space between their two bodies, and rubbed his hand across his face. 'I caught up with them at Aylsham. They'd put up at an inn there. I — I give my name and said I wanted to speak to 'em. There was a long wait and then they sent an answer back saying they didn't know anybody of that name and I was to go away. Well, I kept pressing, and at last the old gentleman — Loveday's grandfather — he come down to see what twas about, and so I started to tell him, about having got to know Loveday and reckoning that was a bad thing taking her away from a place where she was happy . . . something like that. Fact is once I'd got there, I hardly knew what it was I wanted to say. But that didn't signify, for the old gentleman — all stiff and fierce-like he was — he just looked me over and then he rounded on me for — for damned impudence and all the rest of't. I've always believed in holden my head up, and not bowing and scraping to such folks, but he were such a high man, so cool and proud-like — I felt about two foot tall as I stood there . . . And then I tried to kick up a fuss, and say what do Miss Ward have to say about it . . . and all she done was to send down a message saying I was to go home and stop being silly. And then I felt smaller than ever — and I *did* feel silly . . .'

'Oh, Toby — don't judge her hard,' said Charlotte softly, thinking of Loveday last night.

'Nay,' he said. 'I don't reckon I do. Only — only I never thought of her as belonging to them folk at all. And it felt queer — it was like being a younker again, and finding that your mam can't really kiss your bruises better, or finding the little canary-bird in the cage don't live for ever. I come away feeling — well, sore, cut to the heart mebbe, but foolish mostly — just foolish. And what made it worse was knowing that you'd been seeing me like that for a long while — all the time!'

'Like what?'

'Silly,' he said, his eyes on the ground. 'Small.'

'No, Toby,' said she. 'Not you. Not small.'

He gave her a look, fond but unconvinced. 'Oh, Charlotte,' he said, 'still kind even now! And it was you who warned me once before — about going to see them Wards. And I never listened. Always trying to save me from hurt — when it might have been better if you hadn't!'

She only shook her head. He was talking as if from the bottom of a deep well of weariness and despondency, and it seemed to her he would not take in anything she said.

'I *did* reckon I could help Loveday get better,' he said slowly, meditatively, 'that it was just a matter of getting her to take hold of life . . . And even when my eyes told me otherwise, I got more and more stubborn-like inside. Dad always did say I was as stubborn as a dog trying to bite its own tail once I got a notion in my head . . . But then you know that.'

'I can be stubborn too, in my way.'

'You? No, not you . . . My God — thass so strange to think of her gone from Shipden. Yet in a way that don't seem strange at all — like the real place have come back again, like she was only a dream. I wonder where she'll go . . . You know, all the way to Aylsham I was thinking on what you said this mornen − and about you going away. It knocked me back so when you told me that . . . And I kept remembering when my sister Meggy died − and how then I thought, in the way of a younker, that that was my fault somehow, that I was to blame; for I always used to look out for her, and take care on her. I thought twas my punishment for not thinking on her enough − for going about sometimes wi' my head stuck in the clouds, the way I did, and forgetting her. And as I grew older I told myself I must always beware o' losing something I cherished, for it might be took away from me do I not be careful. And now I've let that happen again, haven't I?'

His voice was hollow, dry and thin, like something merely scratched on the windy air and then wiped away again.

'Have you?' Charlotte said.

He regarded her very soberly. 'It's just the same. My head's been in the clouds, and I been chasing after − after what's not real; and now what's real has slipped away, and it's lost.'

'Not lost,' Charlotte said. 'Oh, Toby, not lost.'

He suddenly averted his face, as if to hide from her sight some dreadful deformity. 'Oh, Charlotte,' he groaned, 'don't be kind to me − not now − thass the last thing I can bear. When I stood there waiting in that inn-parlour − that was like I saw myself in a glass, all top to toe, inside and out, and that weren't pretty what I saw. Mebbe some time, when this feeling like I'm all dirty and paltry have worn off a bit, then mebbe I can look you in the face again . . . Except that you're going away.'

'Yes,' she said. 'Very soon. But I didn't go today because—'

'Oh, don't say it, Charlotte,' he said. 'To see you giving, giving still like you always do, when all this time you've had nothing in return − thass what break me. I come through the woods on the way back, and saw all the blossom ruined and lying about where the wind had thrown it — and I saw myself again in that. I wish I could shut the sight of me out — and never see it more.'

His speech had that quality, both disordered and mechanical, of extreme fatigue, and his eyes were glassy. In Charlotte the two sides of love contended — the side that wanted to keep him by her at any price, and the side that wanted him to have comfort and rest. The latter won. 'Come on, Toby,' she said. 'You'd best go home, and get to bed.'

'Aye, home,' he said, stirring. 'No sleep yet though — got to catch the night-tide. Poor ole Dad — I been neglecting our business an' all — I haven't took the *Heartsease* out for a fortnight.'

'Oh, not tonight, Toby,' she said — the wind almost bowling them over as they stood up and began to walk down the street. 'Skipper's not expecting to go out, you know — not wi' this storm brewing.'

Toby looked around him, staggering a little in the blast, as if noticing the weather for the first time. 'Oh — thass nothing the *Heartsease* can't ride,' he said. 'That'll do me good — give me the proper smack in the face I want.'

She said no more: privately she suspected that sleep would overcome him as soon as he got into the warm; and such was his state of baffled self-loathing, bewilderment, contrition and exhaustion that very little could penetrate it. As they parted at the door of his cottage, however, he lifted his eyes to hers, and said: 'When do you leave, Charlotte?'

'Friday,' said she.

He winced. 'So soon! Well — whatever I say now will surely seem too little, too late, but I would say it, Charlotte, if I only knew how!'

He bowed his head again, and went into the house; and the fibres of her heart seemed to be pulled after him like tautening reins, to break at last.

The household at the Crab Pot went to bed soon after her return. After pacing her bedroom for a long while, with the wind hammering mightily at the window-panes and threatening to wrench the protesting signboard from its iron bar, she decided to go down and see if a drink of warm milk would summon sleep. Going past the door of Mr Skeels' room, she heard his voice, wakeful, say, 'Charlotte, is that you?'

She looked in. Silas Skeels was sitting up in his bed by the window overlooking the seafront, with his telescope at his eye.

'Here, gel,' he said, offering the telescope. 'I reckon my old eyes must be cozening me, else I'm in a dream still, and you've tittuped into it. Tell me thass never a crab-boat out there − out in such a storm as make the one that broke my back for me seem no more than the whiffle of a lady's fan!'

Charlotte raised the telescope to her eye. Her hands were already shaking as she did so; and as the bobbing shape flickered into sight against the mass of magnified sea her mouth was filled at once with a ghastly metallic taste.

'Thass the *Heartsease*,' she gasped, and dropping the telescope she ran from the room.

When she stepped out of the front door of the Crab Pot the wind nearly knocked her over. There was rain in it, but it was impossible to distinguish from the spray whipped off the sea; she could only screw up her eyes against the cold needles and make her way in a sort of blind zigzag down to the sea-wall. The onshore wind was beating full against the town, and ramming itself into every lane, and funnelling itself into every cranny and crevice, so that the roof-eaves squealed in unison, and slates could be heard smashing on the cobblestones; and here and there shutters and crab-baskets and crates were grotesquely at large, wildly bowling and skidding amongst the cottages, and fetching up against the flint walls only to be snatched up again and flung round the shrieking corners. As Charlotte descended the path to the beach rags of foam swirled about her, peppered with sand and weed, as if the separate constituents of the coast were by degrees dissolving, and the wind making a broth of creation. Below she could see lights, winking at the margin of the maddened sea; and as she crossed the beach, all churned by the retreating tide and plashy with pools of brine and spume, one of the lights came swiftly towards her, and Skipper Dane was suddenly holding a storm-lantern to her face.

'Oh, Skipper — is it Toby?' she cried.

The lantern-light showed the brown wrinkles in Skipper's face as tremendous furrows, and his eyes were wild. 'I tole him we'd be loobies to put off in such a wind; and he maundered for a while, saying as how he'd been neglecting his work, and he had to change his ways, but then he soodled off to bed, half-asleep, and so I did the same; and next thing I knew he'd slipped out, and roused up our lad Enoch to help him launch the *Heartsease* — but he wouldn't take Enoch with him, saying he'd manage her alone. There's no better sailor atween here and the Point than Toby — but look at the sea! We've beaconed him to come in, and I reckon he think to — but thass one thing to signal, and another to bring her in on such a sea! What come over him, Charlotte? Why'd he do it?'

'He weren't himself, Skipper,' said Charlotte. 'He haven't been himself, these long days, and he know it now.'

'Just let him be brought back to me — self or no self — thass all I ask!' said Skipper.

Some of the watchers on the beach carried ropes, but to run out a line was an impossibility; and they stood helpless, shoulders inclined against the wind as against a wall, and were periodically thrust backward along the sand. As they staggered and recoiled they were pursued by breakers that fell with a roar, and flung up vertical columns of spray which seemed to mount to the very sky before suddenly breaking their backs, and raining down with a hiss and spatter upon the bowed heads below. The sea appeared not a uniform body of water but a chaotic contention between various elemental shapes, in which at one moment huge troughs predominated and seemed to open prospects down to the very seabed, only to be overthrown by the sudden rearing up of a ridge of froth-tipped crags, which in turn were demolished by a seething host of cross-driven wavelets. In the midst of this the *Heartsease* appeared, fleetingly, now broadside, now stern first, as if its dimensions were no more fixed and solid than those momentary illusions of hill and dale created by the frenzied waters. At times even the lights she carried vanished from sight; and each time Charlotte, craning forward with her skirts in the cold surf, felt her heart cease beating entirely until the reappearance of the lights, borne up with a terrible lurch on the shoulders of the sea, set it fitfully going again.

It was the custom of the crab-fishermen to bring in their sturdy, full-bilged little boats right on to the beach; and Toby, who could be glimpsed as a dark shape moving against the pale glimmer of the torn sailcloth, could only try to do likewise. He had put up some sort of a jury-rig, and was coming in by degrees, but the boat was heeling with the smash of the waves; and Skipper Dane, wading into the foam beside Charlotte, cried out above the din of sea and wind, which seemed to rise at that moment as if to howl him down: 'Once get her on her beam-ends, and her keel'll be stove in like a tea-chest — she's too light!'

A swatch of suds hit Charlotte in the face and blinded her for a few moments; and when she had wiped her eyes she saw that the *Heartsease* had struck, stern first. For a moment the boat stood proud, the waves seeming to scurry in retreat from it, and Toby's silhouette was clearly visible on the deck. Then a sidewash, running athwart the tide with a sort of stealthy surge, butted the keel and swung the vessel round, and she was lost to sight again in a geyser of spray.

By now Skipper had fastened a rope around his waist, and plunged into the surf; and Charlotte, seeing the others forming a line and gripping the rope at intervals along its length, hastened to take her place among them. 'That'll tear your hands abroad, mawther, do that goo tight,' one of the fishermen advised her, but she ignored him, looping the rope around her wrist and taking up the slack.

Skipper's head and shoulders could be seen ploughing through the waves, beaten about by the cascades of spume that were thrown off the heeling boat; then they were lost to view. Unable longer to look, Charlotte bowed her head and closed her eyes. Then there was a shout of 'Haul to!' and the rope slithered laceratingly in her hands for a moment before she braced herself against it and pulled. Her hair had been tugged down by the wind, and it made a sodden screen about her face as she heaved and hauled, blinding her again.

The rope went slack, and she almost fell. A fisherman steadied her, and as she mopped her hair out of her eyes she heard the words 'Sorry, Dad – I'm sorry.'

Skipper Dane was supporting a drenched and exhausted Toby on to the beach. As soon as they were clear of the surf the young man fell on to his knees on the sand; then he cast a wild look round at the *Heartsease*. 'She won't break, will she?' he said. 'I tried to bring her in stern first – kept thinking how it'd be if I went and lost our best boat—'

'She'll stand now, she'll stand,' said Skipper, 'the tide's drawing off her. As if thass that blamed ole boot I care for!'

'I'm sorry,' Toby said again. 'I shouldn't have gone out – only thass poor catches we've had lately – wi' me not putting my mind to my work and all – and I got it into my head to start maken up for't . . . You know, I never used to believe that about the yow-yows – I thought that was only an ole gossips' tale; but when I got out there tonight, past the light, I could swear I heard 'em calling out, like thin scranny voices on the wind warning me to go back, and it was hearing that as woke me up to what I was doing . . .' He looked up in astonishment at the girl who was edging her way through the circle of onlookers. 'Charlotte — is that Charlotte there?'

'Yes, Toby,' said she, with a low moan sinking to her knees in the wet sand beside him, and clasping her arms about his neck. 'Oh! Toby — you've come back — thank God — you've come back to me.'

'Come back to you! aye, Charlotte — God bless you, a thousand times! And I shan't never go away from you again, all our two lives — I swear.'

The lashing of the storm was not quite enough to drown out an interested murmur from the spectators, gathered around the twain who clasped each other on the sand, nor even Charlotte's sobs, muffled though they were against Toby's throat.

'There, don't yew take on so, mawther,' spoke up one of the fishermen, phlegmatically. 'Thass all set aroight now, that is.'

Jed met Charlotte at Norwich with his new gig. He had ordered this when he and Marianne were still together, thinking it would please her to be able to go about more. He had never dreamed it would be first used in these circumstances, to bring Charlotte to live in the home that his wife had deserted.

But it was wonderful, wholly wonderful, to see Charlotte again, and to know that this time they would not be separated. He had thought, in the blackest moments of his dark mood, that there was nothing in the world worth loving, but within an instant of Charlotte's waving to him across the yard of the coaching-inn he knew it was quite otherwise. His sister, indeed, redeemed the world for him at a stroke; and he seemed to feel freshening rills playing upon the arid places within him that had threatened drought for ever more.

The first happy greetings over, Charlotte's luggage was

soon loaded into the gig, and they set off.

'I can't hardly believe I'm going to see Heartsease again at last,' said Charlotte, who with her dark trim head was looking as pretty as a blackbird of a year's growth. 'I wonder if I shall recognize all the old places.'

'Well, Plague House will be new to you,' said Jed. 'I hope you'll be comfortable there. Ben have been flying round like a flea in a colander getting it all ready for you; for we neglected the old place a bit, after − well, after Marianne left.'

'My poor Jed!' said Charlotte, laying her hand on his arm a moment. 'It feel so strange to me, for I never met her, and I don't know what to say. I shan't speak of her now, if you'd prefer. But I've been thinking of you, so much, and wishing I could help you.'

'You do,' he said feelingly. 'Just being yourself.'

'And what about that poor fellow you wrote me about? − Todd was his name. You said you were going to his trial.'

'Aye. I went to speak up for him, but that didn't do no good.' Their route out of the city took them past the assize court where Todd Gault had been tried: a bleak reminder. 'The magistrates come down hard on him, and sentenced him to a month's hard labour.'

'For a handful of turnips ? Oh, that's cruel!'

'The sanctity of property must be upheld, my dear,' said Jed bitterly. 'Thass the cant. More sacred than human life, it seem. Aye, Todd's in the Castle prison, Charlotte − where our poor father lay, just for claiming the right to live.'

This was a harsher Jed than the one she knew, with a settled brooding upon him. She said: 'We must try and help him when he comes out of gaol.'

'Oh! they mustn't be mollycoddled, you know: they won't thank you for it; they'll expect feather beds and silk stockings next. Thass what Hemstock would say − I'll wager thass what he did say after he'd watched Todd hauled off to the treadmill.' Jed resisted an urge to spit.

'Well, I shall help Todd — I shall stand against Hemstock till the crack of doom . . . I'm sorry, Charlotte. I shouldn't be taking out my ill-temper on you. So tell me. Did you leave the Skeels and all your friends well? It must have been sad saying goodbye at last.'

'Oh! well — they'd been expecting it for a while, you know,' said Charlotte, conscious of a faint blush on her cheeks. 'And I shall write, and — and it's not so very far to visit.'

'I shall drive you up to Shipden whenever you like,' Jed said. 'What's the news from there? Did it suffer in the spring gales?'

'The news . . . I have got a morsel of news, Jed,' faltered Charlotte. 'It's — I'm engaged to be married.'

Jed started, let out a low whistle. 'Charlotte . . . I had no idea . . . Oh, my dear girl!'

'We've told no one yet,' she said, nervously happy. 'I wanted you to know first. You've — I dare say you've heard me mention Toby Dane.'

'Once or twice. Well, more than once or twice. Time and time again,' smiled Jed. 'A fisherman, I think.'

Charlotte nodded. 'I've known him — well, for years. And now — thass queer how these things happen.'

'I know . . . I'm glad for you, Charlotte: glad because *you're* glad — I thought there was something extra bright about your face when I met you today! Not that he deserve you, whoever he is, because nobody ever could; but I shall be proud to meet him. Oh, but you poor thing — here am I taking you away from Shipden, and—'

'No, no,' Charlotte said. 'Don't think of that, Jed. I've got to be with you at this time — Toby understands; and we're not planning on marrying just yet. He can write, and — and we're sure of each other, you see, Jed — thass what count.'

'Well,' said Jed, giving her hand a squeeze, 'thass a good thing. Thass a fine thing. But like I say, Charlotte, you shall go to Shipden whenever you want; and Toby must come and stay with us in Heartsease too. Well, well – there's hope in this sorry world yet, when it deals kindly with you, my dear!'

They talked more of Shipden and Toby as they drove the lanes to Heartsease: Charlotte haltingly, but with pleasure, telling her brother her heart's tale, the happy ending of which was still a matter of fresh wonder at her every waking. The interval between that reconciliation on the stormy beach and her departure from Shipden had been spent almost entirely with Toby, the unlocking of a great store of mutual love occupying a week that seemed to last only minutes. Sad though the parting had been, it was more than half redeemed by the prospective pleasure of meeting again, and presently being joined for ever. The consciousness of being loved, where she passionately loved in return, uplifted Charlotte every moment; and her present happiness was not of the simplistic kind liable to be overturned by the first contrary indication of fortune. The harmony that prevailed in her mind was enriched by a solemn note that resounded from her last meeting with Loveday Ward, and the thought of the brilliant girl going away to die. She could not smile whenever she thought of her, as Loveday had directed, but her thoughts were tender nevertheless, and opened gates of new understanding.

They came to Heartsease; and the dim recollections of childhood that crowded round her were less powerful in their effect than her sense of the intense significance of this place for her unhappy brother, and of the shadows that now shrouded his view of it. She longed to help him; but all she could say, when he conducted her into Plague House, was, 'Oh, Jed, it's good to be home.'

'Dear Charlotte,' he said, with a catch in his throat, hugging her. 'Thank God you're here.'

This was almost his happiest time in Heartsease. Almost, for there remained the failure of his marriage and the grim condition of the village, over which the deepest happiness was a covering as thin as the quicksilver on a mirror. But in many respects, living with Charlotte at Plague House that late spring and summer came closest to the fulfilment of the dreams he had once dreamed in the Norwich weaver's garret.

He had forgotten how easy she was to live with, to what manageable proportions she reduced life-problems that on his horizon loomed large and forbidding. That she was happy was obvious; obvious too that she had found happiness in those embroilments of the heart which had brought Jed so low; but he was far from drawing resentful comparisons. Certain people could wear their happiness like a rich dowager wearing her silks and jewels — as an insolent taunt at the general sorrow of the human lot; but Charlotte's happiness spread out to those around her. Even Ben Catbush's wooden old face began to smile a little, with an effect as incongruous as if a grandfather clock should break into a jig.

She was interested in all that pertained to the farm, and lent a willing hand with the heifers, the pigs and poultry; and her figure was often to be seen going out to the fields to take the men working there bread and bacon and jugs of ale, or down to the village with batches of baking which she gave to the workless families with the excuse that she had made too much. All the little household arrangements that Marianne had instituted before her interest dwindled were still intact; and Charlotte, though she bore the housekeeping keys, carefully refrained from altering anything, whilst adding some characteristic little touches of her own — fresh-gathered flowers that in the old brown interior of Plague House appeared as lambent as torches. Though by nature an unassuming person, she had no disfiguring shyness, and was soon on good terms with the villagers, who recognized her as one of their own, and some of whom remembered her as the similarly easy-going little girl who had played in the doorway of the Wintergreens' long-vanished cottage.

Usually at eventide she and Jed went out for a walk

about the village. Arm-in-arm they passed down the long curve of the main street, with the sparrows bathing in the dust of the wheel-ruts, deep to them as trenches, or pecking at the grain that had spilt from the nosebags of carters' horses; with the westering sun dividing the street into two-thirds shade and one-third light, so that to cross from Dick Freshwater's Wheatsheaf to the joiner's yard on the other side was to step from night to day. Thus they greeted their neighbours, who hailed them from within their cottages, the doors and windows all being open in the warmth; and thus Charlotte's eye would sometimes fall on some trifling sight that reminded her of her childhood here and that, as she put it, she had forgotten she remembered. Such sights included the great timber hitching-post outside the smith's, which was worn to the shape of an hour-glass by generations of horses rubbing their necks against it while tethered there; the leaning tree that had completely overshadowed the cottage beside it, so that the tipmost twigs were intertwined with the loose thatch of the roof; the footbridge over the stream with the tracery of initials carved on its wooden rails. For Jed, seeing these things afresh through Charlotte's eyes recalled to him his own triumphant return to Heartsease; but all was subtly tarnished for him by events since then. He could not forget Marianne; he could not forget Hemstock, and the distress in the village, especially with the day of Todd Gault's release from gaol approaching.

He went to Norwich in the gig to fetch Todd home. It was a shock to behold the young man, who had the blue-skinned appearance of a nestling bird; but Jed strove to hide his reaction, and to talk reassuringly of the future.

'You'll want to see your mother straight away. I saw her just this morning – she's well and fine. Tonight you must come and eat with us, for Charlotte's looking forward to meeting you, and she's baking something special.'

Todd had lost weight too, and his thickset shoulders were slumped as he sat in the gig and stared about him at the sun-bright country. Nothing that was said to him seemed to register; and Jed was just despairing of finding any more cheerful things to say when the young man stirred and said: 'Have the hay been cut at Heartsease?'

'Mostly. We cut ours a fortnight ago. Twas knocked about a bit by these everlasting winds.'

'I tried—' Todd lost his voice a moment. 'In the gaol I tried to fancy myself out in the hayfield. There was an old speeler in there who told me how to do it. He say you have to shut your eyes and picture the place you want to be, a bit at a time, down to every last blade of grass; and soon you can call it all up, just by squeezing your eyes shut. He reckon you could even do that when you were on the cockchafer.'

'The what?'

'Stepper. Treadmill,' said Todd dully. 'They put you in a stall just like an ox, and the wheel that go round and round, and come the end of your fifteen minutes the air in there's so bad thass like drawing breath through a straw. Twasn't every day,' he said, glancing at Jed's horrified face. 'There was picking oakum and all.' He held up a hand on which the fingernails were broken down to tiny stumps. 'Aye, there was plenty of work in the gaol — work that didn't make nothing, nor grow nothing, nor change nothing, but work all the same; and yet here, where there's not a foot of earth without a crop a-growing on't, there's no work at all for the likes of me!'

'I'll find you work, Todd — I promise, come harvest—'

'Ah, don't you worrit, Jed,' Todd said in a curiously gentle tone. 'I got that all settled in my mind, what I'm going to do.'

That night Elias Hemstock woke with a start from a bad dream. So many of these just lately! — yet all his life his sleep had been dreamless and untroubled. He lay a while gazing at the window of his bedchamber and wondering what time it was. It felt like the middle of the night, yet there was a redness about the square of sky as if the dawn were at hand. Could he be losing his old country instinct for time . . .?

Suddenly he sprang out of bed. That red light was no dawn. He flung up the window, and beheld flames leaping from the largest of the hay-ricks in the yard below. It flashed upon his mind that a farm-servant must have left a lantern burning, or carelessly scattered embers outdoors – when he discerned a movement on the further side of the burning rick.

'Hoy! I see you there! Stop, or I'll have the hide off you!' cried Hemstock.

The figure darted away at once, and was quickly lost to sight in the darkness beyond the ring of light cast by the flames, but Hemstock had recognized the sturdy set of the shoulders, and the curly mass of hair. Flinging on some clothes, while Mrs Hemstock groaned her displeasure from the depths of the bed, he ran out to the landing, hammering on doors and bellowing to the household to wake up, and then hurried downstairs.

In the yard there was no sign of the intruder, and the night was too dark for pursuit. The rick was rapidly being consumed, and though the half-dressed servants were soon at work with buckets and wet rick-cloths, it was past saving, and the only practicable object was to prevent the fire spreading.

'I saw him,' Hemstock said to his son Herbert, who came yawning to his side. 'I saw him clear. The same rogue who was turned loose from gaol this very day – he should have been clapped away for a year! And he will be this time, I'll have him taken in the morning – he needn't think he can go to ground! By God – how *dare* that ruffian bait me in this way!'

Herbert regarded him closely, rumpled and sardonic. 'A deal of fuss over one resentful labourer, isn't it, Father?'

'It seems so, I dare say, to a milksop,' snapped Hemstock. 'You, no doubt, would have me give in to these scum, and say thank-you to 'em for destroying my property.'

'Well, after all, it is a good sign for you, Father,' said Herbert. 'It shows the vulgars hate you quite as much as if you really *were* a gentleman.'

Pivoting at the waist, Hemstock struck his son an open-handed blow across the mouth. Drops of blood arced through the air.

'You asked for that, sir!' Hemstock said, breathing hard.

Herbert staggered, then recovered himself. He held his handkerchief to his bleeding lip and fixed his eyes on his father's.

'Well, Father, that's the last blow you'll ever strike me,' he said. 'A milksop I may be, but I'm not a fool; and a fellow must be a fool to stay here. I shall go in the morning.'

'Go?' said Hemstock with a sneer. 'Why, where's your money? What are you good for?'

'Peary, the auctioneer at Norwich, wants a clerk. I've spoken to him about it. I can go any time I like.'

'Peary? You're mad. A shabby dealer in bad horseflesh and bankrupt stock — you think I'd let a son of mine be seen as the henchman of such a mountebank as that? Get to bed, sir—'

'I shall get to bed,' said Herbert, with a raw look about his thin cheekbones. 'And tomorrow I shall go to Norwich. You make me laugh, Father. You lay about you with your thick fists and in the next breath you're spouting humbug about your good name. Your precious Marianne's really been a credit to it, hasn't she?' He spat blood. 'Your name. I'd pay out gold guineas to be rid of it.'

He left Hemstock shadowed by the dying flames, stiff and without words.

Jed was a light sleeper, and the first tap of the stone thrown at his window-pane woke him.

'Todd?' he said from the window. 'What's the matter?'

'Nothing,' answered Todd breathlessly. 'Sorry, Jed – let me speak to you, just for a minute.'

Charlotte had woken too: she met Jed on the landing and, in spite of his protests, came downstairs with him. She lit more candles while he let Todd in.

'What the devil's going on, Todd?' said Jed. 'You've not been poaching—?'

'Not taking. Giving. Paying back a few old debts,' said Todd, with a hard glitter in his eyes, and his chest heaving with exertion.

'Sit down,' said Charlotte, pressing him into a chair, 'you're worn out – oh, you've hurt your hand!'

'Burnt it,' Todd said. 'Thass nought, miss'es, thank ye. I burnt more than that. Torched Hemstock's hay-rick.'

'What?' said Jed. 'Oh, Todd, no—'

'Flared up as pretty as you like,' Todd said. 'Would have done more, but the bastard saw me. Had to run. Phoo! Lost a bit of wind, I reckon, dinged up in that gaol. Thass why I mustn't stop here – might bring trouble on you an' all. Just wanted to come and tell you I'm off.'

'Where are you going? Where can you go?' said Jed. 'If Hemstock knows—'

'Navvies,' said Todd. 'There's a gret ole 'campment of 'em, where the railway's being cut towards Attleborough way. There's several of my ole mates gone there: they always want labour. And thass well known as the navvies'll shelter a man on the run from the law – they've no love for the law theirselves, and they'll stand by you. No one can get me once I'm there – a navvies' camp's a no-man's-land for them bigwigs. I shall cut across country tonight, and be there by morning. Thank ye, miss'es.' He gulped at the ale that Charlotte brought him, and then submitted as she gently applied goose-grease to his burnt hand. 'This is rare kind of you . . . So – thass what's to do. I wanted to say thank-ye for all you've done for me, Jed, as I doubt I'll be seeing you.

Mind, I don't mean I shall never come to Heartsease again. Hemstock's not finished wi' me yet — thass just a start.'

'Todd, do you really know what you're doing?' said Jed. 'You know how Hemstock came down on you — he don't forget—'

'Aye! And no more do I! I shan't lay down and die at his bidding, Jed — no more than your father did back in 'thirty. Do he make war on us, he needn't be surprised when we fight back.' He looked uncertainly at Jed. 'I thought you'd understand.'

Jed was silent a moment. 'Aye,' he said. 'I do understand, Todd. Forget I said that. And look — if ever you need help, if ever you're in trouble, you come to me here, and I'll stand by you. Thass a promise.'

Todd grasped Jed's hand, with something of the old admiration in his face; then got to his feet. 'I'm off then.'

'Wait,' said Charlotte. She brought him a small bundle from the kitchen. 'Just some bread and bacon. You'll be hungry.'

'I wish there were more Wintergreens in the world,' said Todd, thanking her again; and he slipped out into the night.

'I'm sorry, Charlotte,' Jed said.

'What for?'

He shrugged. 'That don't seem right you should be involved in these quarrels.'

'Well,' said she, 'like Todd said, I'm a Wintergreen too. I remember Father and Mother — not so well as you, but I do. I don't want to judge nobody . . . D'you suppose Mr Hemstock will come here asking after Todd?'

'He can if he likes,' said Jed. 'And if he do I shall tell him I saw Todd and I cheered him to the echo for what he did — and that I wish it had been the house that had gone up in smoke with him in it—'

He stopped, with a dull beating at his temples, and saw the trouble and alarm in Charlotte's candid eyes. He felt ashamed. 'Nay,' he said, 'I—I don't mean that.'

'Just say you don't know nothing about it,' said Charlotte. 'That would be best, eh? No harm in that.'

Her voice gently soothed down the bristling rage that had possessed him. He put his arm round her shoulders and kissed her hair. 'Oh, Charlotte,' he murmured, 'you are my better self — I wish I could always heed you!'

* * *

My dear father,
I am nearing the end of my work here at Heartsease Hall. The topographical views of the estate are all finished and I have only to oversee their mounting and framing. They are very worthy and accurate and deadly dull. Mr Ingamells is in London again — he goes there very frequently of late — but we expect him back today. There is no word from the absconding cousin Mr Deacon. I miss his genial company, though I cannot think of him in the same way after what he did.

I don't know where I am to go next. Things have not turned out here as I had hoped. I almost wish I had never seen Heartsease. No, I don't mean that. I hardly know what I mean. I suppose I used to believe that happiness was like the thimble in hunt-the-thimble — that it was only a matter of looking hard enough and long enough, and then you would find it. Now I believe it is more like the moon in the night sky — always in sight, but never getting any nearer no matter how one tries to pursue it. But there — you have never tried to impose your philosophy upon me, though I know it would be well worth listening to — so I will stop foisting my vapourings on you directly, and merely sign myself,

Your loving son, Pierce

Pierce gave his letter to the servant who collected the post and then wandered downstairs. It was a little while yet till the dinner hour, and he was at a loose end. He was in the library, turning over his estate drawings, when Miss Ingamells came in.

'Well I wonder if Papa may not arrive today after all but has decided to put up overnight somewhere with his guest whoever that may be.'

'Guest?'

'Yes he wrote me that he would be bringing company from London back to Heartsease and I am to order a room made up and a servant's room, he omits to mention the name of the guest but then who am I to be told such things I dare say it is some terribly clubbable friend of his with gout and a red face well whoever it is he can be no worse than Mr Alexander who we do not name Deacon . . . So you are looking over your finished work Mr Coppinger I declare it will be quite strange when you leave where do you suppose you will go forgive my curiosity?'

'I'm not sure. I have a studio still in Norwich . . . but I feel I would rather leave Norfolk. Possibly go abroad,' said Pierce.

'Dear me I wish I might leave Norfolk and go abroad or anywhere almost just so that I might feel that my life had a little more meaning but there the world has rather a habit of thwarting us doesn't it Mr Coppinger?'

'I'm afraid it seems so, Miss Ingamells,' Pierce said. There was a certain community of feeling between them now, for Pierce was deeply unhappy and he perceived that Beatrice Ingamells was likewise. For all her freakishness of manner, Pierce respected her; and the respect was accompanied by a sense of the unfairness of things, as he reflected that the irresponsible heir Mr Deacon had a claim to a great stake in the world which was denied to this intelligent and neglected woman.

'I once saw a caged thrush that had been blinded,' said

Miss Ingamells, 'the poor creature had little holes where its eyes should have been and yet it was singing its heart out gruesome of me I know but it did cause me to wonder whether we all ought not to be blinded at birth and then we would never be tortured with the sight of what we cannot have and we might sing contentedly in our cages . . . But was the bird in fact pouring out its heart for the landscapes it had in its head and longing for them just as if it saw them? Are we forgive my putting it so baldly doomed to desire?'

Before Pierce could frame a reply there was the growl of carriage-wheels in the drive, and he followed Miss Ingamells out into the hall to greet her father.

The guest leaning on Mr Ingamells' arm was not a clubbable gentleman with gout. It was not a gentleman but a lady, very well dressed, very pretty, very archly smiling, and very young.

'My dear Beatrice,' said Mr Ingamells to his daughter, who had gone forward to kiss him and then stopped in her tracks, 'it's wonderful to be home again. You look well, my dear. And Mr Coppinger, how d'you do, sir. I have been greatly looking forward to introducing to you the lady who is to do us the honour of being our guest for a time in our humble corner of old England. The lady who is to confer on me the greater honour – ' he patted the little grey-gloved hand that lay on his arm – 'of becoming the second Mrs Ingamells. Beatrice, Mr Coppinger, this is Miss Harriet Fontayne – soon to be my wife.'

Chapter Fifteen

The Mocking Wind

The salient fact about Alexander Deacon's life was that nothing he had ever done had ever had any ill consequences — at least, not for himself.

At that peculiar institution compounded of brutality and licence called the English public school, Alexander had slipped through the cogs of the system with a minimum of grinding and tearing. He had intelligence to spare, though he only employed it as a last resort; and he was gifted with a tongue which, as an exception to the universal rule, always did what he wanted it to, and never led him into trouble. From an early age he had had a ready humour, and this he used not as an edged weapon — which might have made him enemies — but to fence away the little awkwardnesses of life, and keep at bay those encroaching perplexities that carve lines in the foreheads of other mortals, and ultimately give a furrowed aspect to their souls. Besides this there was, of course, the knowledge that the vagaries of law and genealogy made him heir to a wealthy Norfolk estate — that, through doing nothing but existing, he would one day be rewarded with all the material security a man could desire. It was impossible to say whether it was this reassuring knowledge that formed his personality, or whether his personality was simply of the sort that seems to attract such fortuitous accidents. Certainly Alexander reached manhood confirmed in a feeling that if he had done nothing to deserve the good fortune that would be his when Mr Ingamells died, neither had he done anything to disqualify him for it. His own desultory studies at law revealed to him that justice as it was administered in England was often hidden under a mountain of what looked suspiciously like injustice, and so he came to feel that somewhere in his situation something must be right.

His whole life had thus been an exercise in irresponsibility, which he had carried off by cheerfully admitting it — tempering the admission with the assertion that he did no harm either. And he did not entirely consider that this made moral questions irrelevant to him. Enjoying practically unlimited ease and freedom, he thought it would be a very good thing for everybody to enjoy them, and such thoughts extended into a vague faith in progress and in the more glamorous aspects of political radicalism. In the meantime life unrolled itself before him as an interesting spectacle — sometimes, as when he had been taken with Marianne Wintergreen, engaging his attention more fully, but even when it did not do so, never making him feel frustrated. For even boredom did not strike deep into Alexander; and in this lay a cardinal difference between him and Marianne. Boredom afflicted her to the uttermost degree — as much, indeed, as great grief or anxiety would afflict less volatile natures; and it had afflicted her so much that, driven by it, she had left behind home, husband, country and reputation.

Her motives, of course, had been more complex than that. Alexander's were simple. He found Marianne beautiful and fascinating. Moreover, he liked women — insofar as he regarded them as a different species, and a very diverting one. He was not an outright sensualist — he was too little passionate for that; but he had accepted what his good looks and charm had brought him very willingly, and laughingly confessed to his friends that he was a deplorable fellow. In his way he was a romantic: he relished all the paraphernalia that went with affairs of the heart — and his heart was certainly in it, as much as his heart was ever in anything. For it was one consequence of his position that he viewed the world as a curiosity in which he had no part, and other people as an entertaining study, to be lightly pursued like lepidoptery or the flute. And just as whatever he did in life, whether it was diligently studying the law or drifting pleasurably about the Continent, could make no difference to his ultimate prospects, so he tended to suppose that no action of his could really have any palpable effect on another person with whom he was involved, whether of joy or sorrow; for despite his love affairs, nothing anyone had ever done to him had affected his feelings in the slightest.

He was aware that he had the capacity to inflict pain – his sharp mind and wit could do that admirably; but he saw no reason to use it. He preferred to be liked, and appeared to go to a good deal of trouble to adapt himself to others – appeared, for it was no trouble to his supple nature, which conformed to that of a companion, old or young, high or low, as automatically as water takes on the shape of the vessel it is poured into. And so when an attractive and spirited girl like Marianne Wintergreen threw herself at him – so he phrased it to himself – he was not the man to rebuff her. There was something irresistibly piquant in her air of discontent with that rural backwater to which she had been confined, and which she had clearly been educated beyond; and it seemed to him a pity that she should never see the great world. It would mean, of course, sacrificing her reputation, but that was her choice; and elopement with her could make no difference to his own prospects, which were not vulnerable to scandalized opinion. Alexander abandoned his studies and ran off with Marianne because, in common with every other decision he had ever made, there could be no harm in it.

Paris, then, was where they set up home together, in a set of rooms on the fourth floor of a once-grand, now-decayed building in the Faubourg St Honoré, with peeling posters advertising coaches to the Midi and infallible cures for venereal disease plastered on the blank wall opposite, and women trundling the great barrel-shaped water-carts in the street below. Alexander knew Paris pretty well, and loved it; and if the pleasure of introducing Marianne to the city was mingled with a certain dismay and irritation at her naïveté – much of her polish, he found, was only schoolgirl-deep – then this did not actively disturb him. It would not be for ever, after all: so he had always reasoned, whether squeezing a more generous allowance out of his late father, or enduring the tedium of the Inns of Court. He had become so accustomed to thus referring everything to a redeeming futurity that when one morning, after rising late, he opened and read a letter from Mr Ingamells, the news it contained did not make its full impact on him for some minutes. And then it hit him.

He sprang up from the breakfast-table with a jerk, spilling his coffee. He took the letter over to the window where the light was better, as if he feared his eyes deceived him, and read it again.

He found that his hands were violently shaking. It was the first time Alexander had ever lost his physical poise. But his loss was far greater than that; as he trembled and reeled and steadied himself against the window-frame, it was as if the very foundations of his selfhood were crumbling beneath him. At a stroke he had lost his security; and like a drowning man tormented with a vision of his life, in that moment he knew what that security meant to him. It meant everything.

Mr Ingamells, bland and urbane in writing as in speech, announced to his young cousin that he was to marry again. The lady was of an old Suffolk family and in possession of a modest fortune. Though no one, Mr Ingamells wrote, could take the place of his lamented Euphemia, this was that delightful and unforeseen conjunction of hearts called a love-match . . . All this was of small account to Alexander beside the fact that the lady was young. She was twenty-three, as Mr Ingamells took care to mention. And a woman of twenty-three had years of child-bearing ahead of her. Children. Sons. A son and heir for Heartsease Hall.

Unsteadily Alexander groped for the decanter of brandy and poured himself a stiff measure. It had been another of his fixed habits of mind to regard anyone over forty as a sort of walking corpse; a habit encouraged by Mr Ingamells' conspicuous devotion to the memory of his dead wife. But now here he was taking out a new lease of life, and Alexander was stunned. It still did not occur to him that his own conduct might have had anything to do with this − that in the light of his latest escapade, Mr Ingamells might have taken a long hard look at the man who was to inherit his estate, and decided that something must be done. This news, so innocent, so utterly destructive, appeared to him as random a turn of fortune as a lightning-bolt from the sky.

For the moment his agile mind was paralysed, and he could only gaze dully round the room, at the burnt-down candles, the folding screen with remarkably well-dressed shepherdesses all over it, the English newspaper that Marianne had been reading. She had gone out early, he supposed.

But his paralysis began to wear off as he thought of her. He went and looked at himself in the shabby gilt mirror. What was he doing, amusing himself here with this pretty farmer's wife, whilst in England his real prospects were slipping away? The marriage was spoken of by Mr Ingamells as a settled thing; perhaps there was nothing Alexander could do, but he would not find out by remaining here. With sudden energy he rang for hot water and began to empty the closets of his clothes.

Marianne had risen early to go shopping. They had no servant of their own, and the concierge of the building gave them but grudging service. Alexander would gladly have eaten his every meal at the restaurants of the Palais Royal; but money did not allow, and he was besides the first to complain if their lodgings lacked some little comfort that it would never have occurred to him to buy.

She went out early to avoid any creditors that might be lurking about the outer door. Alexander cheerfully ran up debts with no intention of paying them, as it seemed did many of his English friends in the capital: she understood that there was a certain dash in keeping one step ahead of the duns. Sometimes there were gaming debts, for Paris was full of gambling, and Alexander loved to play. Often he won — perhaps because, as he said, it didn't matter whether he did or not, his prospects being assured; and his winnings went some way to meeting their expenses. When he lost, he shrugged it off: it didn't matter.

But Marianne dreaded to meet those creditors, pressing her in the street for payment. Alexander told her to ignore them, but there were many things about life in Paris that she found difficult to ignore, and which seemed to show that her staid country upbringing was breaking through her thin veneer of sophistication. Though she could make her way about the streets with a fair degree of confidence, she was continually shocked by the boldness of the prostitutes, some of whom were little girls in every physical particular but their haunted eyes, and by the lewd broadsheets thrust under her nose by hawkers. She hated to think of herself as a prude: most of all she did not want Alexander to suppose that he had tied himself to a gauche farmer's daughter who blushed to see what she had read about in books. But sometimes she could not help it. The arcades of the Palais Royal, for instance, were the haunt of the *demi-mondaines*, and at an eating-house there the other week she and Alexander had been joined by several of these with their English escorts. Afterwards, when Marianne reluctantly confessed her discomfort at the situation, Alexander had laughed. 'Why, my dear,' he said, 'you are not, you know, in so very different a position from them. Indeed, in the eyes of the world — which I don't give a damn for — you are no different from those ladies.'

That remark had given her pause; and it had

crystallized what till then she had hesitated to call her disappointment with her new life. Her eternal sense of being betwixt and between returned here in Paris, where she had thought one could simply be oneself. The spectacle of the city was all there, of course – from the dirty streets with their puppet-shows and jugglers and coffee-sellers, to the private carriages thronging the Faubourg St Germain or drawing up with their jewelled loads outside the Opéra; but both these worlds went on without her. She and Alexander made the odd visit to the Théâtre Dramatique (where the obscene playlets, she was afraid, made her blush again); they walked in the Tuileries; they attended an occasional musical evening. But the salons were closed to them. The great musicians and writers of the city might take their mistresses to the glamorous Salle Pleyel, but they were enfranchised by talent. Alexander had no special talent, and only such money as he could raise from gambling and credit. Their society was a half-lit world of expatriate Englishmen and sporting characters and card-tables in shabby-genteel lodgings, where a mistress, though not uncommon, was simply a mistress – something not unlike a wife, but without a wife's claim to consideration. And against such a background Alexander himself was inevitably diminished in Marianne's eyes. As her infatuation with the man had been inextricably tied up with the world he represented, so it was with her disillusion with him.

She went forth into the streets, then, with the feeling that was always upon her lately, a feeling compounded of undeveloped stirrings of doubt, homesickness, guilt, revulsion, and longing. And it was at this hour that her eye fell most keenly upon the faces of the multitude of strangers that passed her by – curiously bare and vulnerable they seemed in the early morning. In them she fancied she read their late sorrows and troubles – the marital quarrel, perhaps; the vigil by the bedside of the sick child; the dreams of fulfilment to which the waking day had presented such a saddening contrast. Her heart ached to be somehow a sharer in their lives, while at the same time the noise of talk that reached her ears, mostly so harshly accented that she could not understand it, emphasized her separation from them.

As lonely as she had ever been in the rural quiet of Heartsease, she came to the flower-market on the banks of the Seine. It was high summer: flowers by the waggonload had come in from the country, and they were spread in profusion on trestles and pallets, in baskets, on high stepladders, so that the eye could scarcely travel six inches without being seduced by some brilliant new variation of colour. Beside the blooms, the flower-sellers themselves looked like the drabbest afterthoughts of creation. They were mostly poor, thin, old, ragged: in every respect the flowers seemed to have had the best of the bargain of existence, except in the matter of consciousness, which for the flower-sellers seemed a dubious advantage. Mechanically they cried their wares, and mechanically the old woman from whom Marianne bought chrysanthemums took her money. Then, as she was depositing the coins in her apron-pocket, the old woman gave a low groan and beat her fist once on her chest. Marianne, about to move on, hesitated; stopped as she saw the old woman sway and stagger.

'What is it?' Marianne said in French. 'Madame, are you ill ? Do you have a pain?'

The old woman motioned her away with one hand, the other pressed to her chest. 'Nothing,' she said. 'Always the chest . . . Nothing, thank you.'

Marianne, despite the old woman's protests, took her arm and helped her to sit down on a stool. To her anxious enquiries whether she could get her some water, the old woman only shook her head, and said, 'My sister'; and Marianne was at last given to understand that it was her sister, working at a stall nearby, that she wanted.

She fetched the other woman to her, more of the flower-sellers gathering round in the meantime with a murmur of concern. The presence of her sister seemed to rally the old woman, who clung to her hand and said something about each attack being worse than the last. In the circle of ragged, commiserating people Marianne found herself quite excluded, and she had to push her way in to ask if there was anything she could do, whether she could call for a doctor.

'Nothing, madame, thank you – we will look after her,' said the sister; and Marianne was aware of several pairs of eyes looking at her, her dress, her manner, not with hostility, but simply with rejection. She retreated. She was not one of the ordinary people, and she could not enter into their lives any more than she could walk into the reception-rooms of Louis Philippe. Clutching her flowers, she withdrew from the ring of people who had already forgotten her, and returned home alone.

As she mounted the stairs to their lodging her sensation of solitude was so intense that she was ready to fling herself into Alexander's arms, and seek comfort even in his fitful absent-minded tenderness. But when she opened the door she found all in such confusion that for a moment she thought they had been burgled.

'Whatever are you doing?' said she, coming upon Alexander in the bedroom, heaping his numerous clothes into a trunk.

'Packing,' he said. 'Must go back to England directly.' He tossed a letter to her. 'Read that.'

'I don't understand,' she said after she had read it. 'Does Mr Ingamells expect you to go back?'

'I don't know what he expects, but I've got to go, and have it out with him.' He checked himself. 'No – not have it out with him. Find out if it's true – if it is, try to reason with him, point out that I've based my life on those expectations . . .' He glanced up at Marianne impatiently. 'Don't you see? If he marries this woman it's pretty well a certainty that there'll be children. She's got years of breeding ahead of her, and I don't suppose Mr Ingamells to be a eunuch.'

'Alexander!'

'Bald words for bald facts, my dear,' said Alexander, continuing with his packing. 'The estate's entailed in the male line — that's why I come in for it. But it only takes one little male issue from Ingamells' loins to cut me out of the inheritance for good and all. What's possessed him to take a new wife on board after all these years I can't guess . . . Wait, though. That's a notion. Perhaps he didn't take kindly to this little adventure of ours, and he's cooked up this story of getting married to give me a scare, and set my feet on the straight and narrow. By God, there's hope yet, if that's the case! All the more reason to hurry back to Heartsease as quick as may be — don't you see, Marianne? I'll eat any amount of humble pie, if that's what he wants. Second helpings. Why so startled, dear?'

'I — I never knew it meant that much to you,' said Marianne.

Alexander laughed. 'You've seen Heartsease Hall, I take it? You've seen the myriads of acres belonging, attaching, appertaining to the same? Of course you have — your father farms them. Does all that strike you as something that doesn't matter very much?'

'No,' she said, watching him, seeing about him a chill briskness she had not seen before. 'That is, if it's something you want desperately.'

He laughed again, more shortly this time. 'Oh, Marianne,' was all he said.

Hardly knowing what she was doing, she began to arrange her flowers in a vase. 'Even if it is true,' she said falteringly, 'it may not happen that way — I mean, there might not be children, or there might not be a son—'

'It's a possibility,' said Alexander, 'but I don't intend to sit back and pin my last hopes on such a possibility as that. God! imagine it — forever living in dread of the news that Mrs Ingamells has dropped a male whelp . . . No, no, my dear, lay not that flattering unction to your soul. I've got to get to the bottom of this. If I can reach the coast this evening I might get a night boat going over . . .'

There was about Alexander, now that the first shock was over, a sort of sprightliness: she could almost see his mind working, as if he could not believe that he would not somehow wriggle out of this one. Looking at him, she experienced a sensation as of turning over the ashes of a spent fire. If he had always been something of an enigma to her, she now faced the possibility that the enigma was all there was to him – a riddle without an answer, a beautiful façade with nothing behind it.

'And what of me?' she said, with tense distinctness.

Alexander took a piece of string out of his mouth long enough to say: 'Come, or stay, as you like.'

'How can I stay? I've no means of my own—'

'True, true. Well, come then.' He tied down the lid of the trunk.

'And then what?' she said, with a quiver in her voice.

'Marianne.' He came over and gently placed his hands on her arms. 'I've told you I suspect my uncle is giving me a hint to mend my ways. I don't see anything wrong in our being together, but the world tends to, and so . . . Look, why did you come away with me?'

'Because I thought you cared for me,' she said whitely, 'and that you understood me.'

'Well, so I did – do. But this—' he pointed to her wedding ring. 'It's not through your nose, but it might as well be. And so whatever we have together can only be . . . temporary. I thought that was understood from the start. After all, we've had our fun, and I've always believed that enough's as good as a feast. And when something as important as this comes up . . .'

She stared down at his hands. 'You mean that it's all over.'

He sighed, shrugged, turned away to resume his packing. 'Nothing lasts for ever, my dear.'

The two of them reached Calais that night; but a gale was

blowing up in the Channel, and it was another whole day before they could get across by packet. It was as if ironical fate was deliberately dragging out their last hours together, and making intolerable what was already painfully awkward.

For Marianne had elected to go back to England with Alexander: she had no choice. And that meant, too, returning to Heartsease, for she had nowhere else to go. She did not know what would be her reception from Jed or from her father, or whether either of them would take her in. For the moment her chief sensation was one of humiliation. She had been humiliatingly unable to adjust to a rakish life in Paris; her daring romance had ended with the humiliating realization that the man for whom she had thrown up everything valued worldly security far more than he valued her; and now she was being drawn back, humiliated, to the very place she had sought to escape. She had grasped at freedom, only to find herself fettered yet more tightly by the iron bonds of circumstance.

And Jed? What had Jed been doing all this time? In Paris it had been possible to think of him scarcely as a living being at all, so alien was that world to his nature; but as they came into Norfolk, every hedgerow and mill and wind-borne rook seemed an emissary of his presence, and the consciousness of what she had done to him, weak at first, fastened on her like an incubus.

From Norwich Alexander hired a post-chaise to take them to Heartsease. He looked more nervous and strung up with each mile; but at last he spared her a glance and, reading her expression, said, 'It won't be as bad as you think, my dear. These little dramas go on all the time, and they usually end happily. Husbands are a forgiving breed – or a forgetting breed, which comes to the same thing in the end.'

She shook her head. 'Jed doesn't forget things,' she said.

Jed had been out in his fields, where the wheat had been badly knocked about by the capricious winds that had persisted into the warm days of midsummer. The same winds had torn a nest from the hawthorn hedge, and a couple of naked baby birds, a second brood, lay lifeless on the ground. Jed covered the little bodies over with earth. Something about the wantonness of this destruction put him in mind of the carter he had seen in Norwich, whipping his old horse till it bled. Yes, he thought, man was cruel, rash, thoughtless, unjust; but there was nothing in the ordering of the universe to teach him to be otherwise.

He went into the house and found luggage standing in the hall. It was as if he had been struck a blow in the chest.

He turned to see Marianne regarding him, holding her bonnet by the strings.

'I'm sorry I – didn't send word I was coming,' said Marianne.

'It doesn't matter,' said Jed. His voice came out quite normally, but he was unprepared for the wave of anger and wretchedness that smote him on seeing his wife standing in the hall of Plague House. He had thought his bitterness had burnt away to a bleak absence of feeling; but now her beauty struck him afresh, and memories that he thought he had done with, of their laughing together in a sun-filled bedroom, gripped and with the devil's own savagery tore him to the heart.

'May I stay?' she said.

'Here? Here, you mean? How long? A day, a week?' He was conscious less of speaking to her than of flinging words at her, like a child with handfuls of stones.

'Until – until we've decided what we're going to do.'

'Who's "we", then, in this case?'

She looked away from him. 'You and I.'

'Ah. I see. That's the way the wind blows now, is it?'

He should, he felt, have laughed at her: petty, childish revenge enough, but something; but laughter was gone from the world. And then there was a footstep on the stair, and Charlotte came hurrying down.

Her eyes took in the situation in a moment. After a fractional hesitation she put out her hand. 'You must be Marianne,' she said.

Marianne nodded.

'I'm Charlotte.' She pressed Marianne's hand. 'Have you had anything to eat?'

'Yes, I – no – I'm not hungry.'

'You must be tired then. I'll make up a room, shall I?' Charlotte's eyes sought Jed's. 'And have Ben take the baggage up.'

'I don't know if I'm staying,' said Marianne awkwardly.

'Well . . . Just for now, eh? And I'll brew a dish of tea. Why not come and help me make the bed up – thass easier wi' two.'

As if she lacked a will of her own, Marianne followed Charlotte upstairs. Once in the spare bedroom she fell into a chair and covered her face with her hands.

'Jed was always talking of you, Charlotte,' she said after a while.

'Was he?' Charlotte drew sheets from the chest.

'I know how dear to each other you are. And so I know – that you must hate me as he does.'

Charlotte shook her head. 'I don't know you. Oh, of course I don't like seeing Jed unhappy. But there's enough hate around . . . and not enough time,' she said, thinking of Loveday.

Marianne wiped her eyes, and got up to help Charlotte. 'Has Jed been dreadfully unhappy?'

'Yes,' Charlotte said. 'But I don't reckon he hate you. Or if he do, that come from love.'

Presently Charlotte went downstairs to find Jed standing at the open back door half in sunlight. He put his hand gently on her shoulder, his eyes still fixed on the summer landscape without.

'There's no reconciling, Charlotte,' he said. 'There can't be.'

'All right, Jed,' she said. 'But no revenging either. Thass best.'

Pierce felt that he had met Miss Harriet Fontayne before: not the individual, but the type. He had often produced wedding-portraits, and had found that there was a certain type of young wives and wives-to-be for whom their status as young wives or wives-to-be assumed such cosmic importance that it swallowed up their identities altogether, and reduced them to a sort of distilled essence of orange-blossom, trousseau, archness and blush.

Not that Miss Fontayne gushed. She was irreproachably well-bred. Her pink-and-white complexion, beautiful expressionless eyes, arched upper lip and diminutive mind were the unmistakable hallmarks of her descent from generations of batteners upon other people's toil. She spoke in a voice like a well-tuned harpsichord, moved with faultless grace, dressed with taste, and was never uncomfortable. Her hands were always occupied with that pointless sewing known as 'work': she netted purses and embroidered handkerchiefs as if no more fulfilling occupation lay within the ken of humankind.

'Ah, the feminine influence, Mr Coppinger — how it sweetens the air of our humble nook,' said Mr Ingamells, coming into the library to look over the mounting of the estate views. 'Bowed down with my nose to the grindstone of duty and responsibility as I have been in late years, I have tended not to notice its absence — or at least to consider it as departed for ever with my irreplaceable Euphemia; but it stole upon me, Mr Coppinger, and was not to be resisted!'

Pierce repeated his congratulations, privately reflecting that for Mr Ingamells to talk of the absence of feminine influence was to be more than a little forgetful of the presence of his own daughter.

'I may as well confess to you, my dear sir, that I wrestled agonizingly with myself over the matter of my

fidelity to the memory of Euphemia,' went on Mr
Ingamells. 'And in thinking upon that sacred dust, do
you know the one idea that stood forth, and made my
decision for me? Duty! Duty, Mr Coppinger – a
lamentably old-fashioned notion, but one which I am
obstinate and unworldly enough to stand by. Duty, you
see, was the most conspicuous of Euphemia's many
virtues: she looked upon submission to her husband as
the pride and privilege of her sex. And was it consonant
with that duty, that glorious spirit of submission that
distinguished her in life, that Euphemia in death should
expect me to mourn her for ever? No, no – insulting to
her memory to think it, insulting to her memory to
suppose that she should seek to assert in death the will
that she had so beautifully relinquished in life! So it was
settled – settled even more satisfactorily, Mr Coppinger,
by the realization that my new bride was of precisely the
same dutiful temper as the old, and would perpetuate her
spirit rather than displace it.'

Turning over the drawings with his smooth hands,
which the white paper seemed to soil rather than the other
way around, Mr Ingamells pursued: 'The new prospects
which my marriage will open up are not, of course,
without their practical aspects, and those not unwelcome.
You cannot have failed to reflect, Mr Coppinger, that the
recent conduct of my relative Mr Deacon does not augur
well for his future stewardship of this estate. It is of
course not for me to judge him, except in one respect; as
a potential possessor of this modest corner of old
England. And I cannot consider him as such, I fear, with
any ease of mind. Thus there is a further argument in
favour of my marrying again – the safeguarding of the
Ingamells' heritage, which can best be achieved by our
raising a new family here, on this ancestral ground to
which I am foolishly attached, and which I hope to teach
a son of my own to treasure as I do.' Mr Ingamells
smiled, and Pierce felt the presence of something shrewd
and steely, like the hard glint of a blade sliding into a

silken sheath. 'Well, my dear sir,' said Mr Ingamells, 'I must leave you for the moment: my solicitor in Norwich requires my signature, I believe, on some papers to do with my shares in the railway. Apparently we have done rather well out of them: ask me not how, for I have no more understanding of such modern devices than the man in the moon!'

Pierce could not feel much pity for Alexander Deacon, who Mr Ingamells said he had informed by letter. It was the reaction of Beatrice Ingamells to this unforeseen event that he was concerned about.

Miss Fontayne declared at once that she and Beatrice would be the best of friends. 'I knew from the moment James told me — pardon me, it comes so natural — from the moment Mr Ingamells told me about you, that we should get on famously,' Miss Fontayne said, making tiny stitches in a tiny piece of cambric. 'What with you being so clever at drawing and music and so on — I absolutely adore those little pastimes. I'm afraid I shan't be able to keep such things up when I'm married — not that I'm anything like as proficient as you, my dear, and it must be such a wonderful resource for you — but all the various duties of a wife in the household, not to mention the social engagements that necessarily come to a married couple, will simply leave no time for them. But you mustn't fear that I shall get in the way of your pursuits, Beatrice dear — may I call you that? I feel as if I know you already — for you must be sure and carry on in your own little way, just as if nothing had changed.'

'Immensely grateful I'm sure but really you mustn't think of my comfort I don't expect anything of the kind indeed I don't,' said Miss Ingamells. Since her father's presentation of his new bride she had been in a state of curious glassy calm, her features permanently composed in a smile. Pierce could only guess at what she was feeling.

'Now, Beatrice, I won't have it,' said Miss Fontayne, holding up a roguish finger, 'for I know we are going to

be the best of friends — we are, you know! — and if I am
to be the mistress of the house — dear me, I can hardly
believe it! — then I shall make you my especial care. And
I won't have you feeling a moment's uneasiness about the
fact of my being your stepmother. Which, of course, I
will be — and younger than you, I believe — how quaint!
Of course, a stepmother is surely entitled to a certain
share of that duty owed by a child to a parent. But having
said that, I don't think we need trouble ourselves about it
any more, my dear. You I'm sure have a perfectly
developed sense of what is right and fitting — that's the
sort of person you are, and I like you for it! — and when
it comes to paying the proper respect to your father's
wife, I'm sure I have nothing to teach you. As for what
you should call me, I really don't see why you shouldn't
call me Harriet, at least in private. When we are in
company, something more formal would be more
appropriate, of course; but that's for other people's
benefit, and you may surely *think* of me as Harriet then
— it will be our little secret!'

This pretty little piece of poison was soon at home in
the Hall: indeed it was as if she was its mistress already.
She was shown all round the estate and the house by her
future husband, leaning on his arm very fetchingly,
turning up her daisy face to laugh at his every quip, and
showing the proper womanly interest in all the domestic
arrangements.

'Well, I have been Papa's little housekeeper for some
time now,' she tinkled, 'and he seems to think I have
some special talent for it — I'm sure I don't know why!
— and is forever praising me to his friends, until I could
quite blush for shame. After all, I'm only doing what
pleases me, for a woman can know no greater satisfaction
than maintaining a neat well-run household, and seeing
that the man of the house has everything just as he likes
it.'

'Beatrice, of course, has filled that capacity,' said Mr
Ingamells, bestowing a smile on his daughter, 'and very

well too; but she will be happy, I'm sure, to surrender the housekeeping keys, and be relieved of those duties.'

'Oh! yes, indeed, Beatrice — you shall have all the time in the world for your own pursuits. In fact, that is one thing I shall insist on,' Miss Fontayne said with an artless laugh. 'There! — I'm being a tyrant to you already, James — but I shall insist, you know, that Beatrice shall never be disturbed. You shall carry on your own little life, Beatrice dear — and trouble yourself no more about the responsibilities of the house than if you were a guest here!'

Thus Pierce watched as Miss Ingamells followed silently in the train of the happy couple — appearing more gaunt and spectral than ever beside the little trim prettiness of her future stepmother. Thus he watched as Miss Ingamells, who was so little valued already, was charmingly condescended to by Miss Fontayne, who was so conspicuously cherished. Thus he saw Miss Ingamells consigned more thoroughly to the margins of life at the Hall; saw what little role and status she had as mistress of the place disappearing into the managing hands of her father's bride.

The effect of all this upon the unhappy woman was plain to Pierce, and it haunted him. His sensitivity to suffering had grown acute, from his own anguish at the loss of Rosa. For there was more involved in that than the simple regret attendant on a failed love affair. He had lost faith in the benevolence, or at least neutrality, of the world: his eyes had been opened to the black shades that enveloped human hopes, and this new consciousness weighed upon him like a physical illness, so that his mirror showed him a face grown thinner, paler, grimmer. His pity for the situation of Miss Ingamells intensified this brooding turn of mind; and it was such thoughts that were occupying him as he worked in the library one afternoon about a fortnight after Miss Fontayne's arrival. Mr Ingamells and his fiancée had gone to call on Mr Ringrose, magnanimously taking Beatrice with them.

The quiet was suddenly broken by the noise of an arrival; and a few moments later Alexander Deacon burst in.

'Pierce, my dear fellow, how are you, thank God somebody's here,' Alexander said, breezing in as if they had met just yesterday. He threw off his dusty travelling-coat impatiently. 'Phoo, it's as hot as hell's kitchen today. Posted all the way from Newmarket.'

'I didn't expect to see you again,' Pierce said.

'Didn't expect to turn up again so soon myself. Does the old fellow keep any liquor in here? Ah! here's soda-water at any rate. I came back as soon as I got my uncle's letter. Now look here, what's the truth of it? The servants have just been giving me some flannel about the master being out visiting with Miss Fontayne. Is she real flesh and blood, then? Can there be any truth in it?'

Pierce told him. 'I believe they're going to London to be married very shortly,' he said. 'Miss Ingamells, of course, is to be left behind.'

'Eh? Oh, Beatrice. Must be a blow for her. She's hardly likely to find an admirer to take her away from it all.' Alexander gulped his drink. 'Pierce. This Fontayne woman can't really be twenty-three. Tell me that was just a fabrication to call me from the errors of my ways. Tell me she's an old dragon past everything but picquet by the fire.'

Pierce shook his head.

'I see.' Alexander examined the crystal glass from which he had drunk; then with an economical movement flung it on the floor so that it shattered to fragments. 'And so this is my punishment for taking a discontented farmer's wife and showing her a bit of life. I see.' He kicked idly at the broken glass. 'I need to wash and dress. I'll send someone to clear this up,' he said, and went out.

Mr Ingamells returned with his fiancée and daughter about an hour later. By that time Alexander was changed, composed, all courtesy as he greeted his relatives, was introduced to Miss Fontayne, and asked if he might speak alone with Mr Ingamells. The two of them retreated into the library, while Pierce went upstairs to dress for dinner. Only a short space of time had elapsed before Alexander barged into his room. His expression was deathly.

'My God,' he said. 'My God, he's going to do it. He really is going to marry that simpering brood-mare downstairs and fill the place with little Ingamells. I told him − I *told* him it wasn't fair when I had always counted on my expectations from this estate − that I was surely entitled to some consideration . . . He just kept smiling and saying he understood my disappointment and my dear sir and all the rest of it. My *God*!' He worked a frantic hand through his hair. The Byronic looks of the unfinished portrait still on the easel in the attic room were gone: Alexander looked like a moody youth. 'Imagine, damn it − imagine coming to this place, over the years; getting to know it; aware that one day it will be yours. And so you adjust your life accordingly. And then suddenly it's taken from you, or as good as. Dear God, that selfish old chiseller's done this to spite me! What am I to do?'

Pierce shrugged. 'Go back to the law?'

'Law? Might as well speak of going back to prison. Ten years of that grind before I reach a grocer's income.' Alexander's eyes narrowed. 'No, no, not for me. I shall have to look for something else. I can't live on a pittance − not when I've been expecting to live in this sort of style. I shall have to think again . . . One thing's certain. I'll not stay here any longer − not to have Ingamells and his little milch-cow crow over me. I'll go now, while they're dressing. I don't consider they've deserved a goodbye from me. I'll go to the inn in the village and if I can't get to Swaffham or Dereham tonight I'll put up with a bed there. Pierce, would you be a good fellow and have the servants send my luggage over to the Wheat-sheaf?'

'Very well,' said Pierce. 'Shall I say anything about where you've gone?'

'Oh! I don't suppose that'll be of any interest to them anyhow − damn them!'

'Wait a moment − what about Mrs Wintergreen?'

'Eh? Oh, back in the arms of loving husband, I presume. Or being beaten by same. My dear fellow, don't give me that look, I beg you. It was never anything but a pleasant little escapade and she knew it. Let's see, your time here's nearly up, isn't it?'

'Yes, I shall be leaving soon.'

'Good luck to you. Believe me, you'll get no joy out of Heartsease.'

Alexander slipped out of a back door of the house, and struck out towards the village across the park. Dusk was at hand, and long shadows lay horizontally among the trees, like felled segments of night, whilst on all sides bees lifted themselves heavily from the clovered grass and sought the warmer upper layers of air. Alexander, absorbed in his thoughts, heard no sound but the brushing of his own footsteps, until a sudden gasp of breath behind him made him realize he was pursued.

He turned to find Beatrice Ingamells running towards him. She was red-cheeked and out of breath, and her skirts were filmed with pollen and grass-seed.

'Wait, Alexander − wait,' she panted. 'I can't run any more . . . I saw you go from my window.'

He stood, impatiently enough, and regarded her as she held her hand to her side and smoothed her dampened hair.

'Where are you going?' she said. 'Did you quarrel with my father? Is that what it's about? Are you leaving?'

'What do you think, Beatrice?' he said. 'You're no fool. You see the position this notion of your father's has put me in. There's no point in my staying at Heartsease Hall any longer. So I'm off. A twitch of my mantle blue, fresh fields and pastures new, et cetera. Perhaps you'll be good enough to say my goodbyes for me.'

Beatrice's lips twitched, and her eyes, pale in the

sunbeams, seemed to strain forth from her skull in the intensity of her stare at him.

'Take me with you,' she said.

Alexander checked himself in a laugh. 'Beatrice,' he said, 'I've always said you are a very entertaining woman. But I'm really not in a fit mood to appreciate the jest just now. Pardon me.'

He made a move, and found her hand clutching his arm.

'I have never been more serious in my life and never shall be again,' Beatrice cried. 'Think, Alexander, think — we are in the same situation, you and I — we both lose by this marriage of my father's; there's nothing left for me here but being forever talked down to by that creature and left to rot in a corner like some poor old relation turned in her wits that everyone will be glad to see despatched to the grave — that's all the future I have here and you know it . . . And I am not to be so disregarded, Alexander! I am a living woman with nerves and senses and a heart, yes a heart though it has been stifled and smothered this many a long year until I have almost longed to go mad and be rid of its yearnings — and now I will suffer it no more, I swear I will not! That heart has loved you desperately for so long, Alexander — you must know it! I have seemed to feel it screaming out like a thing in pain for love of you until I was sure you must hear its cries. There's nothing for me here — where *you* are, there is everything, and I would go barefoot and beg in the streets beside you . . . Take my love, Alexander — it is yours, yours, take it — and take me with you!'

Alexander looked down at the bony hand clutching his arm, and shifted. 'Dear God, Beatrice,' he said, 'this is not one of your better jokes.'

'Ah, of course! Beatrice is always joking — so there is no need ever to take her seriously — no need to suppose that she has feelings! Do you really suppose that there is nothing more to me than this silly mask I show to the world, that I have to show in order for it to tolerate me at all? Because I am plain and drab and have no trifling graces, does that mean I can't know passion? My great God, if that little puss that Father is marrying were to feel one atom of the passion that I have hidden in my breast these past years, it would tear her pretty little body in two!'

'Beatrice, such language, for heaven's sake,' said Alexander, with the libertine's primness.

'Passion for you, Alexander — you!' said Beatrice in a hoarse undertone. To an observer less blinkered by self than Alexander, there would have appeared something imposing, almost exalted, about the figure of the tall woman making her desperate avowal in the summer evening, the half-light of which lent a melting phosphorescence to her still form, as if her irksome flesh were dissolving under the pressure of her spirit. 'Yes, I have hated you too,' she went on, 'hated you for fear that you would discover my secret, and laugh at me — hated you from the very madness of my love for you. But don't you see — what has happened brings us together! I ask for very little, Alexander — only that you let me go with you, and let me love you. It isn't easy for me to declare myself like this — it goes hard with me, very hard, for I have my pride you know — yes, as much pride as a beauty, or more, for a beauty can afford to spare it, and sometimes it has seemed that pride is all that I have to keep the world from grinding me to nothing; but I give it up for you. Doesn't that show that I'm in earnest? I have often thought I would thrust my hand in the fire and watch it being consumed before I would put myself at the mercy of a man like this, but I do it for you. I know you have had lots of women — women who have pretty ways, and know the right things to say and do — but surely none can have offered you love as I do — only let me show you, Alexander — that's all I ask!'

'This is all very interesting, Beatrice,' said Alexander, who had slipped his hands into his pockets, and was regarding her with the air of a man stopped on the corner by a talkative acquaintance. 'Certainly, we both have cause to regret this folly of your father's; and I'm sorry for you, having to go on living at the Hall with him and his little bride, who, I may as well add, has not one-hundredth of your brains. As I say, it's all very interesting in its way, but Beatrice, the only thing I am interested in here is the Hall and the estate — considered in the light of an inheritance, that is. And now that's gone, or as good as, so I'm off. You, I'm afraid, will have to endure this situation, but for me there are surely other possibilities, other ways to the sun, and I must lose no time in taking them. Love in a cottage is not my ideal, Beatrice — either with a beauty or otherwise.'

'Appearance is nothing!' she fervently cried.

'On the contrary, cousin, appearance is *everything* — if only people would realize it!' said he, with a sudden freshness. 'But having said that, I shall not be fussy when I return to London, and look about me. There are plenty of heiresses in the City, Beatrice — marriageable animals whose fathers would be pleased enough to see their daughters wedded to a gentleman with connections like mine. That's my plan for the future. Certainly I shall look out for one with looks as well as a fortune; but, if all else fails, I might even put up with one with a face as ugly as yours, cousin, as long as it has fifty thousand pounds attached.' He smiled, half-turned, then paused, smiling still. 'I don't know though — I couldn't put up with a face like yours at *any* price.'

He held her eyes for a laughing moment, then turned and continued on his way across the park. She did not follow him; and night had completely taken possession of the spot before her motionless figure stirred, and made its slow way back towards the lights of the Hall.

Marianne moved back into Plague House, for the time being. There was nothing else to be done. She made one visit to her father, who received her like a stranger, and gave her to understand that she had made her own bed and must lie in it. Jed not being the sort of man to throw her out, he and Marianne were constrained for the moment to exist beneath the same roof, in an atmosphere as unrestful as an electrical storm.

Without the presence of Charlotte the situation would have been wholly intolerable. The unhappy couple moved in quite separate orbits, Jed rising and breakfasting early before spending the day around the farm, Marianne keeping mostly to her room and only coming downstairs when she knew her husband would be out; and so they met up only by chance, whereupon they would edge round each other with lowered eyes, and muttered greetings – thus by a sad irony replicating the external behaviour of people who are beginning to fall in love. The chief channel of communication between them was Charlotte, who, whatever her natural feelings for her brother, did not take sides, but acted as an unassuming confidante to both of them. It was she who brought her practicality to bear on these two chafing, self-punishing natures, encouraging them to eat and sleep and care for themselves even as they indignantly protested that such things did not matter. She was there to stroke Marianne's hair from her brow when she flung herself stormily on the bed and cried that no woman should have to suffer as she did; she was there to listen quietly when Jed, suddenly brought face to face with a tender memory of their past by some physical reminder about the house or farm, spoke it out loud in a voice cracked by bitterness and regret. In a thousand small ways she stroked down the mental hackles of the pair, and interposed herself between them and the worst scourgings of their pain.

Marianne, so responsive as always to human sympathy, soon came to rely on Charlotte, and unburdened her heart to her – veering between wishing she had met her sooner, and complaining that not even Charlotte's influence could have prevented what had happened. This was not contrariness, but an accurate reflection of Marianne's state of mind: for she was angry, humbled, sorry, and defiant all at once; piteously conscious of having wronged Jed, yet conscious too of being wronged herself, and unable to discern anything that could be called justice in the reduction of such an ambiguous tangle to a single issue of disaster. For she seemed to have come to a termination of all her hopes, and the sheer blank wall which circumstance now presented to her spirit wore such an everlasting aspect that all her young resilience wilted at it, and left her defenceless against a dull despair.

Charlotte's instinct was all towards reconciliation. But she recognized that her view of the situation at Plague House was inevitably conditioned by her own inner happiness, which nothing could quite touch. Grieved as she was for her brother and sister-in-law, she could not deny the buoyancy of her own heart, which leapt at the thought of Toby a hundred times a day, and formed a poignant contrast to the love-blight around her. Toby had visited her at Heartsease twice — meetings the tender sweetness of which remained with her when they were apart, as palpable a talisman as the lucky fairy-loaf that she kept on her window-sill. It was hard, after walking the lanes with Toby wrapped in a rare glow of mutual affection and confidence, to adjust again to the atmosphere of Plague House, and to penetrate to the sad core of that situation. She could only try, fortified by her perception that between Jed and Marianne there had once been an abundance of genuine love.

But their estrangement was so intractable that even Charlotte's healing presence could only soften its harsh edges. Jed's nature, loyal and single-minded, was cloven to the root by his wife's betrayal; and a man of his intense temperament could never subside into the cynical indifference that alone could have made bearable the proximity of a woman who had meant so much to him. Nor could he long suffer this curious suspended manner of their living together. The legal tie was indissoluble, but there were expedients. He knew a decision must be made.

And so the two faced each other at last, Jed coming to see her in her room, with the harvest sun streaming through the open window, and bees straying in and out of the scene of anguish, just as they would indiscriminately hum about the flowers of a wedding or a funeral.

'I've been thinking,' Jed said, 'that the best thing for us to do – the only thing for us to do – is to live apart.'

Marianne inclined her head slightly, more in acknowledgement of his having spoken than in agreement.

'I – I can't talk of what's happened,' Jed said. 'Not – not coolly. I can't see as I ever shall.'

'And I don't wish to,' Marianne said.

'Very well.' Jed suppressed a groan, for it seemed to him that there could hardly have been more butchery in this if they had assailed each other with knives. 'Mr Veazey's away, but I shall go and see him as soon as he returns next week, and consult with him about how it's to be done. Separation, I mean . . . I believe there are rules and so on . . .'

'I believe so,' Marianne said, her face dry, but tears in her voice.

'Is there – what would you like to do? Will your father . . .'

'He won't see me. He may come round, in time. My brother Herbert's left home, and taken lodgings in Norwich. He's written me. I could live with him for the time being.'

'Whatever you wish.'

She waved a bee away from her hair, and the slight movement of her hand was so entirely, uniquely characteristic of her that his soul seemed to plunge into the abyss at the sight of it.

'When do you wish me to go?' she said.

'Whenever – whenever suits you.'

She nodded. 'I – I won't say goodbye,' she said.

Chapter Sixteen

The Blind Hand

Elias Hemstock woke to find that there had been another raid on his property during the night.

This was the third. Last week another of his hay-ricks had been fired; this time the miscreant had tried to set a blaze beneath the first rick of harvested grain. The servants, who took turns in watching every night, had disturbed him before much damage had been done; but before slipping away in the darkness he had left behind him an ill-spelt note which threatened further depredations: *You no who I am and you no what it is I owe you rest ashured you will get it and dont think of trying to ketch me I am were you cant get at me and out of your power*.

Hemstock knew it was Todd Gault, of course; and he had reliable information that the ruffian was hiding out amongst the navvies encamped to the south of the village. Again he cursed the leniency of the magistrates who had only sentenced him to that single month in gaol. Hemstock was about to throw the note on the fire when it occurred to him that he should keep it if he wanted to hunt Gault down for good and all. Mr Ingamells was a magistrate, and the note should surely persuade him to issue a warrant for Gault's arrest. Yes, this time he would have Gault, and see he got the punishment he deserved. It was a sweet prospect; for the thought of the fellow's impudence disturbed Hemstock's rest and haunted his waking hours.

For a moment Hemstock recalled the words of his son Herbert, who had accused him of being obsessed with one discontented labourer, and of thus showing his true coarseness of fibre. But he dismissed the memory, as he had dismissed that of Herbert himself, who had carried out his intention of leaving home, and had ceased all communication with his father. Well, that was that as far as Hemstock was concerned: the boy was gone, and he himself would never admit that there might have been anything in his own behaviour to drive Herbert away. His mind would accept the perpetual loss of his own son before it would concede that he had been wrong in any particular. That was the way he lived: he would abide by the consequences of his own conduct, for he believed it was right, right through and through; he would be burnt at the stake before he would change. And yet sometimes he would come into the house and note the absence of familiar young voices, and be horribly aware of the gap created by the absence of the daughter and son whose names were never even mentioned, and who had been so carefully nurtured only to disappear from his life more completely than if they had died in infancy; and then he would experience a fleeting sensation as of a lone man staring about at the ruin he had made of a fair place.

For therein lay another reason why a grim vengefulness now informed his thoughts of this nobody who was continuing to taunt him: the ignominious return of his disgraced daughter. Just yesterday she had come again to see him, bearing the news that she and Wintergreen intended to live apart, and suggesting that she come back to the family home. And Hemstock had refused to speak a word to her. In a way the news should have been welcome, insofar as it meant Wintergreen would no longer have her; but she would be married to him still, and what had filled Hemstock with a transcendent bitterness, and made him turn speechless away from her, was a vision of Marianne living at home again – a sardonic parody of the state of things before she had met Wintergreen, with the ghastly difference that whereas then all had been proud ambitious hope, now

Hemstock's every sight of her moving poised and lovely about his house would be a reminder of those bright prospects that could never be.

And so he bit on his own misery, like a man under the surgeon's knife biting on the strap. In not revealing that misery to the world lay his only salvation — except, perhaps, for the opportunity to strike back at the world that had ruined him by hunting down Todd Gault. He seemed to discern on the face of fate a sneering expectation that he would merely submit to this latest humiliation — but he was determined to prove fate wrong. He could not bring back Herbert, he could not bring back Marianne as she was, but he would not bow his head before the insults of a gaolbird with scarcely a shirt to his back.

The thing to do was to go and consult Mr Ingamells. He had never felt quite easy about calling at the Hall, except on Quarter Days, and Marianne's disgrace had critically undermined his social confidence; but he equipped himself with the excuse of wishing to offer his congratulations on Mr Ingamells' forthcoming marriage, and rode over to the Hall with the note in his pocket. Mr Ingamells received him genially, and introduced him to his betrothed.

'Mr Hemstock, my dear, is my chief tenant,' he said, 'and I would add, at the risk of discomfiting my worthy friend, my most valued one. I cannot pretend to understand these modern developments in agricultural enterprise, but you can be sure that whatever they are, Mr Hemstock is in the van of them. He is a man much respected amongst his peers, my dear — and deservedly so!'

'I'm glad to meet you, indeed, Mr Hemstock — for where would we be without our farmers?' said Miss Fontayne. 'I am sure nothing pleases me better than to see a working farm, with all the cows and so on; and really, if it had pleased the Almighty to call me to another station, I can think of none better than to be an honest farmer's wife, rising with the lark and busying myself about my tidy kitchen.'

Hemstock made a stiff reply, congratulating the pair, and darkly musing a moment on what it was that this lady had that Marianne had not. An old name, he supposed, but he could have raised his own name through her − so high! He mechanically engaged in some chat − his mind was too austerely practical for him to be good at this − and at last asked Mr Ingamells if he might speak to him on a pressing matter of law.

'Ah! duty, you see, my dear, invades our bower, and so it shall always be,' Mr Ingamells said. 'You would not have it any other way, I know. Will you excuse us?'

In the library Hemstock produced the note and told the story of Todd's raids upon his property.

'A sad business,' Mr Ingamells said, bonelessly reclining in his easy chair, 'but unsurprising, alas, in these times. We may be to blame, I fear, in fostering this greed and cupidity in our lower orders − I do not speak of you, my good friend, who have always shown admirable firmness towards them; but we in authority have erred on the side of leniency, and discontent is the result.'

'Discontent, and insolence,' said Hemstock. 'That is why I came to you, Mr Ingamells. I'm sure you haven't forgotten the outbreak of incendiarism and lawlessness in the year 'thirty − the time of the Swing disturbances; and we put that down very smartly, you'll recall. I feel that this occasion warrants a similar response.'

'Well, there are certain differences. You see, my good friend, I will put out an order for this fellow's arrest very willingly; I shall make the warrant now; but the problem remains of apprehending the culprit. You say he has gone to ground with the railway-navigators − and they, I understand, are a law unto themselves. The parish constables have had difficulties with them before, and it will not be an easy matter for them to hunt out your man, if the navigators do not choose to yield him up. If it were a question of large-scale disturbances, then I would feel empowered to take further action, but as it is . . .'

'I see that,' Hemstock said. 'But I reckon these railway fellows will give him up if they see the law really coming down upon them. And there could be no better indication of that than a word from a magistrate.'

'A word in person, do you mean, Mr Hemstock?'

'Yes,' said Hemstock. 'I've had enough of this fellow, Mr Ingamells; and if you'll make out an order for his arrest, then I shall go to the navvies' camp myself and demand that they hand him over, in the law's name. And if you would be so good as to simply come with me, as Justice of the Peace, the business would be settled — they'll know authority when they see it. I know that your time is much occupied, sir, but—'

'My dear Mr Hemstock, my time is yours to command,' said Mr Ingamells. 'But in this case I am afraid it would simply be wasting *your* time. I am not a man in the forefront of progress like yourself: I know nothing of railway engines and their attendant myrmidons. It is all such an alien world to me, I should simply be of no use — no more use than if I should attempt to parley with Hottentots. No, Mr Hemstock, I am afraid my presence would only be an encumbrance to you, and I have too great a respect for you to pretend otherwise.' He lifted himself elegantly out of his chair. 'Was there anything else, my good friend?'

Hemstock was about to speak, then changed his mind. 'No — thank you, sir. I'm sorry to have taken up your time.'

'Ah, don't be, Mr Hemstock — I am at your disposal, entirely at your disposal! Goodbye, my dear sir!'

Hemstock returned home with a sense of terrible solitude upon him — of being utterly alone in his aims and thoughts and desires; and it was sharpened by yet another loss, the creeping loss of his respect for Mr Ingamells, which had been as fixed and unquestioned a part of his world as his belief in market forces and the Anglican church. But it was characteristic of him that this only stiffened his relentless self-assertion. Another man might have felt himself set back by Mr Ingamells' declining to join his project, but Hemstock only felt more resolute. He would go on with it now even if God and all his angels descended from the sky to forbid it.

He dined early, and then after his single glass of brandy told his wife that he was going over to see the farm bailiff. He had his horse saddled, and rode out of the village at a steady pace, striking out south across the sandy tracks of Madhouse Heath.

The sun was declining on a gaudy deathbed of humid cloud, and the low beams lighting on the expanse of heather and lichen conjured forth a welter of bizarre colour which gave to the scene an unearthly aspect scarcely corresponding to any known season, hour, or landscape, and made the humble rabbits that skipped out of the path of his horse's hooves as quaint and sinister to the eye as imps. Many a doughty man might have found this lurid emptiness unnerving, but Hemstock went on his way in sternest fashion. He had never been afraid.

The landscape took on a scarred and littered appearance as the camp of the railway-builders drew near. Heaps of earth and rubble and cinders interrupted the flat horizon, and the ground was scored with wheel-ruts. A breeze was blowing up from the west, and it brought the smell of the camp to Hemstock's nostrils even before the lights were visible.

It was difficult to know whether the camp would look more unlovely by day or, as now, by lamplit night. The wages the navvies could earn, if their strength was up to it, were comparatively high, but a raw brutality surrounded their lives, in their leisure as in their labour – especially when, as here, there was no permanent accommodation for them, and the contractor was not particular about what became of them when the day's work was done. The straggling shanty of huts and lean-tos and tents was without sanitation, and Hemstock held a handkerchief to his nose against the fevers that must surely breed in it: here and there a crude domesticity manifested itself in lines of washing, in little tin chimneys and even bird-cages hung at shed doors, and one or two down-at-heel women were to be seen; but for the most part the sight that met Hemstock's eye as his horse picked a way through the refuse was as primitive and harshly male as something from the ancient world − as if a slip in time had brought the warriors of the Iceni back to this spot they had inhabited two thousand years ago. And Hemstock was disdainful and conscious of superiority as any Roman as he observed the men squatting about their fires, turning rabbits on spits, smoking clay pipes, their heads turning in unison with a glitter of hard eyes to watch him go by. Others were dicing or gambling at cards: snatches of shouted quarrels floated on the rank air, curses, loud metallic laughter; and around one bonfire a large group of men were drinking from stone jars, while one played frenetic Irish jigs on a fiddle. The illumination of lamps and fires, fitful in the wind and the drifting smoke, gave a peculiar instability to the scene, so that men, shacks, barrels, rubbish-heaps, carts seemed suddenly to stand forth as between parted curtains of darkness and then disappear again; and it was perhaps because of this that Hemstock only slowly realized that the navvies had gathered in a circle about him, and penned him in.

He reined in his horse and stared round at the ring of faces which shone with sweat in the red light, full-whiskered, many of a rugged and inflexible handsomeness not unlike his own. The curiously flamboyant clothes the navvies wore, the brightly patterned neck-cloths and waistcoats and ganseys, added the last weird and dreamlike touch, so that it seemed scarcely possible that only a few miles from this spot cottagers were closing up the shutters in a quiet village world of old timber and thatch. Unconsciously Hemstock gave the arrogant hitch of his chin above his collar before he spoke.

'My name is Hemstock. I am a farmer at Hearts-ease. I have reason to believe that a criminal is in hiding here, a criminal who has committed arson on my property. There is a warrant for his arrest, signed by a magistrate, Mr James Ingamells, of Heartsease Hall. The name of the criminal is Gault, Todd Gault. Is he here?'

No one spoke. There was the sound of a gob of spit hissing on to a fire.

'Gault is to give himself up,' went on Hemstock. 'The law is on to him – he cannot hide for ever. He will be given a fair trial – the longer he holds out the worse it will be for him.'

'He's sick,' a voice said.

Hemstock glared round. In the wayward country-dance of light and shadow it was impossible to tell which man had spoken.

'You admit he is here? Let him face me then, if he is not too much of a coward – which I doubt. Bring him forward!'

'He's here,' a voice said, 'and he's sick. And this ain't your farm, Mester whatever your name is, and we don't take kindly to being ordered about. D'you see?'

Hemstock managed to locate the speaker, and peremptorily pointed his riding-crop at him. 'Don't you address me in that tone, sir. I have the law at my back and the law demands that this rogue give himself up.' Hemstock was not in a passion: his anger, though intense and at that moment seeming to embrace the whole recalcitrant world, was quite controlled, and it did not occur to him for a single moment that his own tone was ill-judged towards these fierce and independent men. It was the only way of speaking that he knew. 'I don't believe Gault is sick. If he is well enough to make criminal attacks on my property, he is well enough to take the consequences. I shall search this place till I find him, do you hear?'

'Uppity bastard – go bugger yourself,' someone grunted, and there was a short laugh like an edged gleam in the darkness.

'You are fools to yourselves,' said Hemstock, his voice growing louder. 'You have nothing to gain by sheltering this villain. It is an offence to harbour a criminal, are you aware of that?'

A hand grabbed the bridle of his horse, and a swarthy face with silver earrings was turned up towards Hemstock's. 'Now you've said your piece,' said the man, 'I reckon you'd best turn your hoss round and poddle your way home. You need telling twice?'

'Take your hand off that bridle,' snapped Hemstock. 'You're guilty of harbouring a criminal, every last man-jack of you, do you hear? I can have the law on you for it and I won't hesitate to do it. You'll all go before the justices if you don't deliver that fellow up – I promise you that here and now.'

'We call that a threat where I come from,' said the navvy grasping the bridle. 'Mebbe it's different down on the farm, but not here . . .'

'Thass always the way with him – trample folk down, swack 'em out of his way!' cried a voice that Hemstock knew. He swung round in the saddle and saw that Todd Gault had appeared out of the shadows. His face was white and drawn, with deep pits under the eyes, and he clutched a blanket about his shoulders.

'You insolent ruffian – you think to escape the law by skulking among this rabble?' said Hemstock. He aimed a stroke with his riding-crop at the hand on the bridle. 'Let me at him – get out of my way—'

'You've said one word too many, friend,' hissed the navvy. Others pressed closer, with a rumble of bass voices, and a foul tobacco spit arced through the chequered light. 'Now you want to cut up rough, you get down off that fine hoss and we'll see what you're made of.'

'Aye, pull him down!' cried Todd, making a rush

forward. 'Pull him down, like he've pulled down many a good man . . .!'

Hemstock's horse shied and side-stepped: it could smell danger in the thick, liquor-tainted air. 'Stand out of my way! You frighten the horse,' Hemstock bellowed, swiping about him with his riding-crop; his fury was mingled with a sort of savage exultation, as if he were hitting out at all the frustrations that life had heaped on him. He felt the crop connect with someone's head, and then a hand shot out and snatched it from his grasp. 'Give that back to me! I'll teach you scum to respect property – I'll have the magistrates clear this camp and commit every one of you to the sessions – I warn you!'

A voice rose above the swelling growl: 'Fetch him off that hoss, boys, and give him what for!'

Hemstock felt hands clawing and pulling at his coat, and his horse whinnied its alarm. He swept his riding-hat from his head and beat about him with it; then suddenly gave his mount a whack on the flank, digging in his heels at the same moment. The horse sprang forward. The navvies fell back before its flailing hooves, but one stood his ground and was ridden down. Hemstock heard a great animal howl go up behind him. He urged his panicked mount on with shouts, but it could not see a clear way through the flickering shapes and forms of the camp and would not smarten its pace. At last a gap opened up between two shacks to reveal the heathland beyond, and Hemstock dug in his heels again; but just as they were about to break for the open ground two figures materialized from the darkness directly in their path, lunging at the bridle. The horse reared with a squeal that Hemstock felt as a perceptible vibration through its sweating body; and in a moment he was pitched from the saddle and hit the ground.

He was on his feet within an instant: his sturdy body, at least, was still obedient to his will, though his horse had made a wild bolt for the heath. Damn the skittish beast, he would have it shot tomorrow! The two men who had leapt out he charged at, head lowered, brandishing his great fists; and flinging them both aside, he ran out of the camp and fled across the heath.

The afterglow had almost faded from the sky, and only a thin acid line marked the horizon: he could not see his horse anywhere. Crickets were chirping in the long turf. Throwing a glance over his shoulder, he perceived a black stream of men issuing forth from the camp in pursuit of him; and in the same moment he realized that his fall must have winded him, and that his breath was short.

Shouts and curses, and a wild excited laughter, filled the air. Hemstock stumbled on some rough ground and nearly fell. He had left the lights of the camp far behind, but the hulking shapes were still advancing towards him, closer now, and fanning out like beaters in a shoot. All at once a sort of horror overcame him, not at his danger, but at the fact that he was running away — for the first time in his life, running away! And from a rabble, when the whole work of his life had been to raise himself so far above them that even to speak to them would be an indignity!

He slowed, and stopped, and turned about to face them, his thick legs planted apart.

'My last warning!' he cried, panting. 'Surrender that man, or I have the magistrates clear this camp! I will see every one of you go to the treadmill — my word on it!'

The navvies had gathered around him. There was a muffled seething, like the lowered sound of a pot just before it begins to boil.

'You are cowards,' Hemstock said.

It was Todd Gault who hit him first. He made a sort of blind rush with both hands, the blanket falling from his shoulders; and Hemstock's mind, with a curious detached surprise, registered the fact that there was no strength at all in the young man's arms, and perceived that he must really be ill after all. He had only to put out his own hand to fend Todd off — but then the other blows began to rain down on him.

The navvies beat Hemstock with fists, and kicked at him with their boots; and presently the big farmer was being tossed back and forth inside the ring of men like a ball in a game. One had brought a storm-lantern, and its weird guttering light made the flying, spraying blood look as black as ink. They went on hitting and kicking, with soft guttural sounds, long after Hemstock had ceased to react to the blows, and had become simply an inert form shunted from fist to boot, with his features reduced to an unrecognizable mass of swelled flesh. They drew off at last, leaving him lying motionless on the turf; and the last to turn away, and trudge back across the heath to the camp, was Todd Gault. He stood looking down at Hemstock for some minutes, hugging himself and shivering, his teeth chattering, before leaving the stark scene to the song of the crickets, and the wind in the grass.

Rosa and Christmas Hubbert were up at first light, and set out across the heath to walk to Attleborough. They had twine and timber to buy, and grain for the poultry, and of all these things Christmas' hands were as good a judge as Rosa's eyes. Rosa held the old man's arm to guide him over the uneven ground of the heath, but she noticed that he needed no steering in the right direction, though even she was hard put to it to recognize features in the purple-tinted waste.

'Well, I feel the sun on my face,' he said, 'and where he is, and how high, tell me all I need to know.'

'Thass clouded this mornen,' Rosa said.

'I know: but I can feel his warmth come through the clouds, and I can tell what mander of clouds they are too – silvery and broken, and moving fast afore the wind, east'ards.'

Rosa smiled, for the description was accurate, and squeezed his arm. 'You are so keen – I sometimes think you see more than I.'

'You only see what you want to see,' said Christmas

cryptically; and she could not tell whether he meant the remark as a comment upon her or as a general observation.

The breeze was steady, and bent the long grass in a single direction like brushed kid; but at a distance ahead of them there was a certain eddy and cross-current in the green surface, as if it were interrupted by a tree-stump or outcropping of rock. As they drew nearer, Rosa saw streaks of red.

'Dear God,' she murmured.

'What do you see, Rosa?' said Christmas.

'There's someone lying there – bloodied – lying there like dead . . .'

'Lead me there,' said Christmas, urging her peremptorily forward.

Elias Hemstock was lying on his side. A halo of dried blood stained the grass about his head. The flesh of his face was puffed out like a grotesque fungus, completely obscuring the eyes.

'My good God, it's Hemstock,' Rosa said, dropping to her knees beside the great still form. 'A farmer at Heartsease. He must have been set upon – beaten terrible . . .'

'Heaven forbid that he've been lying out here all the night through,' said Christmas, kneeling too, and gently exploring Hemstock's body with his hands. 'Ach, here's blood . . . I feel him breathing – 'tis very shallow.' He winced as his fingers lightly touched the face. 'It's a wonder he lives! In the name of pity, what have happened here?'

Rosa's hand was tender enough as she put back the matted hair from Hemstock's brow; but her face was grim as she recalled the death in poverty of her parents, one of many unhappy histories associated with this man. 'Yes – a pity, a crying pity – and so is all suffering,' she said. 'And he should know – he've caused enough of it! And now that come back to him!'

She jumped: Christmas Hubbert had reached out and

struck her hand a sharp blow. 'Get you gone, then!' he said, with a harshness in his voice that she had never heard before. 'Go your ways, girl, and I'll tend him alone. Are you so sure that you'll never stand in need of mercy yourself, Rosa, that you can afford to give none?'

Rosa sat back on her heels, startled and stung. 'I didn't mean . . .' She put her hand to her mouth. The thought that Christmas despised her smote upon her sorely.

'Never mind,' Christmas said. 'We must get help for this man – have his wounds dressed. I fear there are bones broke. He is a big man, I reckon?'

'Yes,' Rosa said. 'We couldn't lift him. I – I'll run to the nearest village and bring help, shall I?'

'Aye. I'll stay by him,' Christmas said. As Rosa got up he put out his hand and touched her fingers. 'I shouldn't have struck you, Rosa. I'm sorry.'

'It don't matter,' said she.

'You're a good woman, Rosa,' Christmas said, taking off his neckerchief and using it to bind a wound on Hemstock's wrist. 'If only you wouldn't starve the good in you, and chill the warmth!'

She set off at a run. Presently she had to slow her pace a little, not only to recover her breath but to wipe the tears from her eyes. She hated to cry, and seldom allowed herself to do so; but now she could not stop.

She brought a man with a cart from the nearest village, and they lifted the massive broken figure of Hemstock on to the cart and drove him home to Heartsease, Christmas cradling his head. From time to time the eyelids, buried amongst bruises, fluttered faintly, and the bloated lips twitched; but Hemstock made no sound, and his limbs did not stir.

Marianne had written to her brother Herbert in Norwich, and arranged to go and stay with him temporarily. She was just making a start on packing her things at Plague House when the news about her father was brought by a servant, despatched by Mrs Hemstock, with a message begging Marianne to come at once.

Jed was afield: Charlotte offered to go with her, but Marianne refused with thanks. She flung on a shawl and ran through the village, though at every step it seemed her legs would give way beneath her. At the farm she found her father had been laid upon a sofa downstairs, and a maid was washing the crusted blood from his face, whilst Mrs Hemstock hovered at a distance, her hands pressed to her temples.

'Marianne — thank God you've come — I have been half out of my senses — I shall not survive this, I know I shall not!' Mrs Hemstock moaned on seeing her daughter.

Marianne stood frozen. 'What happened?'

'Oh, Mr Hemstock, this was not well done! Where is that consideration for my nerves that you have always, with trifling exceptions, shown? He didn't return home last night — the servants searched high and low — and then he was found on the heath this morning, just as you see him now, close to where the railway is building. I had my suspicions when he went out: he has become quite fanatical of late about that young troublemaker Gault, and bringing him to justice, and I had a dreadful feeling that he would go and do something foolish — my poor papa the Major always said I had a sixth sense for such things — but as is my wont, I made no complaint, and here is the result!'

'Sarah, you go about your work — I'll do that,' Marianne said to the maid. She took the bowl and cloth and began to wash her father's face. She had thought at first she was going to faint, but that had passed, and she seemed to have hit upon a resource of strength she never knew she had. 'Have you sent for the doctor, Mama?'

'Thompson has gone to Swaffham on the swiftest horse in the stable,' Mrs Hemstock said. 'Not that I have much faith in Dr Bryant, whose own brother is a common farrier, but one must put up with these things in the country . . . Oh, Mr Hemstock, I wish you would only speak one word to me — I really think my nerves will give way altogether if you do not!'

Hemstock did not speak, or move. He remained unconscious. It was as if that iron self-control that had always characterized him had reached a last, terrible expression. Dr Bryant arrived, and Marianne noticed that even this hardy old surgeon blenched at the examination. Afterwards he took Marianne aside, Mrs Hemstock having gone to lie down and bemoan her lot.

'There are several ribs broke; also the radial bone of the right arm. They will heal — his constitution is remarkably strong. That he has survived at all is proof of that . . . I think the cheekbone is fractured, and the bruising of course is extensive. Several teeth are gone. What internal injuries there may be I can't say: the bleeding from the mouth has stopped, which is a goodish sign. Miss Hemstock—'

'Mrs Wintergreen.'

'Mrs Wintergreen, of course, pardon me,' said the doctor. Marianne saw an embarrassed expression flit across his face — he was remembering her history. 'Mrs Wintergreen, I am bound to tell you that the skull also is fractured. This continued unconsciousness is a blessing in a sense, in sparing him an extreme degree of pain; but it may also indicate injury to the brain.'

Marianne bit off a small sound of anguish. 'Is — is it sure? How can you tell?'

'I can't tell, ma'am. Time alone can tell us . . . But I think you should prepare yourself for your father's condition to remain . . . distressing. I say again, it is a miracle that he has lived. And I am afraid that for the moment I can offer nothing more hopeful than that.'

Dr Bryant advised against trying to move Hemstock upstairs: so the parlour that he had furnished so ostentatiously became the sick-room. Marianne sent the groom to Plague House; and then leaving a maid to watch over her father a moment, went to her mother.

'Mama,' she said, 'I've sent to Plague House for my

things. I shall live here, and nurse Papa. I've come home, Mama.'

The news of what had befallen Hemstock soon reached the Hall. Mr Ingamells, having been told of the farmer's intention of going in person to hunt out Todd Gault in the navvies' camp, realized instantly what must have happened, and interrupted his wedding preparations to act. Elias Hemstock was popular enough amongst other large-scale farmers of the district, and Mr Ingamells had no difficulty in swearing them in as special constables, and organizing a mounted swoop on the navvies' camp which would bring the guilty to justice. He communicated this plan to the Hemstock household in a charming little note, in which he added his hope that his worthy friend Mr Hemstock would be well enough to call on him and his new bride as soon as they returned from their marriage trip.

And Hemstock, meanwhile, lay huge and still, as if with typical obstinacy of purpose he had reached the brink of death and then decided to go no further. Marianne was beside him constantly. The two young children, Wade and Margery, tiptoed solemnly in to see their papa as if they were regarding a felled tree; Mrs Hemstock flitted in and out of the room like a hypochondriacal ghost; Herbert, summoned from Norwich, came and gnawed his nails and watched with pale eyes. Only Marianne was always there. She was there to see her father's eyes flick open, and turn slowly about; to see his fingers twitch, and his tongue inch forward to lick his lips; to trickle a little water into his mouth, and presently a little broth, and see him with convulsive effort swallow it down. And she was there to press her lips close to his ear and whisper: 'Papa, it's Marianne. I'm here to look after you. I shall always be here beside you, Papa. We shall never be parted any more. Can you speak, dear? One word – just one word.' She was there, through the day and the ensuing night; and hers was the burden of knowing, as she watched her father's eyes roam blankly about the room, that the last time she had seen him he had refused to speak to her, and now he could speak to her no more.

Jed was restless at Plague House that day. The final departure of Marianne, though prepared for, was hard enough; the sudden circumstances attending it left him feeling as if his brain were numbed. The attack on Hemstock filled him with horror; yet he kept catching himself in the act of neutrally regarding this stroke that had fallen on his bitterest enemy as a work of Nemesis. The instinctive compassion of his nature contended with the ferocity of his memories; and at last, his mind tugged contrary ways like putty, he sought out Charlotte for guidance.

'I don't know what to think, Charlotte,' he said. 'I've hated that man so desperately that the hate have seemed as much a part of myself as my own right hand; and I keep thinking of Father lying in a convict's grave thousands of miles away, and how mebbe now he'll have rest at last — yet I hate myself for thinking it! And I feel deep down I'd give anything to undo what happened on that heath . . . What do you think?'

'I can't remember Father all that well,' Charlotte said after a moment. 'But I remember he was kind — and I remember he had a deep soft voice, and when I used to fall asleep on his lap I could sort of feel his voice going through me while he talked to Mother, like you can feel the waves breaking when you lie in bed at Shipden, and that was so comforting . . . I don't reckon he would have wanted any man to suffer what Mr Hemstock's suffered — any more than you do really, Jed.'

Jed gazed at her soberly. 'You're rare good to me, Charlotte — and patient too . . . Sometimes I look at the world and it all seem so black — like a botched job that shouldn't have been started; and then I look at you and I know thass wrong to think so, for there's always hope for the world when there's you in it.'

'Dear me, Jed, don't,' she said, laughing and colouring, 'I shall get so swell-headed you won't know me.'

'It's true though. I reckon I don't do enough for you – cherish you right. Or only in a selfish way. You don't see Toby enough, and I know how happy that make you when you do. What do you say we go to Shipden for a long stay? The Skeels will put us up.'

'Oh, Jed, it would be lovely!'

'Aye, we'll go. As soon as – well, soon.'

'You're worried about Todd Gault, aren't you?' she said. 'D'you think he – he had a part in what happened to Mr Hemstock?'

'It looks bad for the lad,' Jed said. 'But I can't – I won't believe he could have . . . And I can't turn against him after what he suffered – I just can't . . . But as soon as we find out the truth of the matter, I promise you we'll be off to Shipden. And we'll drag Toby down to the tailor's, and have him measured for wedding clothes.'

Charlotte's eyes shone at him. 'Jed – when the time comes, will you give me away?'

He smiled and kissed her brow. 'I shall be proud to.'

The harvest at Heartsease was almost in, but that night the winds that had bedevilled this summer swept down again to cuff the stooks standing in the fields, and to pepper them with malicious showers of warm rain. Jed was woken from troubled dreams by the flapping of a loose shutter, and lay staring at the roof-beams for some time, listening to the mischief of the wind without, and thinking of Marianne at her father's bedside.

All at once he jumped out of bed. That was not the wind – there was someone knocking at the back door.

He lit a candle and went down. The wind sprang in with a whoop when he opened the door, extinguishing the candle, and for a moment he thought no one was there. Then Todd Gault fell across the threshold.

'I'm sorry, Jed,' Todd gasped, lurching upright again

and grasping Jed's arm for support, 'I'll go away again if you want — only you said if ever I was in trouble — to come here . . . I'm sorry . . .'

Jed fumbled to light the candle again and then held it up to Todd's face.

'My good God,' he said. 'How long have you been like this?'

'I been sick a few days now — can't seem to shake it off,' said Todd. 'Thass only an ague, they don't bother me no more'n a cra'ling fly usually, I don't know why it is . . .'

Jed helped Todd to a chair, where he slumped back, head lolling. He gulped greedily at the water Jed brought him.

'Better,' he panted. 'Got a thirst like I had my jag at Dick Freshwater's the night before.' He uttered a skewed laugh.

Jed lit another candle. He was examining Todd when Charlotte came down.

'Sorry about this, miss,' Todd said, squinting up at her. 'I won't stay — I'll be off directly . . .'

'Todd, you can't go,' Charlotte said, her eyes meeting Jed's.

'What happened, Todd?' Jed said. 'The truth, now.'

Todd put trembling hands to his head as if he feared it would come off. 'It warn't — it warn't meant to happen . . . not like that. The others had all took a drop too much — and I warn't quite myself wi' this damn fever — and he come to the camp, bullyen and threatenen and — oh, God, it warn't meant to happen . . .'

'It did happen, though, Todd,' said Jed. 'I know.'

Todd nodded. There were tears running down his cheeks. 'I know. There was some as said we'd surely killed him, and the magistrates would be down on us . . . And so they were — they came to the camp this even, and by then some of the navvies were beginning to fall out about it, and were ready to turn in the ones that had joined in, and me with 'em, and so I slipped away — I slipped away and ran, and got across country, knowing the authorities would be on my tail . . . I'm on the run, Jed — they're after me good and proper now — I can't hide it from you . . . If you'll just give me one more drink I'll get gone again . . .'

He pitched forward on to the kitchen table, his head on his forearms. He was shivering from head to foot.

Jed felt Charlotte's hand on his arm. 'Charlotte,' he said, 'if we turn him in . . . We can't send him back to gaol now. No matter what he've done — if he was to go to the gaol like this . . .'

Charlotte nodded. 'I'll go make up a room,' she said.

They put Todd to bed. He was wandering in and out of delirium, coming to himself to protest that he'd be on his way in a minute and then sinking down again. Having removed Todd's clothes, Jed stuffed them in a sack and tied it. 'We'd best burn these,' he said.

'He must have caught it in that camp,' Charlotte said. 'They say it's so filthy there the men are always going down with fevers . . . I wish we could help him better!'

Todd was wriggling about in the bed. His skin was the colour of porridge, and there were purple blotches on his chest and stomach.

'I wonder if we could risk summoning the doctor,' Jed said. 'But I won't turn him in — I won't! I can't change sides now.'

Charlotte bent to mop the sweat from Todd's forehead. 'We'll look after him,' she said.

Charlotte and Jed sat up with Todd throughout that night. For much of the time he was raving: he writhed, cursed, giggled, plucked the covers from the bed. Then there was a period of calm, and Jed fell into a doze in a chair. When he woke it was daylight, and Charlotte was washing Todd down, having stripped the sweat-soiled sheet from the bed.

'You must be worn out, Charlotte,' Jed said. 'Go down and have some breakfast.'

'You go,' she said. 'I'll just finish this. I think he's resting a little easier.'

Except for a few minutes when Jed persuaded her to eat something, Charlotte stayed at Todd's bedside all day, laving away the sweat that poured off him, giving him water, replacing the tossed bedclothes. The young man still alternated between deep, exhausted sleep and fits of feverish talking — showers of wild words in which the names of Hemstock and Jed recurred. It was impossible to tell how much of this was unconscious delirium, how much the unburdening of a troubled mind. But at one point in the day Todd opened his clear boyish eyes and looking straight at Jed said: 'D'you know — d'you know, Jed, some of the village lads were starting to say of you that — that you were just a meddler, come here from the town, nice and comfy yourself, trying to set things right when you didn't really know what twas like in Heartsease and what the young fellers are really thinking . . . But I wouldn't have it! I told 'em so — you've always been a good friend to me and I'll always stand by that — always . . .' He squeezed Jed's arm, then sank back again.

'It's just the fever talking,' Charlotte said.

'Is it, Charlotte?' Jed said, looking on the sick youth with bleak eyes. 'Is it?'

At last, with the sun going down, Todd seemed to be sleeping peacefully, and Jed prevailed on Charlotte to come downstairs for a rest. He ensconced her in an easy chair and brought her beef tea.

'I'll go up again soon,' she said. 'Just shut my eyes for a few minutes . . .'

'No,' Jed said, 'I'll watch him this evening, my dear. You've had enough.' He gnawed his lip and stared at the ashes that the wind was whirling and scattering in the grate. 'I still wonder whether I should get a doctor . . . We'll see how he is tonight.'

Charlotte did not answer: she had fallen asleep. Jed got up and took the cup from her hand and smoothed down her hair. Then he went out to meet Ben Catbush and the harvest workers returning from the fields. He stayed watching the sun descend below the roofs of Heartsease. What had he done for the place, in fact? Were all his good intentions worthless, for example, beside the unpretentious kindness of Charlotte?

He returned to the house deep in thought and went upstairs to check on Todd. He found the bedroom door standing open, and the bed empty.

He called Ben and woke Charlotte, and they searched the house and the farm buildings. There was no sign.

'Oh, if only I hadn't gone to sleep!' Charlotte said. 'I never heard a thing . . . Can he have got far, in his condition?'

Jed shook his head. 'No telling. He must have wandered off, not knowing what he was doing — you saw how he gets those fits of strength when the fever's on him . . . You stay here, my dear, in case he comes back. Ben and me'll search the village.'

It was a long and wearisome business in the rapidly falling dark. At last it was Ben who came upon the news they sought. Todd's errant footsteps had led him to the parish constable's door, where he had brokenly declared that he wanted to give himself up, before collapsing in delirium again. The constable had gone to Mr Ingamells, who had ordered Todd to be lodged overnight at the workhouse infirmary before being committed to Norwich gaol in the morning. Todd was in the untender hands of the authorities now, and there was nothing more Jed could do.

There was a certain guilty relief in Jed's mind, alongside sadder feelings, as he trudged back to Plague House to tell the news to Charlotte. In a way he was glad that Todd had given himself up: he suspected that the young man had done it in a lucid moment in order to spare Charlotte and himself the trouble of harbouring him. But what was there for Todd now? Jed fretted, conscious of the gathering tide of pain in the world and his own helplessness to turn it back. Mr Veazey had warned him against taking the troubles of the world on his shoulders — perhaps he had been right. Perhaps it was time to turn his back and tend his own garden. There was always Charlotte — the one bright ray in a scene shrouded with disillusion and defeat: Charlotte to be loved and cared for, and probably in time Charlotte and Toby's children. Yes, such must be his role, and a worthy one after all. It was a good thought.

Back home he found Charlotte in the scullery boiling up the sheets from Todd's bed in the copper. He briefly told her what had happened.

'Won't they treat him — well, mercifully?' she said.

Jed hesitated. 'Perhaps,' he said. 'Well, my dear, leave that now. You look tired. It's out of our hands. It's just you and me again. Thank God.'

Jed had only just risen next morning, and was about to go out and take a turn in the harvest-field before breakfast, when he had a visitor: Marianne.

Her hair and eyelashes were damp from a shower. Jed had time only for a momentary pang at the sight of her beauty, incandescent in the dark hall, before she burst out: 'I didn't want to come here, Jed. But I need to know the truth. The constable came this morning to tell us about Todd Gault. Apparently he was sick with a fever when they took him and he rambled about having hidden out at Plague House. In a stable, he said. And that you knew nothing about it. I must know the truth — now.'

There was something different about her, he thought. In just a couple of days she looked older. The sparkle had winked out; but a certain dignity had come to the fore. He thought of this, while his lips struggled to frame a lie that would not come. For Jed could not lie. His nature, indeed, had too much of truth in it for his own peace. He shook his head.

'You *did* know of it!' Marianne slowly breathed. 'You hid him here — you hid Todd Gault in this house, knowing what he'd done!' She took a step forward, and Jed braced himself as for a blow across the face; but Marianne merely fixed him with a rigid stare in a way more terrible. 'You knew what he'd done to my father — and yet you took him in . . .! Would you care to see my father, Jed? Would you like to see how he lies there, broken, paralysed, lost in a living death that makes true death seem a blessing?'

'Todd was sick,' Jed said. 'A very sick man.'

Marianne suddenly wrenched at the wedding-band she still wore. It fitted tightly, and a livid red weal appeared as she dragged the ring from her finger and hurled it across the hall. 'Sick!' she cried. 'I feel sick and soiled at wearing this — sick and soiled at the thought that I ever married you!' She rubbed her hands convulsively up and down her sides. 'I feel as if I shall never be clean again!'

'I can't go against my loyalties, Marianne,' Jed said dully. 'My loyalties have always been with Todd and his kind. Thass the way I am.' And as she continued to stare at him and wipe her hands as if he were a thing loathsome beyond bearing he added bitterly: 'Loyalties, Marianne. You wouldn't know about those. I believe there was some mention of them when you put on that ring, but of course you didn't let that stop you.'

There was terrible hurt, recrimination and heart-sickness in the air of that old hall: the very sunlight, fitfully glancing through the leaded window, seemed to flinch at it. Marianne's breast heaved. 'I was afraid of the day when I would stop loving you,' she said. 'I never thought I would see the day when I would begin to hate you.'

'Well, it's variety anyhow,' said Jed. 'And that's what you want, isn't it? Variety at any price.'

Still she steadily regarded him. 'I'm going back to my father now, Jed. He needs me. And I won't forgive you, you know. Ever. All your talk of loyalties won't change it—'

'Go then!' he cried. 'And don't expect me to shed a tear for you or him . . .!'

'Please — please stop.' It was Charlotte's voice. Jed turned to see her descending the staircase. Half-way down she leant against the banister, hugging herself with her arms crossed over her breast, looking curiously shrunken. 'Don't shout — please don't.' She put a trembling hand up to her brow and closed her eyes. 'It's awful to hear it . . . and I've got such a pain. My head — my head's so bad . . .'

With terror at his heart Jed carried Charlotte back to her bedroom and laid her down. A shaft of sunlight pointed out the hectic flush on her cheeks, and two sharp indentations of pain between her eyebrows. Jed sent Ben on horseback for Dr Bryant. Marianne quietly stayed until the doctor arrived, and then as quietly slipped out.

Jed paced the landing while the doctor made his examination. The skittish wind had risen again, a purposeless idiot wind, shaking rain clouds across the sun like a dog worrying a rag. He studied the raindrops on the landing window, and seemed to feel madness rising in his brain.

The doctor was not long. He accepted Jed's offer of a tot of brandy and blew his nose on a silk handkerchief.

'Has she been in any infected places?' he said. 'Norwich, perhaps, the poorer parts. A workhouse. Sick visiting—'

'No,' said Jed. 'She . . .' He thought of Todd, and it was as if a clap of thunder broke over his head. 'Yes,' he said huskily, 'it's possible.'

'Well, anyhow, the fever's taken hold. She's in a lot of pain. I've administered an opiate, but you understand that is a palliative, not a cure. We must wait and see. Keep the windows open, give lots of fluid, preferably milk. I'll return this evening.'

The old doctor picked up his hat, then paused at Jed's wild look.

'Do something,' Jed murmured.

'Sir?'

'You've got to do something!'

'Mr Wintergreen, your sister is in nature's hands. We must let the fever take its course. I have seen many typhus cases this year, though chiefly in the places I have mentioned. We must wait and see.' He glanced uneasily again at Jed's face, and took his leave.

The day that followed was formless, endless, a horrifying sample of infinity. Jed did not leave Charlotte's side. He did not eat or drink. The universe contained nothing but Charlotte's suffering and his own mind, and the latter could do nothing but agonizedly observe the former. He poured water between her cracked lips, he mopped her brow from which the sweat ran in streams, and when a delirious fit came on he held her tightly in his arms and murmured broken consolation to her; but in all this he could not reach her, only try to pursue her down the long corridor of feverish pain. At some point in this amorphous stretch of hellish experience the doctor was there again, and was mixing her a sleeping-draught; at some point then it was night, and Jed was still leaning over the bed, with Charlotte's hand, hot as a live coal, clasped in his. Ben was there for a time, and the little maid, both imploring him to get some rest and saying they would watch over her, and he was distractedly saying: 'You don't understand . . . I've got to take care of her – she is my everything, you see – d'you see?' And then there was a pale light in the room where there had been darkness, and Charlotte was looking at him.

'Poor Jed,' she said weakly, 'you must be tired.'

He shook his head, and lifted her to give her a drink of milk. 'I shan't leave you,' he said.

'Poor Jed,' she said again, with a tremendous sigh. 'Go down just for a little while.'

At last, when she was sleeping again, Ben persuaded Jed to go down and eat. He swallowed a morsel of bread, almost choked, gave it up and went out to the yard to look at the day. A vagrant wind was still at large, and driving shoals of rain-cloud across the sun: at each swift change of light the level fields seemed to change not only colour but form, to swell and bristle, so that all the earth wore a bewitched and eldritch look. Rain began to spit down, and Jed went back into the house, moving like a man who has only just learnt the use of his limbs. His body, indeed, felt foreign and impervious: he wanted to take into it all the pain that Charlotte was feeling, would welcome the pain like a lover if only it could be lifted from her.

The new day grew old, and Charlotte was delirious again. 'Jed — where's Jed?' she moaned, and turned about in the bed with grotesque clockwork motions.

'I'm here,' he said, clasping her. 'Charlotte, my dear one, I'm here.' Then the stiff movements stopped, and she was curled into a ball and giggling — an awful sound, awful in its empty approximation to her real laugh, so cheerful and straightforward. Finally she slept again, blotched and haggard, in the crook of Jed's arm, whilst with the other he clenched his fist till the nails drew blood from the palm, and inwardly railed to see his gentle Charlotte tossed and scourged thus by a power greater than she. Greater in strength only; for from the core of his soul he cursed the mover behind such a world.

The doctor was present, and was ordering warm bricks to be laid at her feet. He bent to study Jed's face. 'Sleep, man,' he said, not unkindly. 'You're at the end of your tether.' Jed did not bother to answer.

Night was in place again, and Jed was still at Charlotte's side. He could not tell whether her ravings, her convulsions and retchings, were any worse: it was all one nightmare continuum. The first staccato notes of birdsong were audible above the wind when Charlotte came out of her delirium and lay very flat and still, breathing hoarsely, her eyes wandering around the room and lighting at last on her brother.

'Jed — will you write to Toby?' she said, in a voice in which only the consonants were really audible.

'Of course,' he said.

'I meant to write to him today — I mean yesterday. What day is it?'

'Thursday — no . . . I don't know.'

'It doesn't matter . . . But if you could write to him . . .'

'I will.' Jed bent to wipe her damp face.

'Poor Jed.' She reached up to touch his cheek, but could not manage it. 'How tired you look. You won't forget . . . about Toby . . . will you?'

'I promise. But you'll be seeing him yourself soon.'

A faint smile appeared on her face. 'That would be lovely.'

Dr Bryant was there again after breakfast, and this time he stayed. Still Jed did not sleep. The day was swept again by sudden overcloudings, which periodically cast the room into a curiously oppressive darkness, as if some vast trap had closed over the house, and clamped it to the earth. Charlotte was worse. The doctor gave her another opiate, but merely shook his head at Jed's questions, and stood by the bed gravely regarding the girl who looked too insubstantial for the weight of agony she bore.

The wind whistled down the chimney, and scattered rain against the window-panes. All at once Charlotte arched her back in the bed, and her tortured eyes sought Jed's. 'Is that the tide?' she said in a whisper.

'No, no. Just the wind. The wind, and a shower of rain.'

'I thought — it was the tide — the sea,' she gasped. Her body made another lurch upward, as if a giant hand had seized and shaken her: there were tears on her cheeks. Jed gave a cry, animal in its note.

'Be calm, Mr Wintergreen,' said Dr Bryant, gripping his shoulder. 'You must be calm . . .'

The wind hooted again, and with a last brief struggle Charlotte died.

* * *

Ben Catbush and the maid were waiting on the landing, and their faces blanched as Jed's cry rang through the house: 'Help me! Oh, help me!'

The doctor presently came forth from the room, shook his head at the two servants and, after a few words of advice, left. Ben went in to his master, while the maid went down to give the news to a knot of people from the village who had come on hearing of Charlotte's illness and were waiting still in the rainy yard.

Others came during the day, as the news spread, to offer condolences: Dick Freshwater, the Widow Thorne, the Rev. Mr Bouverie, Mr Ringrose, many villagers; Marianne also. None saw Jed. He was in the sick-room, stretched face down across Charlotte's body, while Ben stood silent by him. Later Pierce Coppinger, pale and wind-blown, came from the Hall to see his friend.

Eight or nine hours had passed, and it was evening, before Jed was persuaded to lift his head, and get to his feet, and leave his sister at last. Ben took his arm and steadied him downstairs. The village laying-out woman was quietly waiting in the shadowed hall.

'Do you sit yourself down,' Ben said, 'and I'll get you some tea with a nip in it.'

Jed shook his head. He went outside to the yard. A horse grunted in the stable at the sound of his footsteps. The rain had stopped. He opened the gate and went out to his fields.

The rain and wind had dishevelled the stooks, and the corn yet to be cut: it would not be a good harvest. The scene thrust itself upon his vision with insistent detail, as if it recognized no hierarchy of significance. He had just watched his sister die of a disease caught from the man he had brought into the house, and here were ears of wheat and poppies and boot-marks and gateposts and raindrops all demanding to be seen by the same eyes.

A thrush suddenly flew up, so close that he felt the air stirred by its wings, and perched on the hawthorn hedge hard by. There it cocked its head and regarded him with a sharp, hostile look, as if it asked him how he came there. He did not know how he came there: his mind, treading a narrow causeway above an abyss of insane grief, lightless, bottomless, could only grope back towards the past. The cruel deaths of his mother and father, the wreck of a family, the workhouse, the poverty and exile, seemed comprehensible only in terms of some ultimate vindication — a vindication that Abel Jex's legacy had seemed to offer. And it had brought him back to Heartsease, and to a failed marriage, and to the deathbed of the sister who was everything he held most dear. All his life Jed had been preoccupied with justice; now, his spirit stranded in a desolation that stretched featureless from horizon to horizon, he reviewed his past and present in a last frantic search for some manifestation of justice that would save him from despair.

But none appeared: and existence only glittered back at him like a cold pool.

He turned back to the house. Smoke was rising from the kitchen chimney. As he came to the yard the thought of Charlotte lying within hit him like a cudgel and, lost, he broke down.

The uneven surface of the yard was covered with puddles. The reflections in these, of sky and roof and trees, were clear and faithful yet oddly alien: it was like looking through a hole into another, subtly different world. Jed crouched down. 'Oh, let me into that world!' he softly cried. 'This one's awry — all awry!'

At last he forced himself into an upright position, slowly as an old man. In the sky above Plague House he saw that the sun had triumphed. Dark ramparts of cloud were being rent by its full beams, and consumed from within by its penetrating fire, and were toppling to nothingness; a scavenger wind pillaged the cloud-wrack, and like a barbaric conqueror the sun with a flourish drew blood-red streaks across the ruin it had created.

Chapter Seventeen

Pierce's Dreams

Captain Coppinger was walking along the seafront at Torbay with his friend Captain Beeny when the curious feeling struck him.

It was as if a wave had broken over him and receded, a wave of human unhappiness. He stood his ground, stricken and gasping, until Captain Beeny brought him back to himself with a vigorous shake of his arm.

'Coppinger. Coppinger, speak, man. What's amiss?'

Captain Coppinger mopped his nut-brown brow with his handkerchief. 'Nothing, Beeny. It's nothing.'

'Do you take me for a fool, Coppinger?'

'What, sir?'

'I repeat, do you take me for a fool, to be told that there is nothing amiss, when you look as if someone had walked over your grave? A man must be a blockhead not to see it.'

'Why did you say that, Beeny? — about someone walking over my grave,' Captain Coppinger said, not in his usual bark, but almost tremulously.

'Figure of speech,' said Captain Beeny. 'No more. If it gives you an instant's uneasiness, Coppinger, I withdraw it — I trample upon it!'

'No,' Captain Coppinger said. 'That is exactly what it felt like.'

Captain Beeny frowned. 'Coppinger, I am going to dictate. Call me impudent if you like, but I am going to dictate to you, and damn the consequences. You are going to come with me into that inn, Coppinger, and take a stiff tot. And I won't hear you say no.'

But Captain Coppinger did not say no. They went into

the inn, and took a stiff tot together in a bay window overlooking the blue sea.

Captain Coppinger said: 'Do you recall, Beeny, when we were midshipmen on the *Puissant*—'

'Coppinger, I am insulted!'

'What the devil is the matter now?'

'The matter is this, sir: that you could even suggest that I need to be reminded of a time which is branded on my memory by reason of your gallantry – your chivalry, Coppinger – in protecting a boy smaller than yourself from that bullying lieutenant whose name escapes me but whose habit of making water in the midshipmen's hats will remain with me till my dying day. As will the sight of your emptying it over his head and doubling him up with a smart left, Coppinger – God bless you!'

'Beeny, your hand.'

They shook hands, and Captain Coppinger went on after a pull at his grog: 'Well, you remember that time well, Beeny; so you'll remember when we sailed out of Port Royal and left poor old Tommy Ramm there in the hospital. We had scarcely got beyond the harbour mouth when a chill came over us all – you remember?'

'Like yesterday!'

'And someone said: "That's poor Tommy Ramm – that's Tommy Ramm dying." And so we later found it was – he had died in the hospital at that moment . . . Superstition, of course, some might say.'

'Not at all,' said Captain Beeny. 'Common sense . . . Good God, Coppinger, you don't mean to suggest—'

'Not so bad as that,' said Captain Coppinger, shaking his head. 'But I felt something, Beeny, and it makes me worried for my boy again. I told you he leaves Heartsease Hall this week: he wrote me that he may go abroad, may stay in Norwich, may do this or that, all wild words and sad. And I'm chilled . . . If only I might see him, and shake him by the hand, and assure myself that all's well!'

'Coppinger,' said Captain Beeny, pointing his clay pipe like a pistol, 'I'm going to dictate again. There's only one thing to do. You must order him to come home.'

'What do you mean, sir, order?' spluttered Captain Coppinger.

'I mean order – direct – command!'

'Devil take it, Beeny, you know very well I have never ordered my son to do anything in his life! I simply do not believe in it, any more than I believe in those gross impostures my doctor attempts on me. I will not do it.'

'You will, sir,' Captain Beeny said. 'Out of love for your boy. You know all's not well: I have read it in your face every moment these last weeks. It cuts me, sir: I don't care who knows it. Bring him home, Coppinger. Bring him home.'

Mr Ingamells and Miss Fontayne were off to London to be married: the carriage stood before the door, and they were saying their goodbyes. Pierce was to remain one more day at the Hall: he would return to Norwich by carrier in the morning.

'Success attend your endeavours in the future, Mr Coppinger!' Mr Ingamells said, shaking Pierce's hand. 'I speak of artistic rather than worldly success, of course, for that is a vain snare – though too often fallen into, alas, in these acquisitive times!' He paused while the footman handed him his kid gloves, great-coat, travelling-shawl, silver flask, and gold-headed cane. 'Well, it has been a great pleasure, sir: I shall always remember our agreeable conversations, when I contemplate your work hanging on the walls of this unpretentious pile to which I am so foolishly attached. Goodbye!'

Mr Ingamells kissed his daughter, and Miss Fontayne did likewise, remarking, 'I declare, Beatrice, you must be quite relieved to see us go: you shall have the place to yourself, and a little peace at last. Really, getting married involves so many preparations that I am quite exhausted: I almost envy you your unattached state, Beatrice dear!

Well, I'll see you in a fortnight's time — when I shall be your stepmother, goodness me, how quaint! — but of course, in spite of the necessary changes in our relation, we'll be the best of friends!'

Miss Ingamells had presented her cheek to be kissed with the movement and the smile of an automaton; and in the same way she stood waving her hand as the carriage swept away.

'Mr Coppinger,' she said when it was out of sight, 'have you finished your packing?'

'Very nearly,' Pierce said. 'I was just going to finish it now.'

'Perhaps you will walk with me this afternoon, one last time.'

'I shall be glad to.'

He watched her go with a sort of stiff glide into the house, her head up as if she were balancing something on the crown. She had been like this ever since the abrupt departure of Alexander Deacon. Pierce had strong suspicions that something had been said between them then: even stronger suspicions of what was being felt beneath Beatrice's frozen exterior. He was not easy at the thought of her being alone here for the next fortnight, but he had to go. His term of employment was up — and he needed, besides, to get away. Far, far away from Heartsease.

Yesterday he had been to Plague House to offer consolation to Jed in his bereavement, but how could he offer consolation to the literally inconsolable? Jed had shaken his friend's hand and told him always to write and visit, but he had hardly been there at all: Pierce had felt as if he were touching a ghost.

In the afternoon he walked with Miss Ingamells, her dog padding along beside. The bad weather had broken at last, and the sun shone; and often Miss Ingamells turned her painted-doll smile on him and said: 'Isn't it lovely, Mr Coppinger? Isn't it lovely today?' They walked beneath the chestnut trees around the church, and presently she suggested they go in. This lofty Norman building of flint was impressive, but Pierce had little enthusiasm for ecclesiastical architecture. What attracted his eye within were the signs still tenuously linking the church to the life of the community – the Free Seat for the poor at the rear, the wig-stand from the days when gentlemen would slip off their perukes for comfort, the long hooked pole that was stored in the nave in case of fire in the village, when it was used to pull down burning thatch. But already these wore a museum air.

They went into the chancel, where effigied tombs commemorated lords of the medieval manor of Heartsease. Beatrice ran her hand along the cold sculptured stone and abruptly said: 'Have you been disappointed in love, Mr Coppinger?'

Pierce did not blush or prevaricate: self-consciousness was extinct in him now. 'Yes, I have,' he quietly said.

Beatrice's eyes swivelled round to his, and she gave a single listless chuckle. 'I also!' she said. 'Isn't it comical? Isn't it the most comical thing?'

'It is hard to regard it as such,' Pierce said. 'But . . . we are not the first, nor the last, I suppose.'

'But there is the horror of it!' Beatrice cried, suddenly pulsing with energy. 'It is so frighteningly commonplace! That is what seems to bring madness creeping up – the thought that we are mere specks, no more – all our heart-burnings amounting only to a penny candle in an eternity of harsh daylight . . . Even these old Norman frights buried here – dreadful robbers and murderers I dare say – must have yearned and sighed in their day, and felt their sufferings so keenly that it seemed the whole world resounded to the ache of them like the twangings of an almighty harp – and yet what is left?' She rapped upon the lid of an altar-tomb. 'A dull echo!'

She fell silent, and remained so throughout their walk back to the Hall. It seemed very quiet in those huge frigid rooms without Mr Ingamells and his bride, and Pierce feared that dinner would be but a melancholy meal. Miss

Ingamells, however, determined otherwise. She wore a watered-silk evening gown, as if for a grand occasion; and as soon as they were seated she began to talk. If her smile had formerly resembled that of an automaton, now in her unearthly vivacity she was the automaton set going, and overwound too. Her talk had often taken the form of short sprays of nervous flippancy: this was a stream. Pierce tried to reply, but he soon found he was not listened to, and gave it up, letting the words whirl past him. Then she burnt her fingers on a serving-dish, and Pierce started up.

'No no Mr Coppinger it's of no account it doesn't hurt in the least – see?' She held up her hand, high above her head. 'It takes a good deal more than that to hurt me I'm sure and just to prove it I shall play and the most difficult pieces too it will be vastly tedious for you but there you are a captive audience and after all you know tomorrow you shall be free of me for ever and ever amen.'

In the drawing-room she played, fiercely and brilliantly, the most taxing piano pieces one after the other with scarcely a rest between them, her shoulders hunched, her mouth drawn up in a grimace as if she tasted the splendid music like vinegar. Pierce was too deeply disturbed to attend to the barrage of melody, let alone applaud or compliment her; and he had the curious feeling that this was a ritual of private significance, in which his role as audience was entirely nugatory.

Beatrice ceased playing as abruptly as she had begun: sat staring before her for a moment; then rose, and saying, 'Good night, Mr Coppinger,' left him.

He made his way up to bed shortly afterwards, having tried and failed to induce sleepiness with a book. In the passage leading to his bedroom he was arrested by the sight of light coming from the attic room where he had painted Alexander Deacon's portrait. Going to investigate, he found Beatrice there. She had lit the room brightly with a dozen candles, which were so arranged that the unfinished portrait of Alexander, still on its easel, was its glowing centrepiece.

Beatrice twitched at the sound of Pierce's footstep, but did not turn to face him. 'Were you ever paid for this picture, Mr Coppinger?' she said.

'No. But then, it isn't completed.'

'Do you wish to take it away with you?'

Pierce thought of Marianne and Jed, the broken marriage. 'No,' he said. 'I don't care ever to see it again, Miss Ingamells.'

She chuckled: made a sudden movement forward, and picked up the painting in her arms. 'Poor Alexander!' she said. 'Here he is banished to an attic of the house he thought would be his one day. Isn't it a pity?' Her smile now was that of a little girl with a rather naughty idea. 'Let us show him the old place one more time. Let us give him a last tour of his lost inheritance, so his painted eyes can feast on his lost dream! Bring the candles, Mr Coppinger!'

Feeling as if he were in a dream himself, Pierce followed Beatrice Ingamells as, bearing the portrait of Alexander aloft in her arms like a priest with an icon, she glided about the bedrooms of the Hall. She turned the painting this way and that, displaying to the handsome face sketched thereon every grandiose detail, every ceiling-rose and damask curtain and tapestry and gilded chair. 'It's all very beautiful, isn't it, Alexander?' Beatrice crooned. 'And you wanted it very badly, didn't you? Poor Alexander. You lost. And Father won again – he always does!'

They came at last to the master bedroom. Miss Ingamells propped the portrait up on the marble washstand, and taking the candelabra from Pierce's hand studied the picture closely.

'Well, my dear Alexander,' she said at length, 'there it all is: but you are not wanted here, I'm afraid, any more than I am. And so you must go, my darling. I'm sorry!' All at once she thrust the candelabra forward so that the flames licked at the surface of the painting. Brown scorch-marks sprang upward, scarring Alexander's face, and the varnish began to bubble and swelter like the skin of a roast.

'Miss Ingamells, please, not here,' Pierce said, breaking free of his dream-like paralysis and starting forward. 'It will burn fiercely — it's too dangerous.'

She warded him off with an upraised hand, while with the other she continued to apply the candle-flames to the picture, so that the face on it began to blur and distend. Her smile was like the grin of an animal in pain. 'It does burn, doesn't it — wonderfully!' she said excitedly. 'Oh, Alexander, see how your beauty perishes — but it's better this way, isn't it, than waiting for the slow years to do the work? Ah, I still would have loved you, though, Alexander — even then . . .' Suddenly she picked up the crackling picture by its base, and advanced her face so close to it that a stray curl of hair was singed. 'Alexander, I've had the most marvellous idea! You always loved to laugh — you said I was entertaining — and this one is most irresistibly piquant. Here is this house that you and Father have been quarrelling over, here is this precious inheritance that all the fuss is about — and neither of you shall have it!' With febrile speed she bore the burning canvas over to the bed and swept it back and forth across the rich brocade hangings. 'I shall deny it to both of you, Alexander! Isn't that comical? Isn't that an even better jest than the one I told you in the park that day? Not you, not Father, not his little wife — none of you shall have it!'

An acrid smell filled the air as the bed-hangings smouldered and took fire. Pierce made a dart at Beatrice, intending to knock the picture from her grasp and drag her without ceremony away; but she was alert to him, and too quick. She dodged and skimmed past him, and ignoring his cries lifted the canvas, which the oils were now causing to flame like a great torch, to the long window-curtains.

'Please — Beatrice, I beg you, stop, come away for God's sake—'

'Go now, Mr Coppinger!' she cried, as bluish flares began to crawl like panicked rats up the curtains. 'Your heart is not here — this is not your quarrel. You've been kind to me: be kind once more, and go: you have a life, take it!'

He made another lunge at her, but she eluded him: the haze in the air from the heat, the dancing fire-reflection in the silk of her gown, the stinging of his eyes caused by the smoke, all made her into an insubstantial, diaphanous figure, flitting hither and thither brandishing her weird torch, and calling forth a voice of roar and crackle wherever she touched, as if she were a dark fairy waking the house to destructive life. Pierce flung up his hands to cover his face as there was a sudden burst of flame from the bed-hangings that smote him like a dragon's breath; and when he looked again Beatrice was gone.

He ran out to the landing and shouted down the stairwell for the servants; then turned to pursue the distracted woman, who had left a trail of burning fragments of canvas along the passage. He flung open the doors of bedrooms, and came upon smouldering hangings and rugs, but no Beatrice. He could hear the sound of her dog barking, and tried to locate it in the smoke that was filling the passage. Then he blundered into a cabinet with a whipcrack of pain at his hip; staggered and groped blindly for some moments; heard the barking again, and almost by chance put his hand upon the handle of a door that he realized to be that of Beatrice's room.

As he flung open the door there was an inrush of air that pressed him forward like a tail wind, and at the same moment the fire within leaped up with a hoarse growl as if to seize him. Through streaming eyes he beheld Beatrice's own paintings strewn about the room and burning like beacons: flames capered too from bed and drapes and were beginning to shoot from the floor-matting, while scraps of paper and oily canvas swirled and spiralled in the air like fiery hornets. The smoke was already choking him, with a sensation as if his lungs were squeezed flat like closed bellows; but he found breath to cry, 'Beatrice! Come now, for God's sake!'

A low, almost inconsequent laugh startled him, and he turned to see Beatrice, her face shining with tears, emerging from her clothes-closet bearing in her arms a frothy mass of gowns, lace and silk and satin, to which the firelight gave a glamorous aureole as of legendary treasure. Beatrice was grinning as she heaped the rich stuffs on to the floor and then began plucking them up and tossing them round the room, her bare white arms swinging in a wide arc. Pierce smelt the familiar odour of the turpentine they used in their painting, and saw that the gowns too were burning: the oil-soaked frills and flounces bloomed into delicate petals of intensest flame as they billowed upwards and sank with a soft palpitating roar.

'Get away, Mr Coppinger!' Beatrice cried, flourishing a burning shawl, and revealing fingers scorched to the blackness of tar. 'This is not your affair. This is my own self — my own self, at last!'

A crack sounded at the window as a pane of glass shattered: the air funnelling through the hole made a shrieking note above the tumult of the fires, which pulsed with one motion towards it in a great yearning of flame. Beatrice disappeared again into the closet. Pierce heard the voices of the servants down the passage, and ran out to them.

The manservants had brought up pails of water and sand, and heavy blankets and sacking from the stable, and had begun beating out the smouldering fires in the other rooms. 'Miss Ingamells is in here,' Pierce said. 'Quickly — soak that sacking — I think I can get to her.' He flung the wet sacking around his head and shoulders, pressing a corner of it over his nose and mouth with one hand, and shaking off the protests of the footman darted back into Beatrice's bedroom.

A wall of heat hit him. The many fires were meeting, pouncing upon each other and then embracing with an exhilarated whoosh up to the ceiling. Within a handful of seconds, before Pierce's smarting eyes, they had become a single blaze: the scene had ceased to be a room on fire and had become a fire in which a few shimmering remnants of a room remained. He could feel his own clothes scorching despite the wet sacking as he lurched into the closet and shouted Beatrice's name. Figures surrounded him – hanging gowns and cloaks, sheathed in flame: no Beatrice.

She must be somewhere in the bedroom, but nothing was to be seen in the dense smoke. He felt now as if he were breathing pure flame rather than air, and could not bear it much longer: the servants were shouting to him from the doorway. Then he thought he glimpsed a movement on the floor by the bed. He beat a way through the fire towards it, and found himself completely blinded by the smoke. Guided by touch alone he flung the sacking around the prostrate body by the bed: in fiery darkness and pain he dragged himself and the feebly struggling bundle in the direction of the doorway. Hands reached out to grasp him and pull him clear: the fire seemed to relinquish him with a great frustrated exhalation, and he fell breathless on the floor of the landing.

A wet blanket was being thrown around him, and blessedly cool water trickled down his face. He forced his eyelids open with a tearing sensation as of opening a wound: saw the agitated faces of the footman and a maid, kneeling on either side of him, and figures with pails hastening back and forth in the red-lit background.

'Miss Ingamells,' he coughed, 'see to her—'

The footman shook his head, and Pierce threw a wild glance at the bundle beside him. It was her dog, Goldie, that he had dragged forth from the blazing room.

With a baffled cry Pierce staggered to his feet. 'One more try,' he gasped, reeling like a drunkard, but just then the maid screamed and pointed. A woman's silhouette appeared in the doorway of the bedroom and seemed to waver there for a moment in the furnace glow. Then she was thrust forward as if the fire had spewed her out. She came hurtling with a long thin scream across the landing, her clothes one luminous ball of flame, her hair on fire. She hit the banister with hideous force and went over; and unconsciousness came upon Pierce just too late to shut out the sight of Beatrice Ingamells plunging down the stairwell into darkness like a fluttering burning bird.

Pierce sank into a strange subterranean world of dreams and pain intermingled. When he was conscious, a nightmare of pain from his burns descended on him, and made him long for oblivion; when he slept, he dreamt of pain, of the rawness of flame on skin, of Miss Ingamells plunging torch-like out of life. It was as if fire had taken possession of his mind, and was consuming it from within. Only a few external circumstances penetrated the flickering ring of horrors that encircled him: the kindness of the Hall servants, especially the superior manservant of whom he had always been terrified; the smile of the doctor who administered strong opiates that dulled the pain but garishly intensified the dreams, and to whom he drowsily said, his voice coming out slurred and loose: 'I say, you'll be making an opium fiend of me at this rate — like — whatsisname — the poet — Coleridge, that's it — In Xanadu did Kubla Khan a something thingummy decree . . .' And then there was the sight of his own hands, swathed in white bandages, which he lifted up and regarded as if they were something not connected with him at all, and about which he felt some nameless anxiety that his mind could not place. And then there was an impression of sunlight and fresh air, and of a carriage, and of himself being put inside it; of the drawn and furrowed face of Jed looking at him; of another face, so beautiful that he felt like weeping childishly on seeing it. But in all of this he grew less and less certain what was reality and what was dream, for he seemed to slip imperceptibly from one to the other, and to behold indifferently a series of visions that formed only a one-dimensional backdrop to the drama of his pain.

Then all at once he found himself clawing upwards from a maelstrom of fiery images, and rising to the bright serene surface of life; and he opened his eyes with a sensation of clamour being abruptly cut off. He lay still, savouring the delicious wakefulness, and gratefully registering the lucidity of his mind, as palpable as the return of feeling to a dead limb. His eyes slowly explored the ceiling, and the walls, and then the window, where a dark head was framed with gold light.

'I'm not in Heartsease any more,' he said experimentally.

'No,' said a voice.

He licked his dry lips. 'I'm in Norwich,' he said; and with a rush of comfort, 'This is my old studio.'

'Yes,' said the voice; and the dark head moved away from the window, and approached him.

Pierce smiled. 'And you're Rosa,' he said.

Rosa had come to Heartsease to attend Charlotte's funeral, and to offer whatever help she could to Jed. She stayed for several days at her old home, the Widow Thorne's cottage. Heartsease was unutterably strange to her after the isolation of Christmas Hubbert's cottage on the heath: she seemed to feel the pressure of the community's emotions, its manifold sorrows and ardours, like a physical crowd brushing against her. But she rather sought than shrank from this. For a great fear had come upon her: a fear of herself and what she had become.

It had been revealed to her in that moment on the heath, when as they bent over Hemstock's body Christmas had struck her and reproved her with scathing words that had penetrated her like a slow poison. Slow – for she had merely smarted like a hurt child for some time afterwards, and silently taxed Christmas with injustice, and with not understanding her at all – but sure, for she could not long evade the realization that he understood her very well, and that what his blind eyes saw was a girl imprisoned by resentment and mistrust.

Hemstock, she learned, was paralysed, unable to speak, irreparably broken: his rugged body would not die, but he was doomed to lie in a sort of living death, beyond communication, beyond feeling, watched over by his estranged daughter. The harsh words of Christmas and the pity that welled up in her for Hemstock came combustively together.

Nervously, reluctantly, half averting her eyes, Rosa looked upon herself and saw frightening similarities with the stricken Hemstock. Her spirit was as firmly locked away from human contact as his, but in her case it was willed. She had deliberately shunned involvement. She had made her own shell, and hidden in it.

And why not? See what hurts the world inflicted upon the mortals who had been brought unwilling into it – upon guilty and innocent alike – just look around at Heartsease! Was not a hard self-preservation the only sane course? Why should she not withdraw from a world that rent and tore, and in which it was the choicest flowers, those of confidence and intimacy and love, that bore the cruellest thorn-spikes? Thus went her old arguments: she had refined them, indeed, in her solitude. But they could not touch the fear, the fear that she was indeed a creature like the injured Hemstock: crippled, insensate, lost to life. So she forced herself, with characteristic strength of will, to re-enter the turbulent flood of human experience, and feel again its ebb and flow.

It was meant as a trial, no more: already she felt the old defensive tugging; but then she woke one morning to the news of a fire at the Hall. It had been put out at last, with substantial damage to the whole west wing; but Miss Ingamells had perished, and the young drawing-master had been hurt. And from that moment the thought of Pierce – which had in fact been lodged in her mind so firmly that she had been put to all sorts of mental manoeuvres to edge round it – possessed her completely. She ran like a hunted hare to the Hall, prepared to fight her way in, to lay about her and kill, if they would not admit her.

But the servants were in sole possession, and they let her in, and stood sombrely by as she flung herself down by Pierce's bed and kissed his blistered face. Her throat felt like a vice, and for a long time she could not speak, only bury her face in his shoulder and give vent to a burden of tears that seemed to have been confined inside her for twenty years.

He was wandering in and out of consciousness, and did not appear properly to know her. The doctor, who was in attendance, said that the trauma of his burns and the nervous shock had brought on a certain delirium, and this with the strong opiate he had been given meant he was conscious of very little.

Rosa bent over Pierce's gentle, fine-boned face, putting back her heavy hair so that it should not irritate him. 'My poor Pierce,' she whispered. 'You don't know that the girl who have hurt you so is close at hand, and weepen for you! Perhaps thass best!'

She offered herself as a nurse, and stayed by him all that day and the next, changing his bandages, applying the cooling lotion that the doctor prescribed. She refused to let herself cry at the sight of his poor burned hands, for her tenderness and practicality converged, and tears would make her nursing clumsy. The steward, meanwhile, had written to Mr Ingamells, who would surely return immediately on receiving the news. The doctor said Pierce should be well enough tomorrow to be moved; and so Rosa consulted Jed on what to do. Plague House, haunted with mourning, was not the place for the invalid, though Jed, even bruised and grief-dazed as he was, would have taken him. Instead they settled on Pierce's studio in Norwich, which had been closed up during his engagement at the Hall, and Jed paid for the hire of a well-appointed carriage to take him gently there.

And Rosa would go with him. She sent a boy with a message to Christmas Hubbert, explaining, though she had no fear that he would not understand. He had understood all along.

Pierce was still a drugged, hollow-eyed shadow of himself when they put him in the carriage swathed in blankets; but several times on the journey to Norwich he seemed to know Rosa, and murmured sentences in which sense was discernible among the ramblings of shock. When they drew up in Pottergate he was dozing again, and Rosa was wondering how best to get him into his lodgings when a man dressed in black came forth from the ground-floor shop.

'God save us — Mr Coppinger, my good friend!' the man cried, putting his head in at the window. 'Whatever has happened?'

'He've been hurt bad in a fire, and he's still in a poor way,' Rosa said. 'I've brung him home, to nurse him, and take care of him. Will you help me?'

'Help you? My dear madam, anything in my power. Let us get him inside at once. Mr Coppinger, my dear sir, this is a happy reunion, but a most unhappy circumstance! Never fear — you are among friends — we shall soon have you as well and hale as in those halcyon days when you and I shared a glass of negus in my parlour, and you were good enough to lend a sympathetic ear to the story of my downfall at the hands of a fair deceiver — the sorrow of which, though such as to render me incapable of hearing the tones of the violin without unmanly sobbing, was as nothing to my distress on seeing you thus . . . My name is Trunch, miss, Nahum Trunch — I keep the mourning-stationer's below Mr Coppinger's apartments, and quite candidly I would rather see the whole establishment delivered over to the bailiffs — I would rather see it stripped of every last weeper and jet choker before seeing our friend in this condition!'

The kindly Mr Trunch helped in conveying Pierce inside, and in throwing open the dusty studio to air, and brought up from his rooms behind the shop all manner of little comforts and delicacies. He brought too some brandy, which he offered to Rosa before taking a glass himself. 'You'll forgive me, miss — I am not an indulger in strong liquors in general,' he said, with his hair all on end, and his professional expression of commiseration displaced by a touchingly genuine one, 'but in severe trials of my nerves only brandy will do — it's my weakness. Mr Coppinger, my dear sir, here was I imagining you all this time partaking of bucolic bliss, and piping the oaten reed in sylvan glades — many's the evening when I've locked the shop-door, and breathed a sigh of envy for you in your rural retreat far beyond the chimneys of the city, disporting yourself in pasture and mead; not that I can pretend to be entirely at ease in the presence of cows, for though I am assured they are not of a savage disposition, it has always appeared probable to me that nature gave them horns for use rather than ornament, and I am not anxious to test the hypothesis in the field, as it were — you'll forgive the unintended pun, miss, I hardly know what I'm saying — my feelings are so ungovernable in such a situation they are like water scooped up in a knotted handkerchief, and all run out at the corners!'

There was an unused closet-room on the third floor of the house which Mr Trunch swiftly furnished for Rosa's use. She had only a small bundle of clothes with her, the sum of her possessions; and when she had unpacked that, and warmly thanked Mr Trunch for his help, she busied herself making Pierce's room tidy, and setting out the things she would need in her nursing. At last, when she was sure Pierce was sleeping comfortably in the bed, she sat down by the window and regarded him. The afternoon sun was coming levelly into the room, and lay across the bed like a fallen pennant. She had trimmed Pierce's scorched hair, and combed it back, and his profile on the pillow was as clear as a cameo.

'And so now we are alone, my dear, dear love!' she said, addressing him in a voice hardly louder than his own agitated breathing. 'We are quite alone, and shut away from the world and all its cunning ways – and perhaps thass why I can tell my love for you, and let it come out in the light! Ah! I am a cruel girl, you think, to wait until this sorry time to speak the words you so wanted to hear – why you wanted to hear them from such a creature as me I still don't know – but I shan't say that, for you wanted to, and thass enough for me – God bless you for't, do blessing be in his line once in a way, instead of cursing! Oh, I should have said them before, Pierce, my own love – I am a cruel girl indeed; yet I never meant to be! Will you believe that of me, if nothing else? I thought no good could come of't; I thought that'd be better for you if you never saw me no more, and forgot me; I thought we'd only bring each other unhappiness . . . and now see what my fine thoughts have brought you! Oh! but I lied, besides, Pierce: for the truth of't was, I was afraid – afraid to give anything of myself; afraid to let my heart out of the little cold place where I'd hidden it away. I have begun to know better, I hope; and I hope thass not too late, my love – though it may be that when you wake I shall find I have no right to call you so.' She broke off to steal softly forward, and place a kiss on his lips, and then retreated to her window-seat again. 'I've thought of you, often and often,' she went on, her voice dropping lower yet. 'I've thought of you on the bare heath, and I've thought of you in my warm bed; when I've cut the dry broom I've thought of you, and when my coward mind has put me off with lies, and said I should forget, yet I've thought of you still. Oh, my dear, I believed that was best to be heart-free, and keep out o' the way of pain – but how much of your pain I would gladly take now, to give you ease!'

She fell silent; and after a pause, during which the sun sank below the gabled roofs opposite, she got up to change Pierce's bandages, and settle him again in the bed. She made a fire in the grate, and set the kettle on the hob, and then sat down again in her usual place: and it was then that Pierce woke and recognized her.

He was thirsty, and she gave him drink, supporting him on her strong brown arm; and then he sat back against the pillows and gazed at her with clear eyes from which the glaze of delirium had gone.

'Is the pain bad?' said she. 'The doctor left another draught that he say will take the worst off.'

He shook his head. 'I feel the burns,' he said, 'but the pain in my mind has gone now. I hardly knew where I was − I seemed to be lost in a deep cave of dreams, terrible dreams . . .' All at once he smiled, the old light-hearted smile. 'I got the horrors rather badly. Have I been a nuisance − you know, unmanageable and so forth? I can't remember.'

'No, no. Can you eat?'

'D'you know, I think I could . . . Was Mr Ingamells back when we left Heartsease?'

'No. He was expected.'

'It was a terrible thing − nightmarish.' Pierce stirred, threw his bandaged arm across his brow. 'My God, that poor woman . . . How cruel, Rosa, how cruel life is!'

'Hush,' she said, calming him. 'It is so: and we make it crueller, some of us; and thass the one thing that deserve the name of sin!'

He looked at her in surprise. 'When have you ever been cruel?' he said.

She shook her head, unable to speak.

'No, not you,' he said tenderly. 'And here you have been nursing me, and having to change beastly dressings and all . . . But I'm afraid, Rosa, that I'm selfish, and I can't regret it − just to see you close by me . . .!'

'And so I shall stay,' said she, putting her face against

his. 'So I shall stay, Pierce, my only love — do you let me!'

'This is another dream,' he said in wonder. 'It must be.'

'Yes — my dream, Pierce: the dream I smothered, and crushed, and turned my face from — but it lives!'

It was later that evening: Pierce had eaten, and had shaved with Rosa's help, and Mr Trunch had come up to sit with him a while. Now the curtains were drawn, and the sound of the city was only a murmur, and Pierce and Rosa were alone; she sitting on the bed beside him, her arm round his neck, one hand stroking his hair. Their talk had been long, and had reached that still more eloquent stage of loving silence.

Presently Pierce said: 'Rosa — I have been thinking that my father ought to know what has happened.'

'Yes,' she said. She had been thinking of it too.

'Usually I've written to him by now: but—' He lifted his bandaged hands.

'I shall do it,' she said, kissing his brow. She spoke calmly, but she was not calm, and she felt he knew it.

'Thank you,' he said. 'There are letters of his in the bureau — you'll find the address there.'

Yes, she had been thinking of it; and dreading it. She could ask Mr Trunch to write the letter, but she was too proud; and besides, she must face it. For a long time her life had been a pattern of retreat and escape — escape, even, from her own feelings — until she had found herself denying life altogether. Now she had made the decisive turn. She would write the letter; but still she dreaded it.

Pierce's burns remained painful; but his spirit mended hourly in the presence of Rosa, and within two days he was dressed and moving about. For him the pain was an insignificant mote against a sunburst of joy: and Rosa's emotion was scarcely less intense. She could hardly bear to close her eyes in sleep and lose the consciousness of being with him. It was, in a curious way, an idyll; and most poignantly so, because she thought of it as finite. Along the stony bed of her consciousness ran swift eddies of trouble, all relating to the letter that she had laboriously penned to Captain Coppinger in Torbay.

For what would he think of that barely formed scrawl, with its print as large as the letters on Mr Trunch's door? And worst of all – for he would surely hasten to Norwich to see Pierce – what would Captain Coppinger think of the raw country girl who wrote it when he saw her at his son's side? She brooded on this, trying not to show Pierce that she brooded. Here, in these quiet rooms, with the bustling city all indifferent about them, and nothing for her to do but watch over him, and nothing for him to do but recover, and nothing for either of them to do but be together, in an intimacy so perfect that their very eye-beams seemed to rest upon each other like the touch of light fingertips – here no barriers intervened between them, no contagion of a world that thrived on division reached them. The arrival of Captain Coppinger would surely change that. It would bring the hostile world crowding in again on she and Pierce, and she was afraid: afraid he would be lost to her.

But she said nothing: it was a selfish fear, and it seemed to her now that in treading the path of self-preservation she had long been straying into the arid verges of selfishness. And one evening she was shaken with a jolt out of her preoccupations by the sight of Pierce gingerly removing the bandage from his right hand.

'What is it, dear? Is it paining you?'

'Less and less,' said Pierce. 'And the fact is – well, I know this is a small thing . . . but I have been wondering whether I shall still be able to paint.'

'Oh! but you must – surely you must!' she cried. She brought him a pencil and paper, and he tried the pencil in his fingers, wincing a little at the tenderness of the pink skin.

'Ouch,' he said, sketching a few trembling flourishes. 'I'm afraid it will take some time . . . But I don't care, Rosa. With you here — I don't care if it never comes back!'

'It will come back,' she said. 'And when it do, there's one picture that you must paint before all others. The one I wouldn't let you paint — of me.'

'Ah, Rosa! What's a picture, when I shall always have the original!'

Captain Coppinger arrived, very early one morning, having travelled from Torbay without food or sleep.

Mr Trunch came knocking at Pierce's door to announce that his father was here, and was shouldered aside in an instant by a tall, brown-skinned, white-haired, bright-eyed and deep-chested man, sprucely clad in a blue coat and black cravat, the knot of which, however, had worked its way round to the back, either through agitation or a hasty dressing. He darted across the room, very lightly for so large a man, and embraced the startled Pierce as he lay on his couch.

'Thank God, thank God!' Captain Coppinger cried, the emotional vibration in his booming voice transmitting itself physically to Pierce so that he fairly juddered in his father's arms. 'I have been imagining all manner of things on the road — not that this is not bad enough — and what have the doctors been doing to you, my boy? Is that mountebank tribe as perfidiously represented here in Norfolk as it is in Devon? Have those infernal quacks, charlatans, and imbecile cods' heads made you worse?'

'I am nearly recovered, Father,' Pierce said, laughing with tears in his eyes, 'and it's wonderful to see you — and I owe my recovery to the girl you see there, who has been my nurse, and who is so much more to me — more to me than I can say.'

Captain Coppinger released his son, and turned to look

at Rosa, who stood at a distance. 'My dear,' the old man said. He came forward, took her hands in his own great gentle paws, and lifted them to his lips. 'My dear – I am proud . . . Proud!'

The captain's luggage was sent for from the inn where he had put up – he declaring his intention of staying with Pierce, and of shaking down in a corner of the studio. 'Why, I can sleep anywhere there is six foot of space,' he said. 'As long as my feet are facing north it is of no account to me whether my bed be feathers or flint; but these innkeepers – cheats, villains, impostors all – will not accept what is an eminently reasonable demand, and turn their beds about – more fools they!'

After loading Pierce with anxious enquiries, and often brushing away tears without the least embarrassment, and repeatedly shaking his son by the arm in default of his injured hands, Captain Coppinger sent to a cookshop in St Benedict's for some dinner, and they sat down together – Mr Trunch coming up to make a fourth, and giving such vent to his natural geniality, that he said he would never be able to look at a mourning article again. It was a convivial meal. Rosa's diffidence at eating in genteel company was soon overcome by the captain's rather individual manner of pouring onion-sauce on his apple pie – 'Try it, Miss Strickland!' he said. 'The separation of sweet and savoury is a mere tyrannical convention of niminy-piminy society. Our taste buds are our own!' And there was an unexpected, and moving, pleasure in observing the unaffected warmth and love between father and son. Yet she did not feel excluded by this, for the captain was continually referring questions to her, confiding in her aside, and generally treating her as if he had known her for years: a proceeding that charmed her at the same time as it slightly raised her old screen of defensiveness.

Come evening, as the captain smoked his pipe and listened, with occasional volcanic interjections, to Pierce's account of all that had happened to him, Rosa found that more clean bandages were needed; and as the druggist, like most of the city shops, did not close its doors till nine or ten, she made ready to go out and buy some. She would have quietly slipped out, but the captain stopped her.

'My dear, you shall not turn out alone at this hour,' he said. 'I shall go.'

'I'm afraid you won't find the way,' Rosa said. 'Norwich is such a twisty crooked place.'

'I hadn't thought of that,' said the captain very seriously. 'Well, then, we shall leave this poor fellow to rest his head a while, and I shall accompany you.'

She could only assent, of course; but it was with some trepidation about what he was going to say that she stepped forth with the captain into the twilit city. A mist like a swatch of autumn had come down, above which the many church towers appeared to float remotely, while the streets below were awash with filth. Captain Coppinger took her arm very gallantly, but he did not speak at all for some time, and Rosa's tension was such that she burst out: 'You must have been very surprised to get the letter I writ.'

'Not really,' the captain said sturdily. 'I had a presentiment — a most peculiar feeling that Pierce was in some trouble. Thank God it is no worse! You do think he is on the mend, my dear? He seems to improve momently, but then I am an optimist!'

'Yes — yes, I am sure he will soon be quite well,' Rosa said confusedly. She was all too willing to be side-tracked, but she plunged on: 'My letter—'

'And a thousand thanks, my dear, for writing it!' the captain said, squeezing her arm,

'It wasn't well writ,' Rosa persisted. 'And then when you saw me you must have thought . . .'

'My dear girl, whatever is the matter?' Captain Coppinger said, stopping in his tracks, and holding her gently at arm's length to look into her face.

'Sir, I love Pierce dearly—'

'Capital! I too!'

'And he, I think – I know – loves me—'

'Better and better!' said the captain explosively.

'Oh, but Captain Coppinger, you must see . . . I am afraid I made him very unhappy at first . . . I would not believe that our love was right, when there's so much to separate us – and I'm still afraid of that in a way—'

'Afraid? Why, you strike me as a woman who is afraid of nothing – the late Mrs Coppinger was the same: I've seen her row out to the ship when we were in Yarmouth Roads through a sea as high as that chimney-pot—'

'Oh, Captain Coppinger, look – look here at the two of us,' Rosa said, taking his arm and showing him their reflections in a shop window.

'And a very handsome pair we make,' the captain said, smiling. 'But I'm rather afraid you're spoken for.'

'I'm not educated,' Rosa said. 'I barely have my letters. I have worked in the fields all my life, and thought only of food and a roof over my head, and I know nothing more of the world—'

'The *world*?' cried Captain Coppinger, with an emphasis tremendous even for him.

'Yes, the world – the world that has very hard, unforgiving rules – the world that don't take kindly to two people choosing to live their life together regardless of who they are and where they come from—'

'The *world*?' thundered Captain Coppinger. 'Shall I tell you what I say to the world? Go hang yourself! No, I don't – because I don't even speak to it – I don't even acknowledge its existence. It is in *here* – ' he struck his own head with his fist – 'and *here* – ' his breast – 'that the only true standards are to be found. Nowhere else!'

'I wish to believe you,' Rosa said indistinctly, 'but I'm afraid – afraid it won't be so.'

'Why, Rosa,' said the captain, 'don't tell me you are a self-hater. That would be a pity, for I see nothing to hate, and much to admire. And my vision is *perfect*.'

There must have been some truth in the description of

her as a self-hater, for the simple reason that she was about to reject it hastily.

Captain Coppinger forestalled her by turning her to the shop window again and saying: 'Let us look at ourselves again, my dear. For I had my suspicions that Pierce was involved in an affair of the heart; my friend Beeny thought so — estimable fellow, but *dogmatic* in his opinions, and that is the one thing I *cannot* tolerate under any circumstances and *nothing* will change my mind on that . . . I had my suspicions, I say; and I even began to picture the object of his affections. It was not at all like that handsome reflection there. It was of a little baggage in curls, with a prayer-book in her gloved hands — the prayer-book! what a parade of imposture that is — "A man may not marry his grandmother" — really, I protest at such an insult to my understanding — anyhow, that was how I pictured her: leading the poor fellow on a string, and wearing him away to nothing for the sake of one dance in an overheated drawing-room. And instead, there were you, my dear; and the thought that flashed into my mind as I took those fine strong hands of yours was "Thank God, I have brought him up right, and he thinks for himself!"'

Rosa laughed, though there was a catch in her throat. 'I have — I have been so afraid of you,' she said.

'Ha! Afraid of me?' boomed the captain, snatching off his hat, waving it expansively, and laughing too, so that a dray-horse across the way twitched in alarm. 'Who could possibly be afraid of me?'

'Afraid of much,' Rosa said, taking his arm again. 'Too much. But I am learning.'

It was late. Captain Coppinger had gone downstairs to take a warming glass with Mr Trunch, and Pierce and Rosa were alone. They talked of the future: of the threshold Rosa had decided to cross. The captain had proposed that Pierce should go down to Torbay to convalesce. Rosa was going too.

'Will you be sorry to leave Heartsease behind?' Pierce said.

'No,' said Rosa. 'It's what I've been trying to do, one way and another, all my life. Will you?'

Pierce looked into the fire, and Rosa saw a shudder pass across him, the brushing of a nightmare wing. 'I don't know,' said he. 'It seems more like a place I dreamt . . . But no – I shall not be sorry to leave it behind.'

'We are leaving it together,' Rosa said, fitting herself into his arms. 'It don't matter to me where we live.'

'Nor I,' said Pierce, his mouth against her rich hair. ' . . . But not Heartsease.'

'Not Heartsease.'

Epilogue

It is spring in Heartsease: cold, gusty, but flooded with sunlight from that superb dome of Anglian sky.

In the fields the perennial work goes on: weeding the wheat, setting beans and potatoes, stone-picking. More than half a year has passed since Elias Hemstock was struck down, and his son Herbert, uncomfortably enough, directs in his father's place; but the land takes no account of human tragedies, and demands and dictates as of old — demands and dictates just as in the days of Hemstock's illiterate grandfather leading his own plough-team, just as in the days of the Norman lords within their cold tombs in Heartsease church, just as in the days of the Iceni whose flesh has long since returned to this same Norfolk soil, and nourished its harvests, and been dispelled in the pellucid Norfolk air.

Hemstock has been moved to an upstairs room with a broad window, where he may feel the breezes that blow across his fields; but he still lies crippled and silent, and life in him is reduced to the eyes that turn often to gaze at Marianne sitting by his side, and the twitching hand that grasps hers. He is large and bulky still, not diminished, as if his towering will is now set simply upon enduring, like a tree or rock.

Marianne is with him for much of the time; but she is also very busy about the farm, and the hand that she rests in his is rough and unladylike in a way that would formerly have horrified him in his daughter. But he grasps it, tightly.

At the Hall, too, consistency is more in evidence than change. Mr Ingamells has borne up very nobly against the loss of his daughter, of whom he is already accustomed to speak in the same glowingly reverential tones with which he always mentioned his first wife. His second wife, the former Miss Fontayne, is a great stay to him and, as all local society agrees, an ornament to the Hall. The fire-damaged wing of that building has been handsomely restored, thanks to the money realized by Mr Ingamells' railway shares: as he remarks, how wonderful are the workings of Providence!

At Plague House, too, Jed continues to work his land as diligently as ever, though he looks often weary. He does his best still to help the poor of Heartsease; and many have a kind word for him, and pity him as they see him walking, with his strange worn and beaten look, down the village street. At least once a fortnight he goes away to the coast, to Shipden, and stays there a few days. He feels a certain responsibility towards young Toby Dane, and the two bereaved men have become friends. Sometimes he goes out fishing with Toby in the *Heartsease;* and when they are out of sight of land, and the heaving sea is all about them, something of the old uplifted aspiring look faintly appears on Jed's face. But mostly at Shipden he likes to walk about Charlotte's old haunts, and to talk of her with the Skeels, for he feels somehow closer to her there than at Heartsease, where she is buried in the churchyard.

But when he is at home there is one routine that he never breaks, and that is to go to that churchyard each morning, very early, and lay fresh flowers on Charlotte's grave, and stand there quietly for some time. He is not the only one to make this pilgrimage, for Marianne does the same every day, and lays her flowers beside his. But they never go at the same time. Marianne makes her way to the churchyard about noon, and so they never meet.

A day of this cool spring comes, however, when Jed is late. One of his cows is calving, and he waits to see the new life safely into the world before setting out with his flowers. As he emerges from the lane into the village street he comes upon Marianne, a little ahead of him, bent upon the same errand. She turns her head to look at him, with a glint of sun on her fair hair: her pale face, much more beautiful now with its grave composure of expression, just colouring slightly at the sight of him.

'Marianne,' says Jed. 'Are you well?'

'I'm very well,' she says, her face averted. 'Thank you.'

'I'm — taking these to Charlotte,' says Jed.

She nods. 'I'm going there too.'

'Shall I walk with you?' says Jed.

After a moment Marianne inclines her head. A boy with a wooden rattle, returning from bird-scaring in the fields, gives them a glance as they pass.

'I used to do that when I was a lad,' says Jed. 'How long ago it seems!'

'The primroses are very beautiful,' Marianne says, indicating the flowers that Jed carries.

'Yes,' he says. 'She always loved primroses.'

Marianne smiles a little. 'I do too.'

They walk on together, through the cool dancing sunlight: uneasily, a little apart, not quite in step; but slowly moving towards the same destination.

EV THOMPSON

His exotic new saga

Blue Dress Girl

A stirring tale of adventure and a moving and tender love story played out against the exotic background of China at one of the most turbulent periods in its history.

Fleeing from the busy port of Canton to avoid scandal and danger, blue dress girl She-she is caught in crossfire and rescued by Second Lieutenant Kernow Keats of the Royal Marines. Instantly moved by her fragile beauty, the young man takes She-she to Hong Kong, to the home of missionaries Hugh and Hannah Jefferies, where she can regain her strength. As she comes to know the handsome hero, the girl's gratitude becomes love – and her feelings are returned.

But a love affair between a Chinese peasant girl and an English officer seems unthinkable in 1857. And as the Taiping rebellion gets underway, Kernow is torn from She-she's side to do his patriotic duty. Can their great love cross the chasm of race, class and background that divides them?

'Thompson enjoys working his backdrop – lots of chaps fighting on boats, warlords, pirate raids, skirmishes and bloodshed...' *The Sunday Times*

'It will keep you turning the pages and certainly appeal to the vast readership who enjoy top quality historical novels.' *Sunday Independent*

Don't miss E.V. Thompson's poignant saga *Wychwood*, also available from Headline.

FICTION/SAGA   0 7472 4136 8

More Enchanting Fiction from Headline:

VICTOR PEMBERTON

OUR STREET

From the bestselling Cockney author of
OUR FAMILY

The war is five years old and, in bomb-torn North London, fifteen-year-old Frankie Lewis sometimes thinks it will go on for ever. But one foggy night his life takes an extraordinary turn. Inveigled by his mates, 'the Merton Street gang', into playing yet another vindictive prank on the old German-Jewish widow who lives just off the Seven Sisters Road, Frankie finds himself hauled unceremoniously across her doorstep and pulled into a world of books and culture he never knew existed.

Fascinated by Elsa's tales of life before the war, and with her now-dead British officer husband, young Frankie, who, although close to his elder sister Helen, has an unhappy relationship with his own apparently uncaring parents, soon becomes good friends with Elsa, helping out in her chaotic *bric-à-brac* shop and confiding his troubles to her – from his own crush on the pretty Highbury schoolgirl Margaret to his sister's unwanted pregnancy.

But Elsa, determined to give Frankie a start in the world, has plans for his future which he would never have dreamt of, plans that her scheming brother-in-law, local property owner Jack Barclay, is equally determined to thwart...

Don't miss Victor Pemberton's first Cockney saga, OUR FAMILY, 'A wonderful story' Nerys Hughes

FICTION/SAGA 0 7472 4144 9

A selection of bestsellers from Headline

All Headline books are available at your local bookshop or newsagent, or can be ordered direct from the publisher. Just tick the titles you want and fill in the form below. Prices and availability subject to change without notice.

Headline Book Publishing PLC, Cash Sales Department, Bookpoint, 39 Milton Park, Abingdon, OXON, OX14 4TD, UK. If you have a credit card you may order by telephone – 0235 831700.

Please enclose a cheque or postal order made payable to Bookpoint Ltd to the value of the cover price and allow the following for postage and packing:
UK & BFPO: £1.00 for the first book, 50p for the second book and 30p for each additional book ordered up to a maximum charge of £3.00.
OVERSEAS & EIRE: £2.00 for the first book, £1.00 for the second book and 50p for each additional book.

Name ....

Address ....

....

....

If you would prefer to pay by credit card, please complete:
Please debit my Visa/Access/Diner's Card/American Express (delete as applicable) card no:

Signature .... Expiry Date ....